THE WAY IT BREAKS

POLIS LOIZOU

Cloud Lodge Books
London

First published in 2021 by Cloud Lodge Books (CLB)

A CIP catalogue record for this book is available from the British Library.

ISBN 978-1-8380451-5-9

1 3 5 7 9 10 8 6 4 2

Cover Art © Anastasia Loizou

Cloud Lodge Books
51 Holland Street, London W8 7JB
www.cloudlodgebooks.com

To a liberated and united motherland

A Note On The Text

'Ah' and 'Eh' appear as 'A' and 'E' to denote the flat, solid sound of Greek vowels, while most proper names are presented closer to the original rather than colonial versions, e.g. 'Lemesos' instead of 'Limassol'.

'Re' (pronounced like 'red' without the D), used by the Cypriot characters, is an informal interjection, something along the lines of 'hey you', 'man' or 'dude'. Its female equivalent is 'kori' (the K pronounced as a G), which also means 'daughter'.

'Pe' (like 'pen' without the N) is used to denote frustration, annoyance, usually at the ridiculousness of something.

I

One

I t remained to be seen how much he was worth. If the Harley overtook the Toyota before the traffic lights turned amber, the woman in the tortoise-shell sunglasses would leave Orestis a tip. He watched her from behind the glass. She'd lunched on her own in the shade of an umbrella, towel wrapped around her wet swimsuit, and sipped at a glass of pineapple juice as she turned the pages of a bloated paperback. Slow, dainty sips. Some people had all the time in the world. Though the wave of them had ebbed, Orestis guessed her to be a Brit; of all the tourists he'd served, they read the most. But the skin of her shoulders was unfreckled, her hair a midnight black. Maybe a London Cypriot, a Charlie like his mother.

The bike had overtaken the car. He waited for the outcome.

'Excuse me,' said the woman, hand at half-mast. 'The check, please?'

When he returned with her bill, he asked in English: 'It was all OK?'

'Mm. Just what I needed.'

'You are American?'

One side of her mouth curved into a smile. She removed her sunglasses and was older than he'd thought. 'Canadian,

3

actually. But my husband is Scottish. He works at the base, in Akrotiri? Leaves me on my own most days, to frolic at the beach and whatnot.'

North Americans: they shared so much with so little effort. He hadn't managed to catch everything, what with her English spilling out as it did. But she fixed him with a stare so frank that translation was redundant. Orestis' cheeks burned.

'Thank you,' was all he could say.

'Keep the change,' said she, in a different voice.

Still smiling, the woman returned the sunglasses to her eyes and her eyes to the novel. Droplets of sweat dried on her forehead, her neck, the fresh-tanned skin at her bikini straps. The spark-white day was beginning to cool, and she left him to compute his generous tip.

She wasn't short of cash. So why eat here?

On his lunch break, he microwaved his grandma's pasta and took the Tupperware down to the beach, where he settled on a rock to watch the walkers, the swimmers, the joggers. No way had that Canadian been flirting; it was all in his head. Women — at least, not the good ones — weren't in the market for waiters. Aside from the job, there was his weight. You had to offer something to offset your flaws. The fat had snuck on after his Army days like a stowaway, extra filling in his face, extra puff around his middle. It had consumed what muscles he'd built. Not to mention his mother's legacy: the long Greek nose, the large eyes, the things he liked about himself. He recalled his school-day scores when girls would let him touch their legs beneath the desk. When they'd fondle him on nights out, bite his lip, in the blare of a club in the tourist district. In the alleys where Turkish beggarwomen sat on stools inking henna on the arms of tipsy students. Those old conquests were now architects, marketing execs, recruitment consultants. Fuzzy-ended pencils replaced with branded ballpoints. He was a waiter with a paunch, working like a kid in his uncle's taverna.

A guy went jogging past him, shirtless. Orestis lowered his head from the glossy pecs to finish his pasta.

Afterwards, while the restaurant docked in its afternoon slump, his uncle sat him down for a private chat. For the first time, Orestis saw the grey roots in the man's hair.

'You know you're my favourite here,' his uncle said, 'you know that. Not just in the restaurant, in the family, too. I wish I could do more for you, but you know what it's been like. They've fucked us over.' From repetition, Orestis knew that *They* were the government who'd tied the island to Europe. 'Prices are up, everything keeps going up. I remember when you could buy a coffee for seventy-five cents. Now...' He waved the air away.

From his uncle's monologue, Orestis guessed another pay cut was coming.

He was right.

'I wish I didn't have to,' his uncle said more than once, while Orestis, thinking of the man's swimming pool, and the wife and kids sprawled around it in Dolce & Gabbana swimwear, kept a red-faced silence.

* * *

Dinner was stewing in the steamed-up kitchen, a khaki stain of a room that hadn't seen a paintbrush since 1974. As always, the old girl's radio was tuned to the bouzouki classics. She sang along with her trembling murmur to songs that sounded

5

like ghosts.

When he walked up to his grandma she kissed both his cheeks, pinched them. 'My strapping young man.' Then 'A!' — batting his hand away — when he reached for a piece of chopped carrot.

'What? I'm trying to be healthy.'

'Health is for the rich.'

In the garage, his father lay beneath a neighbour's RAV4, which had been everyone's car for a while. Kostas didn't bother to slide out, mumbling instead from under the vehicle. 'Finally, you're here. Get me a Coke.'

Swaddled in the tang of gasoline, Orestis began to calm. He grabbed a can of Coke from the spare fridge and handed it over to his old man. Lowering himself onto a stool, he took a deep breath and came out with it: 'Uncle's cut my pay again.' His finger played with the ring-pull.

Kostas slid out from under the car, face creased and daubed with oil. Instead of an outburst, there was only a gathering cloud. 'Your mother's fucking family...' he said at last. 'Liars and pimps, every single one of them.'

Orestis nodded, tipping the ice-cold Coke down his throat. The rush of gas and bubbles made him choke.

Kostas exploded. 'Didn't I tell you? Didn't I keep telling you not to work for that goddamn crook?'

'I know.'

'Now look.'

'I said I know.'

'If you learned how to fix a car, you could work for me and we'd double our clients. Then you could go to Mercedes or BMW or any of them. Do you know how much they pay?'

'Why don't you work for them, then?'

6

'I'm too old. Who's gonna give me a job?'

'E...' Orestis took another swig of Coke.

'The tourists are gonna stop coming, I promise you. We're not Dubai.'

Orestis' face burned as if his pants had been pulled down before a crowd. 'We won't have customers ei—'

'You still want to own a hotel, are you fucking crazy? For what? So you can clean it up and down for whores like your mother and crooks like your uncle? God have mercy. You'll go there tomorrow and tell him you quit.'

Orestis raised his voice, too. 'Then what? How will we live?'

Kostas was silenced, and unhappy about it. He glared at his son, who gazed at the floor. It was the same conversation between them, again and again. If their circumstances ever changed, the shock of new things to talk about might shut the old man up for good.

Outside on the scorching concrete, a pair of car doors clicked and shut, one of them snagging the leaves of a loquat tree. Uncles Andros and Andrikos waddled over to them.

Andros threw an arm around Orestis, his beard scratched the young man's cheek. 'What's new, gentlemen?'

'Same shit,' said Kostas. 'His uncle's cut his pay again.'

Andrikos made that gesture with his hand, frustration and hopelessness. 'Pe...' That old baseball cap on his head. The Nike tick, *Just do it.*

'Didn't I tell you about that family?' Andros simultaneously ramped up his volume at Kostas and his grip on Orestis' shoulder. 'Arseholes and thieves, the lot of them! Remember your wedding, when her father wouldn't pay the deposit on the venue because he just bought a Lancia? Remember that?'

And the men rehashed the story Orestis had heard at least

7

once a month since birth.

'All right, lads, all right,' said Andrikos in his throaty citrus voice. He patted his nephew's hand. 'He knows this, poor boy. What else can he do, when they're giving all the jobs to Russians and Poles?'

'He could do this!' Kostas said, indicating the garage as if it was the Tsirion stadium.

'And then go to BMW?' Andros cut in. 'Forget it, cuz. Better to stay with the Nazi relative than the Nazis buying Europe.'

Andrikos wheezed a laugh. He looked at Orestis, then leant back. 'Re, you've put on weight.'

Orestis' hand went to his stomach. 'Yeah...' he said, forcing a smile.

'Orestis, get them some Cokes.'

'It's because you don't exercise, am I right?' said Andros.

'Yeah, uncle, probably.'

'Not "probably", I'm right. 'Cause when you were in the Army, you built some muscle, you took care of yourself, didn't you? You were so handsome! How many girlfriends did you have?'

The Army days were an endless slideshow of the barracks. Talking shit with a bunch of guys from his 'enemy' high-school. Drinks and sex jokes and card games, the occasional rifle assembly. Two dead years of service with no reward, while non-Greeks flew abroad to study, earned degrees, got started on their lives in the nick of time. Before house prices burst and restaurants wiped the Greek off their menus.

'Re!' said Andrikos. Though he'd been seated on a plastic chair for the past few minutes, his breath was noisy, a throat full of holes. 'Why don't you go to Pavlos? That gym by the park.'

'Pavlos works at a gym now?'

'What "now", did you forget to put your clocks forward? He's been there since Easter.'

Orestis couldn't picture Andrikos' son working at a gym, or working at all. Selling weed outside the clubs and blasting tunes on the highway, easy. But good honest work? Pavlos was the sort of heavy-lidded fucker that everyone liked but no one could trust.

'Go over there, he'll give you a discount.'

'Yeah? He can do that?'

'E, who knows if he's allowed... But you know him, he does what he wants anyway.' Beyond the smile, the teenage exploits of Andrikos' son fogged the man's eyes.

'Re!' Kostas was back to yelling. 'My son's had a pay cut and you're telling him to go wank around in a gym?'

Andrikos waved his hand again as if to sweep away their troubles. 'Cuz,' he said, 'as our blessed departed grandmother used to say: even poor people need a good time.'

* * *

The old girl had cooked enough for everyone, so they crammed the kitchen with two more plastic chairs for Andrikos and Andros. The woman fussed around them, fetching third and fourth cans of Keo, passing houmous and tahini, pushing everyone to eat more salad. She held her nephews' hands and laughed at anecdotes of times long-gone with their parents. But as she heaped the last of the stew onto their plates, Orestis caught a helpless look in her eyes. She'd made so much, but there'd be nothing left for tomorrow. She crossed herself, mouth tight.

Later in his room, he opened the wardrobe door, still puckered with football stickers from his childhood. His reflection drew its T-shirt up over its wobbling stomach. A bilious ball went up his throat like a lift. The reflection pushed the fat at its sides up and down and sideways. Those shoulders, once rocks that held him upright, had eroded to dunes. Andros was right. Once, not so long ago, Orestis drew the right sort of glance from a stranger. He'd always been grateful for his mother's looks, as his pug-faced father must've been. And those were still there, they would never change. For the moment they were confined, awaiting release. It was up to him to make that happen.

'Worthless,' he whispered at himself. 'Wanker.'

He slapped his stomach.

'You make me sick.'

Another slap, more like a punch.

'Loser.'

Punch.

'Wanker.'

Punch.

He would go to see Pavlos.

Even poor people needed a good time.

Two

Orestis' limbs sagged. He should've been on his break, but the late-shifter was taking the piss. On top of that, every duty in his job description was now worth less per hour. Parents let their kids throw felt-tips to the floor and smear the menus with mustard and vinegar. A couple of Russian wives had repeated their order with obvious eye-rolls as they pointed to the English words. He'd bit his tongue and smiled. Women like them were buffered by a coat of money, legs and status. And they would never get their due. At last, his colleague arrived. Orestis threw off his apron and stomped out. One day he'd carry on walking.

On foot, the road to the gym was longer and busier than he'd anticipated. After what seemed the entirety of his break he arrived at that familiar but intimidating glass-fronted building. He asked for Pavlos at Reception and shut his eyes to the AC as he tried to ease his panting.

'Hey buddy, how's it going?' His cousin strode over with a towel slung over his shoulder, that big grin on his face. Orestis thought too late of their mingled sweat as they hugged. 'Dad told me you would come. It's good to see you, re! I thought we'd have to wait for another wedding.'

Orestis made his usual excuses: work, his grandma's health.

As he did so, Pavlos searched him with those curious eyes, Andrikos' grey-green marble made hazy from weed and peace. Orestis had tried marijuana one night with some guys from the state school. One puff and an icon of the Virgin hanging on the wall had made him think of his grandma. He'd refused another toke and blamed it on feeling queasy.

Now he tried to focus on Pavlos' chitchat, rather than his sculpted torso in a tank-top. Pavlos seemed to have both nothing and everything going for him. A general ease. A Ducati. A sex life. A body to turn heads.

After a while, Orestis cut the chat short. 'I'd better get back to work,' he said. 'I haven't even eaten.'

'OK, buddy. Go eat. Don't stop eating, a? Coz that's dumb.'

Orestis laughed. 'OK.'

'Come whenever you want, I'm always here. Half price for you.'

'Seriously?'

'Yeah, re! Don't even think about it. This is Tinos' place. Half price for family.'

Tinos was the husband of a cousin on Pavlos' mother's side. It was doubtful the offer extended to him, but Pavlos was fixed on it. He squeezed Orestis' bicep and said with a wink and a grin, 'Don't you worry. I'll make you a stud.'

Orestis grabbed a takeaway souvlaki to eat on the move. One of the few things he knew about his mother was that she baulked at people eating on the street. Any mention of the Charlie absentee made his grandma's eyebrows rise, but Orestis secretly sided with his mother. Every so often, he discovered terrible traits he shared with her and kept them to himself. At the kitchen table, where his father and grandma slurped and smacked and guzzled and burped, he zoned out

12

to the empty chair beside them, with its straight back, elbows off the table. Reading between the lines, he concluded his mother was a different breed, with other expectations of life. How bored and alone she must have felt with her husband and mother-in-law. On the other hand, if she'd stayed she might have grown to love her child. He might have been the one to moor her.

Back at the taverna, he noticed a text whose buzz he'd missed. It was from Paris, asking if he was up for post-work drinks in Old Town. On any other day, fatigued and moody as he always seemed to be, Orestis would've declined with a vague lie. But today was wired differently; something about the injection of hope Pavlos had given him, the discounted gym pass and the promise to be moulded and bettered — something told him to accept.

If the approaching woman chatting on her phone was speaking Russian, he'd go for a drink with Paris.

She was, so he did.

* * *

Paris was partial to a bar off the radar. They left his car in a dim lot overseen by a toothless old man, where he squatted to play with a litter of strays. Past the trendy spot around the Pantopoleion, every establishment heaving with smoking, chatting, dressed-up undergrads, they went into a café-bar in one of those vast old houses with high wooden doors and a courtyard; Paris' choice for a coffee and a game of backgammon.

In the light of bulbs draped over a pomegranate tree, Paris did multiple things at once: he smoked, sipped an ice-cold frappé, pushed his glasses up his nose, stroked another stray cat and complained about neoliberalism without once taking his eyes off the game. He'd got first-class honours in Classics from UCL, and could spout whole swathes of *The Iliad* as he scratched his beard. As a teenager, he'd needed Orestis to stand by his side to talk to girls. But now he'd forged his own path, and the awkwardness of youth had transformed into a state of manly tranquillity. For the first time, Orestis felt the less attractive of the two.

'How's your sister?'

'Leave my sister alone,' Paris said, in that priestly drone of a voice.

'How would I get to her? Isn't she in London?'

'Manchester. She's fine, doing her PhD.'

'Serious!'

'Watch what you're doing, re. I'm wiping the floor with you.'

'E, you always win.'

Paris shrugged, smoked, and lifted the frappé to his lips. He moved another chip.

'I saw Pavlos today. My cousin.'

'In prison?'

'No, you wanker, at the gym near the park. He's working there now. He said he could get me in for free. I figured I should go, you know, do some exercise, lose a bit of weight.'

Paris didn't take his eyes off the board. 'Good for you.' Behind him was a painted figure stretching up the stone wall. Shadows fluttered over it, the paws of the cat, spread to bat at Paris' fingers. 'If you want, there's a great spot to shoot some hoops—'

'Orestis!' The voice had come from behind him. He turned,

and Paris looked up from the game, to see Evangelina Ioannidou heading towards them. Teetering on four-inch heels,
her body looked as simultaneously big and tiny as it had at
school. She buzzed, erratic, her perfume splashing everywhere. 'I can't believe it, when did I last see you? Where have
you been?'

'E, what else? Working. You?'

'Where do you think?' she said. 'The beach, the mall, the
bar... How am I supposed to keep track? How are you doing?'

'Fine, yeah. Remember Paris?'

'Oh my God, Paris! I was standing here thinking, "Who is
that Bin Laden over there?" What's with the beard?' Gripping
their arms for balance, she bent at the waist to give each of
them a peck near the cheek.

Paris squirmed at her volume. 'What's new, Evangelina?'

'Cut that "Evangelina" nonsense,' she said, 'I'm "Eva" now.
Haven't you seen my Facebook? You have to, it's a riot. I post
selfies every day, and I use those filters where you look like
a painting, or as if someone took it a hundred years ago. My
mum says, "Kori! What next? Iconography? You on the ceiling
of the Ayia Sophia?" Ooh, hang on!' She answered her ringing
phone. 'Here, you dumbass. In the courtyard, come inside
then out. Past the bar.'

Grabbing a chair from a nearby table, Eva sat herself down
with caution. There was a tight black dress, bulging bust and
fabric-pulling thighs to negotiate. Her body was a full cup of
coffee carried on a tray over people's heads. Though Orestis
had felt a twinge of dread at seeing her, the feeling subsided.
Eva liked him, or at least that's what he suspected, even after
he became too poor to attend their school. More than once
he'd fantasised about her. Of course, he never told the other

15

guys; she was fat, they would mock him. Well, those same people would be laughing about him now no matter what. *So what if she's fat?* his grandma used to say. *With her dad's money, you could own a chain of hotels.* The girl had a certain potency. A pull. And she made Orestis feel comfortable, desirable. Even now.

After about twenty minutes her friend arrived. Skinny, pretty in the usual way, she looked at Orestis, and especially at Paris, like an aristocrat among beggars. When Paris made a leftist comment against austerity, she dragged on a Marlboro and asked if he was a Communist. Her eyebrows were already painted arched. Orestis imagined her pinned to a bed beneath him.

At some point, they started arguing about the development of the old marina, when Eva interrupted to address Orestis. 'Where do you work again?' The drink had clogged her speech a little and lowered what barriers she may have had. She was eyeing him openly; his mouth when he spoke, the parted neck of his shirt as he scratched at his chest hair. For a moment, he wondered if she'd offer to drive him home. They could stop along the beach for a fuck.

He blinked the thought way. 'At the taverna,' he said.

'Ou, that one, your mum's brother, what was he...?'

'Cousin. Yeah.'

'But the pay sucks,' Paris added.

Orestis shot him a look, which Paris ignored.

'Why?' asked Eva.

'His salary keeps getting cut. It's almost half what it used to be.'

'Come on, re...' He glanced at Eva's friend. Face of a woman kidnapped by terrorists.

Eva held his arm. 'Your own uncle would do that to you?'

Orestis tried to laugh it off. 'It's not his fault, prices are going up.'

'Bullshit! There's always money.'

Paris couldn't help himself: 'Not for everyone.'

'Give me your number,' she said to Orestis, slapping the table. 'You know my dad owns hotels. Why didn't you say something before? Give me your number.'

Orestis felt a chill on the back of his neck. 'Don't worry about it, kori...'

'Don't be a moron! Give me your number, I'll get him to put you in somewhere.'

'Seriously?'

'Of course! I only ever call him when I want a favour, he's used to it. Give me your number and give your uncle the finger.' Sipping her Bacardi, she slapped the table again and laughed.

Paris looked down at the interrupted backgammon game and took a drag on his cigarette. It was hard to tell, but Orestis thought his friend was smiling.

Three

It had been a while, but Orestis felt the presence of God. This went against his new beliefs – that he had none – and the godless voice in his head, sounding something like Paris, mocked him. But the past few days had lifted the bonnet and exposed the machine-works of Fate. One thing had led to another and arrived at Eva; Eva whose father owned hotels and might be hiring staff. Orestis' goals were lining up, waiting for him to shoot. A five-star resort on Amathountos Avenue. Corridors walked by men in suits, men who'd press tips into his palm. His wardrobe fatter, his shoes more resistant to holes. He might even buy a car. He'd work his way up to Manager, and watch his bank account climb above zero. No more fights with his dad about the garage. Instead, Kostas would come over to his house – two floors, two reception rooms, a roof garden – to roast lamb on a spit. His grandma bearing bowls of sweet rice pudding sprinkled with cinnamon. Watermelon on the veranda, chatter floating out to the hills to the sea. Orestis' surroundings would finally rise to meet his taste. An oak front door opening to a skylit hall. Iron-railed staircase. Open-plan lounge and dining room. The floors, a cream-and-coffee-coloured marble. Not that speckled pigeon-shit tiling of his grandma's house. Walk-inwardrobes and spare bedrooms, each with its own en-suite. All that space. All that freedom to move, to grow.

Then he'd slap himself out of it. Dreams were for the rich.

Jaw twitching, he'd stare the promise into himself: one day things would change. When the chef at the taverna screamed at him, when a waitress was late, when a kid was snotty, he'd allow himself to daydream. Things would change. They had to. They always did.

'Your cover left,' said the other waiter, Nassis, when Orestis got back from his break. 'They only paid half the bill 'cause they hated the food.'

'What?' Orestis heard himself yelling. 'And you let them?'

'What could I do?'

'That's gonna come out of my pay.'

Nassis shrugged, sad and helpless.

Orestis held his head, shut his eyes. He would never tell his dad of this.

* * *

After hearing about Eva and the possibility of a job, his grandma baked a fanouropita and prayed to the saint. Before she allowed Orestis to have any, she would have to offer a slice to seven women only married once.

'Not many of *them* these days,' she said.

'E, let's pray anyway.'

There was still a chance Eva might've been leading him on. Who was ever nice for nothing? It wasn't as if good things just happened to people like him.

A flash of youth in his grandma's face. 'It's in His hands,' she said and kissed her crucifix.

As was everything. When his mother left, it had been God smiling down on them to push her out of their lives. It had been the will of God that his grandma fall on the steps of the bank and shatter her hip. God decided when his dad received custom and how the books looked at the end of a year. God advised keeping the central heating off in the winter so they might save a few cents. And the Virgin had watched, wilting with shame, as Orestis had smoked that spliff. A sky full of saints had lamented his deeds in cars.

God had made Orestis, but it was Orestis who'd let himself go. By losing his body to his grandma's food, chicken with roast-gilded skin, thick village bread with butter and honey. By succumbing to fatigue and sloth and his uncle's taverna, where his dwindling salary sank him further down a well.

And now, a light had appeared. Follow it, a voice was saying – a different one to the usual.

* * *

Pavlos' tank-top and sweatpants were the dream but Orestis was a realist. Realism drew the line at sleeveless and figure-hugging. People were likely to stare. Shorts would be practical, keep him cool and reduce sweat, but they were also out of the question. His hairy legs out in the open for all to see? No chance. As for trainers, the only pair he owned was over six years old. Others would notice and besides, the soles would die on the treadmill. It shamed him to arrive with bad shoes, XL t-shirt, and a pair of mottled sweatpants, but the discussion was closed by his wallet. He'd packed his uniform in a bag predating the trainers and got his dad to give him a ride to the gym, which only happened after he threatened to call a cab.

'Waste of money,' Kostas said, slamming the horn at a car turning right. 'Just do a hundred push-ups and sit-ups at home.'

'It's not the same. Anyway, Pavlos is giving me a discount.' Orestis had increased that discount by an extra ten euro for his dad's benefit.

They weaved around apartment blocks, bakeries and petrol stations, Kostas' shortcuts that made nothing shorter. Orestis longed for his old Suzuki. They'd had to sell it a few years back to pay the plumber. His dad's better customers began to take their cars to branded garages, the poorer fell behind on their payments. His grandma's medical bills increased. *God willing*, she'd say, *you'll be free of me soon*. Orestis felt a sting in his eyes. He rested his arm on the window of his dad's Toyota and tapped along to the pop on the radio.

'Enough of this shit,' Kostas said, changing the channel when an English song came on.

If his appearance made his cousin think less of him, Pavlos hid it well. He assessed Orestis' physique and prescribed a routine for workouts. He hovered for a whole hour, spotting bench presses, lat pulldowns, flys, lifts and, most awkward of all, the treadmill. He advised working on chest, shoulders and triceps on some days, back and biceps on others, a day on legs and glutes. He talked Orestis through diet and nutrients and wrote him a list of protein sources outside of meat. Pavlos was never supposed to amount to anything. Orestis had spent most of their lives regarding his cousin as a dropout, with a future only in suntanned lethargy. But at the gym, Pavlos spoke with clear eyes and firm hands. His arms were strong, his posture correct. Meanwhile, Orestis had wheezed himself to a near flatline. He'd also forgotten to pack either a towel or a deodorant.

'Wanker,' he hissed to himself. 'Useless prick.'

'Hey, hey,' said Pavlos, hand on his cousin's arm. 'I've got spares of everything. Don't worry.'

He sent Orestis off to a health-food shop to buy the essentials, a place that smelled of earth and wool. Muscle repair, muscle build, maintenance, substitutes, supplements, pills, bars, powders. Thankfully, Pavlos had written a list to hand to the shop assistant. The man was a weedy-looking Greek-Greek, a Kalamaras, so soft-spoken, so languid as to be almost admirable.

'Yes, we have all of these,' said the Kalamaras. 'Please wait here.'

He returned with creatine, whey and vitamins, which he piled on the counter. Tangled cables of veins emerged in his pale arms. Orestis calculated the cost in his head. This was crazy. He ought to stop. Even with the low gym fee, this was a lifestyle beyond his means. He recalled what Pavlos had said about nutrition and refined sugars. Good food costs money. His grandma was right, health was for the rich. Like getting his own place, fitness was another thing that would simply have to wait.

When the Kalamaras ran up the total, Orestis went numb. He ought to say no, ask the guy to put it all back. Instead, he heard himself saying, 'OK.'

'Would you like a loyalty card?'

'Yes, please.'

He watched his hand move to the card machine and punch in his PIN.

The purchase complete, the Kalamaras thanked him for coming. Orestis stood still for a minute, chilled by what he had done.

Back at the taverna, he sprayed and wiped the empty tables. What the fuck did he still care about their cleanliness? Why did he still give a shit about his uncle's business? Let the place fall apart, they could all go to Hell. Set it on fire, fan the flames. Uncle and cousins with their D&G swimwear and holidays in France.

Nassis was chatting football with the barman. He and Orestis were now on the same wage.

Orestis took himself to the bathroom, locked the cubicle and slammed his fist against the door. There in the quiet, he zoned out, eyes locked on a wispy globe of dust behind the toilet bowl.

He never helped his grandma at home.

It wasn't his fault, she wouldn't let him.

He came out of the cubicle and washed his face in the sink.

The old girl would be watching her dubbed South-American soaps, every so often breathing out a *Glory be to God*. She'd walk around the house with a censer, to bless it with the smoke of burning olive leaves. Then she'd sit in her armchair, itself older than his dad, to reminisce about the days before the Turks invaded, before EOKA, before her husband's death. Aniseed tea and a paximadi. Daydreams of a better life to come – thanks to that nice-but-fat Eva and her big-shot dad, who was going to offer Orestis a job, any minute now, in one of his five-star hotels. Orestis would be settled, might even marry the girl. May their troubles go away.

His phone buzzed in his pocket.

Nassis walked in, hand on his flies. He stood at the urinal to piss and groan.

So now both waiters were off the floor. This place was a

fucking joke.

* * *

His last cover had left without so much as a thank you. At least they'd paid their bill. As soon as his shift was over, Orestis dumped his cloth in the bin, threw off his apron and walked out. He took his bag from the staff cupboard and picked up the health-store purchases he'd hidden under his jacket. Out in the open air, he remembered his buzzing phone.

A missed call from Eva. New voicemail.

His heart was loud even against the noise of cars. Inhaling the night, he sat on a low wall to wait for his dad. He stared at the screen for a whole minute, then dialled to play the message.

Re, what are you doing that means you can't answer the phone? Working? Don't shit me. Well, tell your uncle to go fuck himself, because they're looking for receptionists at the Harmonia. Long story short, I got you an interview. You've basically got the job anyway because I told Daddykins to tell the manager you're my very best friend and you saved my life on several occasions with your excellent phone-answering skills, so all you have to do is show up and they'll ask you a couple of questions. And then thank me. Just so you know, I like kalamari...

There was also a text. She'd forgotten to mention the interview was at ten am in two days' time.

He leant back, all breath gone. A breeze ran along his arm, making him spasm. He looked around in case anyone saw. The phone had melded to his hand. In his other was the bag of protein and creatine, the things he couldn't afford – until a mere half-hour later, when Eva had made that call and left

24

that message. No – at around the same time, when she called Daddykins to get him an interview. He ought to message her back, take her out for kalamari, it was the least he could do. But his head was full. An interview in two days. He needed a suit, a good suit, another thing he couldn't afford. When his father turned up, he'd get him to drive to a supermarket, discount outlet, anything, he needed something, at least a good tie.

It made him laugh to himself, and shake his head: money. The fact that it took money to make money. That he should have done this years ago. Should have listened to his gut and leapt into life instead of dipping his toe, watching his step.

The Toyota turned the corner and slowed to a stop a palm-width from his feet. Through the windscreen his old man's mood was clear. Customers.

'What's up?'

'Get in, son.' His father's expression was more gloomy than angry, his voice that of a different man: raspy, soft.

Orestis pulled the seatbelt over his soon-to-be-flat stomach, and Kostas came out with it as if it was nothing: 'Your grandma's at the hospital. I'm taking you to say goodbye.'

Four

The old girl croaked just after midnight. The doctor, a woman, talked them through the motions. Her manner was both warm and businesslike. First came the certificate of the cause of death, on which his grandma's stroke was stated with brutal distance. Then came the undertaker, who talked them through the funeral. Next, it was the priest who'd be conducting the service.

She'd died alone, while Orestis had been at that fucking taverna, scrubbing gum off tables.

People offered their assistance, even their homes for the wake. Andrikos, Andros and their wives came to gently cover the deceased's hands with theirs, and give tearful thanks for the presence she had been in their lives.

'Did you want me to call the relatives?' Auntie Lenia asked Kostas, in a tone that said she'd do it herself.

'I'll call the florist in the morning,' said Maria.

And in the centre of them lay the corpse. His grandma – no, mother; she had been that without question. More than once she'd called herself a burden. *Better if I died.* If she hadn't been so old, so ill and so worthless, she could have helped them earn a living instead of sapping it from them. If only her medication didn't cost so much. If only her trips to the doctor and tests at the hospital hadn't been as frequent. Better dead and cost-free than alive and costly. Orestis' throat was hard and full, his stomach light and empty. She'd had a point. Now there'd be one less mouth and fewer bills. All those glib statements he'd heard over the years, from people who knew nothing: the vacuous lives of the rich, the spiritual wealth of the poor. Idiots. An empty wallet made you long for the vacuum of death.

There, on that white abnormal bed, his grandma lay in a gown so thin he could see her nipples through it. Her bones jutted, another blemish in her weathered skin. He hoped she hadn't been cold in her final moments; she'd often shivered at night, rubbing her arms. God's blessing had passed her by. She'd lowered a young husband into his grave. She'd harboured her siblings' children when their own homes were dark with sickness or violence. She'd spent hours at the sewing machine – before arthritis set in – to cut what little income she had. She'd been afflicted by cholesterol, and a heart murmur, and that corrosive fear and worship of money. There was never enough of it, not at any point. All she'd had were her God and His angels, and the saints who appeared in her dreams bearing news of hope and strength. Orestis heard the words *priest* and *church* and *service*, and he felt the ground tilt. How could he sit there, Paris at his side, and pray, or cross himself, to any of it? Religion, faith. A sham exoskeleton of no more substance than a hospital gown.

'You OK?'

Orestis looked at his father, the new man in his place. His face, already sun-dried by the years, now looked bigger, heavier. Filled up by all those held-back tears, dragged by gravity. In the man's silence, Orestis read the jumble of

27

thoughts; arrangements, adjustments, the whole new way of life they would have to adopt and adapt to. As of today, Kostas was a man without parents. Orestis was all he had.

'E... God willing.'

Both sky and highway were rose-gold by the time they left the hospital. Suddenly, the Harmonia interview had gone from 'two days away' to 'tomorrow'. It was scheduled for before the funeral, so he and his father decided Orestis should take the Toyota. Kostas would get a lift from Andros or Andrikos. They and the cousins' wives would take care of everything. All Orestis had to do was arrive at the service on time. Kostas had begun to suggest he call the hotel and reschedule the interview, but that only sparked a prickly energy between them. It was pretence. Neither father nor son felt the need to sustain it.

At home, a badly-printed notice apologised in advance for a three-day pause in business. The house felt vacated, like those blocks of refugee flats Paris had taken him to a couple of years back. Crucifixes hanging on half-doors, children's exercise books congealing on the floor. What could Orestis find to say to his father now? What would their lives be? He switched on the radio, already tuned to his grandma's folk-ballad station, and let the pining bouzouki fill the room. He took out a pan and tried to recall what the old girl did with eggs. On the counter sat a bottle of olive oil, a prompt. He poured the liquid onto the pan, flicked the gas to a sizzle.

If breakfast turned out well, they'd be OK.

The day felt inherently wrong; as if it was going backwards. After his meal, Kostas fell asleep on his armchair. A fan turned its head around the room, intermittently tickled his remaining hair. Orestis' limbs and eyelids drooped, but he kept himself from falling.

He slapped himself awake. He'd been too hard; the jolt made his jaw lock.

An ice-cube from the freezer helped. Sleep would wait for night-time, he had to be sharp for the following morning. Bolstered by the adequate breakfast, he kept himself busy with chores. He did the washing up, murmuring along to the songs on the radio just as the old girl did. He pulled his and his father's dirty clothes from the laundry bin, the ragged t-shirts and y-fronts, and felt a twinge of regret for what his grandma had had to endure. He made a list of groceries, pulses, rice and pasta, adding a note to shop at a bigger supermarket. Higher chance of discounts there. He responded to calls about flowers, food, and the offers of help and condolences from a ton of relatives, people he'd never even met. 'Thank you,' he said, pushing down the 'leave us alone.' He messaged Paris, who responded instantly. Orestis said nothing about the interview, in case his friend tried to change his mind or contact Eva on the sly. Next, he tackled the cleaning, spending almost an hour on his knees scrubbing cupboards and floors and counters. His face hadn't been so close to a toilet since his army days. Caked in bleach, it made him gag. The sight of his own arm sweeping all his grandma's medicine bottles into a bin bag made his eyes water. Deciding against a local supermarket lest he run into an acquaintance, he drove to a large one on the outskirts of Larnaka. There he wandered as if without purpose; as if hoping to be inspired or illuminated by whatever he found on whichever shelf he passed. When he got back home, Kostas was still asleep on his mother's armchair. From the sofa, Orestis checked on him between glances at the TV. In the evening, they ate sandwiches in silence, watching a Greek sketch show they once found hilarious.

When the sun finally set, Orestis allowed himself to sleep. Settling in bed, he remembered to message Eva to thank her for what she'd done. For minutes, he deliberated about whether to mention his grandma's death. Eva would react like a mother. She'd call the manager himself to reschedule on his behalf. Orestis couldn't say a word to her. He had to make a good impression. He would simply have to do whatever he could to make this work, and give himself the best chance at getting the job. Even if – when – he got it, he wouldn't relax; this was a career to work at. There would always be targets to exceed. He would make something of himself, his life would mean something. He would not lie down and get fucked as his grandma had, as his father had.

His head on the pillow, his mind finally tumbling into sleep, he thought of his mother and felt a sad, damp fury at her absence.

* * *

He woke to a barrage of texts. All were from Eva, and all said exactly the same thing: *You'll slay!!!* Followed by a more sober message, apologising for sending the text a hundred times. He smiled, and for a moment imagined her in bed with him, his hands on her warm naked tits.

His grandma was dead.

Wiping his eyes, Orestis focused on the bright new morning at his window. Voices below and the smell of warm pastry. It wasn't even eight, but already his aunts and uncles were fussing about. They hugged and kissed him and sent him off to the shower, where he cried beneath the running water till he pulled himself together, then out of the door with a pat on the back, after some tugging and tweaking of his jacket and tie.

'God willing,' said the stranger who was formally his father as he kissed his cheek, voice quieter than Orestis was used to. The man even had his hair gelled back, his collar pressed.

Despite two slow double-cabins in front of him, Orestis hit green lights all the way to the hotel. A good sign. He got to the Harmonia in twenty minutes, a third of the amount of time he'd allowed for. He turned into the visitor parking, hands trembling on the wheel. What was he doing here? The last time he'd been to a five-star hotel was for a schoolmate's birthday party, probably Eva's, in the years before his mother left. This wasn't a place for people like him. He lingered in the car, the sun warming his thighs through the wound-down window, and stared up at the building. He counted to twenty.

If there was an odd number of interviewers, the job would be his.

Having forced himself out of the car, to kill time with an amble through the grounds, it struck him how suddenly his life might switch to a different one. Within weeks, he might be arriving at this very hotel on a daily basis. This landmark to everyone in Lemesos, routine. Noisy tourists exchanged for sophisticates with PAs and chauffeurs. The tacky signs of his uncle's taverna replaced with the elegant script of the Harmonia logo, which turned a pleasing cream-white against the sunset. His paycheque would last a full month. His tips would be higher than his uncle's hourly rate. Did people tip receptionists? Here, probably. The rich made their own rules.

Something got hold of him. His breath snagged. His legs gave way, but the only thing to grab was a hedge and it riddled his palms with pockmarks. He held his jaw so that whatever it was would stop; so that the shaking and nausea and fear would go. He thought of his grandma, breathed out, and out, and out, long breaths until at last he felt calm enough to go back to the entrance, and step through the revolving doors.

The Front Desk stood before a wall arrangement of wood and copper panels. Orestis slowed as he approached it and the suited people behind it. Possible future colleagues. His face flared up within the lobby's marbled cool.

'Excuse me... I'm here for an interview?'

He sounded unconfident. The staff might report these minor infractions.

'Good morning. Name?'

A few minutes later, a stout woman, Scandinavian-looking, arrived at the sofa where he'd been instructed to wait and led him to the lift. They travelled up in silence. The woman's hair was a white-blonde filigree at the edges of her face. Her buttocks stretched the fabric of her skirt. He looked away, tugged at his shirt. He adjusted the lucky blue tie he'd remembered, thank God, to buy at the Larnaka supermarket. And he cursed himself. The cologne he'd applied at home had been washed away by his sweat. What a wanker, rushing over like that when he'd had so much time. Another thing he shared with his mother: his punctuality. He ought to mention it in the interview. Or might they have noted it already? Out of the lift, the blonde led him down a corridor and into a boardroom where three suited men sat waiting. Each of them was tailored.

Three. Three men.

Having risen from his seat to shake Orestis' hand, the hotel manager introduced himself. His smile was slick but friendly. Orestis shook hands with all three interviewers, noting the one on the right, who appeared to be gazing at something around Orestis' middle. Orestis smoothed down his tie. He was a waste of their time, an indulgence of Eva's charity. If it was up to the man on the right, the interview would be drawn at once to a close.

'Please, help yourself to some water,' said the manager, indicating a full glass on the desk.

'Thank you.' He gulped down half of it.

Orestis had worn a watch to look smart. Big mistake; it was a thing that begged to be glanced at. Ticked away the seconds to his grandma's burial. The family would never forgive him if he missed the service. He would not forgive himself.

The manager ran through a speech about the importance of the Harmonia in its larger family, the VIP visitors it received from across the globe, the standards it aimed to uphold, all with seamless ease. Orestis did his best to nod when it was right to do so. He would be late to church. Relatives would ask his father where he was, and Kostas could only shrug. The manager carried on. He explained the need for a talented receptionist, someone to be the 'face' of the hotel. Someone presentable and reliable; able to build instant rapport with guests. A person with excellent problem-solving skills. While the manager talked, Orestis nodded. He hoped to show he understood what was required of him, that he'd rise to the challenge. But maybe the nodding was excessive. He ought to sit still. His grandma had been placed in a coffin. She'd been dressed in the baptism gown from her trip to the River Jordan. The undertakers were loading her into the hearse, where she slept in a bed of flowers.

'So,' said the manager. 'Just so you're aware of how this is going to go: we're each going to ask you a few questions, and after we're finished you'll have the chance to ask us about anything we may not have covered. Is that all right?' The sharp smile again. The man's teeth were so white they made Orestis feel overly conscious of his own.

'Of course,' Orestis said. And, thinking of his mother, added: 'Thank you.'

This seemed to please the man.

For the next half-hour, Orestis answered their questions. Of challenges he'd faced at work, the difficult customers he'd had to deal with, goals he had achieved and where he saw himself in five years' time. 'Manager,' he replied without thinking and hoped it hadn't caused offence. The man on the right, whose face had grown no friendlier, shot the toughest questions. He presented ultimatums: would he override instructions from management in favour of a guest's wishes? Whatever came at him, Orestis answered with diplomacy and, imitating the handsome manager, a tone of calm as if nothing could shake his composure. The dryness in his throat would not go away. He refrained from drinking more water. He kept one hand on top of the other. The watch ticked on.

'Do you have any questions for us?'

Orestis realised he'd zoned out. His mind had got tangled in routes to the church.

The men were watching. He ought to ask something, prove initiative, light a spark, reveal a brain, stand himself apart from the other candidates. He was so tired.

'What are the languages spoken here?'

The interviewers blinked.

'I speak English well, but I'd also like to learn Russian. I was... just wondering what you expect of the staff.'

'English and Greek are the main languages,' the manager said with a smile. 'Well, mostly English, of course. But we'd encourage you to learn as many as you like. In fact, the company provides funding for courses relevant to the job role, and that would definitely count.'

The man to the right of the manager, still grim, scribbled a note on Orestis' CV.

The watch ticked against the silence. Orestis' eyes slid to it, but he pulled them back. He kept his smile, heart thumping beneath his new inadequate tie.

'You're Eva's friend, aren't you?' the manager asked, out of nowhere.

The man on the left looked up, the one on the right narrowed his eyes.

'E... yes,' Orestis replied, with a warning pang in his gut. 'We know each other from mutual friends. We used to go to the same school. But I moved to a different one. Ages ago.'

'She's a character, isn't she?'

The manager kept his smile. All three men were still and straight.

'Yes. She's very passionate. Everything means a lot to her. She really cares.'

The other two men glanced at each other, but the manager was looking at Orestis as if he'd just completed a puzzle.

* * *

The drive to the church almost killed him. If it wasn't a Fiat in front of him turning right at a junction, it was a Kawasaki zooming past and missing him by a fingernail. His chest ached. If the next light was still green when he got to it, if the Renault overtook the Mazda, if the Mazda took the second left, families crossing the road, refuse trucks, one after the

35

other, an obstacle course building before him...

He parked outside the church with six minutes to spare. On his way in, adjusting his tie, cursing himself once more for not packing his cologne in the car, useless prick, he caught a low-key greeting from Paris behind him. He swivelled for a brief hug. Inside the church, faces turned towards him from every pew. Andros and Andrikos with their wives, Pavlos in a tight black shirt, all steeped in sorrow. At the front, Kostas lifted the Bible off the space by his leg and Orestis took its place. The man's hand grabbed hold of his son's and remained fixed there throughout the service, breaking only for the sign of the cross on an amen. Bouquets of lilies flanked the altar. Just like the displays around the hotel, he thought. Ashamed, he lowered his head, to think of nothing other than his grandma.

The priest ululated Bible verses in a voice as strong as wine. It drifted upwards with the incense, climbed the pillars and the vaults, flickered the light of the chandeliers. His grandma had told tales of her father, a village candlemaker who'd been blessed by visions of saints. Now those tales would be buried with her, a pillow of words beneath her head. Behind him, he heard Paris sigh. Solemn, respectful, as the word of God filled the room and their bodies, he was a man who didn't believe a thing.

At the cemetery, the priest chanted of sin and forgiveness. He broke a plate and poured olive oil onto the coffin in its grave. Nearby, a group of elderly relatives sobbed into their handkerchiefs. A body returned to the earth, to be swallowed by it, digested.

Orestis looked up to see his bastard uncle with his wife and kids. His hands became fists, his jaw clenched. Whether or not he got this job at the Harmonia, he'd be leaving that damned taverna, and erase any trace of a link to that family – that lesser half of him – for good.

After the wake, he and his father washed the dishes. One dusted, the other hoovered. Kostas put the Pyrex-loads of donated food in Tupperware or tin foil, to be kept in the spare freezer for as long as they needed it. Practicality was a shock, logic an offence. Yet, Orestis told himself, he had coped so well on the previous day, running errands and doing chores he'd never had to consider before as if his soul had switched bodies. As they sat in silence, sipping their cans of Coke to the night-time news, he felt a growing unease. It was just the two of them left: he and his father. A scenario he'd never expected and, to his shame, would've picked last out of any possible choice.

Five

I t was only a matter of days before the Harmonia called. And with the flash of that number on his phone, the pain of waiting was gone. 'Good morning,' said a radio-voiced Cypriot woman from Human Resources, knowing it soon would be. He could hear her smile as she informed him the job was his.

Sputtering his thanks, Orestis assured her he could start as soon as they needed him. He was only working for his uncle, no notice required. He almost added that the wanker deserved no notice.

'Don't worry,' said the woman with an airy laugh. 'There's no rush.'

Maybe not for her. When she ended the call, it was all he could do to keep from jumping up and down with joy or running out of the room shouting *Gooooaaaal!* as he used to when he was little. He messaged Eva, then ran to tell his grandma the news. And it struck him afresh. He shook his head clear. In the garage, his old man was replacing the wipers on a Fiat. When he told him about the job, Kostas only nodded and, with a simple 'Bravo,' brought two Cokes out of the fridge.

'Now, you tell that uncle of yours to go fuck himself,' he

said.

'You think I don't want to? Until I get my first paycheque from the Harmonia, I can't quit.'

'Better to leave with your balls intact, instead of begging for money from that pimp!'

'Yeah? And how would we eat?'

It felt good to spar with his father again, but they were cut short by an approaching Honda. Kostas smiled for the customer.

Eva's response to his message was an eruption of text and smileys. She'd barely been able to contain herself when she'd heard the news from that gorgeous darling manager but she'd been sworn to silence for what felt like decades. Orestis felt the stirrings of something other than amusement as he typed a response, but he pushed it down. He'd take her out for lunch, that kalamari she'd mentioned. It was the polite thing to do. But, from her exclamation-marked reply, he knew he'd be taking Paris as a buffer.

They met her at a restaurant by the Castle. Orestis thought it best for him and Paris to arrive together. On seeing the snap in Eva's expression, he wished he'd informed her beforehand. As always she was friendly. She adapted her deflation into baffled surprise, kissing Paris as if she'd missed him terribly since they'd last crossed paths. Sunlight stretched across the road, vacuum-packing the shops and cafés and bodies within it. They settled down at an outside table with a view of the minaret and ordered three frappés. It seemed to Orestis appropriate that they kept their shades on, for their eyes to be obscured from one another.

'This is how he thanks me for getting him a job,' Eva complained to Paris. Orestis' heart lurched. 'With food!' And

THE WAY IT BREAKS

she spread her hands in disbelief as if it hadn't been her who'd made the suggestion.

'What,' said Paris, 'is kalamari not good enough for you anymore?'

'Re! I'm nearing thirty! I want a marriage proposal, not a squid.' She indicated her naked ring finger.

Orestis laughed, but the words stuck like burrs. Marriage. He drew a blank on forming the right sentence. Thankfully, Paris stepped in. 'What are you going to do with this loser? Can't your dowry get you something better?'

Eva waved him away. 'That's all finished. My dowry's gone to that Russian whore who married my father. Me? I'm left on the shelf, the wretch.'

'A fallen woman?'

Orestis shifted in his seat. Paris was pushing it as if unafraid of causing offence. He even lit a cigarette in his casual manner.

Eva looked unfazed as she lit her own. 'Fallen to sewage. I'll be left with nothing. A couple of Russian godchildren probably, God have mercy.'

'Wow, you were right. Wretched.'

'So come on, Paris! Write that philosophical bestseller and make my father an offer. The clock is ticking.'

Orestis' shoulders loosened. He sank back in his chair and imagined again what it might be like to be with Eva. Hot mornings in bed, on a Greek island, looking out at the Aegean. Drinks on the deck of a yacht, where days rolled on without end or purpose. But then an opposite urge reared up: survival. Eva was born with money, her wish would be his command. Prada purse in hand, she'd build the walls of his life. Golden, but walls all the same. And what he wanted now, more than anything else, was the sky. *Freedom or death*: the mantra they learned in school.

He sat mute through most of the meal, focusing on the rub of the squid at his knife. Eva carried on squeezing a near-depleted lemon over her chips as she talked of the hotel. She gave a run-through of the clients and staff – not the waiters and cleaners; there was too big a turnover to keep up with all those East-Asian, East-European names, she couldn't even understand them let alone pronounce them. Then, out of nowhere, she said to Orestis: 'You're going to need shoes and trousers.'

So they'd been discussing him. That genteel manager must've said to her after the interview, *Nice boy, but needs new clothes.* Or worse, he'd said nothing, and Eva was acting alone. Her protégé was to start with the right equipment. In truth, he owed her that. His hands trembled, so he kept them under the table, but his burning face was out in the open.

Eva offered to take him shopping, right now, after lunch, why not? His instinct was to refuse, to pretend he'd already bought new clothes. It even occurred to him, the idiot, to say he'd been shopping with his girlfriend. But then Paris would ask what girlfriend and the game would be up. It was time for logic, not emotion. As a teen, he'd pictured his head-heart conflict as his mother's genes overriding his father's, like a cowboy breaking a horse. It was a comforting thought, to be genetically wired to take the reins. Eva was right. Might as well cut to the chase, he needed new clothes. Well-tailored suits and crisp shirts, ties of the correct hue. Quality came with its own palette. And it was easy, when you developed your eye, to identify what was cheap, what was a brand, and what was better than both. But he wasn't naive enough to think he could get there on his own.

41

'Sure,' he said, 'let's go shopping. But I'll need another man around me in case you make me look like a fag.'

Paris threw his head back, ejecting a puff of smoke into the air. 'Go fuck yourself. As if I'm going to follow you around the Mall, dressing you up like a Barbie.'

Orestis felt a hollowing-out. He tried to laugh it off. 'Don't you want a new scarf for your poetry readings? A beret?'

'Leave the socialist alone,' Eva said. 'Paris has his own "image"; St John in the cave of Patmos.'

Paris wouldn't budge. Not even when Orestis asked him seriously. At the change in Eva's smile, he dropped it. He excused himself to go to the bathroom, where, alone, he washed his face with cold water, slapped it, and stared himself out in the mirror.

When the waiter brought the bill, Orestis took out his wallet. Eva rebuked him, insisting she would pay. Paris raised his hand to end the discussion, tossing his credit card on the little metal plate. Exhaling his smoke, he said, 'Congratulations to Orestis for his new job... and commiserations to Eva for remaining on the shelf.'

* * *

Before they got to the business of shopping, Eva pulled over at a newsagent's for a couple of Chinos. A welcome plan; the slushed-ice caffeine got them through the heat, remorseless even with the top down in her BMW 3-series convertible. Stretching ahead was an afternoon of boutique after boutique, in each of which the manager greeted her by name and kissed her cheek. While Orestis was allowed to choose his shoes and trousers, Eva would leap at a pair of cuff links or a tie or patterned shirt she simply knew would complete the look. 'They're giving me a uniform shirt,' he would say, but she only shooed his words away, fingernails the size of roof tiles. Whenever he'd complain about his figure, the kilos crowding around his waist, she'd shut him up by pointing at her own. It was a boost to his ego that his physique compared favourably to hers.

'A! What do you think you're doing?'

He felt a mix of sadness, shame, relief and pride when she once again batted away his credit card.

On the drive home after their shopping spree, she sang along to one of Anna Vissi's traditional-lite ditties on the radio. This could be it; everything he needed, here in this person. Would it really be so bad to have everything handed to him? So far in life, he'd worked to get nowhere. With Eva, hard work would be a foreign language, a thing he'd once known but at some point forgotten.

But no, not yet. Independence first, complacency later. *Freedom or death.*

'Are you excited to start?'

'Are you kidding?' The next words paused on his lips. 'To be honest... I'm surprised I got the job at all.'

'What are you talking about, you idiot?'

'E... Let's say I wasn't in the best frame of mind that day. My grandma died. I was on my way to her funeral.'

Eva spun her head, never mind the vehicle she was driving, the road, the other cars.

He laughed, only a little out of nerves. 'Kori! Watch where you're going!'

'Re! What are you telling me? Why didn't you say anything before, are you insane? They could've moved the interview.'

'I didn't want them to move it. I'm gonna be working for them, not them for me.'

Eva shook her head, a cocktail of sadness, disbelief and admiration. 'You're an absolute moron. Listen: stick with me a little while, and see how you get others to work for you.'

Guilt and pride stabbed as one.

'And my condolences about your grandma. I was besotted with mine.' She sucked on her cigarette and exhaled into the blue. Though she was still wearing her sunglasses, he could tell from her voice that there were tears in her eyes as she squeezed his knee. 'Well, one of my grandmas. The other one's crazy.'

Six

Because he wasn't a bastard, Orestis continued to work hard at the taverna. In his last weeks, he was fuelled by the shock on his uncle's face when he'd handed in his notice. There'd been no rebuttal from the man, no attempt to persuade his nephew to stay. What could he offer: his old salary? Every table Orestis cleared was a countdown to that bright new life awaiting him at the hotel. There were moments, while picking up bits of food and plastic dumped by kids on the floor, or carrying dripping refuse sacks to the dustbins out in the back, when his resolve would weaken. Even if he believed, deep down, that he was more than this, he'd be gripped by a sudden terror; of being out of his depth in a five-star hotel, too intimidated by the top rung to start the climb. He'd made a mistake in going for that job. This position, this life, working in his uncle's taverna and living above his father's garage, was the one he was born into, the extent of his world, the extent of his rights. His abilities amounted to resting one plate on his palm and another on his fingertips. This was where he belonged. Ambition was for the favoured. But the moment would pass and he'd shake the doubts away. He would take a few breaths. He would repel negative thoughts. Then the doubts would fly right back at him. It took nerve to go up.

His mind was still reeling on the morning he turned into the staff parking. In his daydreams, he'd arrived immaculate, a tailored copy of the soft-spoken manager who'd given him the job. In reality, he was wrapped in a suit that begged to be worn by someone else. For now, it would have to do. But he'd return to the gym and Pavlos' training, and in no time at all, he'd be trim and fit again. Those protein shakes and supplements, just sitting in the kitchen cupboards... The money he'd spent on them.

There was another expense he had to earn back: his new car. If a battered Honda bought from an acquaintance of his cousin could be called new. When Orestis had gone to pick it up, the man had bragged about buying property in Romania. 'Dirt-poor country,' he'd said. 'easy to buy there. Fix them up, rent them out. I've made enough money to buy a Porsche, I could send all six of my grandkids to university. That's why I can afford to be generous with you.' The money he'd demanded for this tin can was on the wrong side of cheap to be called generous. But Orestis had bitten his tongue and counted to twenty. At least he wouldn't require lifts from his dad anymore.

In the hotel lobby the portly receptionist, that Scandinavian-looking one who'd taken him up to his interview, instructed him to wait on a sunlit sofa. When the manager came to collect him, his warm smile went some way in easing Orestis' nerves. 'Welcome to the Harmonia,' he said, shaking the new recruit's hand. The manager was just shy of his height, and Orestis wasn't very tall. But though a good ten years his senior, the man was in better shape. Trousers belted to a flat stomach, tie draped over a sculpted chest. There was a brightness in his eyes that came from eating and sleeping well, and his coiffed hair was a healthy black with smart dashes of grey at the temples. This was a man who jogged and drank smoothies. 'Call me Thanos,' he said when Orestis greeted him more formally. Having briefly introduced the new recruit to the Front Desk manager and a couple of other colleagues, all of whom greeted him as they might a VIP, Thanos took Orestis on a personal tour. Was he receiving special treatment, as a friend of Eva's? He felt a twinge in his stomach.

'I like to get to know my staff as individuals,' the manager said as if to reassure him. 'And it gives me a chance to further explain our company before you start.'

And so he did, taking Orestis through the panoply of features at the Harmonia. First, there was the hall and adjoining ballroom, with their long buffet tables, a disco ball above the dance floor. Then the restaurant with its enormous mirrors and chandeliers; the kitchens and laundry rooms; the conference rooms; the turquoise mosaic-tiled café, pastries and patisserie; the squash courts, gym and locker-rooms; the infinity pool; another swimming pool and its bar, adorned with bamboo and a cluster of salmon-skinned tourists; the sauna, which the manager recommended with a smile; the meditation room; the multi-faith chapel; the lounge; the offices and utility rooms; and finally, the bedrooms themselves.

These ranged from tasteful but snug single rooms to lavish sea-view suites. Though Orestis, the peasant, knew nothing of interior design or architecture, the rooms made an instant impression. Every detail had been considered, from the coordination of greens on the bedspread and curtains, to the stain of a wooden headboard, to the flecked glass of a pull-switch handle. The jasmine outside the windows.

47

This was it, what separated people; a thing beyond class, beyond status, money or schooling: the quality of detail. The manager not only wore good suits, but he also matched them to his colouring. He accentuated them with his own physique because it works both ways. And the man must have seen the hallmarks of quality in Orestis, for he watched him with naked interest. Orestis' nerves had been unfounded, potentially ruinous. He belonged here. The knowledge of it thrummed within him, electric.

Conscious that his fingers were caressing a bedside-table lamp, Orestis withdrew his hand. It made the manager smile, and Orestis met his gaze, smiling back.

The rest of his shift was swallowed up by the usual first-day admin. A woman from Human Resources – the same one who'd called him, Angela, middle-aged – photocopied his passport and gave him forms to fill out with a black biro. 'What are you more comfortable reading in,' she'd asked, 'English or Greek?' Orestis took offence but hoped it hadn't shown. It took him back to his schooldays. *Charlie* frothing at the mouths of other kids, giggling from the back rows at his English readings in class. A middle finger from his mum across the sea. He swallowed. There were a video and paperwork on Health & Safety, a demonstration of the fire exits and meeting points. He was booked onto a first-aid course. A man escorted him to the staff locker-rooms, where he was issued with a coded padlock and work shirts. Nothing had escaped the attention of Thanos, and he wondered, thinking of the manager's perfect suit, if the man was meeting the hotel's standards or if the Harmonia was meeting his.

In the little time left over, Orestis was taken back to the front desk, sporting his new work shirt, tie, and badge, and reintroduced to his colleagues. The Scandinavian-looking one was actually a Ukrainian called Svetlana. She felt free to chat and joke now and had a mouth full of mischief. Yiorgos, the Front Desk manager, talked him through the Opera system and assessed his tech fluency. To his relief, Yiorgos was unbothered by gaps in Orestis' knowledge. If anything he seemed confident in the new boy's ability to learn.

'You have a way about you,' he said. 'You care about making a good impression.'

It was the kindest thing another man had said to him. 'Thank you.'

'See?' The man laughed and slapped his back. 'It'll serve you well.'

* * *

A breeze lifted the palm fronds along the seafront. Orestis turned the volume up on the radio and, powered by a mix of relief and excitement, sang along. He pictured himself in a BMW 3-series convertible, top down in the lilac evening. He would message Eva to thank her again. It wouldn't even matter if she read too much into it; if she dolled herself up to leap off that shelf.

He parked at his uncle's taverna. It would only be a couple of hours every evening till he got his first Harmonia salary. What were a few more weeks in the chart of his life? Calves throbbing, he went in to start his late shift.

When he got back home, his father sat him down to go through the family finances, and figure out how to diminish their debts. God rest her soul, the old girl's only property was a house in the North lost in the War, not hers anymore but some

Turk's. Forget that. Her husband's orchards had been sold off years before to pay a loan. The chance of being saved by the garage was slim. Thank God they would soon have Orestis' higher salary and with it the prospect of progression, bonuses, perks. For now, the belts would have to stay tight, until the bank accounts could breathe. God willing the monthly interest didn't kill them first.

In Orestis' head was the refrain of his grandma's tears. Her voice followed him everywhere, pathetic, apologizing for her existence, murmuring useless prayers. It would shame her to leave them with debt, but the old girl's contract with life was terminated before she could buy herself out.

Seven

D ays at the Harmonia passed more quickly than they ever had at the taverna. Orestis' hands were always full, his brain always whirring. But while at the taverna he'd been a laden donkey, here he was a cog in a machine. No one stood around idle, and if they chatted football it was while their fingers machine-gunned the keyboards. Yiorgos kept his Front Desk staff occupied but he also entertained them with silly jokes. The work ethic spread to all departments, across all floors.

The pleasantness of the surroundings countered the intensity. If he had to warn a spoilt child, it wasn't about ketchup on a grey floor, but about keeping ping-pong balls from flying into the bar amongst the palms, or over the bridge into the swimming pool, or into the lap of a tanning tourist. The scent of roses and freesias from porcelain vases. Sun-cream mixed with perfume. The clash of colours in cocktails and ice-cream sundaes. The symbiosis of textures, be it sofas or counters or drapes. This was an environment designed to stimulate, to gratify.

Once in a while, he'd encounter Thanos, and they'd exchange a friendly greeting. This mostly took place on the seafront, where the hotel's lawn tapered into beach along a

51

stone path. Orestis had found a good spot to eat his packed lunch; the subsidised meals at the hotel's cafeteria exceeded his daily budget. Wary of getting dirt on his uniform, he'd sit on a smooth rock beneath the bow of a eucalyptus tree to stare out at the gleaming blue. Thanos would appear and stand close by to watch the sea, the swimmers, the cruise ships and tankers in the distance. He beheld it all as if it was both in his possession and a thing beyond his reach. It was the way Orestis' grandma had looked in church: proud and cowed. God was yours but also no one's. Whenever a private yacht drifted into view, the manager's eyes would narrow. Orestis could only eat his tomato pasta and gaze at the object which, like the mermaid tourists in the sea, would stay forever on the horizon. He tried not to stare at the manager, though the man compelled him.

One of the bodies who frequented the beach was about Orestis' age and colouring. That was where the likeness stopped. The swimmer's was a dream physique, chest and abs curved like dunes. The rest of him was both concealed and exhibited by a pair of sleek black trunks. When he rose and sank in the water it was, to Orestis, as if a ghost of his future self were luring him forward. A cosmic cruelty. Thanos' eyes turned to marble when he saw the swimmer. His body stiffened as if to keep him from acting out. Orestis put it down to a shared history between the men. Whatever it was, it was none of his business.

'Some people are lucky,' Thanos said once, with a lightness Orestis knew was feigned. 'Getting to swim, all day every day…
'

It had occurred to him that Thanos might be bent. Aside from his grooming, fine manners and love of beauty, which

52

to Kostas and the rest of the family was proof enough, there was the sense that the manager's smiles were softer to him than they should ever be between men.

Orestis filled the silence. 'I wish I could.'

Thanos turned to appraise him. 'You should.'

It was a running joke between Svetlana and Yiorgos that Orestis was a flirt. She would mimic him: *Can I help you?* in a sultry voice. He would blush, ashamed that someone had noticed these transactions, usually with the girlfriends of rich old men. His assistance for their grateful smiles. His recommendations in exchange for their curves peeked through damp sarongs and oversized shirts. Svetlana would giggle as she slapped his arm. Svetlana, who'd worked her way up the star ratings of hotels along the coast, to land this job after many years of graft.

Nothing was ever got for nothing. Somehow, Orestis knew, he was in debt to someone. And one day they would come to collect.

'The sea is for everyone,' said Thanos after a long, heavy silence.

* * *

After his first Harmonia paycheque, and the final shift at the tavern, Orestis went back to see Pavlos. The hotel's sporting facilities were free of charge for staff, but he felt obliged. It was the right thing to do.

Pavlos erupted with joy. 'How's it going, cuz? My old man says you're working at the Armonia now.'

His dropout cousin had never learnt much English at school, so Orestis ignored the dropped H. Pavlos was one of the

53

few people who'd never spat *Charlie* at him, or mocked his attempts at proper English. Even his grandma pursed her lips when she heard him speak the other tongue. Had Pavlos the chance or aptitude, he might've furthered his education, instead of spending his midnights prowling for potheads and sluts.

'Yeah, re, it's going well.'

'When they make you Manager, make sure you get me in, yeah? Rich people love a personal trainer. Not like these villagers here who want me to train them for free.'

Orestis bristled. 'Give me a few more weeks,' he said, 'let them get to know me, and I'll ask around for jobs.'

Pavlos held one hand up for a shake and with the other slapped Orestis' back. 'My buddy.' But the gesture burst the stench of weed in the air, and Orestis knew he would not be keeping his word.

For the next hour, they shot the breeze over a workout. Pavlos spotted him throughout: bench presses, cable curls, wrist curls, deadlifts. He threw in fifteen minutes of stretches at the end. It was better to work out in the morning, he said, contrary to what Orestis might assume. 'We're more productive early in the day.' This from Pavlos, who'd spent his teen years waking up at four pm. 'That way, you're left with endorphins and higher energy. If you leave the gym till after work, you'll grow tired or bored and never commit.'

The gym had been enforced in the Army, both by sergeants and peer pressure. After his conscription was over, Orestis' motivation had faded with everything else. All that remained was a feeling of loss and waste.

'It depends on my shifts,' Orestis said.

His cousin grinned. 'Fine. Just don't leave it another month before your next visit, yeah?'

'I won't, I swear. And thanks, re – you didn't have to stay and be my trainer. Not when you could get paid for it.'

'E...' Pavlos said, 'you just do a good job at the Armonia and we'll see about that.'

* * *

Whereas Svetlana, following comments from a few Brits, was still learning to smile more and speak less curtly, the Front Desk manager took Orestis aside to praise him. 'You have tact,' said Yiorgos. 'You never rub anyone the wrong way.' At first, the praise was a gift, but it proved a wooden horse. Orestis was handed the worst guests, the most awkward scenarios. Why was Mr So-and-so-from-the-TV's room smaller than his co-star's? What use was the one squash court when it was always booked? If a maid had forgotten a hand-towel, it was Orestis who got yelled at. If a child had wandered off, it was Orestis who was to calm the parent. There were times when his anger rose so close to the surface he had to excuse himself to unleash it in the gents'. He'd slap himself, hard. After a moment or two, his focus would return. He'd lean back to let his breath go in and out. He'd wash his face. Up close on his reflection, he'd check his eyes, his lashes, skin, pores. He'd dissolve himself to a million bits. Eventually, his mood would ebb. He would whisper his goals to himself, over and over. These were only tests to pass. Then he'd return to the Front Desk, and be ready with a smile for the next guest, the next obstacle, the next rung.

'It was such a tough day at work,' he'd tell his father over dinner.

But Kostas would rear his head like an angry horse. 'Your generation is nothing but lazy yobs! Nobody wants to work a single fucking day! How many summers did I have to toil in the orange groves as a boy, for nothing but a few cents? Out there with the snakes. My hands were torn to shreds. For a few *cents*.'

'I know, I'm not saying—'

'I saved every coin! Every coin. Then I gave everything I had to that whore Englishwoman who saw me as a pocket.'

Head filling with brine, Orestis would steer the conversation to the less controversial topic of cars. Maserati, Lamborghini, anything guaranteed to lift the old man's mood.

The one person he could confide in, without getting a kick in the balls, was Paris. At least once a week they'd meet outside the Harmonia – outside because Paris didn't want to see up-close how the Other Half splurged. 'Communist,' Orestis would joke. But his friend was one to talk. Paris, whose family had funded his tuition in England and his jobless existence in Cyprus thereafter, was the Other Half. Together they'd stroll along the lamplit seafront, the moon tapping at the water, towards one of the cafés for a coffee or an ouzo. While Orestis sometimes fancied a flavoured syrup in his drink, he'd learned to condition himself. Any time he felt a craving for sugar he touched his flab. The growling stomach was silenced. These days, even Paris, who saw him once a week, noted a change. 'You've lost weight,' he'd say, matter-of-fact, lighting a cigarette. 'A, wait, it's gone to your arms.'

'Look at my watch,' Orestis would say, and demonstrate how tight it was on his wrist.

One night, Paris asked: 'You seen Eva lately?'

Orestis hadn't. The guilt was a sudden weight.

56

'That's funny. I figured she'd be all over you about the job.'

Orestis shrugged. 'Looks like she's forgotten me.' He focused on stirring his drink.

'Whatever you say.' Paris took a long drag on his cigarette, eyes finding something outside in the dark to focus on.

Orestis didn't want to think of Eva, or see her, or contact her. She had to be reassured of his gratitude without being encouraged. His only shield would be a girlfriend. It was the solution he kept coming back to, weak though it was. Until he had one, he'd keep his messages friendly but sporadic. Even if it took weeks, he would manage Eva Ioannidou out of his day-to-day.

Thankfully, one of her texts came with a lifeline: *Don't go having affairs with all those Russian girlfriends!!*

He seized his chance: *Too late.*

From then on he would casually refer to imaginary ladies who threw themselves at him. In reality, his sole admirer was a Lebanese widow. She'd come to Cyprus as a refugee in the Eighties and now travelled from Paris four times a year, staying weeks at a time. She kissed his cheeks three times hello and praised him to the management. Though other guests smiled back, none had shown any interest beyond the matter of her stay. But if Eva saw him as a skirt-chaser, as most girls did in his school days, she might tell herself she'd never be enough for him. Her attentions would find another target.

When she asked him how he liked her *Daddykins*, Orestis replied: 'To be honest, I'm afraid of him.'

It wasn't untrue. The moment he saw Eva's father step into the lobby, flanked by Thanos and the moody man from his interview, Orestis felt a chill. A portent. Aristos Ioannidou was a giant, dark hair grey at the sides and thin at the top.

Sharp laughter lines gave him a mirthless air. His eyes were like a bird's, flicking here, there, registering and apprising everything. He shared Eva's large nose, not to mention that inexplicable magnetism. The self-assurance that comes with self-sufficiency, confidence stemming from comfort. The staff had been warned in advance of their boss' visit, so the usual standards climbed a few notches. Uniforms pressed, spines upright, voices tuned to a sunnier key. Even Svetlana, who moaned about having to sound like Snow White, was turning on the charm. Orestis had worn his lucky underwear, a stupid new habit he couldn't help. When he greeted his boss with a handshake, the man raised an eyebrow. 'Yes,' said Mr Ioannidou. 'I remember you from my daughter's school. You shook my hand then, too.'

The pause that followed filled Orestis with dread. But the man cracked a smile and slapped him on the back before moving on. Thanos thanked Orestis with his eyes, as did Yiorgos. When the boss moved on to other rooms and floors, Orestis' colleagues pressed him about his connection to their boss. 'It's nothing,' he told them. He and the owner's daughter had known each other in his first school, the international one. He came to one of her birthday parties here. Orestis was quick to add that he'd been forced to leave the school shortly afterwards, due to a lack of funds.

Svetlana squinted but nodded.

At the end of his visit, Mr Ioannidou approached Orestis at the Front Desk. 'I meant to ask: how's your mother?'

Orestis froze. This was a joke. A nasty joke. The boss was angry with him, maybe because of Eva. Eva had complained, and Daddykins had decided to humiliate the cause of her pain in front of his colleagues.

But no. Mr Ioannidou's tone had been friendly, his face was open. He had asked a question and was expecting a response. Orestis' mother wasn't a legend to everyone.

'She's fine, thank you.' And for all he knew, she was.

Mr Ioannidou nodded. 'She's an interesting lady. Very knowledgable. Very polite.' And with that, the visit was over.

Orestis felt hot. His body was drained, suddenly and totally shattered.

* * *

His mother was born to Cypriot migrants in London. While back in the Motherland the remaining family were rebuilding their lives as refugees of the Turkish invasion, she and her parents and aunts were making weekly trips to the Brent Cross shopping centre. In the Eighties, when the debris of war had settled, she took a chance and accepted a job at a Cyprus-based shipping company. There she was in Lemesos, that city she'd heard so much about. She'd go for the occasional coffee with distant relatives in their hastily-erected council flats. She spoke her accented Greek to shopkeepers and received equal amounts of admiration and contempt from men on the streets. When she met Orestis' dad, she was charmed enough to marry him. But, as she explained to her son one night, patting his wet hair dry, that's when her island romance began to fade. 'Your father changed,' she said. He shouted if she so much as talked to another man, he criticised her skirts and shoes. Both her husband and mother-in-law demanded a child to continue their bloodline. It didn't matter what she wanted, nor did they care if she was modern or inept. She began to feel the brunt of their tempers, not only her husband's but also his mother's. Meals became tense, mornings laden with gloom and failure. She would find herself staring out of the window at work, eight months pregnant because they relied on her salary. She would sigh at the sea and the ships that cruised away on it. She had her baby, and time went on. She couldn't be prouder of Orestis, that much she assured him. She was glad to see her genes in him and almost nothing of that hateful other bloodline. Orestis' manners and mannerisms were hers, as was the scale of his dreams. But it wasn't enough to have a wonderful child. She craved escape. In time she heard that her mother, who'd flown to Cyprus twice a year since Orestis was born, had suffered an accident. She'd stepped into a London street when a motorbike sped through a red light and over her foot. The woman was laid up, with only her fragile old husband to care for her. She needed her daughter. This was her ticket out. Orestis' mother kissed him through her tears at the airport, left for England, and never came back. On the phone, she implored him to come and join her. How could he? He was at school here. His friends, his father and grandmother, who loved him fiercely, his aunts and cousins, were all in Cyprus. His father would glower, then take the phone from him and hang it up. 'If she loves you so much, she can come and get you,' he'd say. Instead, she let Easter pass, and then the summer holidays, then Christmas, with only an intermittent phone call to remember her by. She sent him a ruler depicting the London skyline, which Orestis hid at the bottom of his school bag. Without the support of his mother's salary, he was forced to leave the international grammar school for a Greek-speaking state one. His English dwindled – never completely, but enough to widen the trench between him and her. His London grandparents became too old to visit their homeland.

60

His father's and grandmother's fury simmered to bile. Every so often a birthday card or postcard would be waiting in the mailbox at the gate, each one bearing the same words, in English: *Love, Mum xx.* In later years, with the advent of email, she took to sending him more frequent, detailed messages via his aunt. Lenia would print them off and sneak them to him on visits. *It's hard to explain how trapped I felt*, his mother confessed in a particularly lengthy one. *Cyprus oppressed me. The weight of the sun, the mosquitos, those flying cockroaches that scared me to death, people's staring. There, I was The Charlie. The Englishwoman. The whore. To your father, I was always and only those things.* Now she was back home in England, where she belonged. And she was happy. Free. A master of herself. Orestis didn't know how to respond to that email, so he never did. The days simply slipped away. And all that was left now, where once was a sense of awe at the woman who'd appeared only briefly in the life she gave him, was resentment. Sometimes he gave in to nostalgia. A vague memory of sitting in the passenger seat as she drove, just the two of them on the highway in comfortable silence, brought a pain to his chest and throat. He swallowed it down and turned his mind to other things. It didn't matter that she'd sent him a postcard once in a while. The truth was that his mother was happier now. And she'd never come to get him.

* * *

What did Aristos Ioannidou know about his mother that nobody else had known? When had they spoken? He'd used words not typically associated with Orestis' mother: *knowledgeable. Interesting. Polite.* Yet all Orestis could think

61

was that she and the hotel owner must have known each other because, as his real family always said, the woman was a whore.

Eight

J ust after New Year's, one of the night-shifters had to take emergency leave. Elias' brother had been killed in a crash with one of their cousins off the highway. It so happened that Orestis had seen Elias earlier that day, in the changeover from the late to early shifts, and felt an inexplicable shiver. By that point, the brother's corpse had already been collected by an ambulance, his motorbike a crumpled scrap on the side of the road. Elias had been none the wiser.

The hotel had responded with generous compassion, allowing the bereaved all the time off he required. For now, there was the issue of cover, which had to start at once. There was no shortage of daytime staff, but the dark hours required only two receptionists at a time, and the part-timers were unavailable. Orestis stepped forward, which made Yiorgos, both surprised and not, slap his shoulder in thanks. 'That's it, son,' he said. Svetlana leant in to whisper, 'I'm so happy it's not me,' and squeezed his arm. 'Tomorrow I buy you tashinopita.'

Yiorgos spoke with Thanos, who was equally relieved. They sent Orestis home to nap, and to return at ten pm. The other receptionist would talk him through the night routine, but it was nothing he couldn't handle. No surprises.

Orestis rode home on a wave of euphoria. The sky held a promise, he could feel it. Yiorgos and Thanos liked him, valued him. He reached for the radio dials in celebration, then stopped himself. A man had died. Instead of music, he listened only to the noise of traffic, the rustle of the wind in the opened windows. It was nothing, he told himself, he was only being superstitious, but not a single red light stopped him on the way.

By ten pm he was back at the Harmonia, exhausted, having failed to sleep a single minute. Not only was there his father's constant clanking in the garage, and his loud politics with Andros and Andrikos, and the neighbours' TV blaring from their veranda, but there was also the drumming in Orestis' body. Lying in bed, shutters drawn with only pinpricks of sunlight dotting the room, he'd felt intensely aware of himself. A vague sense of power had consumed him. Muscles expanding in his biceps. A firmness in his thighs and pecs. There was still some way to go, but he'd felt, for the first time in a long while, attractive. He shut his eyes, to lie alone in his dark private cinema. Images came on the screen, and among them was Thanos. That well-dressed physique. The crisp shirt. The fitted trousers.

These weren't the thoughts of normal men. But they had kept him from sleeping, the idiot.

The second night-shifter was a guy called Dino, one of those international-school kids whose English was better than his Greek. As usual with his type, their chit-chat ended up Greenglish. They'd seen each other on the crossover, but never really spoken. Shame, Orestis was drawn to him. Here was this lean, sun-deprived character who slumped and slunk about, at odds with the hotel's image. He seemed more out of place in the hotel than Orestis had ever felt. But what Dino lacked in presentation he made up for with charisma. Guests, whether back from a long day or on their way out for the night, greeted him as if he was a friend. He recalled names, no need to fake it, prior requests, itineraries. Some of them asked after Elias and were saddened by his absence. 'Family emergency,' Dino explained. Assuaged, the guests moved on.

'Elias and I were a bit of a double-act,' he said to Orestis in English, which Orestis didn't quite understand but accepted with a nod all the same.

When activity in the lobby slowed, Dino talked him through the 'super-late' shift, a phrase he pronounced in exaggerated Cypriot-accented English which made Orestis laugh.

A little after midnight, a middle-aged man with ruffled hair scrambled to the Front Desk to ask if they had condoms. Dino put his hand on Orestis' shoulder. 'It's all right,' he said in Greek, 'just go to the petrol station down the road.'

The guest slapped a twenty-euro note in Orestis' hand. 'Neither of you has a condom in his pocket? I only need one, for God's sake.'

Dino shrugged. 'We're not allowed to get that intimate with guests.'

The man squinted at him as if reading a number plate from afar.

Out in the light of street-lamps, Orestis made his way through clusters of tourists, joggers and screaming teens to the Petrolina not two hundred metres away. The only packs of condoms he could see hung behind the counter, photos of women baring their tits, leaning on trees or reclining on sand dunes. He requested a pack through a ludicrous display of non-verbal indicating. But what did discretion matter, he told

65

himself as he handed over the twenty, the cashier winking him a good night, when there was nothing discreet about any of this? He power-walked back to the hotel, the plastic carrier bag wrapped tightly in his fist.

The guest snatched the condoms from his hand. His brow creased at the packaging. 'Oh, leave the change,' he said with a distracted air and headed for the lifts, still gawking at the condoms.

'What do I do with this?' Orestis asked Dino, showing the change in his palm.

'What do you mean? Keep it.'

'Seriously?'

Dino laughed.

The next hour gave way to all the things that occupied them during the day shifts. Couples calling from their rooms to slur requests for extra wine, kids trying pranks. The late hour made them even more annoying.

Out of nowhere, sitting on a sofa beneath the chandelier, was a man in a smart suit. Same age as Orestis, give or take a year. Handsome, with his curve of waxed hair, all shades of brown like layers of rock. Bright green eyes, deep tan. It was the latter that clicked a switch: the swimmer. The man Orestis had watched on his breaks, but here in the lobby at night instead of in the sea at noon. The sight of clothes on his body was more of a shock than the sight of him at all. That suit – tailored, tastefully neutral – would've cost Orestis' monthly wage. Had he been a guest all this time? Impossible. He'd been at that beach, doing laps and sunbathing, for months. There was something Middle-Eastern about him; those startling eyes, those long fingers. Maybe Turk. Syrian or Lebanese. One of those Arab playboys you heard about. He could wear out money like the sun could skin.

A woman in her forties joined him on the sofa. Their exchange looked friendly enough, if a little hesitant on her part. Barely a couple of minutes had passed before she and the swimmer got up and moved towards the doors, then out towards the swimming pool.

'Wait for the best part,' Dino said.

Orestis' heart leapt. He'd been caught. But everyone else was free to stare, so why not him too? He played it cool: 'Why? What's going on?'

'For now, they're having a chat. But in a moment she'll give him her room number. Then she'll come back inside on her own and go up to her suite. A few minutes later he'll also come back in, then he'll go to the lift and join her upstairs. And he won't be asking us for condoms.'

Dino was grinning.

Did Thanos know about this?

The night-shifter laughed, startling as a popped balloon. 'Re! You look terrified.'

'I'm not.' Orestis realised he had stammered.

'You've gone white like an Englishman.' Dino's inflexion made the comment ironic.

'I just wasn't expecting it. I didn't think Thanos would allow this sort of wankery.'

There was a silence, in which Dino's face darkened. 'Oh, is that what you thought?' he said, still smiling, but with the same knotted brow and gravel voice of Orestis' father when there were Communists on TV.

For a while there was barely any talk, the night shift punctuated only by Dino's mouse-clicks as he browsed the Internet for trainers.

Outside it was cool, but not cool enough to send him back to the uninspiring staffroom. Figuring the beach would be too dark, Orestis sat by the pool to eat his dinner. With no tourists or sunlight, the water was odd, a mere vacancy. He rubbed his eyes: two am. He shouldn't have sat down; how would he ever stand up again? Sandwiches were a bad idea, too. Costlier than pasta and twice as stodgy. He grabbed his bloated stomach, sickened himself with it, then tossed the rest of his dinner in a bin and vowed to quit bread. A dreadful habit, encouraged by his father and, God rest her soul, his grandma.

No, forget God. Let Him die with her. The old girl was sunk in the earth, alone. Both her corpse and coffin were decomposing to nothingness. Tendons and fibres were melting away. For forty days after her death, her soul had wandered along the beach, searching for the peace that had been denied her. A liberated Cyprus, a reunited homeland; even that dream was buried and vanishing with her.

That woman in the lobby, with the swimmer – was she unfulfilled? Or was that giving her too much sympathy? Was there a cuckold somewhere, maybe even in a different suite? Or waiting in bed for her and the swimmer? These things happened, he'd seen them in porn. Or was she on the shelf, a lost cause in the middle of her life with an appetite for nameless flesh? All that kinkiness bubbling under. The nerve of her, whoring herself out in this five-star hotel.

For a moment, Orestis cast himself in the swimmer's life. Exchanges in the lobby, seductions on the veranda. Following a client in the next lift, to an unfamiliar room; taking off a stranger's clothes; feeling a foreign touch. A fleeting, expensive liaison.

The water licked at the pool tiles. How unreal it looked.

How exhilarating it would be to take off his clothes and fall into it. Someone might come outside, catch him in the act. A colleague. A stranger.

A moth beat its wings against a light. Orestis focused on it to lose his hardon. What a tool, sucked into a fantasy that was foolish and dangerous and wrong. Regardless, it wouldn't let him go. He'd spend the rest of the night with Dino at the Front Desk imagining goings-on in rooms on floors above them, those high-up suites where the curtains were thick and the bedsheets soft as foam. Where the remnants of the night were cleared away by young East Asian chambermaids with fantasies of their own; whose job it was to enable this loud silence.

The transaction in the lobby had been a blessing. Before his break, Orestis couldn't fathom how he'd last the rest of the night shift, but now his mind was spinning, his eyes wide open. A whole new side of the Harmonia had been exposed, as if Dino had unlocked a secret wing of infinite rooms.

He could never speak of this to his father, the old man would never shut up about it. He'd call the whole thing vile, un-Christian. Something a Greek might indulge in, maybe, but never a Cypriot. This was the sort of thing that was spoiling the island, this debauchery. These foreigners with their modern ideas, their affairs and scandals and *ménages a trois*, soiling the beaches where St Paul himself once walked. Orestis tried to agree with that voice, to feel revulsion or at least conflict.

As the end of the shift came into view he kept an eye on the lobby.

'Is he back yet?' he asked.

'What?' said Dino, turning from the screen.

'Nothing.'

69

The swimmer must have left while they were occupied, if not during Orestis' break. Not that it mattered; what further details could he draw from wrinkles on a shirt or lipstick on a neck? Future nights rolled ahead of him, a corridor of mirrors teasing glimpses of another life. Patience. He would learn more in time. He would see the swimmer, if not the swimmer's client, again.

When the early-morning crew strolled in slurping Chinos, Orestis realised the night shift was over. It was bright outside, he was wide awake. 'Go home,' Svetlana said, beaming. 'Go away; don't come back.'

He laughed, but then she clarified: 'Thanos say you go home now and tomorrow you do morning shift. They get someone from agency to cover until Elias comes back.'

Orestis' heart fell.

'Goodnight!' said Svetlana in Greek. 'Bye!'

But Orestis couldn't move. 'I don't have to do it again?'

'No, thanks to God!'

'You wanker,' Dino said with a grin and squeezed his shoulder. 'God's looking out for you.'

Orestis' stomach growled. He went to get his bag from the staffroom and headed out, waving back at Svetlana as he passed through the revolving doors. Outside the hotel, he looked about him: the car park and shrubbery, jasmine and hibiscus. Something told him not to go, not yet. He turned to walk back into the hotel, greeting his colleagues again. 'I need to eat,' he said with a shrug, only half-pretending. He waltzed to the café on the terrace and ordered a subsidised coffee with an apricot danish. The Filipino at the counter smiled at him and dismissed his money. 'Next time,' she said. Thank God. He spent the next few minutes sitting on his own and staring out at the sparkling sea below, the handful of morning swimmers. He couldn't remember the last time he felt such intense freedom. That all could stop right then, with no expectation of more. Even the guilt of eating pastry, now that he was meant to be dieting, fluttered away. He was a vital being, a man of flesh and want.

Having finished his breakfast, he left the building a second time. But now, in the car park, the baked seat of his Honda warming him, his hand lingered on the key in the ignition. If the swimmer stepped out of the hotel before Orestis set off, everything would be fine.

He turned the key. The car started up. He released the handbrake, got into gear, checked his mirrors, indicated. He headed out, no-one stepping through the hotel's doors. And soon his car was on the main road, pulling him away from the Harmonia.

Nine

The hotel was a hub for parties. More often than not these were birthday dos for international-school kids, jelly, gateau and American pop, hosted by stay-at-home mums with husbands abroad. But there were also engagement parties, retirement parties, company functions, christenings, Christmas soirées, fundraisers, end-of-school balls; every branch on the tree of life cultivated by the Events team. *Prices are up, customers are down*, his uncle had said on repeat as if money was an endangered species hunted by Angela Merkel. But the Harmonia proved money was alive and breeding. Quality and expense begot their equals.

For the most part, Orestis' shifts would end before a party was in full swing, splitting him in three: one part was nostalgic for childhood birthdays. Another felt the hollowness of missing out. Both were trumped by the third, the relief of having nothing to do with it. No serving brats, no responsibility for drunkards, no duty to clean up after anyone.

But during the hours where his shift overlapped with an event, he would scan the lobby. He'd patrol the quieter corridors, check the corners between windows and potted plants. Svetlana noticed his distraction and had her fun. 'Dreaming of naked ladies?' she would say, or, 'What's wrong?

You sad you don't get cake?' He would laugh out of politeness, but he resented being spied on. And every day he would sit at the beach, waiting.

The sightings were unexpected. The swimmer would appear at the entrance mid-morning, ready to escort a woman to a waiting tourist coach outside. Or he'd be sitting on a stool at the pool bar, face darkened by the shadows of palm fronds. On the last of their encounters, Orestis thought he caught a knowing look in the swimmer's eyes.

For the first time at the Harmonia, the days dragged. Request and response, greeting and platitude. Daily routine became a flavourless puree. That single night shift was as distant as the oil tankers on the horizon. During silent dinners with his father, Orestis' mind would drift from the sitcoms on-screen to card-keys and blackout curtains in his head, coach trips and shopping sprees.

Then, a Russian billionaire acquainted with Mr Ioannidou booked the ballroom for his sixtieth birthday. There was the usual whirlwind of planning. The Russian's wife, a French-woman, became a daily headache for the team, switching decisions on linen, cutlery and menu. One minute she wanted balloons, the next not. Balloons made a comeback, but the colour palette changed. She demanded musicians who were already booked elsewhere. She wanted the cake flown in from Paris. Orestis heard all about it from an increasingly pale colleague. At last, the party was in sight. Yuri and Svetlana gave impromptu Russian lessons. Eagle-eyes unblinking, Mr Ioannidou greeted every employee to congratulate them in advance for a job well done.

'I will speak with him,' Svetlana said to Orestis, 'so that he will fall in love with me and I become Mrs Ioannidou. Then I will have house in Ayios Athanassis with swimming pool.'

'Then you will adopt me,' Yiorgos said, making her explode with laughter.

Orestis was due to leave before the guests arrived. It only made sense to have the Russian speakers on this shift. But there was a feeling in his gut, a reluctance to leave. A face and body made of angles approached the desk. Shoulders like a coat hanger, thin blonde hair down to her waist, she set her Oakleys down on the counter. She introduced herself as the cellist, while a cab driver staggered in beneath a huge black case. The woman had expressive hands, careful posture, direct speech. She caught Orestis looking and, cheeks flushing, he turned his eyes to the PC.

He brought up her reservation and handed her the room key. She hesitated before she spoke. 'There is a parcel coming for me,' she said. 'It was confiscated at the airport, but my sister is sending it by courier.'

'We will bring it to your room,' he replied.

'But she forgot what hotel I was staying in,' the woman went on, voice raised. 'She sent it to the wrong hotel.'

The one she named was a smaller place, not far along the seafront. Orestis assured her he would sort it out. The cellist only stared. She read his name badge and his collar, the cuffs of his shirt, his watch.

Then she raised her eyes to his. 'You will bring it yourself?'

For a second he forgot the word. 'Yes.'

'Good. You know my room.'

Ignoring the porter, she grabbed her cello case and turned on her heel, heading for the lifts.

* * *

On the way to the cellist's room, he held the parcel as if it might jump from his arms and run away. He tried to look casual as he made his way to the lifts. Everyone was busy with the Russian's party. He turned a corner and stopped dead in front of Mr Ioannidou. The giant man simply nodded and carried on. It made Orestis squirm to remember Eva's face, her messages that went unanswered.

For now, there was the cellist. He told himself that the woman was only being fussy. It meant nothing that she specifically requested him in her room, only that she wished for her issue to be handled by a single member of staff. It was a way to avoid complications, that was all.

The lit-up floor numbers ascended. He recalled the jab of Svetlana's elbow once the cellist had walked away, the wink and giggle. The reflected Orestis' pecs were clear through his shirt. His shoulders were full, his biceps stretched the fabric. Side-on, a pair of basketball glutes. He was near-enough ready and felt a surge of pride. The cellist's age didn't matter; the last time he'd had sex was shortly after the Army, two or three years ago, before he'd gone back to his uncle's taverna. His pride deflated.

The room numbers advanced along the corridor. Orestis slowed his pace, feeling uncertainty and foresight on an equal level. He already knew what the room would look like. It seemed unreal there'd be a living person inside it, maybe waiting for him to join her in the double bed, maybe undressed already. He had the strange sensation that this had already happened, or was predestined. He was only playing his part. It was an out-of-body experience, his mind floating somewhere above himself, viewing him as his body moved. It watched him knock on the cellist's door. It detected the sound of music.

It heard the woman invite him into the room. And it saw her, sitting on a stool at the window with her back to the door, the sunlight blacking her out as she played her instrument. He stood by the door, holding the parcel that had brought them to this junction, and waited. Even with his limited knowledge, he knew she played exquisitely. She handled the cello with the precision he'd noted in her movements beforehand. With her hands she coaxed it to speak, to express itself.

At last, she put down her bow and turned.

'Close the door,' she said as if it was nothing.

As he did so, he heard the sound of the curtains drawn shut and saw the light diminish on the walls. His throat was dry.

'Put it down.'

He placed the parcel on the bedside table, next to her Cartier wristwatch.

'Take off your shirt.'

He heard his breath come out.

He could excuse himself politely, explain that he'd misunderstood. Leave. A hundred thoughts rushed through his head: he was shy, he was imperfect, it would be rude to reject her, it would embarrass her, she could have him fired. But his mind gave way. Had anyone ever looked at him with hunger?

So he unbuttoned his shirt. And she exhaled as if she too had been holding her breath. Once his shirt was off, her eyes went straight to his middle. His face burned. He thought to say something, make light of it, *Too many cheese pies*, but he was wary of sounding like an idiot. This woman wanted a man, not a schoolboy. In any case, he was fine. He was fine, he was fine. He held up his chin, and without being asked, removed his belt.

She didn't say a word, only watched as he unzipped his flies

76

and let his trousers fall to the floor. His blood pulsed. He was getting hard, so he focused his mind on trivial things. Lint on the carpet, the pattern of the bed covers. Dull symmetry. He had that sense of being outside of himself again, his mind above them both. But at the same time, he was present in this body, registering the alarm clock on the bedside table, the sound of people at the pool, outside, below. He wondered when she would leave for the party. He saw how those fingers curled around the cello's neck. He stood in his lucky underwear, facing her. Out of instinct, his hands had gone behind his back as if he was in the Army again, awaiting the sergeant's command. There was a pause, to which she raised an eyebrow.

He heard himself laughing, a short, nervous laugh. But under her glare, he slid his shorts down to his feet and stepped out of them. All of a sudden, she looked afraid of him. He ought to have gone. Instead, he walked towards her.

'No,' she snapped. 'On the bed.'

He caught his reflection in the mirror, his own look of dejection. Orestis looking at Orestis, with Orestis watching from above. 'You don't want—?'

She shook her head. 'No. Go on the bed. By yourself.'

In a blend of reluctance and confusion, he obeyed, never having done it for anyone else's enjoyment before. It was unlike the furtive jacks at his father's place, while his grandma made dinner on the floor below, warbling along to the ancient songs on her radio. Here in this room, with a stranger watching him like a god as if he was performing a ritual, he touched himself. He touched his developed chest, the tightening stomach, the dark hairs thickening as his hand travelled downwards, daring even to tease this woman who could end his career with a snap of her fingers. And, watching himself – from the ceiling, from the mirror, from the cellist's own wide eyes — he enjoyed himself to the end.

Ten

B efore his shift, he donned a vest and a pair of shorts to run along the promenade. Only a couple of months before, he'd been too embarrassed to run in public. He'd kept his cardio to a far corner of the gym, from which he watched the backs of more confident men running endlessly towards the windows. He would shower in the hotel's locker-rooms, though he'd never use the gym there; he'd feel awkward to work out with guests.

The light fell soft on the path and powdered sand. He abandoned the headphones, which kept dropping from his ears, to hear only the shush of waves against the shore and his heartbeat and breath within them.

The last time he saw his cousin, Pavlos squeezed his bicep and said, 'You stud!'

The encounter with the cellist danced around in his head. The woman had even put a few notes in his hand, those hands of hers, as he opened her door to leave. As if it was owed to him. This surprised Orestis; the entire time she'd sat rigid on the stool, one leg over the other, both hands on one knee. Her sole reaction was a look of shock at the end as if she hadn't expected a climax. After he'd wiped himself clean with the hand towel she'd tossed to him, she'd opened the parcel.

Inside was a quaint-looking snow globe, a European mountain village. Flakes fell over miniature houses and cobbles. Her eyes were wet. He'd snuck out of her room, down the stairs, slipped through the doors to the pool and taken the path around to the car park. The following morning, he'd been ready to answer Svetlana's questions. The lies, based on prior experience, came easily. How demanding the cellist had been when he delivered the parcel, how she insisted on opening and inspecting it before she'd let him go. Svetlana had laughed with pained recognition. Over dinner, he was tense with his father as if the man was wise to what had happened, or he might splutter a confession himself. But the thought of his grandma, and what she might say about the whole thing, kept his mouth shut.

The cellist had checked out the next morning, coolly handing her key back to him as if he might be anyone, and left. No other situation presented itself, though Orestis stayed alert. He worried at times he might be overstepping, might be flirting with women, married or not, who'd no desire to see him naked. He recalled details of the cellist, her deportment, physiognomy, anything he might use to identify similar types. There would be more of them out there, people who wanted him.

* * *

Antsy from a mood he couldn't explain, something about the directionless halfway point of twilight, he went to a bar with Paris. He wore a shirt Eva had convinced him to buy, in the hope it would earn its tag.

Paris strolled over with two whiskeys and Coke, as Orestis

locked eyes with a fake blonde on a bar stool. Black dress stuck to her skin as if she'd been tarred, contacts as blue as diamonds. She sipped her drink and batted smiles between him and her girlfriends.

'Re, she's giving you a pass,' said Paris. 'Go.'

'You go.'

'I'm not the one she's looking at.'

'E... She'll want me to buy her a drink.'

'And?'

What could he say? That it ought to be the other way around? 'She's having cocktails. I don't have the money for that shit.'

Paris shook his head, laughing. 'Well, that one's just drinking Keo.'

Standing at the bar was a group of guys. The one Paris was talking about, with white-mousse hair and stud earrings, glanced over. Short but built like a Spartan.

'Fuck you.' He whacked Paris' arm.

'Easy!'

'You think I'm gay?'

'No, re. I was saying men don't cost as much.'

Orestis resisted looking back at the guy who was now eyeing him.

'Anyway, what's wrong with him?' said Paris. 'He looks good. Like Action Man.'

Orestis scoffed and folded his arms, which bulged out his biceps.

They left empty-handed. After Paris drove off, Orestis sat in his own car and watched the street-lamp in the black sky. Instead of driving home, he saw his hands turn the wheel for Amathountos Avenue. He carried on until he reached the good hotels, parked at one, went inside. He saw himself head for the lobby, and take a seat in a leather tub chair. The ceiling was so high the chandelier stopped ten-fifteen metres above him. He tried to draw on something, an allure he could project like a torch. A few minutes went by. None of the well-dressed ladies had done more than glance his way as they passed. Maybe there was a code, some sort of visual signal. A dialect of the underworld. When a member of staff came to clear away a coffee cup, Orestis felt his face go red and stumbled away with a goodnight. He drove back home. In the rearview mirror, his eyes looked frightened.

'Idiot,' he said. 'Useless piece of shit.'

* * *

It had been weeks. The swimmer was gone.

At least Orestis was making strides at work. It was clear he was being prepped for a bigger role. Just a few more months of saving and money would lose its grip on his sleep. He looked better, and it showed in others' faces. As Easter approached he fasted for the first time since he was a kid. His grandma had always been strict about her fast, and gradually conceded defeat when it came to the men in her life. She would dutifully buy and prepare meat for every meal, but it never touched her lips. She served her men yoghurt and eggs and poured milk in their Nescafés. But while she fasted for the love of God, Orestis did so for himself. The diet of pulses and vegetables was potent fuel. The stranglehold of sugar had weakened, no longer did he feel fatigued and heavy. T-shirts now stretched where they flattered.

Without his grandma to make her casseroles, he tackled them himself. Those first few days after her death, he'd been lost. She'd left no recipes, no cookery books to explain the basics. She'd carried all those foods in her head, the way her own mother and grandma would have done back in the village. The old girl went by vague amounts, tossing cups of oil or sugar into a mixing bowl with that intuitive way of an expert. She'd sprinkle cinnamon onto minced meat till it smelled right. His father could roast a lamb, and like his son had picked up basic cooking from his Army days: scrambled eggs, thick chips, fried tomatoes. But Kostas was usually in the garage, often in the company of Andros and Andrikos. Orestis was too old to ask his dad to cook for him, and refused to microwave ready meals. Time to learn. And, he told himself, these were useful skills for when he finally got his own place. Soon.

Aside from calling his aunts for guidance, he found recipes online and printed them off on the 'office' machine in the corridor. Once off-white, now grey, the thing groaned and choked out documents streaked with ink. With confidence came experimentation. The one time his father had sampled a foreign dish his son had made, he'd grimaced and pushed the plate away. 'What is this wankery?' he'd said, and sliced up a round village loaf to make himself a ham sandwich. From then on, Orestis made a meal for himself, and a simplified version of it for his old man. He'd serve it up and eat in silence as Kostas chewed and smacked his lips, knowing that their days together were numbered. With his next paycheque, Orestis bought recipe books, English ones from Kyriakou Bookshops, to make the sort of food they served at the hotel. His father stared at him, dumbstruck, when he expressed these thoughts aloud. 'Good thing they pay you well. They turned you into a European. Soon you'll be talking like a fag Kalamaras.'

Orestis brushed the comment off. Let his father commit to

his tiny world. Born in Cyprus, stay in Cyprus, speak like a Cypriot for the rest of your life – what was the point? Greek spoken by Greeks was refined. Cypriot dialect was rough, ill-mannered; the language of peasants. Sit back and accept your lot in life? Why? And let people lucky enough to be born in a better position horde all the goods? Fuck that. To refuse to cultivate himself would be like leaving a garden as a patch of grass. Or worse, it would be like paving it over, concrete, like most of Lemesos. His body was only the first of the things he would improve.

* * *

Paris had started flicking Orestis' arms and calling him Super-man with an ironic smile.

'Things don't always look as good beneath the surface,' he said.

This came as Orestis spoke of Thanos and his immaculate suits. He baulked at the comment, not just on behalf of his superior, who so far had only revealed more beauty beneath the surface. 'Sometimes, my friend,' Orestis replied, 'things look good on the surface because they're well made.'

Paris looked impressed. He pulled out a pack of cards from his pocket and started dealing.

'No, re, put them away. I can't be arsed.'

'Shut up. You've got to keep your mind alive.'

Orestis smarted. He was about to form a response when Paris continued:

'Studies have shown that it's rejuvenating to keep our minds alive with daily mental workouts. You don't want to end up like our grandparents, do you? Repeating the same old phrases from the Bible because you can't remember anything else?'

Orestis laughed.

They were interrupted by an approaching monologue: Eva, talking to them both as if they'd been chatting for minutes already. She lowered herself to their table, snug in a low-cut dress.

'What happened to your eyes?' Paris said. 'Were you blinded?'

'Shut up, you brick,' she said. 'Contacts are "in" right now. What would you know about trends?'

'That only the brainless follow them.'

She slapped his thigh. 'So what's this about the Bible? Only Paris could bring up the Church in a trendy bar.'

'Nothing,' said Orestis. 'We're talking about our grand-mothers.'

'Mine made the best rice pudding, swear to God!'

'No, mine did.'

'Shut up you villager, what would you know about taste?'

Paris laughed. 'Your eyes are freaking me out. You're like a robot.'

She flicked her hair. 'But a gorgeous robot, yes?'

'Why did you make us come to this place? The coffee's undrinkable.'

'Of course it's undrinkable. This is *the* place to be right now, hello?' She noticed the cards on the table. 'Deal me in.'

'Are you sure cards are "in" this season?' Orestis said.

Eva flicked her unnatural blue eyes at him. 'You're lucky you're so handsome,' she said.

The comment sent a shiver down his spine.

They played a few rounds of poker. Between her turns, Eva asked about the job. Orestis cast flashbacks of the cellist aside.

He settled on vague pleasantries; how much he liked Thanos and Yiorgos (Eva loved them, sweethearts, both of them!), how he recently saw her dad.

'And what do you want to achieve there?'

Orestis was stumped. 'At the hotel?'

Paris' hand churned the air. 'Pe! What is this, an interview?'

'Shut it, re! I'm interested in his career.'

'E... Of course, I want to be Manager...'

'Front Desk or right at the top?'

'So high up he'll be next to God,' said Paris.

Eva crossed herself.

Orestis tasted his words before he spoke them. 'I want to progress as far as I can.'

She looked him in the eye. 'Trust me,' she said, 'you'll go far.'

There was a silence, which Paris filled with a breath of smoke. 'Who needs God,' he said, 'when you have a Ioannidou looking out for you?'

Orestis barely had time to take offence.

* * *

Three am. He and Eva walked through the square towards the half-plot of land where she'd parked her car. The old red-light district, where a teenage Orestis had snuck glances at the sun-drained photos of naked women on the windows of strip-joints. Once he'd found the nerve, he'd approached a lady standing outside the Rialto and she took him to a heat-peeled flat. In those days his virginity was valued in Cyprus Pounds. He noticed there were no boys on the street corners.

Air tickling his collarbone, he became all too aware of

himself. He and Eva were alone. There was a sense of something coming, something to be stopped. He should have driven, even if he'd planned to drink.

'Why did you park all the way over here?'

'This guy only charges two euro.'

They got in her white convertible and headed for his dad's.

'Thanks for taking me home.'

'You're too polite,' she said, in a voice he barely recognised.

They drove the rest of the way in near silence, with only the music from the radio between them. A ballad by Christina Aguilera came on, and Eva turned it up. Something about blaming someone and being sorry about it, the voice and strings like spears. Eva sighed, 'God almighty.' Orestis thought the singer a slut, but scenes from her videos had got him through many a lonely night. He kept his thoughts to himself. Eva was enraptured, a different woman, smoking out of her window and wafting the nicotine away from him as her face emoted along with the song.

When they reached his place, she stopped the car. Then she put her hand on his knee. They sat there for a minute, unspeaking.

'Eva...' he began, not knowing where he would end.

She nodded. 'I know.'

'It's only that Paris...'

She turned, startled.

Now that he'd started, he may as well finish. 'I think he likes you. It makes things a bit difficult for me.'

He bit his tongue. This was wrong. But there was some truth in his words. He'd suspected for a while that Paris might have feelings for Eva, despite his socialism and her entire way of being. But he had no claim on his friend's emotions, no right to use him as a chip. He tried to backtrack, to reform his stance. Blamed his reluctance on the fact that her father owned the hotel. It would complicate things at work, he didn't want others crying nepotism. He wished to succeed on his own merit, not because he was seeing the boss' daughter. The rumours would affect them all. It wasn't fair.

She smiled a thin but warm smile and squeezed his knee in thanks. 'You're too nice. But you need to start thinking of yourself.'

His cheeks burned. 'E, I'm learning.'

'Don't worry,' she said. 'Stick with me and you'll pick it up. You'll always have a Ioannidou looking out for you.'

He stood by his father's garage and watched as she drove away through the shambles of his neighbourhood.

He wouldn't go back inside. Not yet.

Eleven

If his grandma had still been alive, they'd have done seven churches on Good Friday. It had been a sacred duty to kiss the reclining Jesus at seven altars, in seven houses of God. Orestis had assumed they'd at least try, if only for the first Easter since her death, to honour the tradition. But he and his father had managed two churches in the district before pulling over at a bakery for tachinopita. 'Aren't you worried you'll get fat?' his father said, sesame paste at the corners of his mouth. It was the nearest he'd got to a joke. But there, sitting in the car by the beach, Orestis had given in to his hunger. The fast was almost over, the pastry was vegan, he was due a treat.

By nightfall, his father had no intention of leaving the sofa. Orestis set out alone to the nearest church. A group of men carried Jesus from the altar to the grounds outside. He fell into step with the other mourners to follow the procession around the neighbourhood. They passed the pre-war bungalows, where jasmine curled around iron gates. Elderly women got to their feet from plastic white veranda chairs. The smoke from the priest's censer drifted to their bowed heads.

Then it was Saturday, almost midnight on Sunday, and Christ was due to rise. Orestis and his father stood outside the

89

church, too late to claim a seat indoors. The sky was already black. A bunch of youths tossed twigs onto the unlit bonfire, while others around them huddled with their hand-painted candles and protective foil. There came a ripple through the crowd. Rolling out from the doors of the church, a wave of hope and smiles. Of *Christ is risen*, and *Truly he is risen*, as strangers lit each other's candles and spread the holy light. The priest's chant soared to the heavens in thanks. Christ was risen.

* * *

The swimmer returned to the beach. On the last few sightings at the hotel he'd been hidden under winter coats, so to see his flesh was akin to seeing his true form. As he bathed, Orestis watched like a hunter. The man's physical perfection – his abs, that V at his groin – pricked a primal fear.

The swimmer walked out of the sea. His calves dragged the shallow water, his stomach spasmed from the shock of the air. He was already looking at Orestis when the latter spoke.

'Aren't you cold?'

The other man didn't even blink. 'You get used to it.'

Orestis had spoken in Cypriot dialect, but the man had responded with a Greek inflexion. He felt suddenly nervous.

The swimmer carried on: 'Go in, it's fine.'

'A, it's OK. I'm going back to work in a bit.'

'You work at the hotel?'

'Yeah, the Front Desk.'

Those green-gold eyes opened wide. 'A yeah, that's where I've seen you.' He offered his hand. 'Lefteris.'

Orestis shook it and gave his name, too. Not long into their chat, his break was over, so they said their goodbyes. Orestis glanced behind him as he walked the path back to routine. The swimmer had stretched out on a towel to coat his tan with another layer.

For his next early shift, Orestis wore a pair of black swimming trunks beneath his uniform. He'd scoured the city for just the thing, and averted his eyes from the card machine as he bought it. An investment. It transformed him into the sort of man who goes for a swim after work. The confidence lent him a physical ease, or so he hoped: that fluidity and certainty of the cellist. The swimmer – Lefteris – was as controlled as she was. Cypriot, but with speech tuned to a Greek lilt. Few gesticulations. Self-control. This was his power; the force that drew the lonely women who never had to work for anything.

On the beach, Orestis removed his shoes, a sweet relief. The palm fronds swayed above. He removed his uniform, as airborne grains of sand nipped at his body. He cursed himself for not getting changed in the poolside cubicles. It hadn't seemed appropriate for an employee to parade himself through the grounds.

His stomach could have done with more definition, otherwise, he was acceptable. He adjusted himself so that the trunks justified their expense.

Lefteris wasn't there.

Orestis should've come on his break, and used the pool shower afterwards. Trembling, he forced himself into the water and floated, shivered, till his muscles and bones and skin relaxed. How clear the water was, even in a city full of cars. For a moment he allowed himself simply to lie on the surface, eyes closed, to be held by the water. A baptism. The

River Jordan. His grandma asleep in her gown in the grave.

In the distance, there was a yacht. Too far out for him to make anyone out, but he watched the figures walking around on it, shrieking and leaping from it, splashing about in the water around it. Kissing on it. Touching.

He'd drifted too far. He pulled himself towards the shore again, feet kicking up plumes of sand. Felt the gaining emptiness as he stood up and walked out of the sea, its sweet clear water trickling off and away.

Standing in the shade of the eucalyptus trees was a man. Thanos.

The manager looked him up and down with that curious expression of his. His eyes darted back from the wet black trunks.

Orestis bent to grab his towel. 'Hello,' he said, not meeting the manager's eye.

'Good time for a swim.'

'Yes, it's a good temperature.' Orestis could almost hear his dad: *Listen to you. Like a Greek fag.*

'I'm glad you're taking the time to relax. You work hard, Orestis. Don't think I don't notice.' There was a weight to his tone.

'Thank you,' said Orestis.

'You're doing well here. Carry on doing well.'

'Of course.'

The manager looked away, leaving Orestis to grab his things. His heart, his hands, shuddered. He took the path towards the poolside changing rooms. Thanos stayed behind to stare out at the sea; at the orange buoys wobbling on the crests of the waves, and at the yacht where silhouetted figures were moving, parting, intertwining, having the time of their lives.

92

Orestis tried again, this time on his lunch break. Through the foliage on the edge of the lawn, he caught Lefteris in the water. The men waved at each other.

'I'm coming in!'

More eager than he'd intended. As he stripped off his uniform and packed it neatly into his bag, he was aware of eyes on him, real or imagined, but he forced himself to breathe. He trod into the sea, and Lefteris laughed at his flinch when the cool waves slapped his legs. Soon he was immersed. And within touching distance of a perfect being. It was oddly thrilling. To watch the contours and angles of Lefteris' body arching and writhing into and out of the water. To know that a body could be like this. To see what existence could be. The man was a creature of the deep, as part of its ebb and flow as seaweed. Orestis felt the urge to touch him. To feel against his palm this extraordinary thing.

'Where are you from?' he asked.

'Lefkosia,' And, anticipating the follow-up question, Lefteris added: 'I moved here for the sea.'

There followed a tad more info, the bits of peel he discarded to allow Orestis a glimpse. The guy was born rich, it made sense. He'd never needed a job, completed his Army service, studied in England — Brighton, he said, good for gigs and clubs — before coming back to resume a stress-free life. Of course, he'd been to a private international school. He'd spent much of his adulthood at functions, on red carpets, snapped for gossip weeklies next to TV stars in his circle. Droplets of water hung from his lashes. It was hard for Orestis to look him in the eye. Too easy to imagine the body before him in various states, with nameless women, maybe even men. Orestis would never be worth an inch of this being.

And then it struck him: the end of his break.

'I still have to shower!'

Lefteris shrugged and said with a grin, 'They'll manage for a few more minutes.' Part of Orestis wanted to stay, to hell with work and duties. But he trudged away. There would be hours and days of this soon, just him and Lefteris bobbing in their own bubble of time, the need for work a distant, repulsive memory.

From the sea, Lefteris called out: 'I'm going to a party on a boat this Friday. Come.'

Refusal was not an option.

Thankfully, he had no need to change his shift. The minute he got back to the Front Desk, showered and clothed but still tingling with salt, Yiorgos asked if he could do an early on Friday instead. Orestis allowed a moment's hesitation before nodding.

'Oof!' said Svetlana, looking outside. 'We will drown.'

A sudden downpour thumped at the windows. They all stood still for a moment, watching the water that burst and slithered on the glass, hearing the rumblings in the sky. The sky was a violet rage. The tourists gathered to gawp. Orestis had the odd sensation that all of this was for him. This pulsating weather, this clash of colours. A door had been opened.

* * *

It was a given he'd stand out, for all the wrong reasons; non-brand shoes, cheap watch, schooling. Dressed in a cut-price imitation of Lefteris – dark jeans, white shirt, light jacket – he gave himself a pep talk. A strong fragrance, something manly, aquatic, would really set the look off, but he couldn't

94

bring himself to shell out for those French-named scents at the Debenhams counters. Not yet. His usual Axe would do. He hadn't been to a party in years, never to one on a boat. He wouldn't show up in his car. Either leave it somewhere out of sight and walk or take a cab. He appraised himself again.

Who cared what those rich people sipping champagne would think of him?

Just in case, he'd worn his lucky underwear.

He parked near the St Raphael resort and walked down to its marina, where the sun was already sinking pink into the sea. Of all the yachts only one was lit, but it showed no signs of a party. Orestis worried he might be early, so he spent a few minutes pacing the beach. Rows of empty white chairs sat with their umbrellas closed, asleep, and the sea rolled darkly out to the horizon. To think of all the vessels that skimmed its surface, the millions of fish and mammals and crustaceans beneath it... There was so much of the world he could never know or see. Tears came to his eyes. Infinite possibilities, too many for a single person in a single lifetime to catch, were better than none. If it made him feel smaller, good. For if there was a higher power – if not God then something else; Nature, Energy – it was a comfort to imagine that his fate was not his burden. That he might already be cradled in a future security he didn't yet know. *Kismet is a fantasy*, Paris always said. Things were random, not designed. It was man's own actions that impacted his self, and those around him, and those far removed from him. Where Orestis saw an open field, Paris saw a forest of thorns.

Without his watch, Orestis had no clue of the time so he hurried back to the marina just in case. He kept his back straight, took a few deep breaths and, pleased by the bulk of

95

his arms, trod across the dock. Smoking on the deck of a yacht was Lefteris. The man waved at him, flicked his cigarette into the water, and invited him up.

'Handsome devil,' Lefteris said with a whistle.

Orestis laughed. And no sooner had he grabbed onto the railing and heard the splash of water between vessel and dock below his feet than he understood what this evening was. His head filled with air, his eyes with dots of colour.

Kostas would lose his shit.

Lefteris, smelling of flowers and leather, threw his arm around Orestis and led him through the glass doors.

In the lounge, they were greeted first by the hostess, in English. 'Welcome!'

There was a glossy white bar with chrome-and-turquoise stools. A large flat TV on the walls. A bracket of plush white sofas bearing three women and another young man.

'Hello,' he said to the hostess. 'Thank you for having me.'

She kissed him on both cheeks. The women all looked forty or over, all foreign. One had a Russian accent. Orestis didn't process their names, his heartbeat overrode the chat. The other guy was Cypriot too, but fair-haired and blue-eyed. He seemed already acquainted with the women, or at least one of them, one with Germanic looks who swept her hand through his hair as they laughed. The hostess offered drinks. He thought better of asking for Keo. She mixed him a whiskey and Coke at the bar while Lefteris bantered. Not knowing what to say or where to look, Orestis let his eyes wander. They stumbled on the other woman, the Russian. She'd been watching him. They said nothing to each other, but she cast her eyes down and sipped her drink as if she knew something he didn't.

'I have seen you already...' said the host, pointing at Orestis. Before he could respond, Lefteris jumped in: 'He's a model.'

'Ooh! Very nice.'

'He poses for artists, too. Maybe you know someone...?'

'Of course! I know many!'

Orestis shivered. When Lefteris grinned at him, he had no idea what it meant.

Over the next hour or so, thanks to the whiskey or the new identity, he began to feel more at ease. On land, he was Orestis the servant, on the boat he was Orestis the muse. At intervals he suspected he might be mistaken; this was just a party, they were all here to enjoy each other's company, nothing more. Except that the only thing they had in common was the English language. The other two men were by far the more fluent. Their American-accented flow betrayed a lifetime of private schools. Tipsy, Orestis was loose enough to mention his mother's background, which made the Russian woman look at him with interest. The host regaled them with stories of her trips to London. She was large, long wavy hair like tentacles over a bust he couldn't help but glance at. In her bountiful fizz was a trace of the egomaniac. And the woman who stroked the blonde man's thigh, she had the eyes of a hopeful girl in her tightened face. As if Lefteris and his friends might surprise her somehow, disprove what she knew of men.

If the bands on their fingers weren't proof enough, the women dropped mentions of their spouses. The Russian was mostly quiet, and when she spoke her voice was low. Orestis watched her, the sharp jawline and the deep black eyes, the long nose in profile over those mysteriously curled lips. Hers was a slender body, thinner than he'd normally go for, with a dancer's elegant strength.

Suddenly he knew: he was her match. Lefteris had got cosy with his arm around the hostess as she laughed apple-cheeked at a story she was telling. The fair guy's eyes had gone catlike, pupils dilated as the woman next to him squeezed his thigh. Orestis' heartbeat quickened. The Russian got up from her seat, cutting his breath. She let herself out onto the deck. With caution, he followed her outside.

Did she also feel nauseous? Maybe they'd both committed to something beyond their grasp. Outside in the cool air, her back to him as she leant against the railing and smoked against the black night, the foaming waves beneath her, he suspected that wasn't the case. She knew he'd come to join her, and barely turned her head.

'Your mother is English,' she said.

'...Yes.'

'Mm.' She dragged on her cigarette. 'I love England. My husband, he hates it.'

'Your husband is from Cyprus?'

She smiled at this, surprising him. 'So obvious, yes?' Fading, she turned back to the sea. 'He say they have no culture, the English. I say not everyone can be Greek.'

Emboldened by her sudden willingness to chat, he asked more out of courtesy than curiosity: 'Where are you from?'

'You think Russia, yes?'

'Ukraine?'

Her eyebrow shot up in the negative as she inhaled. 'Belarus,' she said, blowing the smoke away.

'A...' He knew nothing about her country, so he kept it at that.

She didn't press him. 'You visit England?'

'Not really.' And, seeing her narrowed eyes, he thought it

best to be honest. 'Actually, I have never been. Never left Cyprus.'

Now she really looked at him. 'Never,' she repeated, softly as if to herself.

She shivered. Something about the darkness, his senses whipped by the sound and spray of the water, the lights from the marina and the rows of other yachts, her eyes averted from him but her body emitting a pull, he longed for the night to reach its point. Even there on the deck would have been fine with him if that was what she wanted. He guessed that it might be. Tentatively, he stretched a finger to the goosepimpled flesh of her arm and stroked it. She responded by allowing him. Then she flicked the stub of her cigarette into the black. Without a word, she took his hand and led him back through the lounge, which had been vacated. The corridor teemed with whispered groans as they headed towards an opened cabin, where the Russian – Belarussian – allowed him to see his attraction through.

* * *

Her name was Darya. At first, this bothered him, because an elderly teller at his bank had the same name, but he cast the thought aside. Belarusian Darya was also older, overtaking him by fifteen – maybe twenty – years. But she lit a fire in him with her own.

After sex, his first taste in a long while, Orestis felt conflicted. Part of him wanted to spend more time with this woman, if only not to appear rude. The rest of him couldn't face returning to his father's house in daylight when there might be customers or uncles to detect his shame. Other guys did it all the time, but Orestis never had and wasn't ready to confront his old man with a new persona. There would be other mornings, he promised himself, to sit on the sunny deck of a yacht, making breakfast and conversation with people who lived free of strings; other mornings to linger in a perfumed bed. Darya understood, no hard feelings. Like other East-Europeans he'd met, she was practical and didn't show much emotion. But she climbed on top of him again before he went, and told him she liked it.

Walking back to his car, he was struck by this otherness. The sun had only dimly begun to rise, which made the jetty, the boats, the St Raphael resort look paused. In all those rooms, all those bodies who weren't him, living lives that weren't his... Even he was a different Orestis now, one who'd stepped through to a different world.

He got into his battered little Honda and sighed, wishing Darya back on his lap. Before setting off again to the flaking plaster of his dad's garage, he counted out the euro the Belarusian had given him. All those notes fanned out in his hands: that was how much he'd pleased her.

Twelve

For his uncle Andrikos' birthday, the family held a lunch at their summer house; an extravagance they could afford back in the Nineties when they lucked out at the stock market weeks before it crashed. Thanks to auntie Lenia, they'd made some wise investments that allowed them to hang on to the house. For most of the year the four-bedroom, four-en-suite property sat empty, a hot topic for Orestis and his father. They rehashed their opinions on every drive up and down the mountain to it. Content to let his old man drive – not that anyone else would've been allowed to – Orestis sat back and watched the view through an increasing density of pines. Ears popping, the sun diluted by his shades, a driver at his side, he felt like someone approaching Lefteris. He would never work a regular job again. He'd say goodbye to the Harmonia, the tourists, the small talk with colleagues, for good. On the other hand, the hotel boosted his ego. Yiorgos had noted his ability to liaise with other departments, his ease with the other managers. The assistant manager, the dark cloud at his interview, was rumoured to be leaving soon, and Yiorgos hinted that some of those duties might be passed to Orestis. More duties, on a day like today, was precisely what he didn't want to think about. The increase in wages, on the other hand...

Andrikos sat in his camping chair in the garden as his wife and sisters-in-law fussed around him. That old baseball cap sat on his head, shielding him from light if not dirt. Andros was over by the spit, watching the chunks of lamb as they slowly turned. Kostas, naturally, went to oversee, having taken his can of Coke from the outstretched hand of a niece.

'You look good,' said uncle Andros, slapping Orestis' back.

Orestis gave a bashful smile.

'He spends all day at that gym,' his father said.

'So when do you work?'

'At night,' Orestis replied.

'I want to move the old fridge from the garage later,' Andros said.

'Sure.'

'Re! You don't think those are real muscles, do you!' said Andrikos with a throaty laugh. 'It's an illusion, he's wearing a costume like the Spidermans at the carnival.'

Orestis left the smoky air to hug and kiss aunts and cousins and in-laws on the veranda.

In the kitchen, Auntie Maria yelled over the din of her cooking. 'My dashing young man!' And she squeezed his cheeks the way his grandma used to. He wondered if she'd ever done what Darya had done. Then he blinked the thought away. The women chopped tomatoes, cucumber and feta into a salad, lashed it with olive oil, popped black-eyed beans out of pods and sliced lemons. Whereas Orestis had never paid attention to their kitchen chores before, today he found himself watching closely. He enquired about ingredients and quantities.

'Good!' Maria said. 'A man who'll cook for his wife.'

Auntie Lenia asked, 'How many girlfriends do you have?'

'None.'

'None?'

'Nobody wants me, auntie.'

'E... What can I say? They're all dizzy from their phones and laptops these days,' she said. 'But find someone before you get too fussy.'

'Dashing young man like this,' Maria said, 'you think he'll have a problem finding someone?'

'That's what I'm saying, he must be fussy!' She turned to Orestis and wagged a finger. 'Don't be. It gets harder the older you get.'

'I'm not fussy,' he said with a grin. 'I'll take anyone.'

A flicker in his auntie's eye made him catch himself.

'Just please promise me,' Maria said, stirring a casserole, 'that you won't be one of those Cypriots with a Russian. I can't abide them leaving their wives for Russians.'

Orestis bristled.

'Agreed,' said Lenia. 'They're all sluts.'

Darya's small pert breasts against his chest. Her fingers squeezing.

'Come on, auntie...'

'What else are they going to take? Our land, our businesses, our men. The things you hear about their ghettos in Paphos, pe...! They've taken over. Before you know it we'll be giving them our twelve points in Eurovision.'

A beast of a laugh from Maria, her cheeks already glossy from the steam of the casserole. 'E,' she said, 'as long as they keep the Turks away...'

'That's something, at least. Just keep them off our boys.'

To shift the topic, Orestis said: 'Better them than English-women, right?'

His aunts blinked and shifted a little. Both smiled kindly.

'Listen,' Lenia said in a softer tone. And he noticed for the first time how thick her hair was. 'Your mother had her faults. She was wrong for what she did, but she isn't a bad person.'

'I know,' he said. And he looked down at her I LOVE CYPRUS apron, with its map of the island, the sketches of Aphrodite and the Kourion. Ammohostos written as Famagusta. *I know*, he'd said, making both the aunts look happy with him. But how could he possibly know?

They took the food outside. Orestis allowed himself a bit of lamb and salad but no potatoes. When his aunts protested that he hadn't eaten their food, Andrikos yelled in his husky voice that they were trying to make him fat, then tell him he was too fat and he should stop eating. Orestis gave in to some of his cravings and helped himself to strips of pitta that he dunked in the tart tahini. After lunch, Pavlos arrived. Not three years ago, his lateness would've been down to late-night clubbing and daytime sleeping. These days it was down to work and training. Orestis still struggled to align his old cousin with the current one. It didn't seem plausible that a man could truly change. He felt a renewed closeness with him as they stood side by side at the mountain edge of the garden, watching Pavlos' remote-controlled helicopter spin away towards the faded peaks. At the other end of the lawn, the younger kids gathered around Andrikos and found everything he said to them hilarious. Orestis wished that his dad was like that. He looked over at his old man, there on the veranda with Lenia and Maria, their daughters and their husbands discussing real estate, and was surprised to find him looking back. A smile on his face. And something approaching pride.

* * *

Almost a week had passed since Darya. During that time, he'd spent every shift at the Front Desk with only half his mind on work, the other half on her sturdy frame. Aside from the images in his head, there was the constant reminder in Yuri and Svetlana's accents. Not to mention the slender wives and girlfriends of VIPs, who with their Marc Jacobs handbags and white-framed Ray-Bans took the lobby, corridors and poolside flagstones like a catwalk. One glance at his position prevented a second. Only his regular, the widow from Lebanon, flirted back. At times she trod close to the edge of taking it further. Orestis dreaded she might overstep.

Once again, the beach was missing Lefteris. He was the conduit for Darya or women like her. Without Lefteris, the portal to that life was closed.

He began to dissect that night on the yacht. She'd seemed to enjoy herself. She'd coolly assessed him, but only in that manner of East-Europeans sizing up a person's personhood, not a man's manhood. In that regard, he knew from his Army days that he was all right. She hadn't shown interest in the brands he wore, despite the obvious quality of her short black dress. He autopsied his technique, and with a grimace recalled that he'd come too soon on the first go. On his second she'd orgasmed, he was sure. The third time, he'd done all he could for her. She had wanted him. She'd told him she liked it. She'd paid him more than he'd ever been paid for a day's work.

There'd been an intensity with the Belarusian that he'd never felt before. As if they'd been split parts of a single object, the proverbial saucepan and lid that had found each other. He could still smell her, taste her. Those fingers on him.

In the meantime, he kept his payment in the box of a Nintendo 64, where there was no chance his father would come across it. What an idiot, when his bank account was hungry for that money, he ought to have deposited it. Yet the idea of spending that wage, to dilute it to digital figures on an ATM screen, made him cold inside. Instead, he kept it in the console box and took it out every night before bed. The notes at his fingertips like Darya's hair, like the skin of her calves. He'd stuff them away in that box he'd had since he was twelve, when the fantasy of a woman was as intangible as the smoke from her mouth, out on the deck, floating off to the dark sea.

After the drought came rainfall. Orestis was eating his salad of pulses, looking out at the waves, when Lefteris walked towards him on the sand.

'Where were you?' Orestis asked, mad at himself for sounding so pleased.

'I spent a few days at my parents'.'

That simple phrase – *a few days* – was a punch. To some people time was a valley that rolled peacefully on; to Orestis it was an escalator, leading up and up to a sheer drop.

'I got a message from Darya,' Lefteris said, peeling off his V-neck top. 'She liked you. She wants you to go to her place on Friday night, while her husband is away.' Grinning, he tweaked Orestis' nipple through his shirt and gave him a wink. 'We can't always choose them.'

'What do you mean?'

'I didn't know she was the friend.'

'Whose friend?'

'Darya. I didn't know it was her you would be getting.'

Orestis frowned. 'Why? What's wrong with her?'

Lefteris' expression was of amused surprise. 'Nothing,' he

said, altering it. 'She's beautiful. You wanker. You're going, right?'

Orestis left a pause. 'Yeah,' he replied with a shrug. 'Why not?'

The swimmer regarded him, a strange smile on his face. Then he waded into the sea, swam out deep enough to dunk his head, and whipped up an arc of water with his hair. He waved to Orestis as the employee went back to his day job, his lunch break finished.

* * *

When he next met up with Paris, they shot some hoops in a public court. Beyond the concrete slab rose yet more concrete — refugee council blocks, offices for businesses now dormant. Their only mark of beauty was the sunset-reflecting windows, scattered like rose petals across their facades.

Paris dribbled the ball, then leapt off the ground in that effortless way of his. His dunk was a whisper through the net. Orestis' steps were heavy, his own dunks a clash of board and pole.

'I'm being promoted,' he said, after another dunk from Paris. 'Kind of. They're giving me assistant manager duties.'

'Bravo.'

Paris had dribbled the ball around him and leapt up to get another shot in.

Orestis almost said her name. *Darya.* How reckless he could be right now, how easy it would be to spill this secret. There was the thrill of dangling over a precipice; a mere push would change everything, forward or backward, it didn't matter – adrenaline was in the state between.

A dog barked, rough, low. It was pressing its face to the wire fence, past which walked a triad of schoolgirls. Orestis hit the ball away from Paris and, seizing it with both hands, tossed it at the net from centre court. It hit the board, the ring, then finally fell through. He lifted his tank top to wipe his face. Paris turned to chase the ball, which was skimming its way along the concrete towards the laughing girls.

Later they went for coffee. It dawned on Orestis that Eva had got more scarce, and not through a lack of invites. He tried not to feel either way about it. The era had simply passed, as others had. Her distraction with people on the lower rungs of the social ladder could only last so long. The last time they saw her, she'd brought along a friend with bleached hair and emerald contacts who set down her handbag on an empty seat with the Fendi logo facing the room. The women had spent most of the night chatting only to each other about mutual friends and going off to the bar alone. 'You went and became a model again,' Eva had said to Orestis. Despite the zing of the cranberry and vodka on her breath, her voice had lacked its usual spark.

Without her, they were free to go to an untrendy spot for a decent coffee. Beneath their table was a pile of old board games, and they settled on Monopoly though neither of them cared for it. Paris smoked with one hand and rolled the dice with the other. He moved his terrier piece along, saying, 'Why are we playing this capitalist shit?'

'When they make one for Communists, we'll play that.'

Paris narrowed his eyes, amused. 'Take it easy, Eva.'

The name hung in the air.

'I have some news,' Paris said, at last, having drained his cup.

'Did you read it in the coffee?'

Paris smirked. He tilted the cup to indicate the dregs. 'Yeah, look here where there's a big dick. It tells me I'm seeing you tonight.'

'What else?'

He took a drag from his cigarette and leaned back. 'I'm publishing a book. Poems.'

'Bravo, re.'

By the swivel in Paris' expression, Orestis' reaction had been more of a comma than an exclamation mark.

'What's it called?'

'*Ananke*, after the mother of the Fates.'

'Never heard of her.'

Paris let the dice drop on the board. 'She was the goddess of necessity, compulsion, inevitability. The world began when she and Chronos intertwined as a serpent and broke the egg of creation to create the sky, land, and sea.'

Orestis waved the air away. 'Pe! I won't understand a word.'

'What are you talking about? Everyone understands poetry.'

'We didn't all go to England.' He stopped himself. Bitterness was ugly. In any case, the night on the yacht, the older women waiting to pay him for a good fuck, it was all sitting in his pocket.

Paris only laughed that low chuckle and stroked his beard. 'You don't have to go that far for poetry,' he said. He leaned forward and recited in dialect a tongue-twister with a dirty finish.

It was such a shock that Orestis' laugh went off like a gun. Paris leant back, content. The waitress came and took another order, and both men caught the way she'd checked Orestis out. Paris glanced sadly at his friend's white shirt.

* * *

He shouldn't have brought the Honda into Darya's neigh-bourhood. Kaloyiri wasn't a place Orestis was ever invited to. Mansion after mansion looked down on him from its slope. Some of them were traditional, simple, beautiful, others mad with modernity. He pulled up outside an equal mix of the old and new, as much glass as concrete, whose flashy effect was supported by sturdy features from days long gone. By the cobalt rectangle of the swimming pool was a sequence of stone arches, topped by a roof of wooden beams. The garden flagstones held enormous clay pots and vines curled around poles, as in a village inn.

It had occurred to him, before he switched off his car, to park in another street and walk. It seemed a smart idea, and he was sure his discretion would impress the Belarusian. But how would he explain himself if a neighbour should happen to see him? He could always pretend to be a lawyer, or insurance broker, an acquaintance of the husband he'd never met. And therein lay another issue: what was the cuckold's name? Orestis' heart beat faster, and it was all he could do to walk casually up the steps to the large front door.

To his surprise, Darya herself answered. He'd expected an Asian maid, as was the norm for these types. Every Sunday the Molos was crowded with Filipino cleaners dressed up for the Catholic church. It was a relief not to have to explain himself to yet another person he'd only just considered. There he'd been, congratulating himself on discretion when so many potential traps could mark him out as an amateur.

'Good afternoon,' said the Belarusian, a small smile on her lips. And when she let him into the house, Orestis wished

110

Lefteris was with him.

Darya wore a long white summer dress, which bared her arms and shoulders. Her hair, dark as a Cypriot's, was pinned up. It was as if she'd woken on a sweltering day in August instead of a mild one in May, whose morning had brought a welcome drizzle to wash the dust off traffic lights and railings.

'Do you want a drink?' she asked in Greek, before turning her back to leave the hall. He followed her through a series of rooms, each wider and more useless than the last. Rich people loved to exhibit empty space; blank square metres where there ought to be signs of life. The only exception he'd seen so far had been Paris' family home, where bookcases covered the walls, vinyl records and artwork patching up any blank spots. No wonder his friend was a poet.

Only one part of Darya's mansion seemed inviting: a small corner turned into a shrine, filled with icons of saints, gold leaf on slabs of wood, the Virgin Mary at the centre. Draped over her icon was a red-and-white patterned fabric he didn't recognise as Greek or Cypriot.

Darya led them to a well-stocked bar by the kitchen. She poured him a whiskey and Coke, saying, 'My husband drinks zivania.' Orestis wasn't sure what to say to this. She poured herself an apple juice.

'Where is your husband?' He had the notion it made him sound manly to ask.

'Dubai,' she said, a full stop. Then she sat down next to him on the black leather sofa, her arm draped over it. He tried not to look at her body. He'd forgotten how well her features hung together. Those black eyes. The sharp nose and jaw. And how piercing her scent was – bergamot. She was a woman who could have any man, so why was she renting one? He filed the

111

question away, to bring out when it felt safe to ask. 'You are free this weekend?' she asked.

'Yes.'

'Good.' She lit a cigarette.

He had half a mind to pull it out of her mouth and kiss her, pin her down on the sofa. He suspected she would like that.

'You live alone?'

'No... With my father.' He stopped before *My grandmother is dead.*

'OK... OK.' And she took a sip of her juice. Her fingers were trembling.

This was his job: to put her at ease, to please her, as he would any guest at the hotel. 'Have you been in Cyprus a long time?'

Her eyes moved in a way that suggested she was leaving the answer out of her answer. 'Yes. It's not so bad.'

'Not so bad? This is the island of Aphrodite, the island of love!'

His ironic tone made her smile. 'I lived in Berlin before. City of sex, more exciting.'

'I've never been,' he said. 'But my friend Paris says it's the best city in the world.'

'A!' she said, with a short laugh. 'Not Lemesos?'

He could have kicked himself for not bouncing off her 'city of sex' remark. Instead, he made a comment about his friend, like a teenager. So now he smiled what he hoped was an attractive grin. 'You speak German?'

'Of course. Your English is very good, I think.'

'Thank you,' he said. Hers was heavily accented. 'And you speak...'

She smiled, not unkindly. 'Belarusian.'

'And Greek?'

All of a sudden, she transformed into a Cypriot; she indicated her middling knowledge with a hand gesture and frown, saying 'a little' in Greek.

He laughed.

'Not so good,' she said. 'But I learn.'

This might be all it would be. Today they might only sit and talk in this vast sitting room, topping up their drinks at the bar. These women were lonely, weren't they? Sometimes all they wanted was a person to talk to.

Then Darya clinked her empty glass on the coffee table. Her eyes went blank. 'You want to swim?'

The change of subject stumped him. 'E... I have no...' But he couldn't think of the English word for swimming trunks.

'It doesn't matter,' she said, with only the suggestion of a smile.

He'd wanted this. Prayed for it.

There must have been an indoor pool in the house somewhere. Maybe a top-floor jacuzzi to mask his sweat. But, taking hold of his hand, she led him out to the garden, where the flagstones covered what would have been a yellow field of snakes.

'Do not worry,' she said. 'No one can see.' She put on her sunglasses.

He looked around to make sure, pulse revving in the silence. All around them were family homes. But all had allowed themselves the luxury of spreading out, unbothered, over the hills, so if he was seen by anyone it would be at a distance of a hundred metres or more. They might make out a naked man, but they'd never know who he was.

Darya waited by the pool. 'You have not done this before,' she said.

113

All of it, none of it, Lefteris' life. 'No.'

The relief was empowering. A charge rippled upwards from his feet. What the hell. He unbuttoned his shirt, thinking of things to calm him. There was a regular at the gym, a broad bald man with a massive beard who must've gone daily for hours. Orestis saw him every single time, no matter when he arrived. The man would take his post-workout shower, then stand dripping on his discarded towel. With all the time in the world, he would slide his briefs on, having first arranged his clothes and sprayed his deodorant. Orestis tried to channel him, that ease with his own body. But the cellist's room had been private, curtained, and on the yacht, he'd undressed in the dark. Here it was broad daylight, the heavens glaring. And Darya's eyes were hidden behind Ray-Bans.

He decided to act as if she wasn't there, reduce her to a voyeur in his private sunbath. His shoes and socks were still on his feet, which thank God he realised after unzipping his chinos. In a gap between one of the stone arches and a wooden beam was a swallow's nest. Poking through it, a small head. If both his socks were off before the swallow flew out—

He gasped. To see the bird fly off, to feel the wafted air of its wings, was a pure delight. He was a creature of this earth, a product of it. His client was waiting. Trousers discarded, underwear the last patch of clothing left, he paused. From above his own head he watched himself as he walked up to the pool. And he saw himself stretch his arms before him, bend at the waist, and dive. The woman stood speechless. Summer dress flapping in the breeze, she stood by as he swam laps in the pool. Let her wait. Who was she, anyway, this foreign wife making a cuckold of his compatriot? This kept woman who'd grown used to having things her way; who'd landed a man with the means to give her everything. He felt a twinge of hatred as he swam past her, a blurred and refracted back of a man in the water. He would show her. He would fuck her till she begged for it. She was no better than he was. Finally, he swam to the ladder and, with all the time in the world, climbed to the surface. His shorts were drenched. He had her total attention. Fixing his eyes on the Ray-Bans, he took her by the hands. He guided them to pull down his soaking trunks and set him free.

They spent the rest of the day in the bedroom. In the light, he could see all of her: freckles on her shoulders, a sprinkling on her breasts. The small scar on her abdomen like a pale burrow, stretch marks on her waist. Shoulder blades sharp as gravestones. For a while, he forgot her role of adulteress. He couldn't understand how her husband failed to keep this woman satisfied, how he was able to leave her alone on this island, or tire of that arch of her back, or those parted lips as her eyes fogged with want.

The answer was simple: he must've been bad in bed. Orestis was not.

As he lay sprawled in the sheets Darya watched him, matter-of-fact. She not only took in his body; she was also analysing his face. The features of his head: his forehead, his nose, his ears. As if she was trying to place or memorise him. He was caught halfway between liking the attention and feeling unnerved by it. Something warned him not to see her again. He brushed it off. Whatever was attracting him to Darya, it existed on a level he'd yet to plumb.

'You please me,' she said. She was sitting up, having stretched to the dresser for a pack of Marlboros.

The ugly bloom of smoke filled his nostrils, stung his eyes.

But he knew his rights, and they didn't include telling her to quit. 'I like pleasing you,' he said.

She gave him a sideways glance. 'You must come to me. Often.'

He must have misunderstood. What she was suggesting was too good to be true. A trick of the universe, a dormant cruelty waiting to strike. The Russian for *thank you* came to mind, but of course, he mustn't say that.

'How do you say "thank you" in Belarusian?'

Amused, she told him, and he repeated it.

In return she said in Greek, 'You're welcome.'

She asked if he could stay until the morning, in a way that implied there was only one correct response. He nodded. In his mind, he turned over the myriad excuses he might give his old man for not spending the night at home.

* * *

If the Mercedes Compressor overtaking from the left was stopped by the traffic lights, everything would be all right.

Red.

He ought to have thought of something better. For everything to be all right was too vague a wish. Incredibly, things were all right. May they continue to be. He slowed to a stop by the Compressor. Its windows were tinted. He sat looking straight ahead, confident that the stranger in the Compressor could sense his accomplishment. It was something you gave off, invisible as pheromones. Now it exuded from him, without effort: sex with an older woman; a good job; money filling his overdraft, soon to seal it for good. He would see to Darya and she would see to him. Sometimes all it took was a different attitude for one's life to click into place.

While his aunts felt attacked by the Eastern women, these vampires, who always seemed to be swooping in to steal something, Orestis was benefiting from one. Darya had come along and given him a future. Better than that: she'd given him access to the true Orestis, the man who'd been languishing in the dungeons of a lesser one. It thrilled him when she bossed him around (*On the floor*, stubbing out her cigarette in a crystal ashtray, eyes like embers) and it drove him wild when she bowed to his commands (pushing her head towards the wall, bending her over her husband's desk).

Amber.

Green.

The Compressor was already a distant smear on the horizon.

He paused. Before driving home, he would pass by his uncle's taverna. He made his way to Enaerio. As the cluster of buildings drew near, he slowed the car. On the outside tables, a handful of tourists sat picking at dips and pitta. From another, a waitress he'd never seen was clearing plates before all the diners had finished. He shook his head. That was once his life, and it did nothing for him to witness it. He'd expected a feeling of elation, superiority, certainty, but all he'd got was a sensation like a ball of lead in his heart.

He drove towards the house on the seafront near the Zoo. He'd always liked it as a child. He was captivated by its overgrown garden and its wooden shuttered windows. Kids in the playground used to say the place was haunted. It belonged to a widow who lived there alone, afraid of ghosts. Looking at it now, all he saw was an ageing bungalow, a pre-War house whose creeping ivy told of its survival. It had borne witness to

English soldiers, to the coup and the Northern refugees of the Turkish invasion, to the Arabs that fled here in the Eighties and Nineties from their own wars, and the businessmen formerly Soviet, formerly Communist, now swimming in coins like that cartoon duck. It shook its head at the crowds stumbling and singing from the Wine Festival every year across the road.

He'd told himself as a child that he would own it one day, that sad haunted house by the sea.

How simple were the dreams of children.

II

One

Darya was getting used to the staring. It was a national pastime, what choice did she have? With her colouring, she'd assumed she'd blend in with the locals, but something was obviously marking her out as foreign. Paler skin? Telling herself it was admiration or envy hadn't worked. Aristos had tried to be charming in those first few months. He'd claimed it was her magnetism forcing people to turn their heads. Over time she'd turned it into a game to predict which women would eyeball her at the supermarket checkouts – one time a mother of four chastised the cashier for allowing Darya to go first, never mind that she was ahead in the queue. She was also learning to shrug off the name-calling. 'Russian whore,' the occasional codger would murmur as she walked past a coffee shop. 'Going to her cabaret,' he'd say to his friend. Little did this dog know, and he might piss himself if he did, that his single insult packed two punches. But that's what they assumed she was: a whore and a Russian. It didn't matter that she knew she was neither. It burned her heart a little every time she caught the neon sign of a *gentlemen's club*, winking suggestively over the roofs of buildings and cars. Because it wasn't Cypriot, or Greek, or even Turkish women being ogled in those dreary establishments. It was women like her, former Soviets. Women she might easily have been, had the wind not blown a certain way on a certain day.

She parked the Lexus at Debenhams, formerly Hermès, formerly Woolworths. It struck her how long she'd been in Cyprus. The past wasn't a thing she dwelt on, but it came rushing at her now, in the noise carried from the sea a hundred metres away. A sight she'd never dreamed would become routine; palms and sandy beaches transposing the silver birches of the woods back home. Rolling fields soared into actual mountains here, so high for such a small island. And between her motherland and current address had come the ruined chic of Berlin, her time with Frau Friedel in that apartment above the unwashed café. There had been bakeries and night clubs and strolls in the Volkspark Friedrichshain, where she'd spent many a lonely evening watching lovers and joggers circling the lake. In Cyprus, she had found some comfort in the similarity of the dominant faith to that of her homeland, at first.

She rubbed her crucifix. Though Orthodox as well, the churches here were different. Instead of golden domes on top of tall white towers was beige brick capped with terracotta. Easter was equally important, but instead of babka, there was flaouna, which she'd grown to look forward to. The services and even the priests were familiar, but their language wasn't hers – *Christ is risen*, met with *Truly he is risen*, but not the way she'd grown up hearing it. It made the sentiment feel less real. At least they also dyed eggs – not to mention the game of striking two against each other to determine whose was toughest. So many Easter mornings she'd spent with Maksim, cracking each other's shells. That number of mornings was finite, it always had been. If only she'd known it then.

Enough. It did no good to wish time bent.

She carried her yoga mat rolled up in her arms like a baby. As she passed a tourist shop, the owner came out from behind his spinners of gaudy magnets and postcards to gaze at her. Men were at ease with their stake in things, they had no need to consider their rights. If they deemed a woman's body in the public domain – which, if visible, it was – then it was their right to admire it. As a member of society, she'd forfeited her right to control the opinions of others. If to them she was a Russian whore, then to them that's what she was. She knew her own truth, and it would only ever exist inside her. The moment she arrived at this conclusion, during an afternoon's meditation overlooking the North Sea, was one of the happiest she'd known. A weight took flight and left her. There was only the here, the now, the self.

The feeling of distraction carried on through her yoga class. Fellow students were moving their limbs too close, breathing too hard, sweating too much. The seafront and cars in the sunlight were too bright in the window, they made her eyes blink and water. And her mind, instead of emptying itself, was filling up.

Orestis. She'd never encountered that name before. Every breath and stretch came with a memory of him, his hands, his biceps. But it was more than a question of physicality. Something about him compelled you to watch, like flames in a fireplace. Yet his vanity threatened his beauty. It made him too obsessed with his flaws to enjoy his attributes. When they slept together, she sensed that it wasn't only her enjoyment that was turning him on, but her enjoyment of him. Yes, he could still stand to trim some fat here and there, but he was

123

close to human perfection. In this country, this city above the rest, she'd seen many a beautiful body in the sunlight. Locals were conscious of their looks in a way that even the West-Germans hadn't been. Aphrodite had found her island, and sunk her claws in deep.

In the hours they'd spent together so far, Darya and Orestis had explored their bodies, but they were still so new to one another that she'd focused on details at the expense of the bigger picture. If he walked into the room with a yoga mat and a pair of sweatpants, would she recognise him? In her mind he was a chest beneath a white shirt, tucked into a pair of chinos. He was an arm around her when she woke, a heat along the length of her back. The brush of stubble at her thighs. A mouth and its breath. He was a voice enquiring about her inner self; about the fields and forests of Belarus, and the languages she'd made her own. Maybe he was why she'd started giving in to nostalgia. She'd managed to go years without thinking of draniki and pork stew, or the kopytka her mother made, yet this morning she'd woken with a wild hunger for it all. She sated herself by recalling their taste. She felt them on her tongue, teeth and throat. And she banished the memory of Maksim by turning the TV up, flooding her head with the Greek patter of the morning talk show host and her ditzy celebrity guests. Darya had even started to recognise some of them.

Maybe this thing she'd started, this thing with the boy, was a mistake.

It wasn't too late to stop.

The class was over and left her with nothing. As she rolled up her mat the teacher touched her arm, gently, to speak with her. Darya flinched.

'Are you OK?' the girl asked in English. Skevi, a young

Cypriot of British descent who mixed her honey-blonde hair with pastels. A pleasing effect. This woman, whom she paid for an hour's peace and contemplation, was the nearest thing to a friend. Aristos had introduced her to several Eastern-bloc wives and girlfriends of colleagues — mostly Ukrainians, the occasional Russian — but she was content to limit their acquaintance to a simple hello at the supermarket. Some of the other girls from the ships had settled in Paphos, they'd lost touch. She had only spent time with the Swedish woman and the German on the yacht that night, they'd probably never meet again.

'Yes, thank you,' she said to Skevi.

'You were looking a bit preoccupied.'

'A...' Darya wished her English was better. 'It's no problem. I think of many things.'

'Yeah,' said Skevi, 'that's the good thing about yoga, it draws everything out of you.'

Darya nodded.

'If there is something wrong,' Skevi said, putting her hand on the older woman's shoulder, 'I also do Reiki.' She lowered her voice a fraction. 'It helps.'

Again, Darya nodded. She'd heard of Reiki. Maybe she needed it, maybe she didn't. But all she said to the girl extending her hand was, 'Thank you. This is enough.'

* * *

In the near-darkness of the room, sunlight bore through the holes of the electric shutters. She stared at it, hypnotised. It brought afternoons, long gone, memories vague and remote enough to be soothing. They lay on the sofa, she against

Orestis' torso. Her hair was matted to her neck, cheek and forehead, and his ribs rose and fell against her skull, and yet she was too comfortable in the discomfort to do anything about it. Her legs, she realised, were quivering as the feeling returned to them, and the warmth of touch gave way to the relative cool of the air. Another evening without her husband.

This time she'd opened the garage for Orestis' car. It was no more conspicuous to let him park there than have a young man walking alone to a married woman's house in the twilight, or a taxi pull up to the drive. Since the lifting of the ban, their neighbour Katina was given to watering her pavement with a hose, and she kept her nose in the air sniffing for gossip. Darya and Orestis had similar colouring, so it occurred to her to pretend he was a younger cousin. But that was foolish; lies always ended in disaster. Better to let the busybody assume what she wanted and act as if nothing unusual was going on. What was the worst Katina could do: call her a Russian whore?

When she opened the door to the garage, Darya met Orestis with a hunger that surprised even her. The young man looked startled, then pleased. And he was not gentle. He picked her up and carried her into the sitting room, where he dropped her on the sofa and yanked off her skirt. It shocked and thrilled her that this boy who was courteous and considerate when clothed, almost to the point of feebleness, could be stripped to the devil at his core. Of the men she'd been with, this was the only one who dropped an act during sex rather than put one on.

Now he murmured to her, half-asleep from his exertion. 'Where is your husband?'

'Dubai,' she said.

Moments passed, ticks of the clock on the unit, their breaths, almost in sync. She heard the sound of fingers on fabric, Orestis caressing the sofa.

'I can't believe he leaves you alone.'

Darya bristled. 'He works. What he can do?'

Orestis put his lips to her ear. 'He can work in Cyprus.'

She exhaled the feeling away. 'He is good.'

Beneath her, his body tensed. Perhaps he was pouting. His expression defaulted to morose when he wasn't charmed or charming.

'Let's not talk about him,' she said, sounding harsh even to her ears. Like a teacher.

'OK...'

Already, she felt, something was dying. A thing more delicate than either of them had realised. This mustn't pass, not yet. Forcing herself to unstick her head from his chest, her back from his abdomen, she faced him. He had indeed been looking darkly at her, but his expression changed. It blossomed. And she knew this was real; this young near-stranger, whose body, whose energy she drew on, he didn't only desire her — he liked her.

'You want jacuzzi?'

He raised an eyebrow, yes. His hand went to her lower back. Hers was coursing down his stomach.

'I make us drinks,' she said.

He remained seated on the sofa, still dazed, as she left the room. Even through the corridor, along the wall of abstracts acquired by her husband on trips to Athens, into the lounge with the kitchen and bar, she felt those eyes of his on her.

Stop this, said a voice. The voice of her babulia, far away inside her head.

She poured the drinks at the bar and paused. There, that

widescreen TV kitted out with surround-sound speakers and the latest Blu-ray player. There, an enormous sound system intended for parties they hardly threw, for people she'd never got to know outside of functions. Couches and stools to take their many guests. And none of this was bought by her, nothing belonged to her. Not even the cash in her wallet that she'd give this young man at the end of the night, in payment for reminding her where she was, what was hers, what she lacked.

She went up to the master bedroom, from which she heard the jacuzzi running. Air from an open window, light from the floor-to-ceiling windows; she gave thanks for it all. The bed was made and waiting. She entered the en-suite with a vague dread. In the doorway, she froze. Something about the sight of Orestis, sitting in the bubbling tub with his back to her, and the view of the hills and sea in the glass before him, chilled her marrow. Perhaps it was the confidence of his shoulders, his head. Like a king on a turret.

This was wrong. It was the same feeling she'd had in her stomach that evening when she lifted her fingers from the piano to answer the phone, to be told that Maksim was dying, to come and say goodbye.

* * *

Orestis hadn't stayed the night. She was dimly aware of his departure, sometime in the violet hours, when she heard the rustle of trousers and shirt. She remembered thinking about how polite he was.

With waking came panic. He'd left without being paid, she hadn't given him a cent. Or worse, he'd stolen from her. This was it, after all. Orestis was a thief, partnered with Lefteris and that blond one, handsome young men trained to fuck old women at night and rob their husbands' homes in the morning. He'd lulled her into complacency. She didn't even know where he lived, or where he worked if he had a day job. But on checking first the bedroom, then the rest of the house room by room, she'd found nothing of any value out of place. Either it had slipped his mind to collect his payment, or he was so sure of her next call that he hadn't been concerned.

The Sri Lankan would be arriving soon. Darya pulled the sheets off the bed and put them straight in the washing machine. She grabbed a bottle of Chanel from her dresser and sprayed the room. It made her laugh, suddenly, loudly as if she were a teenager again and come back with Oleg from the lake.

When the Sri Lankan came, Darya was struck not for the first time by how young she was; as if they'd kidnapped an Asian mother's child. She'd never asked for help in the house; it was all, as with everything, Aristos' doing. But if Darya had had to spend so much of her life folding sheets and bath towels and scrubbing shit from carpets on ships, in hotels, and come out of it all right, then so could this girl.

Leaving the maid to her mop, Darya went out into the garden for her morning meditation. She passed the pool, cheeks flaring at the thought of Orestis' nakedness there the other day, and the way he took her, hands wet, hair wet, chest slick and the hairs of it black. She sat at her cushions in the paved seating area beneath the palms, and let her mind go clear.

Om.

The flutter of a dragonfly hovering by the wall echoed her humming. Nature lent itself to us. Life was a web of balance.

Give and take. Lose something, gain something.

Two

Aristos would soon land in Cyprus, and Darya was to meet him at the airport. Still nervous about driving in the dark, she kept an enormous distance behind every car. Her caution was rewarded; a stray dog bolted across the highway. The lights of her car picked out its sad frightened face on the hard shoulder. Part of her wanted to stop and rescue the beast, but there was no way she could have it in the house. Besides, it was too late now. It had either run off into the fields and salt lakes or been hit by someone less careful. She rubbed her crucifix and gave thanks to the icon on the dashboard.

She waited with a coffee at Arrivals. At some point, a bunch of young men funnelled through the doors yelling English, cheeks red, eyes raw, bulging out of slogan t-shirts and palm-print shorts. Brits on their way to Ayia Napa. You heard tales of the goings-on there; booze-filled kids and foam parties, sex on church grounds. From the look of these boys, the tales were true. Some looked young and sweet, one swung an obvious python in his shorts, but they seemed hollow. Soulless. Moments later, her husband stepped through the same doors, wheeling his carry-on case at his side. A carriage that dwarfed other men. Even in a room this big and full,

Aristos stood out.

He drew her in for a kiss on the cheek. 'How are you?' he asked in Greek, with a knowing hint in his tone.

'Good,' she replied in his tongue, annoyed by the Slavic vowels in her accent.

Aristos didn't want to go straight home. He drove them to a restaurant by the sea, where they sat outdoors and watched the surf roll in and out like ghost hair in the dark.

'You look beautiful,' he said.

A breeze blew a strand of hair to her mouth, so she laughed.

'I mean it.'

'Please,' she said. 'You must speak to me in Greek.'

Now he was the one to laugh. 'Why?'

'I need to know more. Not just say *houmous* and *patates*.'

He grinned at his plate, and she wondered if he slept with other women. Maybe that's what this was, an exercise in deception. Not a handsome man, her husband, but an attractive one. He could hold a conversation with anyone on any subject, his interests were limitless. And self-possession was power. It's what put him above Orestis. The younger man's eagerness was a crutch, he would see that one day.

At tavernas like this, Darya went for the octopus. Whether it was supposed to be healthy or not, who remembered? Was fresh food ever bad? Either way, she sought the warmth of its garlic and wine. And what felt good within was reflected without. Aristos dug into his kleftiko and explained to her, for the third or fourth time in their marriage, the origins of the dish. But now he did so in Greek, and stopped every few seconds to explain words like 'Cretan' and 'rebels'.

When he finished, he raised the subject of an August holiday. A journey through Greece, the mainland or the islands or both.

TWO

'We can go on a cruise,' he said. He knew translation was redundant, and she wondered if that weight of meaning in his eyes and voice was really there. Teacher, translator, maid, wife; she knew what she was and had been, why remind her? She was aware of a streak in her husband that others feared. Perhaps he was beginning to show it to her.

'What do you say?'

Those dark eyes peering out from their long lashes, the face of the man who'd only ever denied her one thing. He did love her, God knew he did. All he wanted was to take her on holiday.

'Good,' she replied in Greek, because what else could she say?

* * *

The sun was gathering strength. Free of its gauze, it roasted the arms hanging out of car windows. It beaded foreheads with sweat, it made every shop turn its AC to maximum. Darya never used AC in the car and drove with the windows shut. She parked the car off Anexartisia Street and evaded the parking attendant's gaze as she paid him. When the old man's voice croaked out a pleasant goodbye in Greek, she felt a wave of guilt. 'Bye,' she said back, glad for the option of a single syllable.

Shopping had become routine, with diminishing returns. Long gone were her days of queuing for sausages she hated and gone were the evenings spent counting Deutsche Marks in Frau Friedel's apartment, and gone were those first months of marriage to Aristos, the freedom and boundlessness of a credit card. Not a single label and not a hundred thousand fabrics were enough. Maybe she was simply getting older, losing her will to please. You looked good for other people, to earn something back; their approval, their respect, their libido, their money. There was nothing she lacked. For that, she remembered to give thanks. *Accept things as they are, for what they are.* Her babulia in the past, and Skevi in the present. There had always been a restless greed in her. Where had it come from? Not her babulia, not her parents, not her country. Be thankful, move on. Her fingers skipped over another row of clutch bags. She might buy a couple if only to mark this day out from the rest.

In the next shop, Darya heard her before she saw her, and by the time she had processed what was happening, it was too late: Eva. There she was, flicking through clothes on a rack, sunglasses pushed up her head and one of those iced coffees from the newsagent in hand. She was with a friend, and it was the other girl who'd spotted Darya first. A sudden drop in their chatter. 'A,' said Eva, seeing her. And that was all. She turned back to the clothes as if Darya had been a passing cat in the window. The salesgirl shifted in anticipation. Young, Cypriot, beautiful, her allegiance was already with Eva. There was one clear outcome: Darya would leave, and the others would talk about her.

They didn't even wait. Eva's friend was first to start, assuming The Russian was unable to follow Greek. The older woman listened as she fondled dresses, the fabric sliding from her fingertips as if she'd no desire to keep it there. She paced around the small boutique, counting out a minute, then another, willing her eyes not to drift to the girls. Eva was all right to look at, in that blunt way, spoiled only by the large nose and that heavy reliance on makeup. She also shared her mother's flabby waistline and huge bust. If she wasn't careful, she'd end up exactly like that bitter old hag. Neither Eva nor her mother deigned so much as to look at Darya, which upset Aristos. He was devoted to his daughter, but Darya never had the chance to find out why. This person, so caring and funny to others, would switch off her lights the moment she beheld her. It took some getting used to, spending chunks of her Christmas, her Easter, alone in the house because Aristos was left with no choice but to see his daughter in private. The girl had despised her from the start, though her parents were already divorced by the time Darya had come along. Eva's love for her father, however, remained. In fact, it had mutated to monstrous proportions. Even now in her twenties, the girl would sit on his lap and call him *Daddykins.* Darya could never fathom acting that way with her father. To her, he was always The Professor. She had watched him dance, cigarette in hand, around the living room, around the gas heater, when Belarus stepped forth from the rubble of the USSR to become its own nation. She blinked the memory away. Had she ever even hugged him, at some point when it might have been possible?

Two minutes. Time to leave the shop and give them the freedom to discuss her openly, maybe even to laugh. 'Bye,' she said to all three – Eva, her friend, the shopgirl – at once, that single blessed syllable, and walked away, having once again bought nothing.

* * *

The pain in her groin intensified. It was like a wild animal, clawing at her, grasping for her stomach, her insides, everything. Good. Game over, her bladder was full. She would park at a hotel and use the toilet.

135

Cars edged forward centimetre by centimetre along the seafront. Some of the mavericks tried to squeeze their cars through impossible gaps or climb over barriers to overtake the sludge. Her bladder was about to burst.

Stupid game. Conceived at her babulia's house, long ago, on an afternoon in the banya whipping each other's backs with birch twigs. She'd needed to urinate, but the steam of the room and her babulia's giggles at her feeble whips were enough to make it wait. When she finally ran to the bathroom, the physical joy of release was so great that her body buckled. Already light-headed from the sauna, she trembled for minutes. At twelve years old, she was already awed by the miracle of the human body. With the tips of her fingers, she'd prodded her veins, searching for a surge of blood coursing through like a river. She'd rubbed her own collarbone till it made her gag. A few days later she pushed her bladder to the limit once more, and derived the same pleasure from it; that painful ecstasy. By the time she'd reached adulthood, and discovered other ways to please herself, the game took a back seat. But recently, a year ago, maybe more, it had returned.

She tried not to think of it. She focused on her breathing, the in and out of it, oxygen to carbon monoxide, which was fundamental, which was the most natural and unconscious thing a human could do.

Outside the car, not a single palm frond stirred.

This would never be her home.

The thought wasn't new. Darya would leave Cyprus. What that would mean for Aristos remained to be seen. Her family had been right, she thought only of herself and her own pleasure. She was greedy. Insatiable. All those years ago, when she dared to turn her back on Belarus, she'd thought she was being sensible. Why deny herself for the rest of her life? What for? In the past few months, the self-reflection of yoga made her face what she truly was: selfish; indulgent; alone.

The torso of a man appeared at her window, making her jump. The driver behind her had got out of his car and, barely containing his stomach in an old vest, stood to glare ahead at the traffic. He shrugged, swore in Greek, then turned to her for solidarity. She mimicked that Cypriot gesture of frustration, *Pe!* expressed through the hand, and the man nodded. But something about her caught his attention. He didn't scowl, but it had registered: an infraction. She checked that the doors were locked.

In a snap, his attention turned back to the traffic. The look of relief on his face said the cars had started to move. 'Finally,' he confirmed through the window and patted the roof of the car as if it was a horse's back. He returned to his own.

Releasing her breath, Darya stepped on the gas, evermore in need of a toilet.

With as straight and unhurried a gait as she could manage, she wound her way through lobbies and corridors in the Myriada to the ladies'. And there, in the haven of a cubicle, she was thankful for the absence of another soul as she gasped, the ache of release more intense than it had ever been.

'Stop this.' Her own voice now.

Who knew what it might do to her body, this senseless test? During puberty, when she began to admire the backs of boys at the summer camps, she feared she'd already done irreparable damage. Had she broken herself? Might she not bear children? These days, she worried about cancers. Of course, she would.

Finished, she sought out the hotel's café. She carried her tea, with honey and lemon, to a window seat from which she could watch the people around the pool below. She recalled that afternoon with Orestis when his shaking fingers betrayed the nerves his face had tried to conceal. He liked to make a good impression, which mattered. To see him revealed bit by bit, at her command but enjoying her attention, brought her a rare joy. She wished she'd been clear-headed enough to request a tease on their first encounter. Instead, a coward herself, she'd switched off the light and ignored the sound of his zip to focus on the noise of the surf.

She'd never done anything like it before. She'd met the woman from Stockholm at one of the hotel functions – birthday, retirement, she couldn't remember. At some point, the Swede locked eyes with a suited young man in a corner. 'You know what he is?' she'd said with a naughty smile. Then that word she'd understand in any language: 'Gigolo.'

When Darya had laughed uncertainly, the Swede had confessed without shame that she knew for certain. Darya had been speechless. Not that she was naive; she'd heard many a tale of the quiet knocks at the doors of Minsk hotels, young ladies offering company to businessmen travelling solo. Of course, it happened here too, and where better than in the five-star resorts along the coast? What shocked her was that such a service existed for women. All she'd ever heard about men of the night was that they sold their bodies to queer perverts. The darkest, quietest sin.

The Swede had pulled an elegant card from her purse and handed it to her. 'Come to my party,' she'd said. There'd be a man for every woman, and if there weren't enough women, she was sure one guy could manage two at once. An explosion of laughter. Darya had been left disconcerted by the encounter, but the memory of it had whispered at the back of her head along the highway, with Aristos driving at her side. Before she'd known it, an evening had been arranged, and three young men had been sourced for three middle-aged women. Darya, the youngest of them, had regretted her decision more with every passing moment. In an attempt not to squirm and betray herself, she'd sat rigid on that leather sofa and focused on her glass of vodka. *He who talks little hears better*, her babulia used to say. And so she'd listened to the charming man with the green-gold eyes, and his fair-haired friend. But mostly she'd been intrigued by the dashing darker one with the nervous smile, whose black eyes, glossy as caviar, took everything in. He would be hers.

Orestis.

He was hers.

Three

Darya gave thanks for the yoga class. For its combination of physical exertion and mental catharsis. For this chance to know herself. And as the summer advanced the evening slots coincided with the sunset, helping her to achieve a calm she seldom managed. There was Skevi's voice, instructing and encouraging, and the rosy light on the metal window frames. In the peace of this no-man's land, her flaws could reason with her rather than attack her. She had been selfish to leave Belarus. She'd abandoned her family, all of them drugged by grief. Yes, she had left, and done so for her sake, but what she'd run away from was not her father, and certainly not her mother and babulia, but the ghost of her older brother.

What she still had to come to terms with, however, was that ghosts could walk. And if something walked, it could also follow.

* * *

She decided she would treat Orestis.

What was the use of hiding, of being kept behind shutters? In any case, her neighbour Katina was bound to have noticed the coming and going of a young stranger. Caught in a morning greeting, Darya had half a mind to mention she was having the interiors redesigned or anything else that might keep suspicion from her door. But she shrugged it off. Who cared what the old cow thought and who she spoke to? Whatever story she made up, the myth that would stick was always the same: Russian whore.

One thing she did wrestle with was exposing her young maid to the arrangement. The girl wasn't stupid; she'd have figured out that Orestis was, at the very least, a lover. But if it brought a sense of guilt or shame to the girl every time she greeted Mr Ioannidou at the door, then Darya would have to find a solution. The only one she came up with, again and again, was to let the maid go. There'd be lots of other work for her in Cyprus, there was no need to feel bad about that. The problem lay more in how to put this suggestion to Aristos.

'When is your next day free?' she asked Orestis one afternoon.

'Friday.'

'Maybe we go somewhere?'

A look of horror in his face. It stung.

'I want to see more,' she continued. 'We go maybe other side of island. Paphos or more far away.'

His eyebrows eased.

So it wasn't Darya he feared. Lemesos was a big city where everyone somehow knew everyone else. This was his only secret. In a country full of yellow grass, Orestis was a green blade.

'Yes...' he said. 'We could go to the shops in Lefkosia, or the theatre if you prefer.'

'It sounds nice.'

'Or sorry, we can go to Paphos like you said. Avagas Gorge, Coral Bay...'

They could hire a boat, he added with meaning. And she felt, as his hands curled around her back, his growing excitement.

They arranged to drive to a beach in the Paphos District, a village called Latchi. Orestis had put on a white shirt, short sleeves rolled shorter. Although he wore sunglasses, she had the sense that his eyes were wide for the sights, as a child marvelling at a dancing bear. And he did remind her of a child at times. Those dimples punctuating his smile, or the way his eyebrows would crease with concern. It was a face that invited a gentle hand.

'I told my father I was with my friend Paris,' he'd said. They'd just set off from their agreed meeting point at a municipal car park. 'It's OK,' he'd added quickly, 'Paris is visiting his cousin in London.'

So the glasses had nothing to do with the sun. His caution amused her. It brought to mind her foolishness in childhood, that fear of the KGB after a trip to Minsk. Those same fears had returned when she left for Poland, then Germany. They'd bounced along the corridors of the ships, and then the hotel. Her heart still raced, even now on an island far away in the middle of the sea, at the sight of a copper-armed cop with a gun.

At one point on the drive, as Orestis looked out at the sprawling city they were leaving behind, his hand travelled as if of its own accord, to rest on her thigh. She blinked a tear away. So far she had paid for every time he'd serviced her. She'd even made up for the time she'd forgotten by paying him double. 'No,' he'd said, 'there's no need, please.' But she'd insisted. 'I want to,' she'd said in Greek, that single

142

word.

But how many euro did it cost for a whole day out, with the expectation of nothing other than the company? How much were his conversation and presence worth? And not only that: what would he anticipate as reward for spending time with her? For at least sex gave him a degree of pleasure – that, she didn't doubt. He got something in return for what he was giving. Who didn't like sex and money? But an afternoon of driving over hills, to a beach where they hoped nobody knew them...?

Now that hand on her thigh. Something inside her had been opened, a gate lifted. Not just today, or even these past few weeks, but over years, maybe the whole preceding decade, since the new century, the new millennium of her new life. She had never been one for sentiment. Nostalgia was for dreamers, people who thought and never did. But where she once rolled her eyes at Hollywood nonsense, these days it took little to move her. A toddler walking next to her mother, or the sight of a ship departing, or a paraglider soaring over the archaeological digs. Yoga was to blame. In forcing her to look within, it pulled without.

They passed churches and petrol stations, dirt tracks off to mountain woodlands and signs to unpronounceable villages. In time they pulled up at a row of beachfront tourist shops peddling snorkels and swimsuits and rubber rings. Once the car was parked, Orestis' brow creased. He scanned the surroundings, then walked up to one of the spinners of baseball caps. He tried one on, turned for her approval, and handed the shopkeeper a five-euro note. 'It's hotter than I thought,' he said to her. She smiled but said nothing, taking her own sunhat out of her wicker bag.

Peak season had yet to arrive, so the beach held only a half-dozen families and sporadic couples. They found a spot away from everyone. Orestis stood for a while, transfixed by the sparkling blue. She watched him. How blessed he was, whether he knew it or not. Despite his carefree image, the shorts and flip-flops, the shoulders loose, the white shirt hanging open, his head was busy. He searched the horizon as if expecting something or someone to appear there.

You could never fully grasp another's life. You could never get inside their minds the way your limbs could enter their bodies.

He remembered she was there and turned to smile. She wanted to touch his face but stopped herself. There hung an unspoken agreement between them: no affection in public. He stripped to his snug black trunks and, to amuse her, ran into the sea with his arms spread out. The shades and baseball cap stayed on his head.

'Come in!' he called.

But she laughed and flicked her head no.

She watched him bob in the water, and she removed her shirt, sarong, sandals, and hat to lie back on her towel. The sunglasses too, so that she might feel the air on her eyelids, never mind if it bore salt and sand. Somewhere further up the beach, a child was pleading with its parents; their response was muted, tired. A perfect time to meditate. Skevi would. Instead, Darya's limbs sank into the ground as if towards the centre of the earth. She stretched her toes into the warm sand. She wished to be alone, just her on the beach with the sun on her body. The light drumming on her eyelids, the water lapping at the sand. Dreaming of this, she drifted into sleep.

And then Orestis' voice came tearing through. Something

in Greek, phrases she couldn't process. But a word she recognised, two, three. In her opened eyes stood a man, elderly and heavy, tan the colour of sandalwood. He was backing away and Orestis, dripping from the sea, was approaching. 'Old man,' that was what she'd heard him say. 'What do you want, old man?'

Orestis stood tense, puffed out chest, face in shadow, hands turned to fists. The other man had left, mumbling, before Darya had even sat up on her elbows. She began to ask a question, barely formed in her head, when Orestis said, 'Don't worry. It's OK.' He grabbed his towel, wrapped it around his waist and took his wallet from his bag. She thought he was checking if they'd been robbed, as she ought to if that's what the strange old man had been up to, but no — he merely took out some cash and said: 'What flavour do you like?'

His head tilted towards an ice-cream van.

She was still too dazed to think. 'No, no!' she said. 'I must not have sweets.'

But he only grinned and went off. And the thought alighted on her, moments later, that she ought to have paid. She would buy lunch to make up for it, and anything else he wanted. She was rubbing sunblock into her shoulder when Orestis returned with two towering ice cream cones. Banana and chocolate chip for himself, rose sorbet for her.

'Sometimes you need a treat,' he said and sat down beside her.

The rose was a welcome bolt, so fresh on her tongue. A treat, as Orestis had said. And in an instant, she understood. Orestis' vanity, his ambition, his willingness to please. At some point in his life, he had struggled with his weight. It made sense. In this country, fatness, ugliness, were inexcusable. Deep scars never healed. Had she taught in Cyprus, she might have met a younger version of this beautiful man, with a belly hanging over his waistband, and he would still have been beautiful. Only less aware of it. How much of someone's journey you missed when you met them along the way.

Another young man, European-looking, walked up the beach towards them. Orestis watched, not in the usual curious way of his compatriots, but with a certain wistfulness. She extended a hand to his thigh, only in consolation, only in understanding, a gesture she hoped might help him be kind to himself. He flinched. First, he looked around, then he gave her half a smile. He moved her hand with a shift of his thigh and left it to fall to the towel.

They got back in the car and drove to the Baths of Aphrodite, which disappointed her. A small waterfall in a rock pool where the goddess of beauty and desire had bathed. Where she was spotted by the beautiful Adonis. Ancient myths were too vast for daily life, they could not be contained to our geography, our buildings, our objects. Nothing on earth could reach the bar set by ancient tales. Orestis, on the other hand, looked dazzled by the water, and the twisted branches that swooped to protect it.

'I forget that Cyprus is beautiful,' he said.

She turned away from his pride. Her love for Belarus was equally strong, but she willed herself free of it. The devotion to a motherland dug as deep as any other, but it was the stupidest, most senseless of all. To be tied to the values of a group, to attribute a sense of identity to a mound of earth, a knot of rivers that had nothing to do with your personhood, was the surest way to lose your self. It made you a horse, broken in by a farmer and kept from roaming free. She'd been in

146

Cyprus long enough to understand the devastation of clashing flags. She'd been raised under Communism, the taking of land and rights, the erasure of God. She'd been subjected to her father's drunken ravings about Russia's knife on Belarus' tongue. It wasn't people who'd been riddled with bullets and electrocuted on fences, it was ideologies. And tragedies became badges. The world saw Chernobyl as Ukraine's cross to bear when the bulk of the damage was done to Belarus. But what did it matter? A group of humans had suffered. Others were to blame for it, others made it worse.

Enough. None of it, not armies, leaders, dictators, language nor faith, mattered to her anymore. If she could live alone in the entire world, she would. Like the goddess Aphrodite, she would bathe in the fresh water falling from the rocks, naked and divine. Only there wouldn't be anyone watching, not even Adonis.

As they walked along the trail, Orestis relaxed enough to let her touch his arm. She bit her tongue. *I pay you for this*, she was about to say when he suddenly pulled her close to him. There in the wilderness, with no-one around but the spirits and creatures of the forest, he put his hand under her skirt and kissed her neck till she came. It made him happy, too.

Afterwards, they made their way to a cheap taverna. It sat on a cliff, overlooking a sea reddening in the sundown. They ordered their early dinner from laminated menus, she choosing the chargrilled octopus and he a chicken salad.

'My babulia – my grandmother – she told me about Aphrodite,' she said. 'She liked to tell all the stories. Aphrodite and Adonis, Zeus, Odysseus, the... Who was the man, half bull?'

'The minotaur,' he said in Greek.

147

'Yes! He was my favourite. For her also, I think.'

'You loved her very much?'

She nodded. And she was grateful when he turned the conversation away from her.

'I loved mine. She was like my mother.'

'When did she die?'

He looked startled. 'Last year. She was old, she had... many illnesses.'

And though he spoke casually, and folded his arms, she saw his glistening eyes and felt a pang in her heart.

Enough. This was too much intimacy. *Stop this*, she should say, as the responsible elder. Of course, she would pay him for the month, but then they must part. Lefteris would supply her with other young men. In fact, she should only have dealt with Orestis through him, as per the initial instruction. Stop this, start again. Meet other men, and only once a month, for sex and nothing else.

Orestis must have read her thoughts, for his expression changed. He lowered his fork. No, he was looking past her. Then he was forcing a smile, and exaggerating enthusiasm, as he rose from his seat to greet a person behind her. 'Hey! What are you doing here?'

She spun to see a middle-aged couple walking towards them, holding out their arms for a quick peck on Orestis' cheek. From the rapids of dialect and tone and gesture, she surmised these were acquaintances or family friends. His baseball cap and sunglasses sat on the table. Her heart raced. But her mind cleared enough to hear Orestis introduce her as his aunt from England, whose Greek was next to nothing.

Acquaintances, not friends.

'Pleased to meet you,' said the older man. His arm extended

for a handshake.

She chose to respond in Greek with a single word: 'Likewise.' For once it didn't matter that her accent was foreign. But might they realise her vowels were more Slavic than British?

'We won't bother you,' the woman said, having kissed Darya on both cheeks. 'We only wanted to say hi.'

'Re!' the man said to Orestis. 'You've lost weight. Bravo!'

'Such a handsome young man you've become,' said the woman.

Orestis responded with a bashful dimpled smile.

She felt a tug at her heart. But she caught herself and looked away; the other woman had been watching her.

When the couple left them to their dinner, Orestis did his best to speak lightly as if Darya really was his English aunt.

'That was one of my dad's customers. They were in the Army together, ouf, years ago.'

But then he trailed off, and when the couple was safely out of sight his face changed. She saw the fear spread like tentacles over his face. The game was not a game. And in a place as small as this, perhaps sex would always come at a price, always with strings. Now was the time to end it. They both knew it was.

Four

The Sri Lankan must have thought her a bored old woman. Darya had taken to spending most of the daylight hours in the garden, slowly pushing her limbs to their limits and allowing her mind to clear in the silence. The time to be outdoors was a gift. She'd seen the swallows build their nests on the house. She'd watched the geckos scurry across the walls.

Days had come and gone. Orestis had messaged her after that afternoon at the Baths: *I had a great day.* But she was resolute. She let his message sit unanswered on her phone, and when she felt the urge to reply she would distract herself; by doing the groceries, or taking the car for its service. There was no doubt: she was a coward. All these years, she had thought herself defiant, independent, strong. She'd spat in the eye of both father and fatherland. But now her reflection showed a person who'd run away, abandoned mother and motherland.

Movement, in the corner of her eye. Her head whipped to the garden wall, where next to a cypress danced a white orb, making noises. Not a trick of the light – a kitten, whose claw had got stuck in the trunk of the tree and was causing it to wail its troubles to the world. Darya lifted herself and ran to it. The kitten flinched and hissed when she held it, but she managed to work its paw free. Baring its teeth pathetically, it wriggled out of her hands and stood with its affronted back to her, fur mussed. She made encouraging noises but the kitten only stared with enormous eyes. She got into the cat pose and laughed. The kitten continued to stare. A white little thing, with blue-grey irises and an orange thumbprint over its nose and mouth.

Strays were still poisoned here. People put out bowls of lethal food. Feeling a pang, she went into the house to fetch a pack of ham slices. She sat as close as the kitten could handle and held out a cool pink ribbon, which set its throat rumbling. It snatched the meat from her, making her gasp, and she watched as it nibbled away noisily. She stroked its spine, which excited its purring.

'Where did you come from?' she asked in her mother tongue. The words stuck in her throat.

Aristos would never allow a pet in his house. But surely there was nothing wrong with feeding one here, in the garden, a space of which she had some kind of ownership, spiritual if not legal. She wasn't willing to risk letting this creature eat from the wrong bowl, and have its life cut short by the whim of a larger being.

* * *

She'd started her game again. Around the aisles, she went in Carrefour as the tension built up in her bladder. And all the while she was placing liquid soap, air fresheners, candles, napkins and fruit in the trolley with a deliberate pace. It wasn't only the throbbing pain that hurt, but the enormous shame that she might lose control in public. A girl with a name badge arrived with a cage of stock to shelve. Darya went to the tills and the door before she could ask her where the toilets were.

On the drive home, the pain became too much. She bent over the steering wheel, on the brink of passing out. With the backs of her hands, she wiped the sweat – or tears – from her face. She took an exit off the roundabout and kept turning till she found an empty plot. Bushes sprang from the earth and rubble. A construction site, either abandoned or never got going. She looked around first, then squatted, and felt the stab of relief.

Finished, she stayed still and stared into space. She didn't know what sort of person she was, what the point of her was ever to be.

At least her father had had plans. That bile in his voice as she repeated scales, E flat minor, F sharp major, it had never left her head. She walked back to the Lexus. Having started the engine, she caught sight of a figure in the distance. A young man, brown, maybe a Turk, spray-painting onto the back of a care home an acronym she recognised from football shirts. He wore an Adidas hoodie and sweatpants whose waistband hugged his buttocks halfway down. Would it be so wrong to fuck a stranger? She could walk up to him now and he'd comply because men never said or heard *no*, and he could take her here in the open plot, against the car her husband had bought, on her hands and knees, by the throat, and not a word would pass between them, not even a cent.

She had crossed a line with Orestis. Arrangement had become affair. In the beginning, it was perfect; she would give him orders to come and do as she wished when she wished it. Lick here, touch there. And he would. But the more they

152

saw each other, the more he'd learned to call the shots. The goat was eating the wolf. How many female escorts got paid to have their way? How many of her former-Soviet sisters were enjoying themselves, satisfied by the hungry eyes of horny old toads in *gentlemen's clubs*? More than likely they'd been brought to Cyprus by gangsters under false pretences, kept on their knees at gunpoint. To service pigs puckered with disease, and to have to be grateful for it. Darya was free, and free to have any man she wanted – any except her husband. Why pay for satisfaction? Here and now, with this young instrument spraying graffiti. Why not?

Why. Not. She knew why her fingers remained on the steering wheel as if welded there. It was what she'd learned, what had come out of her in all those classes in Skevi's studio and out in the garden beneath the gaze of the birds and the geckos: she was nothing but a coward.

* * *

Aristos was home that night. He took her to a taverna somewhere in the mountains, in one of those hundred tiny villages built by stone from a quarry, and whose only choice of an outing was food or church. In the black night, the smoke of cigarettes reached up to the lightbulbs strung from the beams. A table of Scandinavian tourists heaved with the spoils of mezze and Koumandaria. There was a waiter with a stylishly trimmed beard who caught Darya's attention every time he passed. She felt nothing for him, it was a knee-jerk response, but Aristos eyed her with meaning.

She embarked on the topic of the Paphos villas, to which he said, 'Your Greek is getting better.'

She shrugged and made her favourite gesture. 'So-so,' she replied.

He was amused by her Cypriot pastiche. Then he answered her question. The island was doomed, it had got too expensive. Brits and other Europeans would be flocking to Turkey instead; similar landscape and culture and beaches for a fifth of the cost. And the way his countrymen were spending, living beyond their means, the banks' ties to Greece— *pe*! A collapse was on the cards, he would bet his life.

'That's why I keep most of my money abroad,' he said. 'The business, too, move it all away.'

'What about hotels?' Darya asked, meaning his, here.

'Their days are numbered.'

'And people?'

Aristos gave a sad shrug. 'What can we do?' he said.

'Capitalist,' she spat in Russian because she knew he'd understand.

He laughed and drank his wine.

'When there's crisis,' he started, before continuing in English, 'you have to make your own destiny.'

She sipped her wine, to excuse a silence.

He reverted to Greek: 'You have to ask yourself, *How do I make money? What do I have that others would want to buy?* Some people are more clever at figuring it out than others.' And with that, he set his knife and fork down on his plate, and signalled the waiter for another glass of wine. The one with the stylish facial hair. Darya forced herself not to look.

Five

E very day after the first encounter, the kitten came to find her in the garden. That's what you got for encouraging strays. But trouble never comes alone. What would this one bring? She found herself adding cat food to the shopping list, jellied hunks of fish and rabbit and duck that left amber blobs on her hands, which made her gag but the kitten purr. Such a heartwarming sound, with the power to reach inside you. *Ahimsa.*

Orestis would be stewing. He'd be blaming himself for her lack of contact. That was if he wanted to pursue this; if he hadn't been too shaken by bumping into that couple at the cliffside restaurant. For all she knew he had a black book full of clients, and fell into his own bed drained at the end of a night. What had that woman from Stockholm said? One of these men could handle two or three on his own? Aristos was almost right. It wasn't just money you received in return for your assets. Of course, Orestis' looks would get him plenty of that. But they also bought him respect, patience, status, trust... Things denied an ugly man. Things denied a beautiful woman.

The kitten rubbed against her leg, its tail lifted. It arched its bottom to meet her fingertips.

She took out her phone to message Lefteris. If not him, then any of his friends – that catlike blonde from the boat. But her fingers were scrolling to the last exchange with Orestis, and before she knew it they were typing a day, a time and an order to come and make her happy.

* * *

The Sri Lankan had left for the day. As always, Orestis arrived on time. He stood at the doorway in chinos and a black shirt with the top two buttons undone. His face sagged. His hands were in his pockets. And was it her imagination, or did he look slimmer?

'Hello,' he said and ventured a small smile.

Her reply was curt: 'Upstairs.'

His hand went towards her arm, then stopped. He did as he was told, the heels of his loafers tapping every marbled step in an upwards countdown.

In the master bedroom, patchouli burned from incense sticks.

'Take off your clothes.'

He did so. Once they'd been discarded to the floor, his hand went straight to his stomach and hovered there. She felt sick, dizzy. He looked at her with eyes like a bad dog. So she gave him a smile, and the relief brought out his dimples.

'On the bed.'

He obeyed.

'Lie down.'

She walked to the dresser, and from one of its drawers removed two of her husband's belts. Orestis flinched but his eyes glinted. An equal mix of fear and excitement made

156

him stiff as she tied his wrists to the bed. If only she had something tighter than a belt. She stood by the balcony window, untouchable, and drew the curtains open. He tried to blink the sunlight away, so he could watch as she unzipped her dress. She let it slip to the floor. The breath built up in his lungs. The next part she did slowly: she untied the curtain sash from its hook on the wall and walked towards him, pulling it tense as rope in her hands. His body trembled as she neared. And when she put it to his eyes and tied it around his head, his gasp of a laugh made her want him even more.

There he was, trapped like a rabbit. Here was his youth, pulsing back at the elements, his skin exposed and responsive – to the air, to her breath, to her fingers. Her Orestis.

A ball of sadness turned inside her. Nothing lasted. Everything changed.

Her head was a liquid, a gas, it wouldn't solidify to help her stop.

'A,' said a voice from the doorway. 'Hello.'

The room went still.

'Orestis,' said her husband. 'Welcome.'

He ambled to the wardrobe, from which he took out a hanger.

Darya's hands clung to the naked man's thighs, which rapidly cooled. The boy's smile bent to bafflement, and his lips, once his brain had processed the other voice in the room, and to whom it belonged, twitched to form a sequence of words that never came.

His wrists and fingers writhed like a mouse in a snake's jaws. She helped to untie the belts, though they'd barely restrained him. Instead of whipping off the blindfold, he only brought his legs up to cover himself, too late already, and held his head,

157

unable and unwilling to see what he had to face. All he could do, for a protracted minute, was mutter under his breath: 'God have mercy.' The patchouli filled her head with stars.

Aristos placed his jacket on the hanger and tucked it back in the wardrobe before rolling up his sleeves. A man at the office. 'What's wrong?' he said. 'Don't be afraid.'

But for the first time since she'd met her husband, Darya felt a sprinkling of fear.

'Leave us,' he told her in Greek.

Orestis raised his head, that ludicrous blindfold still wrapped around it. It shouldn't have been like this, he would never forgive her. She lay her hand on his heart. Then she got up from the bed and left the room as instructed, his life still beating in her palm.

Outside, the sun was being swallowed by the hills, leaving a trail of red blots. Darya found herself calling for the kitten in Greek, 'Cat, cat, cat.' As if the animal was restricted by linguistic borders. Who knew? But no kitten came running. There was only the hush of darkening walls.

At least one border had been lifted, or at least softened; the arrangement was out in the open, if only within Aristos' house. It was the end and the beginning, so she gave thanks for that. She looked up at the window of the master bedroom but saw nothing, not even a shadow. Aristos would be talking Orestis through the deal, as he would any contract. It brought a flutter of sickness to think of it like that, but that was what it was. She went to the seating area, where she lit the candles and enclosed them in their jars. Here, among the scattered cushions, was comfort. Here was quiet. She was here, and here was peace.

She recalled the peace she'd expected to find in Berlin, peace being the elusive feeling of freedom. All there had been was a paper-chain of days, ready to tear at every glance over her shoulder. *Who was that man? Had she seen that car before?* Though she'd remind herself she was of no importance, that the KGB had more urgent tasks than to hunt down a provincial music teacher, she spent most hours of her week, whatever a week was in those days, unable to move or even open her mouth to eat. Her mother and babulia would assume her dead, or abducted. The sorrow she imagined on their faces and in their hearts made her ill. Her father might have guessed what had happened, but she could count on the silence of his shame. Every once in a while she'd feel a small sadistic glee at the irony of what he'd done to himself. How could he have guessed that those hours, years, at the piano or the cymbaly, yelling at her, slamming his fist against anything until she got the notes, got the scales, *Enough! Again!* over and over, would rear up to bite him as they did? He'd given her a ticket out. All it had taken was a visa to Poland with Tomasz, a concert of folk music by her and her students, to end his tyranny. That bottle in his hand would be the death of him, and her departure was its aid.

She gave thanks for Frau Friedel, who had been a lifeline at a low ebb. Darya's plan had been half-baked, concocted in the striking of a match on the train from Brest into Warsaw as her students laughed and joked. It had gone no further than finding somewhere to stay in Poland, never to return to Belarus.

It went around in her head, that inscription in the fortress: *I'm dying, but not giving up. Farewell, Motherland.*

Half-Polish, half-Russian Tomasz understood what she wanted and helped her to get it. He had acquaintances in Germany, fellow musicians. One of them would put her up.

And one did.

Frau Friedel came with numerous friends. Nights were filled with drink and song and laughter in that little apartment with those deep shadows in the corners. Days at Friedel's café, and nights as a freelance translator, were easy compared with what had come before, and Darya thanked God every day for the mercy He had shown her. That was until she discovered forgiveness could be a guise for vengeance. The ghost of Maksim had followed her. She stared into those deep shadows in the corner of that little apartment until she felt one with them.

Like a hard frost, the USSR had melted away. Belarus had been freed, her father had danced in front of his portable Junost. The Berlin Wall had come down, people had cheered and hugged each other. Everyone foresaw a future of peace, everyone except her. She'd come to the supposed West, she had crossed borders both physical and mental, but nothing had really changed, not inside her. One of Frau Friedel's numerous friends led Darya down the path to Hamburg. There she would board a cruise ship, and become a cleaner for her foreseeable future. Former-Soviet women were known for their work ethic, and her excellent German would carry her over any bumps. Some nights she awoke to her fingers twitching. She put it down to the manual labour. She tried not to hear the yearning of the cymbaly beyond the gentle snoring of the three other women in her cabin, from outside the porthole, somewhere on that fathomless sea.

It was on the ships where she got her first taste of Greek. Katya, the Ukrainian who shared a bunk-bed with her, had a Master's in Greek literature and taught her a phrase or two. These varied in their usefulness. And then, like one card drawn after another from a pack, Life brought a giant of a man to her: a Cypriot by the name of Aristos. She had grown tired of the restlessness of life at sea, the feeling of forever being adrift. Inspired by other colleagues, she began to look for work on land, in hotels. Cyprus was easy to get to, and it appealed: Aphrodite's island, so small it was almost lost in the Mediterranean sea. Someone knew someone who had arranged a job for her as a hotel chambermaid. The hotel was run by Aristos. His first. He would own several more by the end of the decade. He liked to know all his staff, and for whatever reason had developed an affection for her.

Before long he'd got his divorce, and begun negotiations with and about his daughter that would seemingly never end. Darya had prepared herself to sleep with the man, she was even looking forward to it. It amazed her that he'd never even broached the subject of sex but she put it down to honesty, old-fashioned values. It soon became clear that sex had never been Aristos' goal. She heard the passion in his voice when he spoke of closing deals and forcing others into corners. He enjoyed tactics and persuasion, debate and mental athletics. He had a passing knowledge of dozens of subjects and even echoed her father in his passion for history and genealogy. But the one topic that gave him no physical or intellectual stimulus at all was love. She'd assumed his desire not to have more children was because his sole attempt had produced the gorgon Eva.

She wondered at times if her husband was one of those men who lingered in bars to flick glances at the bartender. She noticed types like that, walking around particular coves in Speedos, and licking at dripping ice cream cones while peachy young Englishmen dived off the jetties.

When Darya came to terms with her husband's lack of libido, she resigned herself to living the rest of her life as an old maid's soul in a kept wife's body. She and Aristos had a civil ceremony with acquaintances for witnesses, and she was grateful for her family's absence. Her urges could be suppressed, channelled elsewhere. And in the evenings, when she sat in the smoke of his pipe tobacco, she'd pull up images in her mental projector of men she had seen at the beach that day, the waves on their thighs or the wind at the necks of their shirts.

Of his own accord, Aristos addressed her frustration. He suggested in a roundabout way that she sleep with a friend of his from the local council, a man so discreet that he'd barely uttered a sentence in the several years she'd known him. The proposal made her hairs stand on end. She turned the topic away and, to Aristos' credit, it never came back – until the night of that associate's birthday, when she met the Swedish wife of someone-or-other. Boys for rent, secret parties on the water... a new deck of cards had been spread on the table before her. A couple of hours later, the car lights sweeping signs and rocks along the highway, she confessed her interest to her husband. His response was a warm hand on her thigh, and a gentle squeeze.

She had brought a stranger to her husband's house. She had undressed and enjoyed him. He was her one and only guest, with no determined length of stay. She had no idea what this would mean, for any of them. It felt in equal parts a transgression and a liberation. But that was the nature of borders; they were placed and lifted with little concern for tradition, connection, overlap. Walls were built and walls were destroyed. It didn't matter who was where, and yet it was all that mattered.

Just as she wondered if she ought to go back inside, the patio door slid open and there loomed her husband. The living room light was on, the sun a mere memory. Nights fell so quickly here. Among the cicadas, she heard the sound of a car hacking itself awake. Orestis. The boy would go home, where he would lie in bed, reeling, and be ready to receive her call. In the meantime, he'd consider his future at the day job. Perhaps they would arrange the illusion of a transfer to another hotel, in Paphos perhaps, so as not to arouse suspicion among his colleagues. Or they might promote him to a higher position, in an invisible office, and allow glimpses of his presence every now and then for the sake of pretence.

Aristos came to her and stroked her cheek. And because he knew it was what she wanted to hear, he said in Greek: 'Don't worry. He's fine.'

Six

The first thing Darya saw when she opened her eyes was the rainbow in Skevi's hair. The AC whirred. Was this calm?

There was a second man in the class when usually there was only one. This new one was young, reminiscent of Orestis but more muscled. His brow also furrowed with self-doubt, as he struggled to position his limbs. In time he would learn to master it – if only he'd be kind to himself. At the end of the class, he went up to Skevi for a chat as if they were friends, which explained his sudden appearance. It could well be his last, a one-off trial as a bet or favour. Darya couldn't help but glance at the couple's body language, and the size of the young man's arms. He must have been Maksim's age.

'Thank you,' Darya said to Skevi in Greek as she headed to leave.

The man turned his hazy green eyes on her.

'It's nothing, darling, you're perfect!' Skevi replied in English. Then, in Greek, she introduced her boyfriend Pavlos.

'How are you?' His English was accented.

'Good, thank you,' she replied in Greek because the whole thing was ridiculous and how could she explain that to a stranger?

But Skevi seemed to understand. She laughed, her fingers wrapping around her lover's huge arm.

* * *

For the sake of discretion, he said, from now on Aristos would transfer payment to Orestis via Lefteris. It had been careless of Orestis and Darya to communicate directly. After the boy had had a couple of days to digest the information, Darya called on his services. As the hour approached, she felt a sense of doom. She trod to the front window, on the other side of which were muffled voices. One was Orestis', and the other her neighbour's.

Katina remarked that she'd seen his car several times and wondered whose it was. Nobody in the neighbourhood had a, she paused, Honda. Darya's grasp of Greek came and went with her breaths. She caught snatches of their dialogue and processed some of it. She wished she could move closer to the window, to watch their body language, but the electric shutter was fully rolled up. She'd be exposed at once.

'Doing some jobs,' came from Orestis, and 'For the Russian?' from Katina. 'Architect' or 'architecture' in the neighbour's whine of a tone, a stress on final vowels that made your skin retract.

In the window, a cypress was swaying in the wind. Things lived and died. Darya closed her eyes and breathed.

The doorbell buzzed.

'Good afternoon, Mrs Ioannidou,' Orestis said as she answered, and pointed with his eyes towards the neighbour.

She went along with it and put on her teacher's voice. 'You are late.'

Shutting the door behind him, he pulled her in for a kiss, then laughed.

'What did she say?'

'Nothing, don't worry. She thought I was a relative.'

'Of me?'

'Aristos.'

'What did you say?'

'I told her I was Eva's cousin from England, and I came to Cyprus to do some jobs for my uncle.'

From the way he carried himself, it was clear Orestis was growing used to the idea of fucking his boss' wife. Maybe his brain had compartmentalised what he was doing, added an extra duty to his job description: VIP service. Or, like so many other men, he longed to be half bull.

'Why don't you have any photographs?' he asked one day. 'I've never seen a house without family photos.'

She offered a near-truth: 'I don't like photographs with people. Only paintings with people.'

She'd ignore the betrayal in his voice, which crept in now and again to dampen the mood. Money was a balm for any wound, he'd soon get over it. But his voice had acquired an edge. Why the secrecy? Why not tell him from the start? She dodged not only his questions but her own. Why indeed? Why couldn't she have told him that her husband knew? Why had Aristos insisted on concealing his identity? She didn't want Orestis to view her as scheming, or calculating – whatever was associated with the bogeyman of her kind. Baba Yaga. 'To keep simple,' was her refrain, but even she cringed at that.

Moments later Orestis' edge would fade, the hard light would pass from his eyes. By the end of the month, he was almost his old self. He talked to her in Greek as well as

English and even tried to learn some Russian. More useful than Belarusian, she knew. But he had picked up some of her mother tongue as well and surprised her with it now and again. She gave him little gifts; a watch, which he received with a waning glow.

'My dad will be angry when he sees it.'

'Keep here,' she said.

He liked bending her over the desk in her husband's study, where tobacco lingered on the books and curtains. Afterwards, he'd spin the globe with a gentler finger, and point out all the places he longed to visit. Every so often, Aristos would walk in on them, wherever in the house they were. Sometimes he sat in the corner, watching, and she wondered if he felt anything about it. Orestis would get rougher. At other times Aristos would produce his camera, a Zenit he'd acquired from the Soviet bloc, and the click of the shutter, the whirr of the film inside, would make her heart stop. Orestis didn't seem to mind. He would angle himself to the lens, turn his torso to the light. Satisfied, if that was what he was, Aristos would take his leave to sit in the living-room, mouth smoking with pipe tobacco, and pore over books of history and photos of old Cyprus. Orestis would let himself out of the house, the sound of his little car dimming in the twilight.

For the time being, Orestis would remain at the Harmonia. When Darya pressed the subject, Aristos only said, 'Don't worry. I have plans.' It had taken Darya months to understand what his plan for her was.

Over the weeks, Aristos intercepted the boy as he took his leave and engaged him in conversation. At first, the talk was mundane; work and family, the day-to-day, football. Each time, the conversation grew a little more. On some nights

Orestis cooked for them in the kitchen they barely used. It gave her a sense of pride to find him skilled in other ways – stupid, she knew, but there it was. Her lover could make a three-course dinner and present it with a flourish. 'You should add catering to your resumé,' said Aristos. Was it meant to be a joke? Towards the end of the night, the men would end up side by side on the sofa, leafing through those big coffee table books of the Motherland before she birthed them. Her husband would indicate landmarks long-gone, copper mines long-abandoned, lakes that had evaporated, hotels that had been repurposed or left to be consumed by nature. He would talk of Northern Cyprus, now Turkish, which Orestis was too young to have known unoccupied.

'Have you been?' Aristos asked. The restrictions had been lifted, Southerners were free to cross the border and retread the ground they'd fled.

'I can't,' said Orestis. His entire body clenched. He recalled those protesting cousins, killed on live TV as one tried to pull the Turkish flag down, and then the second to avenge the murder. 'Also, my dad would kill me.'

'Yes,' Aristos said with a chuckle. 'I can't imagine your father would be happy.'

And it struck Darya that the men had a shared history, however weakly linked. Aristos had known Orestis as a child, as a growing teen, and now as a man. On these evenings, she indulged in a fantasy: if only they could live like this, the three of them. A perfect marriage, if far removed from her childhood mroya during lakeside sunsets.

But the dream was foam, it melted away. She was fifteen years his senior. Orestis would leave, and her husband would remain warm but detached. Darya would spend her days wandering around Lemesos, feeling ever more the stranger who never should have come in the first place.

Seven

It was a suggestion Aristos had made before, but it took her by surprise when he brought it up again: a cruise. They were strolling along the Molos with the crowds. It was Kataklysmos, and extra busy. Other countries' customs were always odd – why celebrate a flood? Having run around in the afternoon blasting each other with water-guns, schoolchildren strolled along the lit-up boardwalk with their parents, stopping every so often at stalls of plastic toys and sweets. Kupala was on the next flip of the calendar page. She chased the thought away.

Her tongue was poking at the charcoal salt of corn-on-the-cob, which stuck both pleasantly and unpleasantly between her teeth when Aristos said with an easy air: 'What do you say? How about a cruise?'

There was no reason he'd need to check with her. 'All right,' she replied in Greek regardless. 'That would be nice.'

Her husband's brow rose; the complexity of her phrasing was marginally better.

'I have to confess: there is another reason I want us to go on this cruise,' he said. 'I want you to spend some time with Eva.'

'Eva?' A week, maybe more, on a boat, in the middle of the

sea, with her wicked stepdaughter? 'She will kill me.'

Aristos laughed. 'Don't worry, she'll be fine. I did her a favour when I gave Orestis a job. She owes me this.'

Darya picked at the salt in her teeth. So now she was a favour owed. Maybe it wasn't too late to back out.

'I told her she could bring a friend, to make things easier. She wants to bring Orestis.' Aristos turned to her and smiled as if this news was good.

The moon was bright. It whistled at her, beckoned her thoughts to wander around it, circle it, before drifting off into the depths of the unknown universe, of which she was only a fraction of a morsel of a part.

Orestis would accept the invitation. That was a given.

* * *

Aristos booked a cab to the port. He refused to leave either the Lexus or the BMW sitting in the briny air of the car park for a whole week. The AC was on full blast in the black Mercedes, and though she longed to ask the driver to turn it down she kept her mouth shut. The gleaming road signs passed overhead, along with the new flyovers, another thing she'd seen develop here, over time, over eras, still less than half her life, and as usual, she tried to mouth the Greek she managed to catch. Billboards announced the development of luxury flats and offices. Chinese families beamed at her from sparkling kitchens. New churches were rising from the parched hills, white, terracotta-headed giants.

'More of them?' Aristos muttered to himself. 'Why bother with property developers when we have the Church?'

Before she knew it, they were nearing the port. Even though

that wide blue strip made up every backdrop in Lemesos, there was a thrill about heading for the sea today, with the purpose of travelling on it, across it. The shadows of palm trees brushed the windows, and the jumble of glass-walled office blocks and grey plastered newsagents rolled by until all receded, and the landscape was whittled down to the bare essentials: the road, the port, the sea.

When she got out of the cab, the skin of Darya's cheeks, nose and arms were prickled by the breeze. Inside, it was clear that nothing had been renovated in years – if ever. The terminal was heaving. Tanned bodies waited in long lines for the chance to go elsewhere and tan some more. Middle-aged men with huge bellies yelled unintelligible things at the staff. Suitcases landed on conveyor belts for a scan that nobody seemed to be checking. Children were preemptively dressed in T-shirts of windmills in sunsets or pharaohs' death masks against pyramids. They ran around their mothers' legs, the women sighing with hands on hips.

Aristos surveyed the room for two people. One was an acquaintance who would skip them ahead in the queue. Darya lowered her head. She recalled those hours in hospital waiting-rooms with her babulia, the feeling of relief when the old woman was finally seen to. The second person Aristos searched for was his daughter, who would bring enough luggage to sink the ship.

Time being nothing but a vague concept to her, Eva was always late. Days became nights, with iced coffees along the way. If she missed the embarkation, oh well; Aristos and Darya could spend a week roaming the Islands alone. The nautical miles might help to sever this rope.

Across the room was a familiar light: a rainbow of hair.

Skevi. Darya squirmed at the thought of the woman spotting her, of having to introduce her instructor and husband. Some worlds were best kept apart. Next to Skevi was a young man, stroking the small of her back while the straps of both their duffel bags strained at his shoulders. The muscular boyfriend with the hazy green eyes. They might all end up on the same boat.

'There they are!' came Aristos' sudden voice. He waved at his daughter and Orestis.

Darya was thankful for her sunglasses. She was even thankful for Eva's, though the girl's pout could be seen from Greece.

As he walked up to them, Orestis gave an enthusiastic greeting. They were supposed to be strangers.

Aristos was quick. 'How are you, son? It's been months.'

'Yes, yes...' said the younger man. 'The party at the hotel.'

Orestis flicked a glance at Darya. If only he hadn't.

'Let me introduce you to my wife. Orestis, Darya.'

'What a beautiful name,' said Orestis.

The comment surprised her. She was careful to smile just enough. 'Pleased to meet you,' she said in Greek.

Eva's eyebrows flew over her sunglasses.

Emboldened, Darya went for it. 'Hello, Eva,' she said. 'Are you well?'

The girl sipped on her iced coffee. 'A dream.'

Containers sat waiting to be loaded onto cargo ships. Cranes lifted their necks like giant metal birds and gulls squawked around them, fighting over soggy scraps in the water. Darya steeled herself; for the sight of the ships, for the sea itself, the connector of all her lives. Separation and union. From Cyprus, you could feel the breath of Turkey, whose head

173

touched the Black Sea, who reached up to Ukraine, whose fingers intertwined with Belarus. Closer to Lemesos was Syria, Lebanon. Those poor souls, fleeing the destruction of their world and their selves. Like the victims of Chernobyl. Not only the dead, but those who mourned them. The farmers whose land was suddenly worthless. All she'd had to suffer was her father's words, her fear, her sorrow, and a nose blocked to the bleach she had poured down toilets in cabins and hotel suites.

Maksim's suffering was not her own. Those coloured dots had not been on her skin, those fevers not in her head. The pain she felt was only selfishness. Here she was, fine, with everything she could ever need.

Eva was first to go up the gangway. Orestis, the gentleman, stepped aside for Darya and spread his arm so she would go ahead. She watched her feet on the white iron steps, raised her eyes to Eva's behind, which had reduced in size – but not much – since she'd last seen her. The girl might even wear a bikini.

Just like that, it came to her: Eva loved Orestis.

Within the next few years, they might even be married. That was Aristos' plan.

Darya steadied herself on the railings. She barely breathed a hello to the pleasant girls in uniform that welcomed her aboard. Welcomed her into the lobby, where the polished wood of the reception desk, the surrounding pillars, the curved staircases, their marbled steps, the light filling the tall windows, floor after floor after floor above them, made her head spin. She would lose herself in here.

'Is this how your one looked?'

Eva was talking to her. It took a moment for Darya to understand. Phrases rushed through her head in Greek.

Instead, she settled on a gesture: a wave of the hand and a smirk that said as if.

Eva laughed, despite herself.

Maybe Aristos had been telling the truth. By being forced to spend time with her stepmother, Eva might demote her hatred to apathy. And Orestis, with his kindness and courtesy, might prove to be the key between their locked doors.

Or this would be a disaster. They might trip up. Eva would smell the truth between the prince and the witch. She might be sensitive to auras, shared glances, changed inflexions. Aristos always had been a gambler. But one thing was certain: whatever the outcome of this holiday, Darya would remain the antagonist. Baba Yaga.

Aristos picked up their keys, nodding with approval at his surroundings. A strapping East Asian wheeled a tower of luggage across their path. It was only then that Darya was struck by another thought: Orestis was sleeping with Eva.

But no. Her husband was placing different sets of keys in their hands. The youths were in separate cabins. With a smile, Aristos escorted his wife to their suite. In her gut was a bitter bud.

* * *

The vessel pulled away from the port to a volley of Arabic between the sailors. Bulky, skinny, tall or short, the men passed anacondas of rope as if they were spider webs. Other men yelled in Greek from smaller boats, coast guard or pilots. The whole of Cyprus slid off into the horizon. Would they see the Turkish side at all? Would it be visibly different from the Greek? Her breath soared. Freedom was the sea, the realm of

175

being and nothingness, this deep dark womb from which all life began. She shut her eyes and inhaled it all.

Eva called Orestis to her. 'Come on, let's do *Titanic* like losers.' She stood against the rail with her arms spread out. 'Not like that, what are you doing? He was holding her arms, you brick.'

'You want this ship to be the Titanic?'

'Of course. Don't I look like Kate Winslet?' She struck a pose that Darya vaguely recognised from the film's nude scene. 'I'm telling you, naked we're exactly the same.'

This made Orestis smile in a way Darya had never seen before. He called her Miss Winslet and she thanked Leonardo. A glimpse at their youth, the schoolboy teasing his classmate. Then Eva said, not very quietly, 'And she's the old woman with the diamond.'

The Russian Whore pretended not to have heard.

'Come on, then,' Orestis said. 'Throw the diamond in.'

'Fine.' After a pause, the girl unclasped the silver piece from her wrist and dropped it into the chopped-up waves.

Orestis gasped. He couldn't stop it.

'Don't look at me like that,' said Eva. 'I have others.'

Darya turned from her stare.

An hour later, they were sitting in a lounge of glass walls filled with light. Darya sipped at her grenadine mocktail while the younger two talked of a mutual friend. Orestis had mentioned him before, something about a book of poems. Eva was excited and dropped the names of other poets his book would stand beside on bookshelves. Orestis laughed her down.

'I invited him too,' she said. 'But the idiot made some excuse. I don't know, I think he hates me.'

Darya caught the expression on her face before she changed

it. People couldn't be forced to like those they were supposed
to. Human pieces never fit neatly together.

For his part, Orestis was acting well. He mostly restricted
his attention and conversation to Eva and her father. He was
sharp not to exclude Darya completely and even had enough
clout to ask what part of Russia she was from.

'I am from Belarus, actually.'

Eva narrowed her eyes. '*Pe*! We're like Eurovision in here.'
She looked surprised when Darya laughed.

As for her own performance, Darya was unsure. She knew
she ought to face Orestis once in a while, and engage with him
as a normal person would. But she couldn't look at his arms,
his jaw. Not at his dimpled cheeks. Caught in the no-man's
land of looking and not looking, possessiveness and aloofness,
she stared at the carpet, the pillars, the table, the colour of her
cocktail projected onto the table like an old slide, with only
the occasional glance at whoever had started to speak. She
would have to learn how. She would have to negotiate this.

Aristos' thumb on her hand made her jump. He gave her his
kindest expression, which his daughter scrutinised. The scent
of pipe tobacco lingered on his fingers as Darya brought them
to her lips and kissed them. All would be fine.

They parted ways for the afternoon. Father and daughter
went off to the casino's fruit machines. Orestis took his cue
to work out at the gym, leaving Darya to find her way to the
meditation room. It looked out onto the sea and was so close
to the surface of the water that she felt like a paper boat carried
along by the waves. She might go to the sauna after yoga, to
open her pores and allow the badness out with her sweat. No,
that was dangerous – too much like the banya. Instead, she
focused on the spray of the vessel in the water, the play of

light on the foamy ridges of the waves, willing herself one with them, with everything. *Aparigraha.*

Showered and dressed and perfumed, they reconvened for dinner in a white room of elegant chairs and soft lighting. A trestle table boasted fruit sculptures and chocolate fountains. The rush of the engines played beneath the piped jazz. Eva was funny and effervescent to her two men. And when Orestis exchanged Greek phrases for Russian ones with Darya, she couldn't help but join in. She'd get Darya to repeat Cypriot words, which the woman gathered from the men's reactions were rude, provincial or both, and then cackle with tears in her eyes. Such was the price of peace.

As the others made their way from the dining room to one of the lounges for the evening show, Darya excused herself to go out on the deck for some air. If only she could name what tumbled around inside her, which filled her close to bursting. Resting her arms on the wet wood of the ship's railings, she cast her eye across the whole dark sea. She imagined her soul spreading out to cover it, embrace it, melt into it.

Not ten metres away, a father held his toddler up and pointed out the constellations. She couldn't follow his language, but all the same, she heard the tale of the bear in the sky.

Would a child help? To see yourself, your kin, replicated in a brand new being – it must have some effect. And if it was Aristos', or even Orestis', it would plant her firmly in the country she never called home. But would her child be accepted? Would the blood of his homeland be enough to wash off her Slavic dirt? No. She could not be reborn from foam. She would become a rusalka, wrapping men in her long hair and dragging them down to their watery fate.

After the show, an assault of plucky young Brits with voices like bells, the four of them toasted the first island stop. Then they said goodnight and separated. Aristos' hand was on her back throughout the walk to their suite. When he fell into a satisfied slumber there, she read the message from Orestis for the fifth time and followed the directions to his cabin. The brine walked with her along the corridor, as well as that familiar hush, hush, whirr of the vessel. She knocked gently at the door of his cabin. Orestis answered, dressed only in pyjama bottoms. She sat on his bed and made him get on his knees before she allowed him to take them off.

Eight

The ship wasn't to dock in Santorini till the evening. Over a buffet breakfast on the open deck, bacon and croissants and yoghurt with granola, Aristos told them the myth of the island's birth; a son of Poseidon had dreamt he'd slept with his niece, a nymph. She asked him to throw a clod of earth into the sea, which would turn into a place where she could hide from her father's wrath. Having woken from the dream, the man obeyed its orders. He threw some dirt into the water and, before his eyes, the island of Santorini grew out of it.

'What crazy stories,' Eva said, smoking.

'I like them,' said Darya.

The girl exhaled. 'Me, too.'

The ship being too large for the island's port, small boats were dispatched from shore to fetch passengers in groups. Darya took the steps down to the other vessel, on which deep-tanned Greeks waited, arms held out. Middle-aged men who'd lived it all, and younger ones, their sons, slid around on the rocking wood, their bodies adjusting to the motion of every wave. Her feet were a heartbeat from the sea. She could miss the boat and plunge straight in. The thought of the release sent a shiver through her.

She was first to descend. Orestis had offered to go ahead but she'd sensed he was nervous. 'I did this before,' she told him.

'Mother of God,' Eva said, crossing herself.

When the boat was fully loaded they set off for the island. Eva pulled a digital camera from her handbag. Santorini ahead. A humble dock at the base of a dark cliff, and the lights of a bustling square like lava at its peak. Within the rocky face of the island was a cable car that ferried tourists up to the town. Donkeys carried others up a dirt path.

Eva chose the cable car, as there was no way she'd be using the animal transport. 'No way,' she repeated in English. Darya chose the donkey because here she was, now, and there it was, now. She went alone; Aristos joked that his weight would kill the beast. Orestis was reluctant to let her go as if she might fall to her death, but then Eva said, 'What are you afraid of? Let her go,' so he relented. Darya knew from the girl's narrowed eyes that she may have been looking at Orestis for a little too long.

The donkey's owner was a short old man with a thick moustache and a straw hat, clothes faded by the long days. 'You'll be safe,' he told her, and she knew from his calf muscles that this was a promise. As they ascended, he whistled to the mountains, to the sea, to the tiny pads of land rising out of the blue like thighs in a bath. She regretted choosing the donkey; Aristos' comment reverberated in her head, and she hoped her own figure, though a splinter compared to his, wasn't too much of a burden for the sad-faced beast.

She only knew she had reached the top when there came the sound of a shutter. Her heart lurched. Eva, waiting at the top, lowered her camera. The men came to stand by her side. Darya felt a burst of shame. Was she a joke? She mastered her breathing. *Pranayama.* As the camera clicks continued, she surprised herself: she posed for Eva, throwing one hand up in a carefree swoop.

'Very beautiful,' she said to the donkey's owner in Greek as she dismounted, and joined her hands in thanks. She longed to pat the donkey's head, to caress its melancholy face. Stopped herself.

Whitewashed bubbles of buildings grew out of each other among the stone-paved streets. Cats rubbed their bodies against painted wooden doors and play-fought around the potted cacti. Over the bright blue dome of a church and through the white arch of its bell tower, the sun was beginning to set. Eva tried to photograph it but scrunched her face at whatever she'd produced.

'Aren't you taking pictures?' she asked her father.

'I've done it a hundred times,' he replied.

Night had fallen, but there was still time before the ship departed. They sat down at a restaurant with a view of the houses and churches cascading to the sea. They ordered seafood and dips, a bottle of wine. At some point during the meal, she felt Orestis' hand on her knee beneath the table. Above it, his face betrayed nothing. He continued his talk with Aristos about the future of Cyprus tourism, things she had heard already. The island's state of limbo; both too expensive and not luxurious enough. Tourists would be split between cheaper Turkey and frivolous Dubai, whose hotels were too godly to be confined to five stars.

'And let's not forget we're in the middle of everything,' Aristos said. 'Lebanon here, Turkey there, Syria, Israel, Palestine... Even Bin Laden had a bank account in Cyprus, for God's sake!'

182

Eva clapped with joy. 'I can't believe you're both chatting away like this. Aw, my Daddykins! Just think, a few months ago Orestis was afraid of you.'

Aristos amended the topic. 'What is it you want in life?' he asked Orestis.

'Well, I don't know now. I thought I wanted to own a hotel.' He forced a laugh.

Aristos smiled. 'The smart man always looks at his situation. He stands back and thinks, *How can this work to my advantage?* What do people value? What do they want? Will they pay for it?'

Darya lowered her eyes.

'This is where Cyprus finds herself. Who wants her, what for, what can she offer? Everyone's fighting about Europe and Angela Merkel. But if we weren't in Europe, we'd be back at the bottom of the sea. Europe is why the Russians are in Cyprus. Buy property, get citizenship. Putin keeps the Turks away and he gets something in return. He gets a foot in Europe, a port. We're surrounded by sea. Cyprus is willing to sell herself because she found a buyer.'

His tobacco smoke mingled with Eva's Marlboro. The girl waved it all away from Orestis' face. 'I'm willing to pay for anything,' she said. Then: 'With my father's money, of course.' Her laugh was so huge it made the other diners turn to look.

On their way back to the ship, Orestis kept touching his forehead. By the time they'd stepped off the cable-car down the rocks and onto the dock, he'd turned pale. With obvious effort, he tried to retain an easy, jovial air.

'Are you all right?' Darya asked.

'I'm not... feeling too good.'

She watched as he gripped the stepladder up from the small boat onto the ship and swayed, despite his attempts not to, up to the entrance and the lobby.

Eva was concerned. Was it the food, her voice, did she drive him insane? He tried to laugh. It was nothing, a little dizziness. 'It happens sometimes. I'm not used to travelling.' She would fetch the doctor, she said, but he refused, insisting he'd be fine in the morning.

Those eyebrows of his were knotted, his eyes wet. Darya felt an ache in her chest. Orestis turned in, but not before accepting some pills from Eva's handbag. Father and daughter took the change of plan in their stride and went out on the deck to watch the ship depart. The lights on the tip of Santorini, like lava at the mouth of the volcano, faded away. When her husband and stepdaughter headed off for the lounge to catch the late show, Darya scanned the blackness for signs of life. She could think of nothing worse than loud pop and dance routines. She yawned, counting on Eva to be happy of her father's company all to herself.

Instead of returning to the suite, she watched her feet walk down a different corridor, through other doorways. Glass panels slid apart to let her through, nothing like her old ships, till she was rounding a corner for Orestis' cabin. She passed an officer in his smart white suit, and though he nodded politely she turned her face from him. Bleach. She tried to block the smell, the memory – not in the cabins or suites she cleaned, but in the hospital. The white labyrinth where her mother had worked, where Maksim had died. He'd only been Orestis' age.

The cabin was dark, the curtains drawn over the porthole. Sickness hung in the air. The sheets and quilt were a bundle in the single bed. Orestis was somewhere within it, his body still the same but folded up and obscured, its head turned towards the wall. She sat on the edge of the bed and placed a hand where his thigh would be. She had never seen him like this, a ball of cotton with a tousle of hair. She sat in that thin hum from the bathroom, the dim thump of music from the lounge. The walls, the floor vibrated. A cotton swan, discarded onto the carpet where it keeled and transformed back into a towel, trembled as if it was cold.

Why was she here? If she could leave, she would. But she was a tiny thing in a small space, the cabin a walnut containing her, floating on the wide expanse of the sea, on a large planet in the immense universe.

Samota.

She stared into the darkness of the room, focusing on nothing but her and Orestis' breathing.

Nine

During her days as a cabin stewardess, she'd felt a pleasant ache at the sight of a new port. Each took her further on her journey, further from home. In a cabin filled with three other girls' breaths, she would peek from her lower bunk at whichever foreign dock was in the porthole. Oslo, Algeciras, Port Said, Funchal, Agadir. From behind the glass would come the bickering of gulls and dockworkers speaking words she couldn't know.

The ship had docked in Syros while they'd slept. This time Darya saw its port not as a miniature in a porthole, but as a vista from a suite above sea level; a room large enough for her and those three other girls to have danced in.

'Let's go out for breakfast,' Aristos said. 'I'll ask Eva to check on Orestis.' His tone suggested Orestis had been lying about his illness, or that Darya might be the cause of it.

They convened in the lobby. A voice came over the tannoy to announce first in Greek and then in accented English the imminent Bingo. What did he look like, this man who was speaking? Had she passed him in the corridors?

Eva wore a dress with a bold floral print, which Darya complimented.

'Thank God you got rid of those contacts,' Orestis added.

'Re! She pays me a compliment and all you can talk about is the colour of my eyes? That was the fashion at the time!'

It was as close to a thank you as Darya would get. When Orestis turned to her and made a point of saying, 'You look very nice,' she gave a small thankful nod. That would do.

Eva slapped his arm.

'You feel better?' Darya asked in Greek.

And before he could answer, Eva said in English: 'Don't worry, he's OK.'

Then they were out in Syros – the streets, the roads, marble. 'Fitting for the ancient capital of the Cyclades,' said Aristos. And he reeled off bits of history as her eyes skipped up alleys of marble steps flecked with cats and chrysanthemums. She hoped the kitten was all right back in Cyprus. The Sri Lankan had been given strict instructions on feeding, and the girl only ever needed to be told a thing once.

Eva pointed at various signs along the harbour and chal-lenged her stepmother to read them aloud: photographer, pharmacy, boat hire. The Greek alphabet was similar enough to Cyrillic that it wasn't much of a challenge. She could read the words, even if they meant nothing.

'Bravo!' Eva would say each time. Thank God she was in good spirits, but those same spirits were annoying as hell. Darya had no interest in playing the amusing foreigner. Aristos distracted his daughter with boutiques.

Orestis was distracted himself. Walked close to the harbour, where dozens of boats were docked. Did he also recall their day in Latchi, the fishing boats strung on the boardwalk like lights from a beam? Here, among the bright bobbing speedboats were a handful of luxury yachts, standing up in the water like big white cliffs. Orestis looked chastened by them. She could buy him one, why not? A mere sliver off Aristos' bank account. They'd take trips around the coast of Cyprus. Fruit and wine on the deck, sex in the open air, naps in the sun, all in the privacy of their own property. Their own floating island.

Two boys stood on the curb, on the point of crossing the marbled road. Not quite twenty, skin browned and hair bleached by the sun. On the other side of the road was an elderly gentleman, in a straw boater and a light expensive scarf. In an instant, Darya knew what they were, what the old man was. His eyes were trained on Orestis, and the boys had turned their heads to follow his gaze. As if by some wire between them all, Orestis lifted his eyes to acknowledge them. Understanding between the men expanded into a net, a net that caught everything. Darya's heart stopped. The air thrummed with violence.

And then, the net between the men was clipped. The boys hadn't crossed the road but perched on a stone wall. Gorgeous birds. The man waited for the traffic lights to change.

Darya understood, more with every breath, that she and Orestis were finished. Emotions were transient, as everything was.

Orestis turned and saw her, and his soft smile said he'd been thinking the same thing.

* * *

They took a late lunch on the ship. The horde of passengers, some in shorts and flip-flops, others dressed as if for the ballet, heaped meat and fish and pasta onto their plates, jelly and ice-cream and cake in side bowls. Beasts. She had to force herself to eat a small portion of potato salad.

188

Orestis had removed his baseball cap when they re-embarked. Minutes later, running his fingers through his hair, he excused himself from the table to go to the bathroom, and she wondered if she was showing the appropriate amount of concern as he left. He returned with his hair in better shape. On his way back to the table, he checked his reflection wherever it was, calling to him from between the pillars like a sprite in a forest. He sat back down. His cheeks looked red.

During lunch, that anxious little frown made plough lines in his forehead. Then he straightened his back. 'Mr Ioannidou, I just want to say again how grateful I am for this trip. I've always wanted to visit the Islands but never been able to.' His shirt was more buttoned up than before.

Eva waved away his gratitude. 'He did it for me, not you! Don't think you're special.'

They all laughed.

'Your father never brought you to Greece?' There was a hardness in Aristos' tone.

'No. Well, we were going to go to Athens when I was little, but then... Anyway.'

'Well, for now, you're seeing the Islands. Next time you can do the mainland. Peloponnisos, Delphi, Thessaloniki.' Her husband flourished, he expanded with every sentence. Out of his mouth blew the North East, where, he told them, Muslims and Christians and Jews once lived in harmony. Ioannina, with its forests and lakes and wildlife; the boars, the scorpions.

Darya recalled the lakes back home. The storks rising from their nests on telephone poles. A memory of her life or a memory of a dream? Either way, it didn't matter. It was all real and it was all gone.

'Is your family in Russia?'

The question surprised her. More surprising still, it had come from Eva.

Darya cleared her throat. 'Belarus.'

'A, yes. Do you see them?'

Darya bought time by pretending to clear her throat. 'We speak,' she said. That old lie. It had been ages since she'd called on it. She averted her eyes from Aristos.

'You should see them.'

'Yes...' And she couldn't think of any other words, not for a long, long, time. 'It's difficult.'

That anxious expression of Orestis' came back, this time for her.

Eva babbled about her departed grandmother, which prompted Orestis to remember his, and Aristos his. From the way the memories converged, the three dead women had God and the kitchen at their centre. Darya's babulia had been the same because of course she was. People were always the same, here and there, in the past and the future. It was only in the present where they differed.

When Eva asked her, 'Is your grandma still alive?' Darya froze.

She lowered her fork, dabbed her mouth with the napkin.

'Still alive,' she said. But how could she know?

Darya had never told her husband about Maksim. The existence of relatives back home was the extent of his knowledge. He inquired once about her father, and she didn't want to discuss it. So she mimed drinking from a bottle and let that be that. Aristos nodded and allowed the subject to rest. But if that's where his judgment had settled, it was a great injustice. Her father could have no knowledge of her betrayal, but all the same. Darya felt as if, with that single gesture, she had brought the Professor to the guillotine and removed his head. To reduce him to an alcoholic, to the cartoon mime of a bending wrist, was unfair. He drank vodka, so what? So did everybody. Her babulia could knock it back as if it was water. The Professor's problem was his impatience, and the drink only aggravated it. He wanted Belarus to be independent, for its language to be saved from the brink of death, for those government bastards to pay for their lies, for God to be dead, for Darya to be good, for Darya to play well, for Darya to learn, for Darya to become what he wanted, now, now, now, now, now.

But it wasn't who he always was. Sometimes he taught Literature, he read poems to their friends on winter nights and they sang. Sometimes he was a comedian, whose thick triangular eyebrows would point up to the sky after a dig at his mother-in-law. But the time came when all his personas would ball into one: a sick misery. The day they received the phone call, Maksim was breathing his last, the professor-father-clown was consumed. He railed against the power plant, against the military, against the government. He yelled his accusations and conspiracies at his family, wife, daughter, mother-in-law, what did it matter, they were all a single woman, and his screams were so loud that her mother threw uneasy glances at the kitchen wall. She who had seen so many bodies expire, death coming through the skin as red stars, he didn't even care what his anger was doing to her. For years, there was only that buzzing lump of energy in the house, a dangerous planet whose orbit the women avoided. When the USSR collapsed and Lukashenka took over, they thought: 'At last! A reprieve.' Here was a President who addressed his nation in its native tongue, the Professor could finally be more than one persona again. How wrong they were. None of this brought Maksim back. Nothing erased the damage done to his country. All those infected bodies, all those empty deaths. Heroes of the USSR, leaving only golden stars in their place.

On the one hand, Darya felt guilt for dismissing her past, she felt shame for the pain she caused her mother and babulia by leaving. When she pictured them, their eyes were filled with tears. But on the other hand, she felt an enormous relief to reject everything that had come before, to turn it away and say, *Enough.*

Move on.

Start again.

* * *

It seemed as if Tinos was drifting towards them instead of the other way around. Even from this vantage point, the island was dwarfed by its massive church. Officers barked instructions at sailors, sailors shouted to each other, officers called to men on the docks, who caught the mooring ropes. The anchor came clanking down. Given the go-ahead, Darya and the others gathered in the lobby to disembark. Down the gangway they went, holding on to their hats. In the temper of the afternoon sun, they crawled up the slope towards the church, the path to God marked out with tourist shops. Aside from the usual plastic magnets of windmills and beaches, which could apply to any of the Islands, there were icons. The best of them sat in woven baskets on the ground. These weren't the usual, prints on card glued to planks of wood; they were thick slabs of tree trunk, hand-painted and finished with gold leaf. Jesus saw into you. The Virgin's sorrow reached out for your hand. Darya watched one of the shopkeepers. Her face reflected the icons' sobriety, the sense that you could only stand by and watch as life went on the way it did, as people acted the way they would.

Oh, white birch...

That song. How did she even think of it?

'You probably know, Orestis,' Aristos said, which Darya translated as *You probably don't know, Darya*, 'this is the most important pilgrimage of the Greek Orthodox world. But do you know how this church came to be?'

'I only know it was a miracle,' answered the younger man. Good pupil.

'E, yes, basically. One night, a hundred years ago, a nun dreamt of the Virgin Mary. The virgin guided her to a place where, buried in the dirt, was her icon. The nun related her dream to the monastery. When they dug up the site she had been guided to, they discovered the foundations of an old church. This one standing before us was built in tribute to that miracle.'

Orestis nodded. 'That's a nice story.'

'Nice story? God have mercy!' said Eva. 'It's a miracle.' She crossed herself.

Aristos winked at Orestis.

The church itself was not in the image Darya had come to expect, but more Western. Through the carved marble gate, embellished with flowing relief, was an immense forecourt. Large staircases with intermittent streams of blood-red carpet led to arched colonnades of marble columns, a cream facade and a bell tower that soared to Heaven. Our Lady of Tinos.

But there were no chants and psalms in her head, only that

193

plaintive song:

Oh, white birch, why are you not green?

Inside, the church was more typically Greek: icons and gold. Except there also stood a glass plinth, like an upright fairytale coffin, with an icon of the Virgin inside. A throng of tourists queued to kiss it. Orestis had removed his baseball cap before they'd even passed the ornate gate. Eva was crossing herself. Aristos simply was, thinking whatever it was that he thought. She would never truly know her husband.

As Eva and her father admired the icons, the golden chandeliers, the sky-bound ceiling, Orestis and Darya found themselves queuing for the sacred icon. Sitting on a stool was a priest with a long black beard, who wiped the glass after every pilgrim's kiss. Darya felt a bloom of discomfort. She kept a shrine in the house, over which she'd draped the rushnyk she'd bought from a vendor in Warsaw – a souvenir, a sign. But there was something about walking up to this holy picture, and this holy man, that left her exposed, afraid. Maksim was watching from Heaven, and he was sad. Sad to have been excluded from her life, to be dismissed from the telling of her story. She had denied him, eroded him. That made her no better than the Army, the government, those men in their brown suits, that had sent him to the plant. They were all culpable, united in their crime.

Then it was her turn to kiss the Virgin. She couldn't bring her lips to the case, not quite. The priest caught her eye and brought his cloth up to wipe the glass regardless, to wipe away what hadn't ever been there.

She and Orestis waited outside for father and daughter. Other tourists chatted and posed for photos. Somewhere here there might be other Belarusians. Darya would know them on sight, as you're always able to tell your own. There was that time in Sigma when she'd bumped her basket into another woman's, and had known in her gut that they shared a homeland. But she'd excused herself in Greek, and hurried to the cashier.

An elderly local walked through the gate of the church. She staggered up the steps, both her headscarf and eyes a burning blue.

'Do you believe?' Orestis asked. He wasn't looking at Darya, but at the miracle site before them. 'In God?'

'Of course.' Unconsciously, her hand went for the cross around her neck.

Orestis looked surprised, even a little hurt. 'I thought maybe because of the yoga...'

'No, I mean...' But she didn't know what she meant, what anything she ever did or thought meant. 'Yes,' she said at last. 'I understand.' It wasn't what she wanted to say at all.

Did he know about the USSR, about state atheism? About what God could mean? If only he'd remove his sunglasses, the baseball cap, if only they could face and see into each other. Her little finger stretched to his hand. Stroked the skin. For a few seconds, he allowed it.

'Why you don't believe?' she said.

He didn't turn. 'E... Never mind.'

'No, why? It's your grandmother?'

His body tensed.

'Some things make sense,' he said after a while, the words taking their time to form. 'If there was God, He would do things to always make sense. Some people suffer for nothing, die for nothing. *God's will.* Other people are bad but they get rich, die happy. *God's will.* His plan. What sort of plan—?'

His throat closed itself to words. Then he swallowed and tried a lighter voice. 'My friend Paris... You should meet him. He says there's nothing as bad as the Church, throughout history. God is fear, control. God is people. We are the ones who make things happen, we do things ourselves, even decide who lives and dies. Whose life has value and whose doesn't.'

What she saw was a sort of sinking. Orestis sinking into the ground, away from her. 'You cannot believe this!'

Orestis laughed and turned to face her. 'Why?'

'Because...' But she could think of nothing to say other than, *Because God.* And then it came to her: 'You know Fabergé?'

He repeated the word, but blankly, like a robot.

'He makes eggs, the... golden ones, and with the diamonds... the ones there are only a few. Maybe fifty, in whole world. For tsar and tsarina.' Orestis nodded, more out of politeness than recognition. 'Some, you touch them and they break— sorry, open. And little things come outside, like a picture of Tsar Nikolai, or flowers. They are inside all the time. You think it is you, you are one who breaks the egg, you are one who makes things come. But it was like this already made. The way it breaks, it is the...' She struggles for the word. '...The design.'

She made out his narrowed eyes behind the sunglasses. Felt the urge to kiss those lips, hold him. But they were here, among people, outside the church. She stopped herself.

'Hmm,' was all he said.

She thought of a ship departing; a mooring rope set loose, an anchor drawn.

'I know is true,' she said. 'Believe me. I know.'

Now was not the time to say more. But she wanted to tell him. She knew with sudden clarity that if anyone would ever hear it, would ever listen to her, it was Orestis. This was why he was brought to her, this was why their paths had crossed. God wished to absolve her. He was giving her a chance to wipe her soul clean.

Eva and her father stepped out of the church. The girl looked at Darya as if she was Judas, caught.

Before the ship departed, they had time to sit at a café, of course, because what else did Cypriots do? Eva demanded lokmades, and her father had said Tinos served the best. Fried dough balls finished with streaks of honey and chopped nuts; the very thought of them repulsed Darya. 'No sugar,' she said.

'Mash'allah,' said Eva.

Why had this girl been so indulged? Everything was about and for her. All her father's attention and affection, all the money and status she'd got for nothing, even the acquisition of Orestis – everything had been sown and harvested for her consumption. This fat spoiled child from a fable. But unlike make-believe children, she would never receive her comeuppance, she would never be taught a lesson.

The waiter came to inform Darya that they were out of the ginger tea she'd ordered. Apologising with a hand on his heart, so dramatic, he offered mint instead.

Darya shrugged, yes, whatever.

Eva found this hilarious. 'She really doesn't care, does she?' she said to her father and carried on laughing.

No. Enough. She didn't care. She wouldn't care again.

* * *

Darya left the others to watch the sun set from the meditation room. Her body and soul were wrung together like a wet rag, twisting her almost to tears. Sadness advanced and receded, anger swelled, then frustration, a sense of loss, grief, which faded to wistfulness, then apathy, as the water rolled out ahead of her, pink and golden and blank as if nothing had ever been troubled there; as if the sea was a vacuum of feeling, a lifeless and soulless mirror for existence.

She returned to the suite to shower while Aristos napped. The water ran over a lifeless body, a plinth of bones. The woman was gone. What was Orestis for, if not to come and satisfy her now, to fuck her and do whatever she asked him to do, to earn the money her husband was paying? But she wanted nothing. Her energies were dimming, her soul departing. A paper boat.

But that was all she had to be. She sat in the armchair, licking her lips and swallowing, slowly, repeatedly, and watched her husband as he slept. The giant, with his toes dangling over the bed frame. He'd got himself a trinket in her. She'd grown wise to it early on, she'd been complicit. Aristos had never wanted sex. A man born without that switch for arousal. Eva was the product of a fluke experiment, if not a different father. What Aristos needed, after the divorce from his wife, was a beautiful ambassador. East-Europeans were Other, and Other, though hated, was exotic. Investors, partners, rivals were always men, always middle-aged and curious for foreign flesh. At first there came a dread, that Aristos might expect her to sleep with them – after all, there must be some reward for his expenditure, the clothes and spas and shoes and house. But her presence alone was enough. Already he held the prize, already he was powerful and envied. Why would you not trust him, align yourself with him, emulate him? It didn't matter if she was actually a gold-digger, a common slut. She was there to remind the room that the man who'd bought her was a force to be reckoned with. He was potent. Giant.

But she wouldn't stay dissatisfied.

God have mercy, she was never satisfied.

Ten

I n Mykonos, they were again guided off the ship into smaller boats. This time the light had gone, and the sea billowed with complaint. Women fell into prayer while their husbands and sons affected nonchalance. Darya was unafraid. She all but jumped into the boat on the cold black water.

The island was pulsing. Lit-up restaurants and cafés bulged with bodies and music. Tourists swarmed the cobbled streets past white-washed houses with blue doors and shutters, potted flowers of coral and pink. In the distance, those famous windmills rose from the hills. Souvenir shops sold magnets, icons and replica vases of three-thousand-year-old porn, comical erections, postcards of feline orgies. People spoke of Mykonos as if it was Soddom, and the island winked at its own bad name.

Eva took pictures. She showed a preference for the painted windows and the cats that sprawled on their sills. The crowded square enraptured her, as did whatever she spent most of her time trying to capture but which, judging by her expression, remained elusive. You couldn't catch life. Moments were more than split-seconds, feelings more than a single moment.

An art shop caught her eye, rammed with paintings, oils and

sheet copper embossed with hairline patterns. The proprietor sat on the steps in a brilliant skirt, her turquoise ring and earrings casting back light. On the step by her folded leg was a spread of oracle cards with pictures of angels. This was for her, nobody else. In the window was a sign, on which Darya recognised the words *yoga* and *reiki.* The woman looked up. She would speak to her. But as she mustered the words another tourist arrived, an Englishwoman enquiring about the paintings, saying *lovely* and *unique*, and the moment was snatched away.

She joined the others in a tourist shop, where Eva was choosing between souvenirs for her mother. A silk scarf or a blue clutch bag, why not both? Orestis bought a little wooden boat with the word MYKONOS painted on its prow.

'For your father?' Darya asked.

He smiled. 'For me.'

They paid and left. Darya noted that the others had dropped their dialect to put on the accent and rhythms of Greece. Easier for the men, whose jobs required them to buff their edges daily. Despite her schooling, Eva struggled to reign herself in, to keep that native tongue from poking through her mouth.

Orestis teased her about it when they'd left the shop. Together they cackled at anecdotes of fellow Cypriots, always someone's friend or cousin, who'd translated literally from dialect. Orestis' eyes creased, dimples deepened, more with Eva than they ever had with her. It wasn't only their age, their upbringing. It was something that ran through them. But what was language, and dialect, when bodies and souls became one in the dark? Orestis' face had expressed itself to her in ways that Eva could only dream of. What of his hazy look of seduction; what of his reddening cheeks when he was too aroused to catch his breath; what of the relief of his release; what of the way his lips looked fuller as he finally exhaled; what of the smile that came after that?

He pulled his phone from his shorts to call his father, a man who must be closer to her own age. She wondered what expressions and inflexions he made with him, what sides he showed that he didn't show Aristos. How different Orestis was when he was naked, someone else again when clothed.

They went down another cobbled street. The scent of roses and the noise of local voices. A flight of steps led up to the turquoise balcony of a two-storey house, on which stood a slender man in nothing but a pair of white briefs. He leant on the rail, smoking, staring into the distance. Noticing them, he glanced down. His eyes moved around the group till they found Orestis. Orestis slowed his pace. From behind, she watched his posture adapt to the other man's gaze. Shoulders fell back, chest pushed out. Man as bird. And as they passed the balcony, its owner put his cigarette to his lips without taking his eyes off the body below.

The cool air made her arm hairs stand on end.

'Darya,' Eva swivelled back to say. 'You know what means *poushtis*?' And her face was vicious with delight.

* * *

The ship would depart the next day. Some of the passengers stayed to revel in the island's night-life. Middle-aged English-women flirted with barmen and waiters, roared with laughter over their cocktails. Hundreds of young men gathered in bars for beer in bottles and shots of ouzo. They tossed them back with a flex of tanned bicep and a flash of midriff. She could take her pick of these stags. She wouldn't even need to pay them. (Aristos – Aristos wouldn't need to pay.) A few of them appraised her but most only had eyes for each other. Eva could barely contain her glee. She slapped her Daddykins' arm, *Look!* 'E, OK,' was his response. 'That's the way it is here.'

Darya had seen gays before, but not so many in a single place. Unnatural. The white crosses of churches stood stark against the night. Many of these peacocks cast a glance at Orestis, which he pretended not to notice as he strutted past. A pretty one raised his eyebrow and took his straw in his mouth. If he was willing to pay, would Orestis accept? Would the price be higher? She remembered his Godless words – he saw himself as a thing without a soul, a vessel or tool to do and to use, to affect and enjoy. Or perhaps only viewed. Yes. He'd be happy to spend the remainder of his life as a statue in a museum, a temple, where people could pay to come and worship him.

By the time they sat down to dine al fresco, the straw seat of the wooden chair rough against the backs of her thighs, her face was burning. Aristos ordered a bottle of red. When it was brought to him he sipped it, shook his head, asked for another, sampled it, and finally nodded. He poured out a glass for each of them. Darya downed hers in one.

It was mostly the men who did the talking, football and politics, the EU, Angela Merkel and Greece. Eva was strangely quiet, limiting herself to expressing how good the pizza was and how pretty the island looked at night. But then she turned to Darya. 'You do yoga, don't you?' She only ever spoke to her stepmother in English, so what was this Cypriot dialect now – not to mention this detail of Darya's life? The wine stood up from the girl's breath.

'Yes,' Darya replied in Greek. 'I have a teacher.'

'I'm thinking of starting,' Eva said. 'Does it really do you good?'

Darya nodded. 'I feel better.'

'I have a lot on my mind.'

Darya didn't know how to phrase what she wanted to say, so again she nodded. And then she took a gamble: the girl's hand was on the table, she put hers on top of it. Eva didn't respond. Nor did she remove her hand.

Eventually, Darya did so herself. 'You... photographs.' She mimed clicking a camera with her index finger close to her eye.

'I like it,' said Eva. 'It relaxes me. Do you want to see?'

She reached down to fish her camera out from her handbag. Rolls of fat at her shoulder straps, she really ought to watch herself. When Eva reemerged, she angled her camera towards her stepmother and flicked through the recent shots. No pretend admiration needed; Eva was good.

'Look at this one, the shadows and the light,' the girl was saying and proceeded to give a brief commentary that placed each photo in the context of the day. She had not been taking pictures of flowers and sunsets. She picked out details, composed stories. In Tinos, she hadn't taken photos of the miracle church as much as the pilgrims heading towards it. A middle-aged woman with patchy brown hair looking up with a mixture of fear, awe and hope. The effect was so intimate that Darya became one with the stranger. Maybe feelings could be moments, maybe they could be captured. 'I'm very good at people,' Eva said.

And she flicked along to the image of another stranger: Darya.

Her cigarette paused in the air. Eva had photographed her

while she watched the artist with her angel cards laid out on the steps. The experience of it returned. It was all in her face, and inside her now, again.

'You have a good face,' said Eva, cigarette aloft.

Darya knew she ought to stop looking at the photo. 'You make good photographs.'

'Take,' Eva corrected. She drew on her cigarette and added: 'Yes, I do. I have a lot of talent, but I need to go further. I need to get a better camera, enough of this kiddy one.'

Darya wouldn't have known the difference.

'You can have my Zenit,' Aristos said.

'Keep it. It's all about digital now.' She grinned at her father, winked. Then, 'You know who else has a good face?'

Orestis brightened.

Eva lifted the camera while he posed, jokingly but perfectly, in his open blue shirt and tight white vest, and she clicked, clicked, clicked.

Yes, please, somebody document it: the beauty of him. So that people in the future, his grandchildren, could see how precious he was. So that when he was dead there would continue a snapshot of his prime. She finished the wine in her glass. Of course, there were those other photos – taken by her husband in half-lit rooms, pictures that could never be seen by anyone. Darya had felt unsure, then obedient, then potent in those moments, in charge of someone's interest. She had never held Aristos' attention so completely. Eva's photo, on the other hand, had exposed her for who she truly was. She'd forgotten to look over her shoulder. May as well be dead, shot in the back.

Enough. She looked away from them all. On the floor was a chunk of chicken a tourist had tossed, for three stray kittens

THE WAY IT BREAKS

to run and fight for. The wind blew strands of hair into her face, it was too much for the clips. As soon as they got back to Cyprus she'd chop it all off.

When the waiter brought the bill, Orestis insisted he pay his share.

Aristos batted him down.

'Why you want to pay?' Darya heard herself saying. 'You know Aristos will pay, this is how it is. My husband will pay for you.' That teacher tone.

For a second, Orestis had looked hurt. But then the charm crept over his face. 'I feel bad,' he said. 'But I promise: one day I'll repay you.'

Eva blinked as if something had fallen. Then she dragged on her cigarette, looking at all three of them as if that something had fallen into place.

* * *

Back on the ship, they had a nightcap at one of the bars. Orestis chatted to a Filipino waiter, somehow they'd become acquainted. He whispered to the others in Greek that the man was a qualified doctor. 'This is the best he can get here,' indicating the bar, the ship. What about her, had he forgotten? Or was this his way of reminding her? The best was sometimes the only.

When the others had turned in, she went to Orestis' cabin. He opened the door as if surprised there'd been a knock. She removed the belt from his shorts and tied it around his eyes. Here was a joy reserved only for her. She made him kiss and lick his way up her legs and under her dress, and she held his head there. He tried to remove his boxers but she wouldn't let him. 'Please,' she instructed him to say, in Belarusian. And 'Please,' he would parrot back. Then he said it in Greek, and she knew he meant it. When she finally allowed him to, he entered her. She slapped him. She dug her nails into his back, she wanted to be inside him. Her finger slid between his buttocks and his face was seized by a delighted shock. He turned her over then, pressed her face into the pillow, and was more forceful than he'd ever been.

Men were so feeble after their violence. Orestis lay there, wincing, depleted, as she patted his chest. Only part of the room was lit by the ghostly face of the moon in the porthole. Only part of him.

'You are beautiful,' she said. She didn't know if she was speaking of his looks. She hardly knew if she meant it as a compliment.

Orestis was taken aback. Then contentment stole over his features, he looked at peace. They lay together for a while, not talking, simply staring at the cabin ceiling, rocked by the infinite sea. The ship's engine thrummed below, closer here than in her suite.

'Eva likes you,' she said.

He took a moment to answer. 'Yes, I know.'

'You sleep with her?'

'No. No!'

He would think her jealous, so she took a different path. 'Why not?' And she added in Cypriot dialect: 'She has big boobs.'

Orestis laughed, surprised. 'You've learned the basics.'

'Of course.'

He propped himself up on his side to look at her as nobody had. In awe. With satisfaction. That she was who she was.

And this being, this Adonis... he was hers.

But she couldn't help her mind, her tongue. His words in Tinos, outside the church – surely there was more than just a face here, more than the sum of moonlit parts. There was an energy, a spirit, a thing that could project itself and leave imprints, like the tracks of a deer in the woods, after all flesh and sinew and marrow dissolved.

'Why you don't believe?'

'Believe?'

'It makes me sad.'

His expression dimmed. 'When you were talking about God,' he said, 'what did you mean, you know? You know what? How?'

She should have stayed quiet. 'It's OK,' she said, waving away the discussion. 'It's OK.'

'No,' he said, 'not *It's OK* — what?'

'Why it matters? It doesn't matter.' Her fingers reached for his naked leg. In Tinos, feet planted on the ground on an island, she felt a longing to tell him. Now, drifting in the middle of the sea, there was only fear. 'It doesn't matter.'

He let the silence fall again. And at last, he spoke. 'My grandma used to see saints.'

'Yes?'

'She told me she saw Ayios Nektarios once. And the Virgin. They appeared in front of her, to tell her she would be OK.'

'She was ill?'

'Yes, but I mean— just... in life. She would be OK in life.'

A pause.

'Did you see something? Is that how you know?' And he looked at her as if he himself wasn't proof enough of God.

'No,' she said. And she heard herself groan into the dark

room. Maksim was up there, past the ceiling and the decks and the stars. 'I had brother.' She was so startled by her own words that she was silent, for an age. 'He died.'

'I'm sorry. How?'

Nobody had heard this, nobody since Belarus. But Orestis was hers. He was the only one who could hear it, who would. 'You know Chernobyl?'

He furrowed his brow and nodded.

'My brother was in Army. They make him and other boys go to Chernobyl after... fire. After explosion. Factory was in Ukraine, but close. Belarus was...' She felt his name clog her throat. She had to push it out, set it free. When was the last time she'd said that name aloud? How much power could there be in consonants and vowels? 'His name was Maksim.' Her eyes burned. Itched. 'He and other boys, they clear mess in Chernobyl, but the... soil, the things, the air... Everything poison. Maksim got sick. Very sick. And afterwards, he died.'

Her father had cried as he kissed the shell of a boy in the hospital bed. Darya herself had leant in to kiss her brother's hollow cheek, and been entranced by the whiteness of the little hairs there. A piglet's skin. She recalled the shame of her thoughts.

'I'm sorry,' Orestis said, and he was wiping tears from her cheeks that she hadn't even known were there.

'It's OK. It's OK.'

That's what the authorities had said. It was OK, nothing to worry about.

'No,' said Orestis. 'No. It's not OK.'

He kissed her, softly. He kissed her mouth, her cheeks, her forehead.

She wanted to say more, but what could she say? In what

vocabulary, Greek or Russian, Cypriot or Belarusian, limited or limitless, could she express why Maksim's death meant the presence of God? Why the punishment for abandoning her loved ones was to live like this, a body that looked alive but was sleeping inside.

She was a bad person. She deserved the existence of God.

Eleven

How different Mykonos looked in the daylight, like a hibernating bear. They drank frappés at a café, all smoking except Orestis. Aristos ordered a confection of semolina custard and filo pastry for them to share. Of course, Eva took her frappé sweet. Darya bit her tongue.

Orestis excused himself to make a phone call to his father. 'The old man will be worried, even if he doesn't show it.'

His father had been told this was a trip with friends, by plane and ferries and sleeping on acquaintances' sofas; an expense Orestis could afford with his recent pay rise. All the same, his father had raged about the waste of money, when he should feel blessed that his son was calling home.

'How are your parents?' she asked when Orestis returned.

It took him a moment to recover from his confusion. 'It's only the old man and me now,' he said. 'I don't really speak to my mother.'

Eva grimaced.

Aristos swooped in to alter the mood. 'The memory I have of your father is from one of Eva's parties at the Harmonia – you were eleven, possibly twelve. It was carnival time, and he came to pick you up dressed as a gangster.'

Orestis' smile was out of politeness. Anyone would have known.

The ship set sail in the afternoon. Lethargic from all the food and sun, they retired to their cabins. Even Orestis, for the first day since they embarked, forewent the gym. Aristos fell asleep as soon as he lay down, but Darya struggled. As the minutes piled up, she became more conscious of the heat, her limbs, the sheets, the bed, the pillows. She deconstructed every sensation until the very notion of comfort was lost. It was no use, tired as she was she would not sleep. She left the suite, and Aristos to his slumber.

She found herself walking through the corridors, where uniformed girls worked in near silence. They wheeled their trolleys, whispering in Russian and Polish. They cleared the sick bags waiting outside cabins. Eventually, there was a lounge, where Darya sat on a barstool and ordered a mocktail. There was the barman Orestis had chatted with, the Filipino doctor. Should she say hello? Of course not. The grenadine syrup in her drink made her wince, but the piano in the background soothed her. Carried her thoughts away. There came the intermittent static of walkie-talkies from the hips of white-suited officers sitting in leather tub chairs. Reality. Jobs. Money. It was all so mundane. Why could the world not exist on pleasure and beauty alone?

The music, it dawned on her, was live. At her back, on a corner of the raised stage where solo acts and Bingo took place, stood a mini grand. At the piano sat a silver-haired gentleman whom she guessed to be German, maybe Swiss. She didn't recognise the tune he was playing, but his touch on the keys showed ability, experience. She only realised she'd been staring into space when she caught the wave of his hand

and the nod of his head.

A Russian. Or worse, someone from home.

Nobody she knew, of that she was certain. He lifted his right hand from the piano to beckon her over, his left one continuing to play. Why not? She moved closer, pulled up the chair nearest to his corner of the stage. He wore beige cargo shorts and some heft around the middle.

'What song would you like?' he asked in Greek, accented.

'I'm not Greek,' she replied in English.

'Russian?'

Why not. She would never see this man again. 'Yes,' she said.

'Ah. I'm German, but I know a little bit.'

'It's OK,' she replied in German. 'I know a lot.'

'Wonderful!'

They carried on in his native tongue.

'What would you like to hear?'

'What's this one?'

He cocked his head and smiled as if she was crazy. 'You don't know Celine Dion?' His eyes were a shocking blue, boyishly round.

Darya shrugged.

'How long have you been in Cyprus?' he said and laughed. 'I'm playing this one because everyone loves it.'

She liked his manner. It was good to speak with someone else for a change, someone she didn't know well enough to have to manage. He drew the song to its end, his short stubby fingers surprising her by tiptoeing beautifully over the keys.

'You play well,' she said. 'Do you do the shows?'

'No! I don't even work here. Johnny just lets me play.' He winked and pointed at the barman, who winked and pointed back.

Darya laughed. Even this man had befriended the barman doctor.

'Are you on your own?'

She could say anything, anything at all. She felt a rush along her arms as if pulling off the sleeves of a blouse. 'I'm with my family. They're all sleeping, but I don't sleep well.'

'My children are playing video games,' he said. 'Can you believe it? We came out to the middle of the Mediterranean and all they want is their Playstations.'

She shrugged. What would kids find interesting about the sea?

'Do you play?' the German asked.

'Playstation?'

He laughed heartily at that. She looked around to see if anyone was watching.

'No. The piano.'

She went numb. Her mouth had lost its function, she couldn't quite close it. The longer the silence went on, the harder it was to break.

'Aha... So you do.'

That wooden bulk in the corner of the living room, casting shadows against the walls, the floor, her life. All those years in its service. All those long afternoons of her fingers on keys, foot on pedal, again and again and again. The echoes of the notes, the echo of that angry voice. She'd kept her foot pressed on the pedal till the notes stretched and bent and wound to a death. The Professor had been doing the same to her, pressing her down, pressing the life out of her. Deciding what she was to be.

'Yes,' she said at last. 'Many years ago.'

'Why did you stop?'

She licked her lips and brought the mocktail to them.

'You don't forget,' he said, softly.

'Don't you? Shame.' She tried not to look at him, the middle-aged boy whose hair might be curly if it wasn't cropped. But then she couldn't help catching, in the corner of her eye, his hand coming up. He was holding it out for her, and before she could stop herself she took it, and her feet were climbing up to the little stage, and she was lowering herself onto the piano seat. A shock bolted through her. How did this man treat his children?

'Play me something,' the German said. 'Whatever you remember.'

At first, she only stared at the black and white trail before her. Her hands hovered over it, then descended on it, fingers gently alighting on the keys. She stumbled over Rachmaninov, *Prelude in C Sharp Minor.*

'Wow!' He chuckled. 'No Celine Dion for you.'

A few bars in, her shoulders began to shake. They shook along with his laughter. And something else was shaking up with them, out of her. Something bitter and desperate. Her mouth twitched, her breath rattled in her teeth.

For half a minute she couldn't speak, and he watched her, equally speechless. Nobody was speaking, nobody in the room.

She gripped the stool, then righted her back, her self. 'Thank you,' she said, 'but I'm too tired. It was a pleasure to meet you.'

She stumbled off the stage, forgetting the steps, and left the half-drunk mocktail on the table as she headed out of the lounge, away from the stranger she hoped never to see again.

* * *

Viktar. She hadn't thought of him in years. During her time as a teacher there'd been numerous schoolboys who'd eyed her with meaning, but none more than Viktar. For someone so young, his spine had been rigid with adult assurance. A prime athlete, groomed for the Olympics. As if the boy hadn't enough on his shoulders, his father had approached Darya about after-school cymbaly lessons. She'd accepted, though with reservations. She had seen the way Viktar stood in the corridors, palm pinned to the wall above any female head. To her surprise, he'd been well-behaved in the hour of private tuition. His hands brought such tender precision to the kruchki on the strings that it had been hard to imagine the other things he did with them. One day she'd learned why: when he wasn't gentle enough, his father would beat him with a ruler. She'd asked him to take part in the Poland concert, and his father had relented. When the idea had come to Darya never to return to Belarus, she'd paused to consider taking Viktar with her.

At first, she had been wary of him. Then she'd worried for him. Then she'd forgotten him. Now she worried again. She hoped life treated him as gently as he did the cymbaly.

'Something wrong?' asked Orestis.

It was easy to explain your mind being lost in the sea. She nodded, coolly.

A mood had brewed, a cloud in her mind. They descended on Kos in their usual foursome, but Darya kept her distance. She either sped up on her own or lagged behind, pretending to be entranced by bougainvillaea, or cats playing around the old stone walls of the harbour. Whatever the others said, however they said it, made her angry. She found fault with everything.

She'd been to many parts of the world with the ships she cleaned, but never to Greece. From the islands they'd done so far, it didn't seem different from Cyprus; beaches, promenades, cafés, signs in Greek and English, kiosks with the Coca Cola logo in their signage. She'd never admit it, but she was still unsure of the relations between the countries. Cyprus seemed to flit between idolising and dismissing Greece. Sometimes it was her beloved mother, sometimes a wayward brat that ought to be disciplined. Some people longed for union, others preferred their separation.

She was grateful for the hat. The sun breathed on her bare arms all along the promenade, where cartoonists drew portraits of tourists that bordered on insults. Orestis and Eva had got ahead of her and from this distance, his broad back, strolling through an unknown landscape, looked of a different person. One who was unfiltered, unthinking, natural.

How much he performed for her. How hollow he was. No, not hollow – the opposite. Loaded. So loaded, with all those faces and mannerisms and niceties, Orestis within Orestis within Orestis, a matryoshka doll of different patterns. Individuals in a set, so pretty, so finely made. But inside? Nothing.

That wasn't fair. After all, he had listened to her.

Every few steps they took, Eva would turn to share her observations with him. White shorts stretching over her backside, she was radiant. The shadow fingers of palm fronds passed over her panama. She took out her camera. And now Darya knew how good the photos would be. But she couldn't imagine the compositions, she lacked that ability. She would have to wait and see, and then she would know. Oh yes, that was it; that was the image, the design, the perfect framing waiting for someone to claim it. Eva stopped Orestis by a tree for a photo. First, one of him alone, then one with the two of them, her arm extended in front of them.

'Let me take it,' said Aristos.

'Leave us, Daddykins! We look stupider this way.'

Darya rolled her eyes. Her babulia's voice in her ear: 'You're acting like a child.' And she knew it was right, she was wrong. But how can you fix something when you don't know what's broken, or how it broke?

Aristos took them to an ancient plane tree in the square. 'This is where Hippocrates sat. Imagine, all those thoughts... first thought right here.'

She was relieved when they stepped out of the heat and into the shade of a bougainvillaea for an ice-cold drink. Then she got up, not saying a word as she went to the bathroom, only so that she might stand in a cool white space, not speaking, not hearing, not having anyone look at her. Just being.

Breathing.

Being.

* * *

She'd wanted to see the castle ruins, as recommended by the itinerary back in the suite. Orestis would have agreed. They ended up at a beach, fifteen minutes by cab from the harbour town. It was a wide-open space with thatch umbrellas along the front. Eva laughed at a sign banning nudists, took a photo. 'The stupid ones are for Facebook.' Then she watched Orestis as he took off his shirt and shorts and ran into the water. Her face fell. What had been anticipated, and now was, was too good, was too much, was too soon. She wasn't equal to it, and maybe never would be. Darya felt a pang of guilt.

Did Aristos?

Her gorge rose. Whatever the point of this trip was, it wasn't worth it. All this hidden knowledge, these disguised emotions, it was a poison to the soul. Ink in a glass of water.

'It's so bright. Makes you want to sleep,' said Aristos. And he lay back, pulling his hat further over his forehead and sunglasses, both to block out and give in to the offensive sun. Arms behind his head, towel between his bulk and the sand, he was the king of everything. Zeus.

How could he so easily be? It was making her crazy.

Skevi would do her yoga. Right here, on the beach. She would take herself into her own hands, calm herself. After all, that was the pleasure of it. That's where the contentment came: to recognise your body's achievement, its abilities and limitations. To set a goal and make it. To commune with yourself. To push yourself. To know yourself.

She started with some cat-cow stretches and felt their work in her spine. She pushed a little further with the downwards-facing dog pose. And then, with a bend of her knees and slow roll, she stood in the mountain pose. She bent at her waist and let her torso sink towards the sand. As smoothly as she could, she let one leg slide back while the other bent at the knee. She then arched herself as if pinched from the middle, plucked off the earth by an invisible deity. By the time she'd raised her arms to the sun, spread them, and finally joined her hands in prayer, her head was swimming in lightness. She could be something above all this. A spirit, an energy that moved beyond its corporeal confines. Limited to nothing. Not this beach, not this mess, not the house her husband had put her

219

in, not his country, not any country, not names nor identities, not those who would use any of those factors against her. She was a being without borders. She was free.

That familiar click. A few metres away, Eva lowered her camera. For a moment she only stared, then said: 'Perfect.' She'd used the feminine, which could mean either Darya or the photograph – whatever she meant by the word itself. Perfect.

Enough. Enough photographs. Darya had come to under-stand that old fear of them, of the soul being trapped in the frame. What could she do but counter with politeness to mask her sense of doom? Eva would find out about her and Orestis, it was written. Maybe that was Aristos' plan. He arranged for all of this to force the truth into the light. He'd always resented her, and now he would destroy her. He'd never wanted her to take a lover; it had all been a test. A trap. She would be exposed as a whore, Orestis a pig, and Aristos a martyr.

'I am going to walk,' she said in English, catching her breath. 'You want?' But she knew, prayed, the girl would refuse.

'No, you go. I might swim.'

There came those clicks of the camera again, as well as Orestis' calls, teasing the girl from the water. 'Come in!' he was saying, and Eva was yelling back, 'Stand still so I can take a picture of you. Perfect! Calvin Klein.' Of course, she wouldn't join him in the sea. And of course, he could call only to her. Darya told herself not to look back at them, not to see Orestis rising from the sea like a god.

She wandered further along the beach, as far as it would take her. If it circled the entire island, so be it. The ship could depart, with everyone else on board, that was fine by her. Something held her throat. Samota. No, something worse. A noise escaped her mouth, surprising her. A hiccup, of a laugh or a sob – whatever it was, it came with the intent to hurt. There was a sea, dark and full of salt, swirling around inside her. She'd allowed this, this effect on her. She'd allowed too many negative energies to close in, they'd eroded her defences. How stupid she had been, a woman in her forties with the bubblegum heart of a child. She was alone, fighting a battle she couldn't see, no allies at her side. That frightened white kitten, its claw snagged in the tree. Viktar playing gently, beaten horribly. Her lips quivered, her tears gathered.

The air was full of salt. Ravaging, cleansing. May it fill her completely, as it would a balloon, and may she float away. In and out her breath, in the way that was meant to relax you, in through the nostrils and out through the mouth. She would cut through the brambles and thickets and thorns, finally through to clarity. Only you can help yourself. Only your mind and your body hold your spirit back.

At her feet, the water fanning out to the shore was so clear she could see every pebble, every grain of sand. In the distance were windsurfers, but on land, around her, only the occasional tree. Behind the sea there were hills. She could even make out houses. Those tin signs in the town square earlier, the boat trips to Turkey. These homes, so close she might see figures at the windows, they might not even be Greek.

The wind carried her name with it. A man's voice.

Aristos.

He walked towards her, bare feet on the wet ground.

In the moment she beheld her husband, her mind turned from sand to glass. Mr Ioannidou. Of course, this was his plan. Of *course*, this was the point of it all, and she was an idiot not to have realised it. He had led her to want a lover as if it had ever been her choice at all. As if it hadn't been his will.

He would make her unfaithful to make himself a cuckold, a martyr from which she must beg forgiveness. He gave her Orestis, only so that he could take him away. To expose her weakness, make her see and admit her own powerlessness. Because that's what her husband was: a man who would be God.

'Where are you going?' he said, daring to smile. 'We've got to head back.'

'No,' she said in Greek.

'What *no*? You want to stay?'

She couldn't answer.

He placed a hand on her shoulder. 'What's wrong, my love? You want to stay here?'

He knew. He knew so much more than anyone. The anger, the frustration, his lies, everything made her silent. She knocked his hand away. 'You make all of this,' she burst. 'You make all happen like this. Why?'

'I don't understand you,' he said. His eyes narrowed behind his sunglasses.

With all this light she could see.

'What do you mean?'

'Why you do this?'

'Do what?'

'Me! Orestis! What do you want?'

Her husband spun his head and hissed. 'Keep your voice down!'

She wanted to fight him, *No!* But she knew he was right. 'What do you want?' she said again, quieter.

'What do I want? Are you joking? It's only what you want. What you want, what Eva wants. Every day, always. Just like with her mother.'

'No,' she said, already weakening. She would never win against him. Nobody did.

'Yes.'

'Why you bring Orestis here?'

'Eva wanted him to come. She invited him. What was I supposed to do, say no? Why would I? For God's sake, Darya, use your brain.'

'Then why Eva comes?'

'She's my daughter. You're my wife.'

'And Orestis? He is your son?'

Aristos scowled. 'He's a young man, Darya. He and my daughter have known each other since they were children. If they want to be together, we can't force them not to be. We'll find you someone else.'

He made to touch her again, but she slapped his arm away. For a long moment, there was only the sound of the water at their feet.

'You're being ungrateful,' he said. 'Do you understand? I take you out of the hotel, I give you a beautiful house, a maid, even another damned man to satisfy you. Only so you can spit in my face. I'm a perfect idiot.'

She turned her face to the sea. Nobody ever won.

'You want to go? A? You want to go off on your own, no more money and security, no family, nothing?'

No family. It didn't matter how little she'd said of them, he'd figured it out. He knew from her silence that she'd done wrong. And now he pulled it out like a gun. She did her best to look directly at him, but the sun flicked at her eyes.

'You make everything,' she said. She could hear her voice, that strained whine. Brambles and thorns. She hated herself. He saw her as a child, jealous and crying for a toy. And he was better than her. Bigger, more powerful next to her mortal self.

'Come,' he said, extending his hand.

She didn't take it. But this was a time to be practical, to retain what little she had. She would show no pain, no emotion at all. Head held up, she walked past him, and back to the others, expelling the negative energy inside her to the air, to the sand, to the sea, step, by step, by step, by step.

In the taxi back to the harbour, Darya climbed straight into the passenger seat. Even the hot stare of the driver didn't faze her. In the back seats, the others spoke about nothing in particular, but at one point she heard Eva asking her father, in a volume that was low by her standards and no-one else's, 'What's up with her?'

'Leave her, kori,' whispered Orestis.

Darya almost felt his hand on her shoulder.

Twelve

Rhodos was the last stop. From the deck, Darya watched where the ship sliced the water to send foam spreading outwards. She'd started her game again. Something inside her body beat against its cage, it begged to be released. She squirmed, pushed her legs together. If she wasn't able to stop it at this age, what would happen by the time she was sixty? Would nature take care of it, remove all control of her body from her? It happened to everyone, so why not. Just before she'd left home, her babulia had begun to struggle to rise from her seat. You can will yourself anything, but there it stops: at the will. Whether you achieve it or not is out of your hands, all you can actually do is want. And want prevented peace. Accept things as they are, don't wish them to be what they aren't. *Aparigraha*. But then where did that leave her? Not doing, not getting, not wanting; simply being. Let God move her as He wished, to people and places that were meant to happen to her. It was for the best. Look what her own free movements had done; they'd only resulted in pain.

The wind made her feel exposed. If the German pianist saw her again, he might approach her. She would have to explain his acquaintance to her group, and her unusual family to him. He might mention the piano, the fact that she played, something not even Aristos knew about. She used to find romance in living separate lives. Like one of those many-headed goddesses, she was mysterious and barely glimpsed. But now she was only tired.

Women lay in rows on deckchairs, rubbing sunscreen into their limbs, reading books with detectives on the covers. Who were they?

A sudden grip on her arm cut her breath. Orestis. He was pointing at the sea, his face an eruption of delight.

Dolphins.

A school of them swam along with the ship, leaping in and out of the waves as if trying to catch it, like dogs with a ball.

'Sweethearts!' said Eva, running to the railings. 'My God, they're so cute!' Then she winced. 'My camera. Damn it, it's in my cabin.'

'E, go get it,' said Aristos.

'And miss this? By the time I go and get lost like an imbecile...'

Her forehead creased. The poor spoiled girl didn't know where happiness was, which path to take to reach it. She took out her phone to snap photos on that, then reviewed them, scowled, and gave up.

They stood to watch the squeaking lovely creatures. More and more passengers gathered. Orestis was so overjoyed that Darya laughed, and before she knew it her hand was patting his arm. He turned to her then, his soul leapt out to meet hers. It was a spark beyond flesh, beyond pleasure, or language, or history. And it unnerved her. Almost as much as the tears that gathered at his eyes.

Darya was about to say something, *Are you all right?* But Eva got there first: 'Re, for God's sake! What's the matter with you?'

'I don't know,' he said, and he was still smiling, then laughing, as he wiped his eyes. 'I don't know, just...'

But the spectacle in the water kept him from finding the words.

The humans went back to their lives. Aristos summoned a waitress to order frappés. When she returned with their drinks, Darya wondered if the girl might be a trained lawyer or an architect.

'E, Orestis, animal lover,' said Eva. 'I see you're still drinking milk. You didn't go and turn vegetarian on me like Paris.'

Orestis' jaw dropped. 'What are you talking about? Paris is a vegetarian?'

'Hello!' she said in English, as Cypriots do when someone's being a fool. 'As if it's a recent thing.'

'He never said.'

'You didn't notice. But me, I'm observant.' She lit a cigarette.

'A vegetarian poet,' Aristos said. 'What a surprise.'

Eva slapped his arm, and blew out her smoke to the immense sky. 'Leave him, Daddy! He's a darling. But God almighty, how can anyone be vegetarian? I couldn't even fast for one day when you sent me to grandma's that Easter.'

'It's easy,' said Orestis. 'There's tons of food that isn't meat.'

'Don't tell me you are too!'

'E, no, but it's healthy.'

'That's how you lost the weight, a? OK.' Eva took a drag of her cigarette. Then she turned to her stepmother. 'And you, Darya? The Buddhist.'

Darya didn't understand, so Eva repeated her words.

'Buddhist,' said Aristos in English. 'You know, Buddha.'

'Not Buddhist,' she said to the girl. She had the feeling of something needing to be held back, or stopped. 'Vegetarian is good. Why not?'

'Mercy!' said Eva. 'God made animals so we can eat them, and you're all telling me to stop the souvlaki.' She added in English, 'Sorry, no way,' and shook her head as the smoke flew out of it.

Orestis looked down at the table.

'If you're doing it for your health,' Eva carried on, 'then it's worth it. But for animal rights? God's sake.'

'So nothing else is worth it?' Orestis asked, lightly as if he was joking. Darya understood that he wasn't. She hadn't followed a conversation so clearly since her chat with the German. She felt plugged in, electric.

'No,' said Eva. More smoke blew out of her mouth. 'An animal has no value besides the food it provides us.'

'Tell that to your ancestors,' said Aristos with a chortle.

'E, I'm not a farmer!' said Eva. 'I'm not dragging donkeys up mountains.'

Orestis laughed, thankful for something he could tease her with, something easier than meaningful debate. He joked about Eva living as a peasant in a Troodos village.

It wasn't that he was superficial; he was afraid. He felt and thought, deeply, maybe all the time, but what he wanted above all else was to be liked. To be rated like a good hotel.

'The cow was worth something to your grandparents,' Eva said to her father, 'because it helped them with their work. I don't need the cow for anything other than milk. A burger. It's serving me in a different way.'

All life has value: Skevi's refrain. Darya said the words in her head and repeated them aloud.

The other three looked at her. To her surprise, Eva nodded, cigarette aloft, and pointed. 'Exactly.'

For the next few minutes, Darya let the others' chatter sail over her. Her eyes rolled over to other life forms, other groups. There were dads with kids in rubber rings, about to take a shrieking leap into the pool. And in the pool were white-haired couples, three or four in a row, taking their cues from the thin instructor standing on the edge. Behind him, a girl she recognised as a dancer from the show led a treasure hunt. Her face opened wide for the children, eyes and mouth clearly expressing joy, excitement, danger. This was wrong. Children should be taught that no emotion is clear.

'What day is it?' said Eva. 'My God, you forget everything when you do nothing all day.'

'It's the sea, that's what it does to you.'

'You're always doing nothing,' Orestis said.

'Comedian.'

The sixth of July. Kupala. It opened inside her. Maksim in his white tunic with the embroidered collar, eyes reflecting the blaze of the bonfire as he leapt over it. His feet at the flames. Then her brave big brother telling her, grinning into his beer, that he would search the forest for the fern flower. He'd seemed so much older than her then. But now, through the inverted telescope of time, she could see how young he truly was, how little in life. A boy, not a man. A boy with a burning desire for his classmate Maryia, with those round green eyes that bore into your core, with their slow lids as if she didn't care what she found there. A boy who smoked side-by-side with skinny spotty Yaraslau on his father's tractor. And her own girlish hands, thousands of days in the past, dozens of lifetimes, making wreaths of flowers to float, candlelit, down the river, as she dreamed of her future husband. She'd had no idea of the future that was on its way, already swimming upriver towards her.

A motion woke her from her spell. Orestis' hand, waving. Those friendly eyes.

She was on the deck, the ship. A woman in uniform darted to pin a plastic chair from sliding off in a gust of wind.

'What were you thinking about?' Aristos said. 'We lost you.'

Now they were watching her, all of them. 'Is important day,' she said in English. 'Today, in Belarus. Today and tomorrow.'

'What day?' asked Orestis. 'A saint?'

'No, is... Old.' It was beyond her. 'Very old,' she added, throwing her hand over her shoulder to indicate the centuries.

'E,' said Eva, 'whatever it is: cheers.' And she raised her glass for them all to clink.

* * *

That night Darya went to the show. The last thing she wanted was to be left on her own, staring out into an unlit sea. Aristos laced his fingers through hers on the table. With everyone's attention on the stage, she was free to watch the lights flash and move across the room, and over the living bust that was Orestis. Waiters rushed around with cocktails, coffees and sundaes, communicating over all that bass-weighted noise. A man stood next to her, balancing a sleeping child on his shoulder. He filmed the English dancers on his camcorder. Darya scanned the room for the German. If he was in the room, he was lost amid the shades of blue that made up the audience. And so, then, was she.

A pounding pop number. Eva swivelled in her seat. 'I love this song!'

Darya shrugged, she'd never heard it.

It was enough to make Eva slap the table with glee. 'You're something else!'

During a lively bouzouki set, the audience clapped along. The evening turned Greek, the compere's voice booming 'Opa!' over the sweet tang of the strings. Men leapt onto the dance floor, landing with perfect balance to perform their sweeping gestures. Women joined them, arms around each other's necks, moving their feet as if kicking up sand. Eva was one of them. Without a thought or care, she'd stood up, put her arm around a Cypriot stranger and together their bodies expressed the music. It was beautiful, a people's ballet. Aristos applauded his daughter. Orestis put his fingers in his mouth and whistled. Darya, amazed at him, laughed.

'Come on,' he said, getting up.

And for a moment she forgot herself.

She let him take her up to the dance floor and join a group of people unconnected to her, all of them following an ancient ritual. She took his direction, feeling his hand on her back, on her waist. Her own hand was on his shoulder; here, it was allowed to be. And she picked up the steps. Soon she was dancing. A girl again. As if she would make a wreath of flowers to float along the river. And it stung her eyes. She would soak up the lights, moving and blinking, and she would soak up the sound, which made her limbs, her heart, vibrate because she was a spirit, an entity, borderless, free, above all this. She was outside of her body, looking down. And the woman down there looked happy.

Thirteen

I f Santorini, with its tangle of lights at the dark summit, was the dream, Rhodos was the moment before waking. It was the island most like Cyprus so far. Stone piers at the harbour; medieval structures rising from them like yet more rocks; squares full of tourists browsing spinners of magnets and postcards; chain hotels and shops; restaurants peddling Greek, Italian and English food, within touching distance of Russian furriers.

Back in their cabin, Darya had told Aristos she was going on a guided tour this time, with or without them. She wanted to see something other than cafés by the beach. Part of her had hoped he would reject the plan, and let her go alone. Another part of her hoped that her husband and stepdaughter would go off shopping and eating together, and leave Orestis with her. 'That's a wonderful idea,' Aristos had said. 'I assumed nobody else would want to go.' He suggested it to the others over breakfast, then, after speaking to someone in Reception, wangled four places on a coach. Because they were so late in booking, the only available tour group was for Russian speakers.

'You can translate for us,' said Aristos.

'Pe!' Eva threw her hand up. 'Who cares? Old rock here,

column there, whores there, we'll get it.'

Darya was almost thankful.

Orestis phoned his father for the last time as they waited to board the coach. At the front stood a perfect blonde with a microphone. Between cheery banter with the driver, she pointed out the passing landmarks and sites in familiar words and cadences. Darya was on a coach full of former comrades, some maybe even from Belarus. Please God, nobody she knew. The world could be so small.

An elderly Ukrainian, travelling alone, leaned over to ask Orestis if he knew how long the journey was. Orestis apologised in English and explained he wasn't Russian. He and the woman laughed about it, and he indulged her for the rest of the journey. In careful English, the Ukrainian spoke of her children, grandchildren, departed husband. His questions opened her heart. Darya pulled her eyes away. The sweaty fabric of the seats and the rancid WC, unleashing a stench every time its door swung open, were bringing on a headache.

Eva was watching her. There was no suspicion there, but something softer. Exhausted, Darya turned to the window, where Rhodos floated by.

'Mash'allah!' Eva gushed to Orestis as they shuffled off the coach. 'A friend of beasts and old biddies!'

The sunlight was a slap. They'd been tricked by the tinted windows of the coach. Darya had worn a short dress with spaghetti straps and was now cursing herself. All this skin exposed to the rays. And why was she wearing black? She tended to tan rather than burn, but still: her skin had not developed under this glare. Aristos never even thought to wear sunscreen, he was dark as tea. This was why she wondered at times if Eva was his daughter at all. Beneath the mound of makeup, hers was a creamy complexion, which deepened with a coppery undertone. Orestis was the same. Today he wore a vest, no shirt. And she felt nothing.

What an idiot she'd been to tell him about Maksim. It was that face of his, that face that opened your heart.

Oh, white birch...

Not that again, taking over her thoughts. Floating along this brown earth here, around the ruined ancient columns, over the heads of other tourists to the dry hills in the distance and beyond, to the sea.

Oh, white birch, why are you not green?

Aristos extended his hand to hers, took it. She rejected it. After a long sleep, at last, she was awake. This was not affection; the man was incapable, a mere husk. No, worse: he was a parasite, a vampire. All these years, she thought she'd been immune, that she was somehow favoured. As if she had ever been special, as if she had ever been more than a tool. In this way, Eva had a point. Darya's value to her husband was that of a cow; to milk, and ultimately to sacrifice.

They followed the Russian tour group, as a courtesy to the blonde with the microphone who kept scanning the horizon for them. Darya translated nothing, heard nothing. Aristos knew enough about the place and structures to give the tour himself. An amphitheatre nestled in the side of a hill, and a stone stadium leant against the surrounding trees. It reminded her of the way her father leant back in his armchair. The surroundings simply moved to make room.

She'd visited Rhuzany once, the palace ruins. Those windows, those arches, standing like burned-out matches against the dying sunlight – were they only so haunting because they were of her land? Did your ancestors' lives continue through

234

yours? Would hers extend to her children? She thought of the little bodies swallowed and spat by Chernobyl, of their twisted limbs and hole-punched hearts.

Enough. If someone offered her a pill to erase her brain, she'd take it.

Maybe there were other cures. Skevi had mentioned reiki. Let the girl with the rainbow hair infuse her with positive energy, withdraw the negative old. Nothing else had worked.

Eva framed a shot. Darya stood back. Orestis, on the other hand, played at spoiling the photos. He posed as a runner on the track, then angled his torso to hurl an invisible discus. Darya lacked the ability to fill empty spaces with history. It was beyond her to envision the smattering of columns and steps and platforms culminating in a building that was supposed to have stood here. She couldn't picture the athletes or their screaming fans, regardless of Aristos' many descriptions. But she saw Orestis, standing amongst the earth and trees and stone, and felt the rush of millennia passing through. He carried more in him than even these ruins did, even more than the work of craftsmen who'd died thousands of years before he was born.

But a life could start again. She was a soul, not a corpse. Rebirth was as much a part of life as death. She watched the others gather round something ahead, and knew in her gut that she would leave them all.

On the coach back to the town centre, Aristos leant over to whisper that her mood was affecting the holiday. 'One more day,' he spat. 'One.'

She didn't know if this meant she ought to suck it up for one more day, be pleasant for one more day, or that she only had one more day as his wife before his patience ran out.

She would wait and see.
One more day.

* * *

They sat down at a restaurant for what Aristos promised was the finest souvlaki in the world. Darya didn't have the appetite, and said so, but Orestis wouldn't take no for an answer. It was his treat, he insisted, enough freebies from his boss. Eva ordered a chicken gyro for herself and one for her stepmother. 'Don't worry,' she said. 'If you don't want it I'll have both.'

A pointless gesture, but the older woman gave the impression of a smile all the same. When the food arrived, the smell cut right through her. She took a bite, then another, then another. The sauce dripped out of the pitta, fatter and more succulent than the Cypriot kind. The tender meat, the shredded lettuce, the yoghurt, cucumber, mint, lemon: an eruption. She became a wild boar. But she had always been like this. It was a truth she must stop denying, try as she might to mask it with yoga, with health, with denial, with her silly little game. Everything she did, she did for her own pleasure. Even anger, when she felt it, was another way to satisfy herself. She was sick, demented, impure. A reckless hedonist. And an idiot. She would trade her head for a feast.

On a slow roasting street, she spotted a bookshop. Maybe they stocked Russian novels, it would be something at least. Or she could buy a book she'd read before, translated into Greek. On entering the shop, she abandoned that dream; the place was barely bigger than a cabin. Wooden brackets propped each other up like a house of cards. They leant and sagged over the proprietor, a man of advanced years whose shirt was tucked neatly into high-waisted chinos. Swallowing her pride, she approached him. Greek came more easily with strangers.

'Excuse me,' she said in his language. 'I am looking for Janka Kupała.'

The man looked up at her, expressionless.

'Poem?' she said, drawing a blank on the word for poetry.

She thought the man was being dismissive, but no – the wheels in his brain were turning.

'I apologise, but I don't know the name,' he said in a gentle voice.

'It's OK...'

'We have a book of Russian poetry,' he continued. 'And of course, there's Dostoevsky, Chekov, the usual ones. Alexievich. I like her work.'

'Yes,' she said, feeling a chill.

The bell rang with the opening of the door. Aristos stood in the doorway. 'There you are!' he said. 'We turned around and you'd vanished.'

She bit her tongue.

She thanked the proprietor. It pained her to disappoint the man after his service, but she wouldn't buy anything in front of her husband, especially not Russian literature.

Out on the street, Aristos' eyes were alight. 'Tell us next time you decide to vanish.'

'Only there,' she said in Greek, gesturing at the bookshop.

'Come on, Daddykins,' said Eva. 'She's a grown woman, for God's sake. She can go wherever she wants.'

Aristos raised his eyebrows, rolled his eyes. He turned to the younger man, whose eyes were flitting between them all, and then he feigned a lightness. 'You see, Orestis? This is what awaits you.'

And there it was, out in the open. Aristos' first acknowledge-ment of the stud being groomed in the stables. But nobody said a word, and Orestis' nervous laugh hung in the air.

Eva stopped at the window of a boutique. 'Mother of God!' she said. 'I want it.' She was talking about any one of a half-dozen cocktail dresses slung over the half-headed mannequins. She ran inside, dragging Darya with her. If she'd been in her right mind, Darya would've refused. But she was still mired. In any case, what could she say? With half a head herself, she mastered her breathing and left the men. Orestis looked back at the women, wishing he could join them. After all, he was only a boy, a boy left alone with the headmaster.

For a few minutes at least, Eva kept up the charade of shopping. The heels of her mules clipped along the wooden floorboard. It was the sound of a confident step, a woman who knew what she wanted, what she could afford – everything, of course. Darya stroked the hanging dresses, simply to feel the cool of the AC. She might lie on the floor, press her cheek against its wood. And it was then she felt a familiar demon grow inside her. A judder of pleasure, but also of fear, sickness.

She would run away.

Eva had a comment for every garment. And while Darya nodded or shook her head, she calculated her escape. Run away. Yes. Why not? She could do it today, now, in a snap of the fingers as she had done in Poland. Again she saw the faces of her mother and babulia. The former in that dark kitchen of long ago, asking her to peel potatoes, when a bird flew into the room and made them both scream, then laugh, then scream again. The latter's mouth trembling as she reminisced of nights in the park in the days of Stalin when she danced with a young East-German to the music of an accordionist. Sitting by the gas heater, warbling Vysotsky's war songs. Darya had known for a while she'd be leaving Cyprus – what if she already had? This was a different country, here, now. She didn't have to board the ship. No one could force her. She could go to the bathroom and never return.

But where could she go?

'This one's a doll!' Eva said with a gasp. A red cocktail dress came rippling off the rail.

The boats. Those tin signs in the square, by the harbour. Boat rides to Turkey. Turkey was so close.

'Can I tell you something?' Eva turned, her face, her stance, steady.

Darya nodded. Had those signs and boats been here in Rhodos, or had they been in Kos?

'My father is clever. I know him. He knows how to come out on top.' The girl must have noted something in her response, for she lightly slapped her arm. 'My God, Darya, you really amuse me. You always show exactly how you feel.' Then, 'At least, that's what I hope.'

'I'm clean,' said Darya, because she couldn't think of the word for transparent.

'I'm not so sure. I think there's more to you.'

Darya's cheeks burned.

'Don't worry,' said the girl, 'everyone's like that. You think I don't know, a Russian coming to Cyprus, that something must be up?'

The girl behind the counter was intrigued. She looked away when Darya noticed.

'I am not happy,' Darya said. 'In Belarus. I leave.' She was aware of having stressed Belarus. Somewhere, her father was clapping. Maybe even from Heaven, because who knew what

239

had happened to him, to any of them? They might all be dead and buried.

Eva put a hand to her heart. 'God have mercy, don't think I'm asking you about that! Please. Honestly, your life is your life. But that's what I mean: don't let my father tell you how to live.'

Darya wished she could understand. She heard the words, recognised them as individual parts, but together...? How would she ever be on equal footing with Aristos' daughter? This had to be a trick. Eva was gathering rifles, ready to put her on trial and stand her against the wall. Well, she needn't trouble herself. A boat to Turkey. Then who knows where. *Anywhere.* She was capable, and nobody – not even Orestis – had any idea that she was.

But Aristos...

Somehow, Aristos would stop her.

'I know my father,' Eva continued. 'He does that. Believe me, I know. He pulled the same shit on my mother.' The girl paused, considered her words, and reached a decision. 'I don't know what he's told you about her. But I can imagine. That she was lazy, stupid, fat... But, you see, she understood him. She knew who he was, even when others couldn't see it. She was scared of him. And he used that.'

Eva's eyes were wet and glowing. Darya remembered the hateful things the girl had said about her in the past. The tears of a girl whose parents had broken up. Of course, Darya had been evil. It didn't matter that she'd only met Aristos after the fact. What mattered was that he had chosen her and discarded his wife. What mattered was that she had never been one of them.

'Do you understand what I'm saying?' Eva placed a hand on

her arm.

Darya realised she was shaking. She pretended it was the AC, and hugged herself. 'I understand,' she replied. 'Thank you.'

'I don't let him get to me.' Eva's eyes sharpened to bullets. 'And neither should you.'

'OK.' And she nodded, to show the girl she had listened. Squeezing Eva's arm, she felt a hardening resolve. She would not be boarding that ship back to Cyprus. Her life under Aristos was over.

They left the boutique laden with bags. Even Darya had been coerced by a summer dress. It wasn't her money, so why not? They walked over to the bench in a small park, where the men were sitting with ice cream cones. Orestis' face lit up.

Behind him was a small group of people, their clothes unlike everyone else's. Something about them was from a different time, out of step with this world. They approached the surrounding tourists with open palms. One of them held a baby, whose cries rang out across the park. Beggars, like the Roma she'd seen in the cities. People's eyebrows would press on their eyes as they watched them.

'Finally!' said Aristos. 'Did my darling's credit card melt?'

'Yes, Daddykins! Will you give me yours?'

'As if there's a difference.'

Darya could see it now. She heard as if for the first time, how Eva spoke to her father. The irony hiding a sternness. The tone of an animal handler.

'Want some ice-cream?' asked Orestis. 'My treat.'

A voice called Aristos' name.

Eva was first to respond: 'Oh my God! What are you doing here?'

A middle-aged couple were walking up to them, Eva spread her arms for a hug. Darya's heart lurched. The same old couple that had recognised Orestis, that day at Latchi, she was sure. She could not play his English aunt now. This was how it would end – everything gone with the strike of a match.

Fine, let it be.

But no.

They weren't those people. The couple were friends of Aristos. They barely acknowledged Orestis in the scramble of conversation, between the man, the woman, Aristos and Eva.

'What are you doing here? Are you living here now?'

The woman said something about America, they were here on holiday.

Eva grabbed the woman's hand. 'You remember Orestis?'

The man did a double-take. He held out his hand in a grand show. 'This handsome young man? That's Orestis, the fat one?'

Darya noted the flicker in Orestis' face, like static on an old TV.

'That's me!' he said, laughing. 'Orestis the fat one.' And he was on his feet, shoulders back, clamping the other man's hand in his.

'Re, you've changed so much! I never would've recognised you.'

'Oh, I'm sorry!' said Aristos, meeting her eye. 'Let me introduce my wife.'

The older couple stood back, angled themselves to greet her properly. Something registered in their eyes, was filed away. It was the look bureaucrats gave you in Minsk.

'This is Darya,' he said in English. It dawned on her that he always introduced her like this.

So she greeted them in Greek. 'Pleased to meet you.'

'Likewise.'

The man turned to Aristos. 'What has it been, five years?'

'Since we saw you? Nine or ten.'

'You don't say!'

'It's true.'

'I only got married a few years ago.'

'Christ.'

The rest happened quickly. First, another voice came through the tangle. Orestis' head perked up in her direction, then there was a tug at Darya's arm. Next to her, another face she didn't know, another's skin on hers. Young or old, who knew. It happened so fast. A woman with black hair and a shawl, gold hoops, eyes full of water, spittle in the corners of her mouth, and she was speaking in another language – not Greek, not English. There was a baby in her arms. *Take the baby.* That's what she was saying, it must have been. *Take the baby.* Urgent, desperate. There were cries, they pierced her ears. The baby's or its mother's. Both. Orestis spoke in English, he was barking at the woman, *Get away from her! Go!* The beggar woman, a mother with her baby. *Go!* Darya trying to stop them, *No.* And someone was pulling Darya away, someone yanking the other woman's hand off hers, unclenching the fingers, the nails from her skin, *Get away from her!* At least that's what she thought she heard. She didn't know. None of it sounded real, none of it was real. *Please, God, please may it not be real.*

* * *

On the pavement, past window displays and wing-mirrors,

243

she felt outside of herself. No longer a body. Only a breath of a human; condensation left on a pane of glass.

The others had put it behind them. Already, it was simply an odd thing that happened, destined to become an anecdote, guaranteed to earn five whole minutes' attention at parties.

At the time they'd been concerned. That other wife, whose name she was told but could not remember, she'd said, on seeing her staring vacantly at the bark of a tree, 'Get her some water. She's gone into shock.' Then she'd lowered her onto a bench. 'Let her sit. Sit down, love.' Eva and Aristos had flanked her on the bench and held a hand each. They'd asked if she was OK, they'd told her that the woman with the baby was gone. A memory fluttered. A young policeman – no, two of them – were dragging the woman off her, and people around them were staring, gasping, hands at mouths and mouths moving with speech. The police had seen the beggars, the travellers, whatever they were, and were already on their way when the woman pushed her baby at her and said, *Take him, please. Take him.* Of course, that was what she'd said, in her native tongue. Of course, it was. A plea to give her child a life. Darya understood it, then and now. But look what she'd done.

Everyone else had moved on. They'd watched her breathe, and breathe, and compose herself until her breath became normal. Until she'd lost that edge to it, that sound like a slip. And they'd had coffee together, she, her husband, her stepdaughter, her lover and these two new old friends as if life was always like this, which it was. Of course, it was. These things came and went. These moments between people; reaching, touching, breaking away. Like her father reaching out to squeeze the skin on the back of her neck like a kitten, giggling as she did. Like her kitten back in Cyprus. Like the maid from another land, more distant than hers, come to serve a woman she couldn't know. Like her mother kissing icons, a crucifix on a silver chain, her fingers as she told her she loved her. Like the sweet strong voice of her babulia singing in church, her voice wrapping vine-like around the priest's. Like Maksim peering out through that body diffusing to bones. Like the blood that always emptied. Like the soul that rose to meet her, then kiss her goodbye, and leave.

III

One

As a child, Aristos had always preferred puzzles to sports. He would sit in the shade of a plane tree overlooking what was, in his young eyes, the entire world. In fact, it was only a patch of mountainside in the Lemesos district, their village just a fragment of a fragment of Earth. But he would spread his sights to the blue-grey slopes in the distance and wonder about the villages there. How would he get there? Which path could he take? More often he'd search the valley for the city, where he knew his future lay, the terracotta roof tiles of a house here and there acting as stepping-stones for his eyes amongst the dusty green hills. Pantelis, whose taverna hunched close by, would spot him sitting beneath the boughs of that tree, self-exiled from the games of the other children running up the steep dirt streets, and he would call out to him: *Little Hippocrates*. The boy who sat in lonely contemplation beneath a plane tree. Aristos liked the nickname, and so he liked Pantelis.

The man was as poorly educated as anyone else in the village, but he'd learned the words of Homer off by heart. He claimed that his father and his father's father and his grandfather's grandfather's father would tell the tales, passing them on down the generations. So Pantelis would set plates of roasted lamb and potatoes at his tables, and on command recite whole passages from *The Odyssey*.

Men are so quick to blame the gods: they say
that we devise their misery. But they
themselves — in their depravity — design
grief greater than the griefs that fate assigns.

Aristos had always preferred that tale to *The Iliad*, whose violence and bloodshed were too close to his experience for comfort. He'd grown up with EOKA's nationalism, the fight against the Brits, then bloodshed between brothers. Better were the exploits of Odysseus the trickster, and the gods and monsters who met him on his journey. Its wisdom lived on through the ages. It was a tale that could turn a boy, obeying his master's orders, into a man who commandeered his ship.

In some ways, Aristos reflected, it was Pantelis who had instilled in him this yearning to venture forth, explore, take charge.

Now he was in Greece, the Motherland. He didn't like to think of the country that way – that was for the flag-wavers, the men with *ENOSIS* stickers on their pickup trucks. Those men longed for a past that never was; one in which Cypriots were all Greeks until the Ottomans invaded. Even as a child he knew that no country could possibly be just one thing, in the same way a person could not be just one thing. Humans were compounds of their geography, their history, their produce, their climates, the effects of their neighbours and friends and enemies. But try as he might to fight the imagined spiritual connection with Greece – or, more accurately, to the Ancients who informed his education, his view, and European history since – he couldn't help but feel a stirring in his blood. He'd visited countless times in the past. He knew the mainland and the islands off by heart, cafés and tavernas and bars, the best spots to watch the sun set, where to watch for scorpions and where you were likely to encounter a wolf. And he had never felt anything other than Cypriot, neither Greek nor Turk.

He wondered if, perhaps, he was delving into his past because he was settling his future. Darya had been upset to share the boat with Eva. But his daughter was attached to Orestis, it would have been foolish not to act on it. There was no one better for his little girl; a young man who was dutiful, considerate, polite – and handsome! Nothing like the youths who spilt their parents' money on branded swimwear, and their nights joyriding through the tourist district. That receptionist – Elias – lost his brother in a car crash not too long ago. And the one who stepped up for the night shift? Orestis. One man's recklessness revealed another's maturity. Thank God, despite the bumpy road of his adolescence, Orestis had turned out more like his mother than his father.

She was a rare person, Melina – intelligent, inquisitive, charming. Among the other mothers at parties and fairs and recitals, she stood out for her lack of airs. Her departure was a loss, and a shock to Aristos, though that was shameful to admit. His first wife bore the brunt of his moods. When Orestis was removed from the international school, Aristos' heart dropped. He got close to approaching Kostas at the garage to offer the payment for the boy's tuition, but he held himself back. What would it have achieved? To Kostas, the school had become a symbol of his wife's Britishness. Nothing would make him prouder than to spit on it. Aristos kept out of their lives, but he monitored the boy's development. Lemesos was a small place, it wasn't difficult to bump into acquaintances, to ask after others. Over the years he noted with relief that

251

Orestis was fine. He hit a snag after the Army when he put on that weight and worked for his uncle. But who was Aristos to judge? He'd always enjoyed a meal himself, and he hadn't been born with a list of hotels to his name. When Eva put Orestis forward for a job, Aristos created a vacancy. And Thanos would hire the boy because Aristos knew his character. He'd known the woman who'd sown it.

He dragged his feet as they made their way back, along the old castle walls, the palms, past the hundred cats, towards the SS Astraea. In the dappled shade, artists drew caricatures of tourists who had only just arrived.

'*Keep Ithaki always in your mind,*' he quoted as they boarded the vessel. '*Arriving there is what you are destined for.*'

Eva, on a higher step, turned to face him. 'Pe!' she said. 'We're on holiday, don't take us back to school.'

Aristos laughed, and so did Orestis. Perfect boy. Who else would have his daughter, look after her when Aristos was gone? He loved his Eva, she was vibrant and – in her own way – beautiful, but there was no getting around the fact she was a handful.

There was, however, that uncomfortable truth: Orestis was servicing Darya. Bad luck. But his wife needn't sulk, there were other men to fill the part. Perhaps it was better this way; the young buck would've had his fill of women before he settled down to family life.

As they walked into the ship's grand lobby, a redhead in a low-cut top gave Orestis the once-over, and the young man tossed a glance back at her. Much as it disappointed him, Aristos had to confront another truth: not only was Orestis a man who would always attract attention, but he would always seek it. Aristos was resigning his daughter to the role of the

252

cheated housewife, which even her mother had never played.

Damn it. Nothing was ever perfect.

* * *

Knowing the Captain had its perks. Aside from the first choice of seating for dinner, table reservations for the nightly cabaret and complimentary drinks at the bar, they were now to be granted a tour of the bridge. It might lift Darya out of whatever state she seemed hell-bent to stay in. It was unclear if the others were oblivious to it or attempting to blow it away with good cheer, but Aristos was tired of his wife's foul mood. She was a person whose emotions were clear, it's what he liked about her, and one of the reasons he chose her. Whether the emotion was worry, distraction, or pleasure, nothing was performed. A person straight as a javelin. But this, now? Baffling. At first, after their fight on the beach in Kos, he'd thought she was jealous of Eva, possessive of Orestis. But she hadn't gone to his cabin, though he told her she could. *Thank you*, she'd spat in response, her Greek vowels perfect. Now, she barely looked at the boy, or at any other male for that matter. Instead, she glanced over her shoulder as if something might attack from the corners of her vision.

It wouldn't have been the baby, not that beggar-woman. Darya had never wanted to be a mother, that was another reason he'd married her. Yes, the incident had been unsettling. Perhaps that was it. She was disturbed by a stranger's sudden touch. In the early days, she would flinch at his fingers on her skin. *I'm not use*, she would explain in English, drawing the subject closed. He suspected a history of abuse, perhaps by the drunkard father.

They were out on the open deck. The smell of salt hit him, all at once. The music of the after-show disco having dimmed to a thrum as they walked from rooms to corridors to those slick wooden floors outside, there was now the sound only of waves, and the light only of stars. Then, in the endless black, grew the orb of an officer's torch.

The lanky man appeared to know Aristos, whether by prior introduction or purely by reputation. The bigger man did what he always did when unsure of someone's acquaintance; he put his hand on the officer's back and said, 'Thank you, my friend.' Most responded well to physical contact. In a handshake, using both hands was better than one – *You're safe, I'm friendly.* Of course, in his travels on the job he'd picked up on cultural differences. Sometimes it was handshakes, other times bowing, sometimes it was two kisses on the cheek and other times three; whatever ingratiated him to his hosts.

The Captain stood by the door to greet them. He shook their hands, though the custom had been banned, as each stepped through to the bridge, a space that felt cramped to such a tall man as Aristos. Eva pointed out maps and compasses on the walls, a brass barometer. Meanwhile, his wife stared into the green light of a screen. 'That's the radar,' the Captain said, 'to warn us of any other vessels.' Orestis was wide-eyed at the view beyond the wheel and the glass facade: the dark water, rolling onwards to mist.

'I've seen some things, I can tell you,' said the Captain. His face, with its deep lines in patchy skin and its faded eyes, had already said it for him.

'I swear to God,' Eva interrupted, 'if we see an iceberg now...'

The Captain laughed.

254

Aristos was proud of his daughter; she had her own ways of ingratiating herself. But she was not to be taken for a fool. A manager without a boss. She would be all right without him.

'Is it easy to steer the ship?' Orestis asked the captain.

'You want to try?'

The boy couldn't have looked more pleased. That charming smile of his, so like his mother in many ways, with the Greek nose and those warm eyes, was the only thing to make Darya look up from the radar. The low green light cast shadows around her features, distorting her face like a cubist portrait. That's exactly what she was: cubist. Her every side was on show, but instead of being clearer, she was more obscured. He would never truly know his wife. But she had better not make trouble for him now. Not when it had all been going so well.

Two

His wife didn't so much as look at him in the taxi
home. When Aristos moved his hand across the
cool back seat to cover hers, he expected her to pull
away, and to have to be stern about it. Instead, she did nothing,
not even flinch. Her hand sat there under his, dead. If she kept
this up, he would be forced to take steps. Aristos had never
been the sort of man to hit a woman – he didn't even hate
them – but people must be taught to learn their place and
respect boundaries. If his employees knew not to be petulant,
so should the woman who'd sworn to love him.

The highway and the cars streamed past, the sea in the distance now, no longer beneath their feet. But she continued to
wink from between the buildings, shrubs and signs. Billboards
boasted of developments soon to rise from the yellow fields.
Panthea was once a peaceful hill, a couple of houses at the
top, now it buckled under family mansions and blocks of flats
spoiling for a view. Prices had risen, the time was right. One
of his cousins had sold an inherited bungalow in the centre of
town, for a sum too mad to have been believed just a couple
of years beforehand. And what was Aristos doing, holding
on to his hotels, when every part of him was yelling to sell?
He ought to build luxury flats on the new marina. The city

was stretching out into the sea, again. Full of swagger, safe in the hands of the European Union, Cyprus was presenting herself as a five-star resort. She would attract businesses instead of families, the moneyed seeking money. Interest rates were favourable, criminals kept their bank accounts here. The Russians had come and stayed, established their neighbourhoods in Paphos, even their radio stations. Money for a visa, and another EU citizen was born. Next, it would be the Chinese. And if the talk of offshore oil was true...

It drained him. Perhaps it was the afternoon light on his eyelids. Or, call a spade a spade, he was getting old. Ambition was the blood of youth, and Aristos had never been greedy. He'd wanted to make money and dictate his own life. He'd achieved that by thirty-five. Leave business to the kids and get out while he could still enjoy himself. Sitting with Orestis in the living room, lifting page after page of a coffee-table book, chatting about all they remembered and felt and thought – that was living. Seeing his only child get married, maybe even give him a grandchild...

And Darya?

He'd imagined her next to him, propping him up in his dying days; that Soviet stoicism of hers a cure for any weakness. But now, seeing her profile against the car window, a shadow portrait of the woman he thought he knew... Who even was she?

Back at home, her silence filled the house. It filled the dining room meant for friends they never invited; the salon meant for parties they rarely threw, and from which his wife would frequently absent herself; the hallway in which he'd let her make that shrine of hers, with the Slavic fabric draped over icons and candles; the garden she used for meditation, yoga, sunning herself, whatever she did out there; the bedroom where the young stud he'd hired specifically to cuckold him, for her, would fulfil her every desire. For her pleasure. For her needs. For her, for her, for her.

'Darya?'

She went straight to the kitchen. He heard the door slide open and he felt, for a second, a panic that she was about to do something crazy. Run away. Leap into the pool. She who had always been so steady, so calm.

He walked to a reception room to watch from the window. In the frame, he saw her go towards the seating area, to its enormous cushions and candles in jars. She searched around it. She bent over to peer into a tree. Her shoulders slumped, she began to walk back. Then she stopped. She dithered, went back to the tree. She checked a bush. Then she looked over the garden wall.

Was she looking for the cat? Christ, it would've gone by now. Someone would have run it over, if not poisoned it. That still happened.

Darya walked off the frame. Soon he heard the door slide shut again, and her footsteps on the tiles. She was heading for the hallway.

'Darya,' he said, stepping out of the room. 'Come here.'

She paused at the staircase. What turned to face him was a maddening mix of confusion and defiance. The veins throbbed in his head. He was too old for games and so was she. But he would play all the same, a game for thinking men who liked to sit beneath plane trees. After all, life was chess.

'Darling,' he said, 'are you OK?'

'Yes.' She didn't even blink. To his surprise, she went on to offer something of an explanation: 'I am thinking.'

He nodded. 'You know,' he said with a gentle voice, 'I only want your happiness. Whatever you want I'll give to you.'

Only a fool would not understand. She was no fool.

Whatever thought had come to her, the words to express it never did. Her eyes moved, in a way that made him think of a printer spreading ink on a page. She allowed the silence to grow, and grow, and cover them both.

Waking, he pulled away from it, her spell, whatever it was. 'I'm going to get a drink.'

And when he glanced back, he saw that she was staring at something in the distance, somewhere by the front door.

* * *

He had a meeting with Thanos at the Harmonia. Aristos wore a Tom Ford suit he had picked up in London, which the hotel manager correctly identified. Thanos was a man of detail. His judgment had been an asset to the chain, and he must be assured that he was valued. But he was also to be reminded that some things were beyond him, and so Aristos had paired the shirt with gold and onyx cufflinks that cost nearly as much as the suit. Once in a while, the manager's eyes would travel to them.

They were sitting at one of the cafés overlooking the pool. Aristos had passed Orestis at the Front Desk, and the boy had blended his greeting with the other staff. 'Good morning, Mr Ioannidou.' But he couldn't help wondering how much Thanos had noticed or indeed suspected. The manager was an intuitive man, little escaped him. It must not be forgotten that he'd known almost at once what Lefteris was. He'd requested a private talk with Aristos then, in which he'd raised his concern

259

of solicitation on the hotel grounds. There was nothing they could do about businessmen renting girls off the street, but this…? *There are men in suits who wait in the lobby*, Thanos had said, his tone full of portent. *One in particular.* Aristos had seen no point in feigning ignorance. *Yes*, he'd replied, and watched the manager's face as it had filled in the blanks. Thanos, with his well-bred posture in a tailored waistcoat, had not been happy about the arrangement – an extra service he believed to be tarnishing the hotels' good names – but Aristos assured him the men were being closely monitored. Male prostitution was far less messy than the alternative. Firstly, these handsome young bucks were always willing, and they got to choose the women or men they serviced; they were not foreign girls who'd been tricked into leaving their families for what they'd been told was legitimate work in Europe. Secondly, female prostitution was a side racket for drug-dealers and Mafiosi. Lefteris, and other men of his ilk, were sole traders. Female clients didn't make trouble. As long as drugs were kept off the premises, the hotels' doors were open to these sons of Aphrodite. In Orestis, Lefteris had seen an opportunity to earn some extra income. Notwithstanding that messy beginning when Darya had paid in cash, Aristos' money passed as a housekeeping expense from him to Lefteris, who took his percentage before handing the remainder to Orestis. Aristos contended that this was, in no uncertain terms, hush money. On some nights the dread kept him from sleeping. But he comforted himself that Lefteris was of wealthy stock – rich families were the most fearful. While the young man's father might get a secondhand ego boost in private, in public he'd be horrified at where the extra income had come from. Reputation was currency, and scandals were depressions. Aristos had to protect himself. If news of gigolos operating at the hotels were to spread to the general public, he could feign ignorance and make a grand show of stamping them out of his establishments. It was his word against that of creatures of the night. But then, who would leak the news in the first place? Employees for whom the hotel was a glittering line on a resumé? Male clients concealing their sin? Or women revealing theirs?

At times he worried about Orestis. The boy could almost certainly be trusted, but he was also vain, and still unpractised. He might let slip to a friend about his work on the side. A friend of Orestis' was likely to be a friend of Eva's. And if Darya's name got bandied about... This was why he had taken the photos. Orestis had been flattered, the poor fool; it hadn't even occurred to him to conceal his face.

Thanos thanked the waitress by name when she brought their pastries and coffees. Aristos took his in the traditional way, thick and unsweetened, the kind his late mother would have 'read' in the emptied cups of her visitors. Thanos was of the younger generation, who liked their fancy brews with milk and foam and sprinkles. Whatever kept him youthful.

To begin with, the men made small talk, 'How was the holiday?' followed by 'Wonderful,' followed by a recap of the Islands. How light it all sounded without mention of his wife.

'How about you? What news?'

'Nothing exciting to tell,' said the manager.

'A, come now. Dashing man like you. You must have a line of ladies.'

Nerves made a wave of the younger man's smile, as Aristos predicted. An old army buddy had spotted Thanos walking into a gay bar. *I'll give you a hundred euro for a photo of him there,* Aristos had said. *Double for any kissing or touching.* The friend had obliged. Aristos had paid double.

'E... I get on OK,' Thanos said.

For a moment, Aristos reflected on how good it might be to have a more open relationship with this man; if only Thanos could be honest about himself, if only Aristos could be the sort of man who encouraged honesty. People were too afraid of him to reveal themselves completely. Everything he knew of them he had to divine. He had the talent to do it, like his mother discerning fortunes from the dregs of her visitors' coffee cups, but whereas hers was a warm, inviting way to fathom people, his was cold. It was as if he'd only read about them rather than spoken to them. And information was rarely useless. That was what people feared in him: they could sense their own dissection.

'There's something I wanted to speak with you about,' said Aristos. 'It's something to which I've given a lot of thought.'

The manager sat up straight.

'As you know, I've been travelling here and there in the past few months, sorting things out abroad. Long story short... I sold them. Munich, Amsterdam, Dubai, I sold them.'

Thanos' eyes widened.

'I'm taking a step back. I've been working away so much these past few years, my poor wife thinks there's an intruder whenever she finds me home.' A good touch, he thought. 'The truth is, I'm getting tired. But don't worry,' – he threw a hand up – 'I swear on my life that I am never selling the Harmonia.'

Thanos nodded.

'As you know, I've been keeping a close eye on the hotels. It's how we've sustained our standards, our quality, across the chain. But now I'd like someone else to take over for me. You.'

A kaleidoscope of emotions in Thanos' face. He was speechless.

'I feel lucky to have found you,' Aristos went on. 'You have demonstrated over the years that your standards, your expectations, your leadership, are second to none. I can think of no-one else I would trust to do this for me.'

'Mr Ioannidou,' said Thanos, though he'd already been permitted to use the Christian name, 'I don't know how to thank you. That's more than I ever hoped for.' His voice had been reduced to a fraction of its usual body, it was a mere breath.

'Don't hope for anything,' said Aristos. 'Want it. Then do everything you can to get it.'

The manager conceded with a nod and a raise of his eyebrow. 'But will I still be based at the Harmonia?'

'If it suits you to use it as a base, then by all means. But someone else will take on your duties.'

The manager didn't blink. 'Do you mean Orestis?'

Aristos kept a casual tone. 'Why not? He's a strong employee, isn't he? He's coped well with assisting you, according to his performance reviews. He's established good relationships with all departments. As far as I can tell, he also has the hotel's interests at heart.' He lifted his coffee to his mouth, cufflinks catching the light.

'Yes,' said Thanos. 'He has an eye for quality. I knew it when I first showed him around.'

'He gets it from his mother,' said the older man.

A mistake. The fool.

Thankfully, Orestis had proved a boon to the Harmonia.

The staff appeared to have forgotten his link to Eva, if they ever knew of it, and his tenacity was a natural path to a good career. The various department managers thought highly of him, even Tina. Plus, on several occasions, the guests had made a point of singling out his service. Aristos only hoped he hadn't extended that service beyond what was appropriate. The thought had occurred to him before and he'd dismissed it, but now, with Thanos in front of him, and that expression on his face, it returned as a possibility.

'In the next few months,' Aristos continued, regaining his footing, 'I'd like you to train him. He needs to be at your level before you start your new role.'

'I'm not worried about him,' said Thanos, voice low. But then he raised his eyes to give Aristos a strange smile. 'He wants things and he gets them.'

The older man sipped his coffee.

'How long do we have?' asked Thanos.

'I reckon October, but I'm willing to leave it to you.' He drained the cup. 'As for your salary, it goes up today.'

Three

A woman was screaming and another was in tears. As he got out of the car the sound became clearer, and it dawned on him who the voices belonged to. Ice ran down his back. He had never heard his wife like this. The noise took him back to the village, where everyone's business was broadcast to the street. His face burned with shame, here in this fine neighbourhood.

Inside, Darya was yelling at the maid to get out. A clatter of broken English and Greek, then, between breaths, whispers to herself in her mother tongue. The maid was on her knees. 'I need job,' she was saying, the tears streaming into her mouth. 'Please, madame. Not me.'

Aristos shut the door behind him. 'What's all this fuss about?' He kept his own voice level.

On seeing him, Darya switched off, to glare silently at nothing.

The Sri Lankan crawled to him. 'Mr Ioannidou, please! I didn't do this. I didn't do this.' Her Greek was lumpy with sobs.

'Don't worry, my girl,' he said, lifting her up from the floor. He held her by the shoulders and spoke close to her face. 'Whatever happened, let me try to sort it out. You go home. Go home and rest, it's OK.'

Did she have enough Greek to understand him? She stared at him, unsure if she should leave.

'It's OK,' he assured her. 'Tomorrow.'

'Tomorrow,' she repeated. Then she tried to catch Darya's eye. Her mouth quivered. 'I'm sorry, madame. Not me. Not me.' The door open, she hesitated on the veranda. Then she turned, took a last look inside, and shut the badness in.

'Darya...'

But his wife was pacing the hall. 'I fire her. She's idiot.'

The sight of her was unreal. That straight nose, those high cheekbones, all her edges were sharper. Face as red as if she'd been strangled.

'What are you talking about? She's good. You had no problems with her.'

'No Filipino,' she spat because she thought it was Greek for 'maid'.

'What do you mean, *no maid*? Who's going to clean?'

'Me.'

'You!'

'I clean! I like it.'

'Darya, come...'

She slipped from his grasp. She was walking away, too close to the wall, so close to the glass of the picture frame. Her whole head looked fit to burst, something swelling inside it. Rattling breath, shaking shoulders. Then she puffed, puffed, a sound from her mouth that in time he realised was crying. Her eyes began to stream, and she stood, pathetic, in the middle of the hallway, overcome. Her hands floated about her like seaweed in water, and at last, they came to her face.

He approached her with caution. No longer spouse but

suicide bomber.

'What is it?' he cooed. 'What is it, my love?' Gently, he put his hand on her. But she didn't flinch or throw him off. She rolled into his hug and, clutching his arm, cried into his shirt.

It was fine. She would be fine. Something had upset her, and she'd kept it inside. But she wasn't a person who could let things ferment. She was used to expressing her passions. Now it was coming out, all the bile she'd felt, all the anger and bitterness, and she would feel better for it. His wife would be empty and clear once more.

She spent the remainder of the evening in the garden. She'd taken a bowl of cat food outside and placed it on the paving. Aristos stayed in the living room, leafing through his newspaper. He would have to call the agency for a new maid. Pity, the Sri Lankan had been good. But Darya would refuse to see her again. Aristos had grown to resent his ex-wife for the way she treated the maids. The woman had changed when Eva was born, she had transformed into a face forever caustic and sniping. As far as Aristos was concerned, there was no adequate reason to be unkind to service staff, and he'd never have expected it of Darya. After all, she'd been a cleaner herself. He wondered if it had been a mistake to take her with them on the cruise. Perhaps it had brought back memories of her former life and blurred her place in the new one.

Once in a while, he lifted his eyes to the window, where his wife was sitting on a patch of grass. She looked from the garden wall to the tree against it, to the ground. It was all she had done for hours.

* * *

There were even more cars in Cyprus than stray cats. He coasted around Old Town, searching for a place to park. Some vehicles had been dumped where there were no markings, while others blocked them in. Eventually, he found one of those cheap spots run by old men with husky voices who spent all day sitting under the sun in plastic chairs. En route to his appointment he saw a familiar figure: his wife, walking through the shadows of oaks. What was she doing here? A rendezvous with Orestis? Or perhaps she'd taken his advice and called Lefteris for another man.

Aristos followed. It was only to check she was all right, God knew she never explained herself. What use were obvious emotions when their motivations remained obscured? That was no way to achieve anything.

Her pace was unhurried. With a distance of ten-twenty metres between them, he tailed her through the old Turkish neighbourhoods, the minaret of the mosque serving as a compass. She led him through the British-Venetian network whose architecture he hadn't stopped to admire in years. At best the majority of his compatriots were blind to it, at worst dismissive. Culture had barely scraped through that dreadful post-War period when historic structures were thumped down like cockroaches. It shamed him that he'd played a part in that, however unwitting, on those muscle-tearing construction sites of his youth.

Darya passed government buildings with painted wooden shutters, and beneath the iron balconies of flats and offices. She ignored the tourist shops selling vulgar mugs and post-cards and pens, cheap reproductions of classical sculpture. The better of them sold machine-made Lefkara lace, for those turned off by the expense of the handmade. The paradox made his head hurt. People were content to spend thousands of euro on machine-made branded handbags, yet baulked at the idea of spending less on something that took more time, effort and talent to produce.

A man sat on a graffitied bollard, stroking a cockatiel.

A stunted beep, a screech of brakes and 'Fuck you!' said a man on his moped, for Aristos had stepped off the curb without even looking.

He apologised to the man, eyes still on Darya. She hadn't turned.

If his wife was going shopping, she was taking an odd route. She turned past an old tailor's, towards a pedestrian avenue of bars and restaurants, where people sat smoking and sipping frappés in the fractured sunlight under trees and awnings. The street ended at the Pantopoleion, its arched entranceways like giant gaping mouths. One swallowed her up. Aristos quickened his pace. So far he'd been walking casually so that if she turned and saw him he might greet her and marvel at the coincidence.

It had been at least a decade since he'd last been in the Pantopoleion. It looked lighter than before, a new lick of yellow up its cavernous walls and a light green skin on its iron skeleton. Fresh fruit and vegetables in crates formed a circuit around the place, the food inside that giant mouth. Every so often, a stall selling honey, candies and local crafts. Evil Eye pendants hung from wooden stands. Necklaces, earrings and bracelets reflected the sunlight pouring in from up high.

His wife passed a choir of woven baskets, the type his mother had used in the village. The departed woman would sit on the veranda with one in her lap, breaking pods and popping out the black-eyed beans. He could share this part of himself with

Darya, together they might start afresh in their relationship, on the same step. Though she kept her past under lock and key, Aristos suspected a similar upbringing to his; rural and, if not destitute, at least more deprived than the average. It was the USSR – she would have queued for what was now readily available at convenience stores, she knew the meaning of gratitude. Or so he'd thought. After all, he'd assumed she'd be an atheist.

Aristos' mother had always made sure he had shoes. There were children in his class that walked along the dirt track from their homes to the school on bare feet, who laughed about jumping from cowpat to cowpat in the summer so as not to feel the burning earth. Though his mother was widowed young, his father came from a big, guilty family that never let her fall down the well of abject poverty. Their support earned her the trust of a village she hadn't grown up in. She was, therefore, able on countless occasions, to defer payments on groceries or eke out grants and favours. One of her chief teachings was not to underestimate charm. She remembered the details of people's lives, enquired after the health of their loved ones and kissed them on their name days. She identified what it was that mattered most to people, and stored it in her mind. If the butcher was flattered by reference to his strength, she made reference to his strength. If the baker wanted to complain about his wife, she listened and nodded. And if the priest required women to be humble, she confessed her worthlessness once a week. People always needed clothes, so she made them. The Seamstress, they called her in the village, with something approaching reverence. She taught herself new techniques, challenged herself, picked apart garments to see how a thing was achieved before putting them back together again, often better. An uneducated woman, widowed at thirty and having lost all her children but one, she'd survived on the merits of mind, will and people skills.

Aristos checked his watch. Still a few minutes before his appointment.

But Darya—

He'd lost her. Perhaps she had spotted him, and run away. He remembered again their spat on the beach in Kos, the look in her eyes and the tremble in her voice that had never been there before. A woman possessed. And Jesus, it had angered him. All that he had given her, and for what? Nothing. How much can a person want? She had everything he worked for. Everyone else dismissed her as a gold-digger, especially Eva, then, but he'd always given her the benefit of the doubt. Because he knew when he first met her that there was something different there. Perhaps her own history, that Red blood beneath her pale skin. Strength was in her fibre. Her goals were humble, money not among them. He could take away the house, the possessions, the help – the absence of them would never make her search the garden in despair. None of it meant as much as that goddamned cat.

There she was. Standing in the doorway. She simply stood looking outside, this way and that.

What had he done? Forty years old she was, with the spirit of someone half that age and the restrictions of someone double it.

But she needed him. He needed her to.

She went across the street, to gaze into the dusty window of an antique shop. In it, the hallmarks of different people's differing homes. There were old irons, the kind he remembered his mother pressing over skirts, steam billowing beyond the candlelight. But there were also shepherds' crooks, which he'd never needed in his life. There were radios and televisions they couldn't afford until after his Army service, after '74. There was a portrait of Queen Elizabeth II, like the one a neighbour hung on her wall when the Brits patrolled in the days of EOKA. Patterned trays and coffee cups with logos he recognised from long ago. None of them would mean a thing to Darya.

She stood looking into a workshop next door. The elderly, olive-skinned artisan kept his focus on his moulds. He sat on a stool amongst effigies of limbs in wax; a hand, a foot, and what Aristos assumed was an elbow. Votives for church, in exchange for healing. Hanging to dry was a trio of half-formed babies. Embryos. Darya was staring at them.

With a feeling like missing a step, Aristos realised how close he'd got. Time to go, or he'd end up too far to make his appointment in time. He glanced back at his wife and felt a coldness take shape in his gut like a snowball.

Did his wife want a child?

If so, she would not get one from him. And if it wasn't his, it would be Orestis'. Or worse...

The thoughts tumbled around his head, all the way to his solicitor's office.

Four

The crackle of gunfire. Screams of agony, yells, instructions, stuttering breath and then relief. Beneath his boots, the red earth of the Northern territories, merging with the steps of the Central Library. Bodies strewn across the streets. Men without eyes, hanging out of open car doors. From a megaphone strapped to his truck, the nasal calls of a fruit seller. The statue of Archbishop Makarios, around his shoulders a cloak. No, not a cloak. A youthful corpse. Turkish eyes staring, getting closer. The mewling of cats gargling the air. Tangled together on the pavement, a tortoiseshell clash of fur slapping the blood with a myriad of paws. The young Turk's eyes drained to white. The sound of life escaping, emanating from Aristos' wrists, his hands thrust into the unknown flesh—

He clung to the sheets, struggled to catch his breath. Had he woken himself? It was something he'd been able to do once; to recognise he was in a dream and turn himself away from the worst of it. But no; from the window came the dying rev of a motorbike in the early light.

Darya lay beside him, still beneath the thumb of sleep. His wife, so detached from him now that his terror hadn't registered. What would his mother have made of this marriage?

Once awakened, there was little point in returning to sleep. Aristos got out of bed and went down to his study. From the bookcase, he picked a volume on the British Colonial years and set it on his desk. In the kitchen, as he brewed himself a coffee on the hob he heard the pat of bare feet on the marble. At the doorway stood Darya.

'You wake,' she said in Greek. Those tenses of hers.

'Sorry, my love. Did I wake you?'

She flicked her head up.

When she began walking towards him, he waited for her to put her arms around him, as she once would have. Instead, she went past him, to slide the doors open and sit in her spot in the garden.

* * *

It felt unreal to have no meetings to attend, no flights to catch. A new life. But he would not stay in the house, not with Darya's mood growing over it like fungus. He drove to Enaerio, where he picked up an ice-cream cone with gargantuan scoops of rose and mastic for a stroll along the seafront. This could be his daily existence now: an endless holiday, just an old man enjoying himself. All that money, and all that planning for it, would finally count towards the present rather than the future. It wouldn't be long before he died; the years had a way of sliding off out of one's reach. Live while you're alive.

He kept close to the eucalyptus trees, in case he should spot an acquaintance. People were swimming in the sea. Not as many as there once were. Cyprus' golden years were brief and gone. The dust of the civil war and the Turkish invasion had settled. The South had picked herself up, provided for her refugees, and raised her head to new prospects. First, the wealthy Arabs came, some of them refugees from their own wars. Then it was the wealthy Russians, after the collapse of a wall, of a whole system. And always there were English tourists, and Germans and whoever else sought the sun and sea.

Aristos had never been a fan of the English. Not solely because of the general feeling against them back in the village – so clever, their soldiers luring children to their jeeps with sweets; who would shoot at them then? – but because he thought them an arrogant tribe. They had conquered the world and broken it up, poured their language into the cracks. And yet they acted the heroes. They showed no remorse for their Empire, nor any knowledge that they'd been aided by allies in the Wars. They saw themselves above; as a goal for others to stretch for but never to reach. And now, it pained him to think that Cyprus needed them.

He would sell the Cyprus hotels, too. He had written them over to Eva in his will, but he would speak to her about it soon. All of a sudden he felt a rush: the urge to reach for something, hold onto something, go back to someplace. But how far back would he have to go for peace? To before '74, before the Army had recruited him to shoot at invading Turks? When they scrambled to the nearest crater, and huddled there because nobody would bomb the same place twice? To the protests, each of them pulsing with vigour and meaning? To the brief emancipation years, when the Brits were forced to let them go? To the years of EOKA, when Greek-speaking neighbours talked of rebels as if they were saints? To when he danced to Turkish songs at neighbours' weddings? To those days in school when boys talked with glowing eyes about the teacher?

To when he shared thick slabs of bread and cheese with the kids who had no shoes? To when he confused *phi* and *theta* in his alphabet?

Or he might go back to his first hotel, the promise of that time spreading out like a blanket. He might return to his daughter's birth if only the memories attached to it were good. Eva's mother was a person he'd rather forget. When they met as students in Athens, she had shown just one of her sides: the one full of life. The one who blazed with art and politics, and ambitions to open museums, heritage centres. But the birth of Eva had exposed her for what she was: a kept wife who expected her husband to do all the work. Who wished only to lie on the sofa, shop, eat, anything but what she'd been promising the world for years she would do. Her wit fomented to sarcasm, her beauty shrivelled to a permanent grimace. The more his businesses and status grew, the more she demanded, the more she sniped. Aristos had no patience for people who didn't help themselves. It was one thing to dream and another to wake up and go.

He'd been charmed by Darya's simplicity. Physically, she was a queen. But her dreams were small, her needs basic, stability her only request. A result of her upbringing, no doubt, the attitude he'd encountered in many Slavic people: be grateful for what you have. He would give her a life, and all she had to do was be there for him, at his side, grateful.

Aristos ordered a lot and ate large portions. He devoured books and information. His companies swallowed others. But when it came to sex, he had never had much of an appetite. In the Army, the men talked about their girlfriends and the things they had done to them. At school, the other boys laughed like donkeys at a dirty song about a Turk with huge breasts and,

276

weeks later, at a picture one had found in his father's desk. In these moments Aristos mimicked the expected behaviours. But in truth, women didn't interest him. He remembered the immense guilt he felt when his father had died, the relief. The man had pestered him, relentlessly, when he was soused. *Where's your girlfriend?* The zivania on his breath poking him, too. *When I was your age, I had dozens.* According to village gossip, he'd still had them. But Little Hippocrates contemplated everything other than girlfriends. When talk spread about the butcher and a young bricklayer, Aristos worried he himself might be homosexual. He felt the shame of it during confession, and the priest was stern. The years came and went, but he never felt a moment's desire for another man. He decided he was simply abnormal and would have to learn to hide it.

His first wife was a virgin when they married. In the lead-up to the wedding, he let her mind fill in his story. He'd tried sex one night with a prostitute, in a crumbling flat in the red-light district, but he hadn't enjoyed it. His friends in the other room were having much more fun with theirs. He tried it again with his wife because now he had a goal in mind: to father a child. From that point on, his wife assumed he had a mistress or two, and he let her believe it.

Darya had understood at once what he was. Perhaps because she was so in touch with her own desires, she could detect the absence of them in others. The miracle was that it didn't faze her. It was almost as if it was what she wanted; for someone to leave her alone.

He couldn't risk losing her. They were made for each other.

* * *

The power was out. They lay in bed, sheets pasted to their limbs. Perhaps it was a good thing. He would only have dreamt of death, as had become the norm in the past few weeks. Every couple of minutes, his wife's sighs would soar above the noise of crickets. She was unused to the Mediterranean heat, still. A pine in the desert. Yet she raised the heating in her car as if forever in the grip of a Siberian winter. Would she ever acclimatise to his country? He recalled her first experience of an earthquake, her confusion when the ground slid beneath her feet. It made him smile.

'We've got so used to the air conditioning,' he said into the dark.

Nothing.

'In the village, in the days before we had electric fans, we used to go outside when it was too hot. We'd go out and sleep under the stars.'

This time she made a noise; an acknowledgement but also, he was almost certain, a sound of pleasure.

A shift in the mattress, the sound of bedsprings and cotton. Her silhouette rose before the moonlit curtains and slid through the room, to the door, and out. He leapt out of bed and followed, a pain thumping in his chest.

He found her outside, by the pool. She lowered herself as if to sit by it, and that's when he realised his wife was naked. With the merest whisper of a splash, she slipped into the water. Her head came up again, hair like ink, like henna, on her skull. And she let a big breath out to the night. Was that a laugh? Relief?

He walked over to her, and she turned at the thud of his heavy steps. He couldn't make her face out, but the stiffness of her neck, her body, was that of an animal guarding its territory.

She stood still. Slowly, he removed his own underwear, and again he heard a sort of laugh. No, not a laugh. It was a mixture of disbelief and delight. He went to the steps and gingerly climbed into the pool.

She didn't come to him, and he let her keep a distance. For the next few minutes, they only bobbed in the water. Occasionally, she would dip her head below the surface and rise again, beautiful. Why not tell her so?

'Beautiful,' he said in Russian. It was one of the few words he knew.

He could've sworn she was smiling.

Five

He never replaced the maid. When he rang, the agency informed him that Mrs Ioannidou had beaten him to it, to say she no longer required their services. Stunned, he hung up. If this was what Darya wanted, why did he feel this flush of anger, this embarrassment? Let her clean the house then. Let her throw his kindness in his face. More money saved.

Truth be told, his wife seemed happier without the maid. She even sang to herself as she gathered freshly laundered clothes and sheets and pillowcases into her arms. She forewent the dryer entirely, choosing clothes-pegs outside. She washed the plates and forks by hand instead of using the dishwasher.

This was almost his mother's ghost toiling away at the sink, in that tiny house of many summers gone. He approached her, wrapped his arms around her, and rested his head on her shoulder. She flinched but stayed. She would have to be watched.

* * *

The temperature climbed. He suggested they rent a holiday

home in the mountains till the autumn. The freshness of the woods might appease his troubled wife. Not to mention she could put some distance between herself and her daily worries, whatever they could be. People always spoke of how curative the mountain air was, perhaps there was some truth to it. At the very least the serenity would calm a stormy head.

The treatment seemed to work. He'd found a cabin in Platres, in whose panelled rooms the sound of water was always close. Their neighbours were invisible. Nights were filled with the whistling of wind and the flapping of batwings. Darya's movements had begun to lose that recent edginess, which had made her walk as if stitched together limb by limb. Her scowl had almost vanished. She was smoking less, again.

'I'm so happy here,' he said, prompting her.

She said nothing back, but her expression was one of agreement.

At times he would find her staring at a corner of the living room, lost in the empty space. At other times a sadness would cloud her eyes, and he assumed she was thinking of that little white kitten. Let her have a stray if it would help her get over the other one. As long as it was here in the country house, where the fresh air would diffuse the smell. Yes – he should buy a house in the mountains. People with far less money had done so, why hadn't he?

She made dinner, stews with potatoes. Not exactly appropriate for the end of summer, but she devoured them. For the most part, they ate in silence, and he found himself longing for Orestis' company, his presence in the kitchen, the boy running his finger along those printed-out recipes with that furrowed brow that haunted his face. Who could've known those days would die so young? Aristos never spoke a word of this to Darya. It might annoy her. Then where would they be?

It had been weeks since they'd seen Orestis. As far as Aristos knew, Darya hadn't called on his services. Knowing him, the boy would be growing agitated. But there were other men for her and other prospects for Orestis. In many respects, Darya's loss of interest solved the problem of the boy's transition from wife's lover to daughter's suitor.

Orestis was likely to be his heir. Sometimes the thought came as a shock as if it was new. Aristos tried not to think about the two women sharing the one man. This was especially difficult where Eva was concerned, spoiled and sheltered and innocent as she was. But it wasn't as if they shared him in the same way, on the same level. Physical closeness and emotional connection were different states of being. One woman communicated with Orestis through his youth, the beauty of his flesh, while the other spoke to him in dialect, she communicated with words and gestures in shorthand. Eva was linked to him through a past, both personal and social, rooted in the geography and history of their motherland. It was why parents insisted their children marry within a community; the foundations of a relationship were already lain, not to mention the traditions that would never be negotiated, never bargained away. Other than him and Orestis, the women had no link to each other. It went without saying that many would be scandalised by the arrangement, and it would damage the Ioannidou reputation for generations to come if it was ever found out. But was it immoral? Of course not.

As if his peers were in any position to claim a moral high ground. How many stories had he heard during and since the island's rise from the ashes of war? So-called Christians praying for others' ruin so they might succeed. *God willing,* they would say of their future fortune, while docking the salaries of their employees or cutting corners in health and safety as if there were any other purveyor of fate than them. They called Russian women whores but had no qualms about ogling them in strip bars, or gave a thought to how the women got there in the first place. One of his own cousins had hired an Arab contractor for his garage extension, then called the police to report him as an illegal migrant.

If a young man was sharp enough to invest in his body and earn some extra income from hiring it out, then that was a sign of nous. And if Aristos earned a percentage of that through his mediating hotels, that was good business. After all, what was society, from business to friendships to sex to the Church to councils and town planning, but investment and reward, plus interest?

'I'm going to Munich next week,' Aristos told his wife between sips of stew.

She nodded.

'And I was thinking that perhaps we might go together sometime.'

'Again holiday?' she said, which made him laugh.

'Or maybe something more permanent...'

She didn't quite register that word.

'I don't know if I want to stay in Cyprus,' he explained. 'I like Germany, I like Germans. I think you feel the same...'

Over the course of his sentence, her eyes widened. She nodded, to show she'd understood, and a smile hovered around her mouth.

He'd caught her. She'd been about to leave. He knew it.

* * *

Aristos didn't speak with Orestis again until the wine festival. Thousands of people gathered in the park, around the
sculpture of the wine-grower. How many of the younger
generation had ever seen a man actually dressed like that,
with a waistcoat and vraka? Orestis and Eva walked around
the Municipal Garden hand-in-hand beneath the light bulbs
strung between the trees, their friend Paris with his hands in
his pockets at their side.

At first, the latter man was reticent and watched Aristos as
if assessing a predator. But as the evening wore on and the
plentiful booze filled their systems, the vegetarian poet began
to thaw and yelled his political commentary over the music
and song. Their Communist president alighted different fires
in each. Orestis looked concerned that they might come to
blows but Aristos was having a great time and even slapped
Paris on the back for a game well played. He'd missed that
ardour of youth; the belief that human nature had the capacity
for change. Together they toasted the future of Cyprus, with
wine from Ayia Mavri.

Aristos raised his voice over the noise. 'This is from my
village.' There was a pain in his heart after that, a pain that
didn't leave for the rest of the night.

The youths reminisced about the Zoo next door.

'Remember the lion cubs? What were they called—'

'The darlings! Of course, I do, I took photos with them like
a superstar.'

'Of course you did. You probably drugged them yourself.'

'God have mercy, Paris! Can't a little girl hold a lion cub
without wondering if the zookeeper doped it up?'

'As if it would've bothered you.'

'E, true. I'll probably wear them to your book launch.'

They talked about his poetry. Aristos was impressed, though the book was doomed to earn little.

At some point in the night, Eva asked her father about Darya.

It was the first time she had ever enquired after his wife and, if he wasn't mistaken, called her by her name. He was almost too surprised to reply. 'She's unwell, sadly.' And, seeing that the excuse had registered as lazy, he prepared to expand on it.

Eva cut him off: 'I noticed she doesn't drink.'

Aristos' shoulder seized. 'To be honest,' he said, 'she doesn't like to see drunkenness.' He recalled that gesture she'd made of her father drinking. 'There was a lot of it where she's from.'

Eva narrowed her eyes and lit her cigarette. He didn't know if he ought to be suspicious.

Orestis looked from father to daughter, seeking a moment to connect with Aristos.

'A!' said the older man. 'Toffee apples. I haven't had one in years. Who wants one?'

'No thanks,' Eva said in English, her preferred language to express disgust. 'It gets stuck to my teeth.'

Paris also passed on the offer.

Orestis accepted and followed him to the stand. Around them were men with bellies bulging under old T-shirts, faces red with drink and laughter. Children ran around, playing Catch among the tables and chairs. Some of them belted dialect with mighty lungs – *Provincials*, his first wife would've called them with a sneer.

Orestis laughed at what they overheard.

'What? Don't you like the Cypriot tongue?' Aristos asked with a smile.

'We learned proper Greek,' said the young man.

285

'It's in there somewhere, too.'

Aristos asked the vendor for two apples. Orestis put up his hands to decline.

'Eat it, son,' said Aristos. 'Drop the diet. As my grandma used to say, you don't want to die hungry.'

Orestis faded. 'How's Darya?'

No answer that would satisfy the gored bull. No answer full-stop. 'She does what she wants,' he said.

Orestis' eyes dropped to the ground. How beautiful he was, a different sort of man. The Ancients used to dazzle their opponents. They combed their hair before a battle, to be perfect physical specimens in glittering armour. They instilled the dread of awe in their enemy. Sex was a power. Nothing weakened a man more than an attack on his ego, his libido. Even the Church understood this; its promotion of a sexless existence wrestled guilt into subjugation. God for your impure thoughts, a perfect trade. Money, property, land for your place in Heaven. The boy had finally learned to use his beauty to his advantage, to look beyond himself. That evening in Mykonos, when they strolled past the clubs and bars full of gays, Orestis had absorbed the stares of others and projected their energy to make himself known, wanted, feared. Desire and intimidation were cousins. A man assumed to be well-endowed was a threat, an other male equipped to steal the lessor's property. That's why the stories persisted about Africans and Arabs. A potent assault force.

One of the boys in the barracks had earned himself the nickname Sterling. The others tried to joke about his gift from God, but humour was a thin mask. It was hard not to be entranced by his gift in the showers. Not that it had saved him once the Turkish bullets flew.

286

How far from the Ancients they had come, to remove even the beauty from war.

Orestis turned, looking caught. Someone called Aristos' name. He racked his brains to identify his neighbour Katina. He'd spent enough time with the woman so as not to require more of it but still failed to see the reason for Darya's hatred of her. Loosely attached to Katina was a teenaged daughter, who tapped on her phone and couldn't look less interested in what the adults were saying. To Aristos' surprise, the woman squinted and pointed at Orestis. 'You're the nephew.'

In an instant, Aristos understood. 'A! You've already met.'

'E,' said Katina. Then she turned to Aristos. 'I saw your wife the other day, in that music shop in Ayia Zoni. I was driving past and saw her from the window.'

'Music shop?'

'Yeah. I didn't know she could play the piano.'

'My Darya? She doesn't play.'

'God as my witness, it was her.' Off his baffled expression, the woman decided not to push the point. 'E, OK, maybe I didn't see right.'

'Or she has a twin,' said Orestis.

'God have mercy,' said Katina.

They bade her goodnight and walked back to the others. A man with a coffee-stained voice was crooning Hadjis, Aristos' favourite. He'd seen him at the Kourion back in the '90s, or was it '80s, with Marinella. The bittersweet melodies, the yearning guitar, none of it took his mind off what Katina had told him.

Her words stuck to him all through the drive back home. With every stop at a traffic light that gave him yet more space to think, he felt a growing resentment for his neighbour. What did she mean by claiming that his wife played music, that she was hiding something from him? Was she trying to make him a fool? Did Katina know the truth about Orestis and decided to tease them all? Darya didn't play the piano. Of course, she didn't.

She did. Of course, she did.

There was so much he didn't know about his own damned wife. He'd had her investigated before they got married, it was only logical. Her story of leaving Belarus after its liberation checked out, the details of her family, her father, her mother, her grandmother and a dead brother he never brought up because she never had – something he thought perfectly understandable till now. He knew she'd gone to Germany via Poland, and had discovered which ships she'd worked on before she'd landed the job at his hotel. Everything pointed to a person in search of a better life.

But this? That she was spotted doing things he had no clue she could do, not a damned clue, made his fingers clench. Did she hate him so much that she hid her truth? What else was she keeping from him? He had caught that look in her eyes when he mentioned a future in Germany. It was hope. Hope. As if she'd been drugged and caged like those lion cubs. As if he was such a dictator that she couldn't wait to defect. She was on the brink of it, he was certain. Ran, that's what she did, that's what the details of her past revealed. And how else would she have left Belarus, if not with a man? No prior marriage had turned up, but who was to say what she'd done to get out of the Eastern bloc, what she'd done to cross those borders, how far she would go to betray him by leaving him too? The next time a traffic light stopped him on the seafront, the questions that burned him erupted from his hands, thumped against the steering wheel. He beat the BMW, making his horn blow loud, making a passing tourist jump.

The lights of fast-food restaurants and English pubs, karaoke bars, buzzed in his eyes, the club music thudding in his bones.

Whore, he thought of his wife. *Whore.*

Six

His voice echoed in the hall. He tried again. Nothing. She'd done it already. Left. The damned woman hadn't even waited till the promised Munich.

That little shrine of hers was still in the corner. He ought to tear it down, rip that red-and-white fabric in two. He went upstairs, hoping to find her in bed with another man.

The room was dark. His wife was indeed in bed, but only with Hypnos – no doubt escaping her husband in sleep.

* * *

Sipping her tropical smoothie in the early-morning light, she looked maddeningly content. The rain prevented her from sitting outside, so she sat at the kitchen table and stared into space as if in meditation.

'You are free today?'

It had been a while since she'd posed a question first.

'I have to see my solicitor. Other than that, yes.'

She nodded.

'You?' They both knew what he meant by that.

'I see Skevi later,' she said.

'Skevi?'

'Yoga teacher. She does for me reiki.'

He lowered his coffee cup harder than intended, the clink almost shattered it. 'Reiki? Please don't tell me you're paying for such a thing.'

She turned her head to stare, all contentment gone. 'Why not?'

'What the hell is reiki going to do?'

'Feel good.'

'You feel bad?'

She didn't answer. She'd already said more than she'd meant to.

'You feel bad?'

'I want to feel good.'

She'd used the feminine for 'good' as if she meant to be a good woman. He smiled. 'You know what will make you feel good...'

Her eyes lit up. 'No.'

'Call Orestis. Or Lefteris, anyone you want. Don't waste my money on nonsense.'

'No more boys.'

'Darya, what do you want? What is it that you want?'

What she wanted, and she made it clear, was not to look at him. Her neck was tense, fingers tight around the still-full glass.

'Do you want a child? Is that why you're being like this?'

She rolled her eyes.

He couldn't help himself. It burst from him in a voice he barely recognised, one he hadn't used since the breakdown of his prior marriage: 'Darya, do you play the piano?'

At first, she looked afraid. Then incredulous. Finally, a hopeless misery crawled over her features. Something inside her had snapped. Not in a violent, mad way, not like a fresh twig; it was more like old rope, the fibres detaching, letting go to unravel the whole. In a quiet voice, she said, 'I want to go away.'

At last, there it was.

'You want to leave me.' They both heard his tremble. 'You want to go home?'

She flicked her head up. 'We still go Germany?'

'Is that what you really want?' His hand reached for hers.

After a pause, she said, 'Yes.'

'Then that's what we'll do. Just give me some time to settle things here.'

Her head, almost as if despite the rest of her body, swung slightly towards him, lowered. An affectionate cat. He put his hand on the back of her neck and leaned forward to kiss her forehead. The action left the taste of sweat on his lip, and the froth of her smoothie on his shirt.

Let her believe they were going if it meant a peaceful home. In the meantime, he'd come up with another plan.

* * *

He let her go to her reiki, whatever kept her quiet. He had no problem with yoga and meditation, their physical and mental effects were proven. He'd even dabbled in the latter, having learned from an older friend who'd travelled to the East, but it had been years since he'd last done it. Massages and treatments were of equal benefit if outrageously priced — not that Darya much indulged in them. But reiki? It was invisible as ghosts, as lacking in fact. She might as well have paid a shaman.

'Christ,' he said to the windscreen.

His wife out of the house, his solicitor dealt with, his conference calls made, he dropped in on the Harmonia. Orestis had mentioned he'd be working that weekend, so Aristos called ahead to arrange a meeting between the managers. Svetlana beamed at him from the front desk, and within minutes a thick Cypriot coffee had been fetched for him in the meeting room where the other men sat waiting. Over the next hour, they discussed individual achievements, team adjustments, objectives and timeframes, schedules, and set a date at the end of October for handovers, and the official start of Thanos' new role. Aristos noted that Yiorgos was looking sullen.

'What is it?' he asked.

'Nothing,' said Yiorgos. And he couldn't help but flick his eyes at Orestis, fresh in a crisp white shirt. The look Aristos gave Yiorgos drew the meeting to a close.

The owner was escorted to the lift and went in first.

'The mirror's looking old,' he said. 'There's a crack in the top-left corner.'

Thanos whipped out his notebook. On the ground floor, Aristos dismissed the others, telling Yiorgos there was an urgent matter he wished to discuss with Orestis. That served the dual purpose of putting the Front Desk manager in his place, and Orestis on edge.

'Let's walk to the beach.'

The young man threw a glance at his former manager, then promptly back at their superior. He followed.

They walked past the pool, past the bar at its edge, the showers and the ping-pong tables. Aristos took his time. When they approached the stone path through the trees to the sand, he said, 'You can feel the weather changing.'

'The water's good,' Orestis said. 'I come for a swim on my breaks.' He was standing with his hands behind his back. Clothes tight against his body, head high, he could have been holding a spear, or a plumed helmet made of bronze.

Aristos smiled. 'My old boss used to swim every morning before work. It's good discipline.'

'Has something happened to Darya?'

'This doesn't concern her. In fact, it's about Eva.'

The boy was unable to mask his feelings.

'You may think that, when Eva approached me about a job for you, I was doing her a favour. To tell you the truth, it was she who was doing me the favour.'

A punch would have shocked him less. Nevertheless, the boy shook his head as if reeling from a physical blow. 'I don't know what to say.'

Poor lad. When had that yokel father last paid him a compliment? 'I mean it. I remembered how presentable and polite you always were. I was happy to have such a person working in my hotel.' He allowed a moment. 'Also, it was a pleasure to spend more time with you lately. To get to know you better.'

At this Orestis shifted a little. A smile straddled his face, not knowing where to land. 'Likewise,' he said.

'You have also been a good friend to my daughter. I know she's not the easiest person to deal with, but she's always been fond of you, and I'm pleased to see you've been getting closer.'

'If it's upsetting Darya—'

'Forget Darya.' It was louder than he'd meant. 'She's satisfied.'

Orestis swallowed.

'Eva feels strongly about you. I know she does. And what a father wants most in the world is for his child to be happy.'

The young man nodded, as he was supposed to.

'It would make me happy, too, to welcome you into our family.'

'Sir—'

'Think about it, Orestis. A man like you, looking after my Eva, responsible, handsome, sturdy. By marrying her, you will have everything. You will have money, a house, a new car, whatever I can't currently give you. And one day, you'll even have the Harmonia. You won't have to answer to your old man anymore, you won't have anything to worry about. And you will be loved. Not just by my daughter, but by me, too. You have my word – I would be proud to call you my son.'

Silence. The boy turned to face the sea as if an answer was waiting there. 'Thank you, sir.'

Aristos placed his hand on the young man's back. 'I know it's a lot to take in. I'm sorry to have surprised you like this, but at my age, I have to think not only of my own future but also my daughter's. My family's.'

At length, Orestis responded. 'I understand.'

'Good. And don't worry – Eva will never find out about you and Darya. You won't say anything, Darya won't say anything, and I... I keep the photos locked away.'

For a moment, Orestis looked baffled. His reaction came slowly: the face went white, the pupils shrank as if something had been emptied from him. Then another face appeared: a demon, within that perfect head. Aristos had only ever been struck by one man: his father. Nobody else had dared. He steeled himself.

But Orestis' fury faded. He looked down at the ground.

'Think about it,' Aristos said. 'When you're ready to propose to my daughter, you have my blessing.'

Keeping his gait unhurried, he walked back up the stone path. Then, remembering, he turned.

'Tell Yiorgos that I found out you were dating my daughter, and that's why I wanted to speak with you. I gave you a stern warning about treating her well. You don't have to say anything more.'

This was a good excuse. It would assuage the Front Desk manager, who would have felt diminished; it would relieve Orestis of coming up with a suitable lie; and lastly, it would plant in the staff the knowledge that Aristos was firm but fair, a boss who had had no personal reason for an employee's progress. All was in order.

Seven

On Sunday, Darya got up early to don a smart skirt, blouse and navy jacket. She sprayed herself with Yves Saint Laurent. When he asked her where she was going dressed like that she said, without a moment's hesitation, 'Church.' As if this was a weekly occurrence. She didn't even give him the time to question her. Her back was turned, the Lexus reversed out of the driveway before he could even blink.

Dumbstruck, he went to his study to stew, and pinch the bridge of his nose while he sat at his desk. He tried to read a passage from his latest purchase, a book about the invention of the Phoenicians, but struggled to concentrate. Damn that woman. He'd vowed never to let anyone affect him.

He would go for a drive. Perhaps to Amathous, or the Kourion, the Tombs of the Kings, somewhere with ruins where he could sit and contemplate the infinite stretch of time, the long reach of the ancients, the proof of legacy. On the highway, however, came an intervention. The soft-voiced DJ in the speakers was taking his listeners on a journey through the rebetika. Those decades-old songs of loss and longing spoke through the static. Giorgos Vidalis, Marika Papagika, Markos Vamvakaris, a haunting of voices. Crime, prostitution, drugs;

the lyrics painted portraits of people as they really were, the things that made and unmade them, in places as distant in the memory as Constantinople, Smyrna. To think that these voices were ever censored or silenced. That was the real crime: when humanity was hidden from humans if it was regarded as dirty rather than true.

Aristos found himself singing along to the songs, the words came readily. They took him back to the village, where his elders had sung with smoke-filled throats. He ignored the signs to the Kourion and turned off from Erimi towards Kilani. His ears clogged as the road steepened. He swallowed to make them pop.

In the village, he parked at the most central spot he could find. He couldn't even remember the last time he'd come. A construction job in Lemesos had carried him away from it, and he'd moved his mother into a care home as soon as her dementia was diagnosed. She'd referred to the village on every visit, even on her bad days. *I want to go home*, she'd beg, as the woman in the next room relived her son's funeral, wailing, pulling out her hair. How could he ever have left his mother there? At the time he'd convinced himself the staff would give her what he could not. But what thanks was that? In the end, what had he given the woman in return for all she had given him?

He went into a newly-refurbished café, once a house, if only he could remember whose, where the proprietors were total strangers. He ordered a soumada, and the almond heat filled his throat till at last his ears popped.

'Excuse me,' he said to the couple behind the counter. 'I wonder if you remember my family.' He gave his father's surname. It sent a shiver up his arms to hear it aloud after all this time.

The couple explained they'd only recently moved to the village, the café a retirement whim. Most of the inhabitants had left for the cities years before. But they directed him to the little square across the road, where an old man in a starched blue shirt sat in the shade of vines playing backgammon with a round bearded youth.

'Of course,' the old man said when asked about Aristos' mother. 'Of course, I remember her.' His face was alight, the near-blind eyes almost blue. 'The Seamstress.'

It was clear he didn't recognise Aristos, nor did he ask his name. Instead, he pointed to a corner and gave instructions to The Seamstress' place. Aristos thanked him anyway and set off.

Good God.

It was small, so much smaller than he remembered. The stone abode, with that low roof of corrugated iron, no more than a shack. Tears stung his eyes, so he didn't look for long. What pained him most was not the thought of his poor widowed mother, stunted in what should have been the prime of her life, mending clothes and praying every day to forgive the gambling, womanising, drunken ways of her departed husband. It was the thought that if he took Darya out of their house in Kaloyiri and brought her to this pile of rocks in Kilani, she might even be happy.

He had been so hard on his wife. But that was only to keep her.

He could dissuade her from going to Germany. After all, she'd been calmer in that holiday house in Platres. She might accept Kilani instead. She might see that she had more in common with her husband than not. She would feel less apart.

He walked on. He went past that house with the brightly coloured wooden door and shutters, which had always been brightly coloured. The family in it owned the first television he'd ever seen. For half an hour a day, they would let the other villagers watch from the open window. *I Love Lucy.* He remembered the show, the protagonist's elastic face. He could almost see it through the shutters now.

He walked past his teacher's house, the woman who'd aroused his pubescent classmates. A Greek flag hung outside it now and, though not as obnoxious and provocative as the Turkish flag painted on the Kerynia mountains, it offended him. He'd never had time for nationalists. To be proud of achievements attributed to a whole group? Where was the self-worth in that? Why take pride in what was only yours in the abstract? Nationalism attracted people who in some way had failed to make their own mark; who had the need of living vicariously through the successes of a larger entity. As if Cypriots were only either Greek or Turkish, Christian or Muslim. This was a tiny rock between Europe, Asia and Africa. It wasn't only Greeks and Ottomans who'd come here, it was also Francs, Venetians, Armenians, Kurds, Turks, Syrians, Brits, Roma... Now the Russian businessmen, the Chinese families, the imported maids from all around. Catholics and Jews and Jehovah's Witnesses held tight among the Orthodox Christians. The priest in this very village – God rest his soul – read both the Bible and the Quran. Cypriot was a blend of every tongue that ever talked here. He'd even read of a Maronite community in the North, whose dialect was a composite of Latin and Aramaic. To diminish such a wealth, such a broad and varied heritage to narrow-minded flag-waving was near enough to blasphemy. How dare anyone break it into pieces.

He wanted to go further. No, not only further. Deeper. He wanted to extend his arms and reach back through the vines of time, to the fields where shepherds herded their flocks, where women with coloured beads and headscarves ferried dough into stone ovens, to makeshift Orthodox churches hidden in caves from the Ottomans, and further back, to Richard the Lionheart and Berengaria, further, to traders from distant lands mingling on the docks, to philosophers and the dawning of the Greek alphabet, to Chirokitia, to the beginnings of European civilisation, to Aphrodite stepping out of the sea.

'Good afternoon.'

Aristos turned to find a man slightly older than him, perhaps not quite as tall, definitely thinner, dressed in camouflage trousers and a black jumper. Next to him huffed the donkey he led up a slope.

'Good afternoon,' Aristos said back.

'Are you from Lemesos?'

On closer inspection, the man's stubble was patchy, the hairs greying, his eyes crusted with sleep. But there was also a child's curiosity there.

'Yes,' he said. 'But I used to live here.'

'You went to Lemesos?'

'Ou, it's been years now.'

The donkey's ears twitched. A couple of flies were circling its head, which the man tried to waft away.

'May I...?' said Aristos, raising his hand, and the man indicated yes. For the first time in years, Aristos felt the hide of a donkey. The touch brought back neighbours, the crowing of cockerels, the scent of warm bread from the ovens. Perhaps it was the animal's face, that hopeless air of drudgery in every donkey – whatever the reason, he felt a deep longing. Darya riding her way up Santorini. Eva's words about a creature's use.

'Do they have Cadbury's in Lemesos?'

Aristos laughed. But almost at once, off the man's expression, felt remorse. He smiled what he hoped was a gentle smile. 'Of course. Surely you have it here.'

The man made a face that said either *No* or *Not enough.* 'Will you bring me some when you next come back?'

'I promise.'

'Only Cadbury's, though.'

Those British soldiers patrolling in their jeeps; handing out chocolates, coaxing the local children to be their shields; they'd done their job.

* * *

Across from a restaurant leaning over the wooded hillside, where a trio of men sat with cups of coffee, smoking, and sipping at glasses of water, stood the church. His grandma had told him stories of the eponymous saint, Ayia Mavri. So many versions of a single person's life, none of them likely to be true. Yet for some, they still were, as real as the gods and Jesus and Christmas goblins. Aristos went to the side, where the building grew out of the hill and the plane tree. Water ran from a spring beneath the chapel. He had to duck to step through the entrance.

In the dim light of candles, he made out the beautiful gates, hand-painted saints in gold leaf. His eyes travelled upwards, to the walls, the ceiling, where Christians hundreds of years ago had made their frescoes; a dark sky of martyrs watching from above. At his size, Aristos should have felt oppressed by this tiny space, but he felt embraced. All that love, that devotion unique to religious art, coddled him in its womb. Here he was, a logical, atheist Christian. He never wore a cross, so as not to draw overt lines between himself and a foreign associate. He never prayed, and only went to church for the fireworks at Easter. He baulked to hear of countrymen leaving their land and money to the Church. He almost spat at St Raphael, the Church-owned hotel resort. Who accepted such a thing? But he did believe in God. There had to be someone in charge of this. And that someone would choose to reward or punish him in the end. There was a small wooden table covered in red cloth, processional crosses glinting from it. Another table bore an icon of Ayia Mavri herself. Next to it stood a small wax head, a votive for a sick child perhaps. That head could be Darya's. It could be his.

He spent half an hour beneath the plane tree where Pantelis' taverna used to be. The memories came, wave upon wave. That villager with the donkey, who'd asked about chocolate, was like Melis, the son of a local carpenter. In retrospect, Melis must have lacked oxygen when he was born. His mother had died from the birth, leaving behind a child with impaired abilities to speak, move, perhaps even to think, who could say? Aristos was not like the other boys. He did not taunt Melis, did not call him names like Sleepy or Dopey or kick him and flee as the others did. His mother had raised him to be kind. Otherwise, God would rage, you'd be denied your place in Heaven.

But Aristos learned that compassion could attract more earthbound rewards. Melis' father, Dionysos, nodded friendly greetings at the teenaged Aristos though he scowled at other boys. Aristos took his kindness – which so far consisted, paradoxically, of doing nothing – further. He sought out Melis to engage him in one-sided chitchat. The boy began to look for him too and smiled with a mouth open wide when he found him. This kindness was hard for Aristos. He had no tolerance for people's failings and an impatience with anyone who couldn't keep up. He felt sick at the drool and snot that came out of Melis. The boy hadn't deserved to be bullied, but did he deserve Aristos' time and effort? Dionysos was so grateful that he'd give Aristos a bag of oranges from his grove, to his mother's glee, and sing his praises to everyone. It was easy, therefore, to ask the man for a job in his workshop. And in time, for a pay rise. Dionysos taught him skills that would prove to be invaluable. They would take him out of the village, enable him to get by in the city. That first job had led to other jobs, then to better jobs. Without any knowledge of his role, Melis had lain the foundations for Aristos to provide for his family and, ultimately, for himself.

He didn't even know if Melis was alive or dead. And if he saw him now, would his mouth open wide with joy?

Eight

Orestis had proposed to Eva. Aristos answered the phone expecting ear-bursting excitement, but the voice that greeted him was sedate. 'Did you pressure him?' Eva said instead of *Hello*.

'I only told him it would make me happy to see you married.'

'Right. Like a rifle to his head.'

He knew then that for the rest of her life, his daughter would wonder if her husband truly loved her. He assured her they were a perfect match, that he had believed so for a while. She had even known it herself, back when they were children.

'The only child who ever knew what was good for him was you,' she said.

Then she thanked her father and hung up.

The engagement couldn't have come at a better time. Orestis had requested to speak to him privately on one of his visits, and in the boardroom, he confessed as if to a priest: all the cash he'd received from Darya in those early days, he'd been keeping in the box of an old games console. His old man had discovered it while clearing out the house, looking for things to dump or sell at the car boot sale. Kostas had raged, yelling the house down about his son's mendacity. What had he been doing? Selling drugs with his cousin, the hash addict? Stealing

THE WAY IT BREAKS

purses at the tourist bars? Here he was, an honest man trying
to scrape by and pay back loans and remortgage his business,
while his son was stashing away euro like a politician with
a Swiss bank account. In a panic, Orestis had blurted to his
father that the money was meant for an engagement ring: he
would be asking Eva Ioannidou to marry him.

The mood shifted. Kostas slapped him on the back, kissed
him on both cheeks. Aristos bristled at the thought of this
peasant being linked to Orestis. The idea that those genes
would live on in his future grandchildren... He hoped Melina
had actually cheated on him; that there was a better man in
Orestis' DNA.

'Bravo, my son,' he said, shaking Orestis' hand and patting
his back.

That bashful, dimpled smile.

Eva would be fine.

Dismissing the boy to his duties, Aristos thought of that
money, money from his own wallet, sitting in an old box only
to return – even indirectly – to him in the form of a ring. A
circular economy indeed.

When he broke the news to Darya, he did it casually. It was
better that she found out soon, and the less fuss the better. She
simply nodded, the sunlight dimming in the window behind
her. Nothing mattered. This was the way she was of late,
taking everything in her stride. She had been doing her yoga,
her meditation, even that reiki nonsense. But if this was its
effect, then who was to say if it was good or bad, when a
man could not even tell what his wife was feeling or thinking
anymore? She had become stricter with her diet, a full-time
vegetarian. When he took her to a taverna, she even refused
the octopus. He asked her what good it did to deny yourself

pleasure. She replied, 'I am not the only life.'

* * *

A date had been set for the wedding, the end of September on the following year. The perfect time, according to Eva, who didn't want to sweat through a fabric meringue, or shiver when she whipped it off to dance. In the meantime, preparations for the engagement party were underway. The Harmonia's Events team took care of everything, with special attention now that their client was Mr Ioannidou himself. As far as Aristos could tell from reports, Orestis' colleagues appeared to be happy for him. He had stepped up to the position of manager and was handling himself as well as expected, with Thanos and Yiorgos on hand for support. Whereas Yiorgos frightened the employees who didn't catch his humour, Orestis adapted himself to each person. He was palatable, popular. But his standards remained high.

Though Eva occasionally asked after Darya, his wife showed no interest in anyone. Aristos found others' perception of her increasingly hard to manage. Her behaviour must not reflect badly on him. He readied himself to be strict if she refused to attend the engagement party but, to his surprise, she was willing to go. She wore a patterned dress that Eva instantly recognised, it was one she'd picked out for her in Rhodos. The women spoke only for a moment, but he saw Eva lean in to whisper in Darya's ear.

'Bravo,' his first wife said to him at the buffet table. 'She's like a statue. Galatea.'

It didn't matter, he let it go. 'You look beautiful,' he said in response. Because here, in this exquisite hall full of food

307

and friends and music, where their daughter was celebrating her union with a man in a million, he could bat away his first wife's arrows as if they were flies. He could even feel sorry for her. Especially now, as she watched her daughter with the evil stepmother, trying to calculate who was hurting her more.

In a corner of the room, standing by himself, was Lefteris.

Mastering his breath, Aristos went up to him. He put his face so close that he could see the flecks of bronze in those liquid green irises. 'This isn't the time or place for your business.'

Lefteris smiled, his arrogance firmly rooted. 'I'm here as a friend of your son-in-law's,' he said.

'He invited you?'

'Relax, my friend. I don't know why you're annoyed to see me. Don't forget I'm the one who brought him to you.'

'By accident. I've known him since he was a child.'

'You knew what you could make of him. Not who he actually is.'

Aristos left him standing there. He made his way to the doors, where Eva tried to intercept him. She begged him to come to the dance floor, the bouzouki was about to start. But he excused himself, saying he'd be back in a moment, and left the room to get some air.

In the car home, he turned his head at every red light to check on his wife, who gazed out of the passenger window. She had behaved well. People had complimented her and received a reply in decent Greek. Though Orestis had spent the evening trying to catch her in the crowds, she had kept her contact with him to a single moment. Shaking his hand, she'd said, 'Congratulations.' He'd asked her how to say it in Belarusian, but she'd only smiled, looking down.

'What did Eva whisper to you?' he asked.

She looked dazed.

'Eva. She whispered something in your ear.'

It took her a few seconds, but his wife did reply. 'Nothing,' she said. 'I could not hear.'

Nine

The sale of the Munich hotel went through. A collar released from his neck. Dubai would be next, though it would be painful to lose his biggest money-earner. He wondered if he should do it at all, especially now that his daughter was getting married. But it wasn't as if he'd be leaving her nothing. Eva had shown minimum interest in the businesses and, provided she didn't shop it all away, the proceeds from the sales alone would provide for several generations of Ioannidous. Between them, Thanos, Orestis and the other managers would take care of the Harmonia and the smaller hotels. The villas in Paphos would see to them themselves.

His money was safe, locked away in a foreign bank. *Switzerland*, a friend in finance had said to him. *The interest is good. And now with this atheist Communist for president, who knows what will happen to your money here?*

Despite himself, Aristos had harboured some hope in the election of a left-wing president. Almost every Greek-Cypriot politician had promised to find a solution to the Problem, to negotiate a reunification of this blood-stained isle. This time might be it. As the years since '74, and Aristos' life, passed, reunification stayed stubbornly trembling, a near flatline.

He'd even considered voting for that UN proposal a few years before if only to see the thing done at last. But how could he cross the box to breaches in human rights and international law; a freeze on freedom of movement; the presence of Greek and Turkish military on a land still shaken from the violence of both? The episode felt like subterfuge, a clearing of Turkey's path to the EU, with no regard for Cypriots' best interests – whether so-called Turks or Greeks.

Just a year before the Anan plan, the borders between the free South and occupied North had been opened. Where once the Turks shot anyone who so much as hunted snails in an occupied field, now, at last, the people could return to their former towns and villages. They wept, seeing childhood homes again. They laughed, reunited with Turkish-speaking neighbours. A seed had been planted. The olive branches promised by the flag were beginning to grow.

He cancelled an appointment in Paphos to go for a drive to the opposite end of the island; to Cape Greco, a place he hadn't been to since Eva was a child. This time he asked Darya if she wanted to come. Her expression cleared, like sunlight poking through the clouds. She was on the brink of saying *Yes*, he was sure of it. But then something changed. She hesitated.

'Fine,' he'd snapped, and set off alone.

Now he regretted it and wished he'd waited for her to agree. Perhaps she still would have.

On the way, he stopped by his first hotel. A mere pebble compared to the jewel in his crown a few hundred metres along the avenue, yet it still gave him joy to see.

He turned off for the highway. The road spread open before him, he pressed on the accelerator. He didn't care. Let the cameras snap him, he could afford the slap on the wrist.

Houses on hills looking down at the sea, apartment blocks and holiday flats, so many buildings he'd helped to construct. He passed the naval base at Mari, where friends of his had been stationed. He passed signs for Larnaka, Lefkosia and the British bases, that appalling Turkish flag on the mountainside, and before long he was driving through Ayia Napa, what used to be a village, a smattering of watermelon farms. Now it was a clubber's paradise, crawling with youths so drunk and high they barely knew what country they were in. Then there was the waterpark, which Eva had begged him to take her to one summer. Ten or eleven years old she'd been, plodding along in her tight pink swimsuit with the silly frills, and the attendant at the slide assessing her as if she was an elephant trying to fit through a straw. He should have chastised that boy. He should have hugged his daughter. What he wouldn't give to see her at that age again, her soft unpainted cheeks and big brown eyes.

He drove along the beachfront, in this season a near wasteland of bars and restaurants waiting for party-loving tourists. Nightclubs on a long siesta.

At last, he arrived. The sky was blank as paper and the sea was a blue that roared. The cape filled the horizon. Rocks scattered along down to the water's edge, sometimes wrinkled, sometimes cracked, like blackened petrified sponge.

He'd forgotten to lock the BMW. The keys were still inside, probably still in the ignition.

It didn't matter. Almost no one else was here, and the few bodies that were, were equally dazzled, equally buoyed by the air of the sea, and the immaculate turquoise where the shore rose to meet it. He was carried along to a small white chapel, where stray cats gathered around a water fountain.

Little bowls of food had been left for them.

He ought to take one home. That would be the perfect bridge to his wife now, why hadn't he done it already? Why did he always feel such a need to keep her down?

Why did he feel the need to own things? Now, here, he wanted this place to be his. He wanted to grab it and keep it inside him. It was the nomad's need for adventure, for experience at the same time as settlement, as stability. People wanted land so they could feel the existence of home, a patch of Earth to belong to them and them to it. But they were doomed to roaming, no single existence perfect.

He carried on, stepping carefully over rocks to sit close to the sea. This raw patch of Earth, it existed regardless of anything or anyone but itself. It was rocks affected by water, water affected by rocks. A clash of chemicals, of pure being and being in the presence of nothing, beholden to no-one. It was a landscape without a calendar, without a clock, without currency, without nationality, without arbitrary walls. Even the sea, that enormous force with a trillion lives inside it, sliced into separate territories on maps. Here it simply was and lived regardless. Here you could almost believe in the gods, the dawn of everything. Ananke and Chronos, intertwined as a serpents around the egg of creation, breaking it, and out came land, sky and sea. Produce or progeny, all emerged from the twinning of desire and compulsion over time, the knowledge of transience. And then there were Ananke's daughters: Clotho, Lachesis, Atropos. One spinning the thread of your life, the other measuring it, the last cutting it off.

The words on Kazantzakis' grave came back to him. He felt them in his body, expelled in a breath across the world:

I hope for nothing

I fear nothing

I am free

Freedom. That old obsession. Of his, of his country's. But freedom shifted from grasp to grasp. One man's freedom might depend on another's capture. Money was a release for some, oppression for others. Freedom could be control or release, the tourist's discarded bikini or the woman's burqa. America's flag waved over a bombed Baghdad. A man with the right to vote, voting for dictators. It was the thing everyone wanted but no-one granted. Its acquisition meant its theft. When did you have it, and if you had it did you know it? Was that what you'd call it? The acceptance of things as they were, that was the road to happiness. But was acceptance a freedom or was it willing enslavement? God – no, not God; the gods, the many – decided your griefs but you were the one who led yourself to or away from them. *Freedom or death.* The refrain of Greek independence expressed in the very flag. He learned it at school. Freedom or death, in stripes of blue and white. A cross in the corner, God always watching.

Hope for nothing.

Fear nothing.

Be free.

IV

One

If Darya answered the door, everything would be all right. It circled Orestis' head as he took the turning for Kaloyiri. The last time he'd driven here, it was in his dented little Honda.

The engagement had already borne previews of his life to come. One of the first things Eva had done was to take him shopping for a new car. 'Finally,' she'd said. 'It's within my rights to express an opinion on this tin can. Even Mr Bean would spit on it.' Orestis had protested, but not with much force; she swept him along to the nearest showroom. What would his old man say to see him turn up in a BMW, a car he wouldn't be allowed to service? By the time the new convertible was ready to collect – 'Why collect? They deliver to you.' – Orestis had decided he no longer cared what his father said or thought or wanted from him. He was a Ioannidou now, in spirit if not in name.

His fiancée had also taken him clothes shopping, once again in preparation for a new job. This time she'd purchased more than work trousers and the smart black shoes to go beneath them. She'd added chinos, shorts, sweaters and sunglasses to the basket on his arm, Valentino, Dolce & Gabbana, whatever he'd liked, whatever had made him look good, and she'd charged it all to her credit card.

One thing, however, was still off the table. Though she would sometimes let him touch her in places no one else had seen, Eva was still a virgin. It was idiotic – she said it herself, she knew it was idiotic – to hold on to archaic traditions. Yes, she believed in God but her God wasn't one to vilify female pleasure. She had her reasons for celibacy, and they were unshakable. Orestis would simply have to put his libido on hold.

How could he? The past few months had been the most physically gratifying of his life. What even was a life without stimulation? After introducing him to Darya, Lefteris would invite him over to his place, a villa close to the Amathous ruins. He took Orestis on boat rides, where they would lie on the deck, eating grapes and melon, and smoke nargile. Cigarettes turned his stomach, but the apple tobacco made him dizzy in a way that felt like an orgasm. Lefteris would also bring women on board, clients, and on occasion men. If it was their preference, he would service them while Orestis watched, or service Orestis while they watched. One time he'd asked Orestis to take part in mutual masturbation for a kinky American on the Internet. Orestis had almost accepted, but the thought of his image travelling abroad, being downloaded, then possibly uploaded onto porn sites, gave him pause. Lefteris had found someone else. 'You should think about porn, though,' he'd said. 'You'd make a lot of money from it.' But even this side-gig had been too much of a risk. To his credit, Lefteris had understood, and been careful to match him to clients with no link to the hotel.

If Eva thought he would wait another year for sex, then she'd be disappointed. Orestis was a man, one at his peak. At first, he'd tried to put it out of his mind, out of respect and affection. Some nights he still went out with Paris to a café, and Eva was content to leave them alone while she went clubbing with her shallow friends. Paris would spark a conversation with a pretty barista, and the girl would be charmed at first. But then she'd catch sight of Orestis, and Paris would step aside with a look on his face that was best ignored. If the girl didn't have a place of her own they would end up fucking in his bright new car. It gave him a sense of power, to lure the ones with diamonds in their eyes with a flash of his keys at the bar. It was out of the question to take the car to the beach, the salty air would scrub away its veneer, so he'd drive to the spot under the bridge by the old Lunar Park where his mum used to treat him to the Ferris wheel. But after these easy lays he was always, for a fleeting moment, surprised that the girl would call it a night.

He hadn't heard from Darya since the cruise. To begin with, he felt guilty, then neglected. He had let her down. She no longer desired him. In bed, that conversation in his cabin came back to him; the mourning in her voice as she spoke of her brother's death, her anger at the waste of life. That was the last time she had called on him.

Had he not been enough in her time of need? She had come to him, not for sex but compassion. He'd listened, he was sure he had listened. But the more he thought about that night, the more he heard a useless wanker, saying nothing of any help. She may as well have confessed to the linen.

He'd been lucky to land Darya: a beautiful, thoughtful stranger whose company he enjoyed. Lefteris had regaled him with many a tale of clients with freakish fantasies, fetishes that made him queasy. But with Darya, he'd felt a connection. They could be more than lovers, maybe even more than

319

friends.

He had to see her. She had to speak to him again.

The car rolled up to the familiar neighbourhood, up to the side of that garden wall which had made his hands shake on that first day. If that neighbour were to spot him now, she might not even recognise him.

He made his way up to the front door and counted to twenty before ringing the bell. A van made a three-point turn in the street. If it completed the manoeuvre before the door opened—

Darya. From the change in her expression, she hadn't even thought to check through the peephole. And he had registered her look: one of unwelcome surprise, after what had been serenity.

But the surprise faded into something else. It became disbelief, then tenderness.

He stood silent, the ability to speak leaving him entirely as her eyes filled with tears. She turned her head away. She was shutting the door.

'Please,' he said. 'Darya. Please.'

She only stopped because he said it in Belarusian.

* * *

They sat in the lounge, where she made him a whiskey and Coke at the bar. For herself, she poured an apple juice.

'Are you well?' she said in Greek.

'Yes, thank you.'

'I see it goes well at Harmonia.'

'Yes, very well.'

'Good. I'm glad.'

That last phrase came out wrong. She'd used the words for 'pleased to meet you'. He caught her smile; so it had been a kindness. But it was his supposed job to put her at ease. All this time, he should've been paying her.

'Look, Darya—'

Her hand came up to block him. A traffic warden, a crossing guard. 'I don't want,' she said, her voice soft. 'I don't want.'

In her fist, she held the cross that hung around her neck. He felt a steep, sudden sadness.

A ringing made him blink, and he realised his eyes were wet. Darya was already up. She answered the phone on the wall behind the bar.

The next few minutes blurred in his memory. She'd said 'Yes,' as if confirming something. Then 'No' with mounting dread. 'No. No. No, no, no.' The phone dropped from her hand and he remembered sprinting to her. It was like that incident in Rhodos, with the beggar and the baby. Darya rattled to the core.

'What is it? What happened? Darya? What happened?'

When she spoke it was in another tongue.

'I don't understand. Darya, I don't understand. Is it your family? Is something wrong?'

She croaked the word: 'Aristos.'

His blood ran cold. She had slid to the floor, and he had knelt down to her. But his knee was damp. And when he held her hand, it was slick. At first, he thought she'd spilt her apple juice. But he hadn't heard the glass break, or even fall. It was still on the coffee table. Then there came that unmistakable smell.

'I'm sorry,' he kept saying. 'I'm sorry. I'm sorry.'

'God have mercy,' said the widow.

Two

The police got a statement from a tourist who'd been walking nearby, a French Ecology undergrad doing a semester abroad. She first spotted Aristos by the chapel, where he was watching the kittens play. A man of his height and stature, he was easy to notice. She walked down the wooden steps to get as close to the water as possible, and when she came back up she caught sight of the impressive man further along the rocks. Almost at once, she saw him slip. She ran to help. He was older, he might have broken something and there was nobody else around, the few other tourists had walked ahead in the opposite direction. He'd hit his head. There wasn't any blood, but she could tell it wasn't good. He insisted he was all right, and then his face went red. She felt his wrist, his pulse was slow. Trying not to show her panic, she asked him the number for emergency services, but he couldn't remember, or couldn't understand. His car was in the parking space, it had to be his. 'Hospital,' she said in French, but he understood. She searched his pockets for his keys, but they were still in the ignition. By the time she realised, his pulse had got slower. She sped on the highway, she didn't care if he got a ticket, she would pay. She barely even thought about driving on the other side of the road, the other side of the car, they might have died together. By the time she'd got him to a hospital, she knew it was too late. He was dead before they'd got him on a gurney. His last words were muffled. Nobody could make them out.

Eva pored over the details, again and again. For all her intensity, Orestis had never seen her cry before. Not that she sobbed and wailed; the tears ran in a continuous silent stream. The room echoed with the absence of her loudness. She stayed glued to the sofa in her mother's house, leaning into the woman's hug like a child. It was then that he realised he might love her.

'How's Darya?' she asked. 'Is somebody with her?'

'Don't worry,' her mother replied, patting her head.

Eva stared into space until her breath became lighter, and her body gave in to sleep.

* * *

Darya opened the door, slowly. This time she wasn't surprised. Without letting him in, she extended her hand to his chest. He thought she was trying to push him away until he felt the beat of his own heart against her palm. He held her there, saying nothing until she took her hand away and shut the door.

The funeral was well attended. Not only were the hotel managers there, but so was Svetlana, who'd come to pay her respects to the man who paid her well and was always so pleas-ant. Aristos' friends were worthy of headlines, politicians from the news, celebrities from music and sport. One man he spoke to was an old boss of Aristos', who'd employed him as a contractor for one of the glass blocks by the seafront. He was the one to advise him on buying his first hotel. A rundown place at the time, but with plenty of potential. Investment. That was the key. Aristos had made a success of it. Of course, he had. Because he was a man who knew what people wanted.

Orestis' father had insisted on attending. They'd bought him a sharp new suit, the best-fitting one he'd ever worn. His hair was gelled back and he was clean-shaven. Though his face drooped at the loss of a future in-law, Orestis felt there was something obscene about his presence there.

Darya kept her sunglasses on. No matter who came up to kiss her and offer their condolences, she stood still as a statue.

* * *

'Do you ever miss grandma?' Pavlos asked him at the gym. They sat sweating out five sets of bench presses. Though his cousin had never actually met Aristos, and like the rest of the family emitted an amazed laugh at the engagement to Eva, he'd looked heartbroken as he kissed his crucifix, *God rest his soul.*

'Of course,' Orestis replied. 'I think of her every day.'

'She raised you.'

'Yeah.'

'Remember when she used to tell us about the archangel coming to cut off our heads?'

'With the scythe, yeah.'

'E, more to me than you.'

Orestis gave something between a breath and a laugh.

'How's Eva doing?'

This unpacked so much. Guilt, for one: Orestis had yet to introduce his fiancée to Pavlos. Either out of embarrassment, or concern that Eva would dismiss his cousin as a waste of space. Not that she would have a leg to stand on; whatever he used to be, Pavlos provided health and wellbeing now, while up to her father's death Eva spent every day indulging herself. In any case, Orestis didn't know how she was doing other than living her grief. How could he pick through the viper's nest of a person's despair?

'She's coping,' he said. Then, to deflect, he asked after Skevi.

'She's good. Oh hey, she keeps trying to get me to go to this trendy spa in Paphos, she says Anna Vissi goes there, even Sakis Rouvas. I tell her I'm not up for any gay shit with Sakis. But I don't know, it might be a laugh. Wanna go? They'll give us massages, wax our legs.'

'What type of massage? Don't forget I'm engaged.' He wondered what counted as gay in his cousin's mind.

'Ou, I forgot to tell you, I met her! Your mother-in-law.'

'Who do you mean? Eva's mum?' But as soon as Orestis said it, he felt a chill.

'No, re, Ioannidou's wife. The Russian.'

'A. You don't say. How?' For a moment he feared the worst.

'I did a yoga class. Don't laugh!'

Orestis forced a grin. 'You do yoga?'

'E, only a few times so far. But it's good, re! It's nice to clear your mind a bit. You know how I get really anxious.'

He didn't, but Orestis nodded all the same.

'They say it helps. Yoga and stuff.' Then he leaned in. 'I mean, so does the weed.' And he laughed.

Orestis was dying to ask more, but he kept his mouth shut. They carried on with their workout.

'It's really difficult to bend for those poses, though,' said Pavlos. 'Like a Russian at the circus.'

With every pulldown and raise, Orestis felt a rising panic. The ground was parting. He'd thought he'd been digging a tunnel out of his prison, but he'd only dug a hole. Fate stood by and watched as he worked it into a grave. And Death, as he had seen twice since the start of his new life, was the visitor who called in unannounced. It didn't care if you hadn't prepared. He'd already lost whole nights' sleep recalling what Aristos had said about the photos. Those evenings in half-lit rooms, turning to the camera, posing, the wanker, the idiot wanker, as the deceased clicked, flash, clicked, flash, documenting all of it. He pictured the photos in the hands of his colleagues. Svetlana, Yiorgos, who would stare at him as if they'd never known him at all. Night-shift Dino who'd be unsurprised, he'd known of the goings-on at the Harmonia and guessed that Orestis wanted his share. Thanos – his disappointment would be devastating.

He had to get those pictures, destroy them. He would speak to Darya, then sever all ties with her. He would have to lose her, too.

Three

With Aristos gone, Thanos called a meeting for the department managers. They already knew of the sales abroad. Dubai had gone through. The Paphos villas were to be handled by a Russian agency. The Lemesos residences would carry on as they were. The deceased had prepared for the handover. 'As if he had known,' the manager said in a fragile voice. Lastly, Aristos had made out his will, in which he ensured that all his staff would receive double their usual Christmas bonus in the event of his death. 'So that they might have a good time on my behalf,' as Thanos quoted. Tina from Events and Sia from Housekeeping dabbed at their eyes.

For the duration of the meeting, Orestis was outside his head. He watched himself from above, in his Armani suit, sitting at a polished table in the boardroom of a five-star hotel. He was a manager, convening with other managers, most of them a decade or more his senior. As a child he had been taken out of his good school, as a teenager snared by the Army, as a twenty-something consigned to his uncle's taverna, dragging out heavy soggy refuse bags from bins, and now, a true man, at last, he had achieved his ideal body, he had been on a cruise, he drove a BMW, women wanted him, they had paid for him, those men in Greece had ogled him, his fiancée was a Ioannidou. And people were eulogising a powerful man he had cuckolded – a man who had not only watched him doing so but had paid him to. Orestis was both horse and cowboy.

An ornate clock hung on the boardroom wall: the sun, with rays fashioned out of sheet copper. If Thanos called the meeting to an end before quarter past three, everything would be all right.

* * *

This time, Darya didn't answer. A few moments' wait, another attempt, nothing. He followed the stone path around to the garden. In the pool, he saw a black smudge — the back of her head, rising to the surface.

The sound of his voice startled her. Even when she saw who he was, she stayed floating in the water, watching with caution.

'Aren't you cold?' he asked.

'Not here.'

'How long have you been in there?'

She looked away, shrugged.

'Come out.'

She lowered her head so that the water covered her mouth. He sat on one of the poolside deckchairs.

'You are manager now,' Darya said when she raised her head again.

These days he wore his own suits, good ones, not that green branded shirt. The only sign of a uniform was a metallic badge with his name and position engraved on it. 'Yes.'

'I knew this would happen.'

He didn't know whether that was a compliment or not.

'Why you are here, Orestis?'

'To see you.'

On saying it, he knew it was true. What he had come for were the photos. He'd imagined searching the house, like a cop in a raid. But his offence fell to pieces when he saw her. This woman before him was not a vindictive person. If she found the photos, she would destroy them herself. Or she would keep them, to look at whenever she felt the desire. A part of him hoped she would.

'Don't marry Eva.'

She'd spoken so quietly he thought he'd misheard. The hairs on his arms stood on end.

'I've known her since we were children.'

'But this is not life. Your life – it mean something. It matters you are alive.'

His eyes stung. 'What else can I do?'

'Leave. Go away. Start again.'

'Like you?'

Her voice was low. 'Yes, like me.'

'This is my home, Darya. My friends, my family...'

She looked away.

'What will you do?' he asked. The two of them together, on a boat, sailing away on her husband's inheritance. He would cook for her, clean, whatever she wanted.

'I will see what comes,' she said.

She was planning to leave. The realisation shook him.

What was there to keep her here? What roots did she have, what ties without Aristos? She and Eva had made progress since the cruise, but no-one would call it friendship. There was nobody else around, not a Russian or a Ukrainian or even that Swede on the yacht. Yet she never looked weak, never unsure of herself. Was she free, or was she simply alone?

'Will you sell the house? Will you leave?'

'The house is not mine.'

'E... I'm sure Aristos—'

'No.'

It was so final.

'Come on, Darya... Surely... It must—'

'Everything goes to Eva.'

Orestis felt the deckchair fall away from him, his well-dressed legs dangling in space. 'Are you sure?'

She nodded.

'E, Eva will give you something. No question. I'll ask her. Let me give you something.'

'I don't want,' she said with a shrug. 'This is Aristos' gift for me.'

He didn't understand. He only heard his jagged breath.

'Do you remember Rhodos? Woman with baby?'

He nodded. It came back to him often.

'This was God for me.'

'What are you talking about?'

'He gives me a chance.'

Her idea of God differed from his. Never mind what would always divide them, he wanted to hold her, as he had done in his cabin. He wanted her to open to him. But all he said was the only thing he could think to say: 'Come out of the water. Please.'

This time, she did. She floated to the edge of the pool and, gripping the metal rails, rose from the water. Her body shivered, her hair stuck to it. Her eyes were locked on his.

There was the sound of her wet feet on the tiles, and the touch of her soaking hair at his neck as she bent to kiss his cheek. 'Do not worry.' She stroked his forehead with her fingertips. 'You always worry.'

It was good to see her happy. He kissed her wrist as she lifted his chin.

'My Orestis,' she said.

Then she slid the patio doors open and went back into her dark, empty house.

V

As you are is as you'll find it, her grandma used to say, and Eva knew the words would follow her to the grave. It came from a story that varied with each telling, but its moral was ultimately the same: the world gave back what you gave to it. That was something her father had understood and used to his advantage. People remember kindness, he would tell her. And most of them — not all of them, but most — repay it.

When she thought of her father now, Eva could assess him as she might a stuffed lion in a museum. That was the curious legacy of death, this privilege to look without fear at what once might have killed you. Not that her father had ever scared her. He dominated, that was who he was; a man so big you were bound to look up. She admired him for bettering himself. He went from a childhood in the village, in that shack with a hole in the ground for a toilet, to an adulthood in which his name had spread throughout the island and across the sea. But his success made him impatient with others' slow progress, intolerant of their demons.

He had been vile to her mother. He put his dreams before hers, and for him to rise unimpeded she had to be suppressed, pinned like a butterfly on a board. When she was depressed, he was mad that she wasn't buoyant. If she was lonely, why wasn't she throwing a party? Why cry, and not at least try to be beautiful? Eva remembered him yelling at his wife, to get up and walk, stop being lazy, do something, which made her limbs too limp to move. By the time he'd married Darya, he appeared to have mellowed. It annoyed Eva that this Russian slut might have changed him. What did this woman have that her mother didn't? It wasn't until they went on the cruise that she saw the film repeat itself. He'd pinned Darya just as neatly, and his technique had improved. Who knows what he had promised the poor woman? An escape from the Eastern bloc probably. Why have nothing as a Communist, when you could have everything as a Capitalist?

It was not the lesson her father had taught her. For all his amassed wealth, his views remained more or less socialist. It wouldn't have surprised her if he'd voted for this bumbling fool of a president. He always paid his taxes, as confirmed by his accountant and solicitor. And unlike everyone else with a job she'd ever met, he never once complained about the refugee tax.

He'd raised her to reject racism, nationalism, xenophobia. It was why he'd sent her to an international school rather than a state one, cost and status were a bonus. He wanted her to see for herself how big the world was, how tiny she was within it. But in some ways, the experiment had failed. She loved Cyprus. If it was idiotic to love a concept, and to be proud of what you hadn't achieved, then she was an idiot. She compared the traits of her people to others and they fared well. She loved the way Cypriots stared at strangers and welcomed them. She loved that they fed and ate too much. She loved that they danced together in a circle and sang without inhibition. She loved that they mocked everything and everyone, including themselves. And she felt for this country, this cursed little island, which had barely scraped together fourteen years of independence in its history.

Fourteen was how old she was when she started to claim ownership of herself. When she told her mother she was seeing grownup films at the cinema, or piercing her ears, or staying up past her bedtime. When she accepted her size and the gossip it would fuel. At least she had big tits, even if it made clothes-shopping awkward. It was when she finally told her father that she didn't care if she was fat, as long as she loved herself. It was when she started to learn how to play his game.

* * *

Paris' book launch was at a poetry café in Old Town. Nestled in one of those Venetian buildings with the tall doorways, it was a cosy room of dim lights and the smell of wine and food in its walls. Paris took his place at the microphone stand and with a clear voice read his poems as if they were breathing inside her head. Though teachers and classmates had presumed him shy, Eva had always known that the opposite was true. Paris didn't care about how he was perceived, in fact, he was an anarchist. A symbolic brick here, metaphorical graffiti there. She had teased him about it once and he'd called her a princess. 'A,' she'd said, 'and you'll shoot me like the Romanovs.' But even she had been unprepared for the ability and comfort he showed in his readings. A natural. She felt a warmth in her heart as the room applauded his work. If he wasn't such a Communist who antagonised everyone, then who knows... He

337

might even have been the one to meet her at the altar.

She queued to get her copies of his book signed, one for her and one for her new friend the lesbian who liked this sort of thing but was in Azerbaijan designing shopping centres. She told him what a weirdo he was, what was this book jacket? A snake breaking an egg? God have mercy. Paris smirked. Eva felt a sudden urge to stroke his stubbled cheek and thank God, the very shock of it kept her paralysed. Paris had a girlfriend now, a pretty Greek-Bulgarian who cared passionately about renewable energy. Her honey wave of hair tumbled over his head as the girlfriend leant to kiss his temple. The proud owner.

'I didn't understand a word,' Orestis said of the reading.

Eva laughed, slapping his arm. It helped to keep the sadness down. Laughter and cocktails. Regardless of what he said, Orestis had watched his friend in awe and put his fingers in his mouth to whistle loudly at the end. That was enough.

* * *

The idea came to her to have a traditional wedding, in tribute to her father. He may not have been a nationalist, but the man had still been fond of his heritage. Orestis joked it would be traditional-lite, like the bouzouki pop she blasted in her car. She told him not to try her.

One day she drove up to his village of Kilani. To see the jumble of paved slopes, the stone houses with painted wooden shutters, the pagoda of vine leaves over an alley, old men with walking sticks sitting on wooden chairs with straw seats, she felt a nostalgic ache. Stupid; she'd never even lived here. She took photos. When anyone passed her, she'd engage them in conversation and explain her project: she was documenting her father's life, and a Cyprus of the past that she hoped would remain in the future. Then she'd invite them to her wedding. She wanted the reception to be right there in the village. On the streets, if the inhabitants allowed it. She hoped that an invitation to the feast would tempt them. Big deal, they only numbered a couple of hundred souls. One by one, she knocked on doors or, if they went unanswered, left notecards with her phone number on them, asking for people's permission to have her banquet here. God have mercy, the majority of the residents was over sixty. And most of them remembered her grandma fondly. The Seamstress. They were thrilled to be invited to her descendant's wedding.

There was one person she wished to invite, but it would take all her powers of persuasion to do so: Orestis' mother. She got the sense that her fiancé felt the same. No matter how dismissive a front he presented, he couldn't quite hide the hurt of her departure, his curiosity to know her. 'Leave it,' he'd say when Eva brought her up, but each time his tone softened, weathered like stone by water. She realised that the biggest part of the problem was Kostas, that perhaps he was the reason Orestis feigned aloofness. Eva knew her future father-in-law's faults – quick-tempered, unwilling to be educated, immoveable, xenophobic, sexist – but she knew how to make him laugh, or at least raise his eyebrow as a sign of mirth. It was how she got away with her bullshit.

'If you invite that whore to the wedding, I'm not going!' he said when she raised the subject at a family barbecue.

'So many whores in my family are coming to this wedding, isn't Orestis allowed *one*?'

A shocked silence. Then an explosion of laughter from the

339

rest of the family, and even Kostas was amused. What stunned him was his pride. Eva knew that if she pushed her agenda, played the role of the interfering bride, he would finally relent. He wanted to see her again, too.

'And me, the poor wretch. I want to know what genes are going to make up your grandchildren. I want to know where this gorgeous human being came from.' She held Orestis' hand.

'What,' said Kostas, softening, 'you don't think it came from this?' He was indicating himself, an eyebrow raised.

'Excuse me,' Andrikos interjected. 'Who is the one who brought the supermodel genes into this family?' He made a show of presenting himself, from the dirty Nike cap to the protruding belly and the navy flip-flops.

She joined him in laughing. But he was right, Pavlos was probably even more good-looking than Orestis. Those green-grey eyes, that lazy smile – my God, who made these beings? Demigods. They bore no resemblance to their fathers.

In the kitchen, Lenia whispered to Eva: 'I have Melina's email address. I'll give it to you.'

'Thank you, auntie.'

'Don't mention it. What mother would want to miss her only son's wedding?'

It was Easter. They played at cracking dyed eggs, a dozen pairs broken down to semi-finalists, then finalists, and at last, a winner. Orestis held up his champion egg to prove that its red veneer was unscathed. Lunch was a table covered in roasted lamb and salad, broad beans, green beans, olives, feta, taramosalata, tahini, moussaka, roast potatoes. Of course, she ate, none of that diet nonsense. While the younger cousins ran around, the adults talked and laughed and listened to music.

One of Orestis' cousins tried to tell her about property, that her husband was a genius at it. He had bought a house to let in Romania, dirt-cheap country. He could advise her. Eva had already hired an architect and bought a cute apartment with huge windows on the seafront to serve until the house was built. To the cousin, she simply said, 'I have plans,' and shut the conversation down by asking about the kids. One of her plans was to buy shares in smartphones, invest in new media. People were embracing technology more and more as a life enhancement. This was a connected world. People wanted everything on their phones, the less to carry the better; as if they were nomads or refugees. But she would always, God willing with her mind intact, keep up with trends; if you didn't move with the times, you were a dinosaur, extinct. She'd driven past the concrete ghost of the Ariel cinema enough times in her life to understand the ephemeral nature of a status quo. She had broken into the abandoned Fysco Lotus mall, to document the process of decay; weeds where once was commerce. There, she had found the shop of a local artisan, his small-scale reproductions of ancient statues left in cobwebs on rotten shelves. These predated everything she thought she knew about her motherland, even Aphrodite herself. Female forms with enlarged vaginas, what looked like penis heads, babies worn as necklaces. She photographed them, breath stilled. They barely looked Greek.

The other part of her plan was to sell the properties, maybe even the Harmonia. But she would ensure the staff remained. The new owners would be crazy not to have those sweethearts Thanos and Yiorgos in their establishments. Times had changed. If Cyprus was going to be too expensive for the penny-pinchers, then she would aim to focus inwards, on

341

affordable luxury. With her inheritance, she would open spas and gyms, on sliding scales of expense. People always wanted to feel and look good, no matter their lot in life. She might even open a yoga and meditation retreat, somewhere in the mountains where the sound of running water was all around and the air was fresh. Orestis was keen to have Pavlos run one of the gyms, and she agreed he should. Judging from his work with Orestis, he was a good personal trainer, and his looks would boost sales. But she would not end up with a hash-den empire under her nose. Pavlos had better keep his other business outside of hers, or else.

* * *

It was a sunny September morning on the day of their wedding. They had rented an old-style country home, with a courtyard of large clay pots bursting with flowers instead of grains, and a four-poster bed that took up the room in which, that very night, she was to give herself to her husband. Orestis and Eva went through the rituals of separate preparation. Musicians stood playing their fiddles and flutes while Pavlos, as best man, shaved his cousin. After the bride's hair and make-up were done, Eva's mum and maid of honour wrapped the sash around her waist and head. In a church full of souls, the priest blessed their union. He gave them bread and Koumandaria. He led them around the table three times after they placed the rings three times on each other's fingers. They'd worn their headbands, a design of fig leaves out of silver, copper and crystals. Like the bridesmaids' dresses, they had been made in London.

The invitations had been printed on paper from Lebanon,

the flowers imported from France, the favours from Athens. She was a Ioannidou after all, and her name carried certain branding duties. But her wedding dress was of Lefkara lace, handmade by a local craftswoman. At the reception the beer was Keo, and the wine brewed at the Ayia Mavri next door. The food was also her people's: spit-roasted lamb, stuffed peppers and vine leaves, grilled halloumi and salad. Dessert was a mountain on a trestle table: loukoumades, daktyla, yoghurt with honey and fruit salad. Some of the villagers had even gifted glass amphorae of their own homemade spoon sweets: bitter orange, bergamot, walnut, cherries and watermelon peel preserved in syrup and lime.

Music was provided by the live bouzouki band, instructed to play a melange of old folk songs and recent pop. People danced, Orestis throwing himself into the middle with Pavlos and Paris as people cheered. Guests pinned money to the bride and groom. Her mother's South African relatives were touchingly generous.

'It takes me back to old times,' an elderly villager said to Eva with tears in her eyes. 'Any minute now, we'll be hearing Turkish.'

How different one generation could be from the next. Even in the space between hers and her father's, Greek had been modernised. Then kids were typing Cypriot words in English letters. This old biddy was missing neighbours that some of Eva's peers would spit on.

Taking a break from dancing, Eva sat with Orestis' mother. She had emailed Melina to introduce herself and to request a postal address. The woman, as Lenia had predicted, was delighted to hear from her. What sort of woman would want to miss her son's wedding, yes, but also: what sort of woman

343

could leave her son in a different country, to stew in worry and regret and confusion without her? Who in their right mind abandons their child? At least that beggar in Rhodos was trying to give hers a better life. Though Eva had gone against Kostas' wishes by inviting his ex to the wedding, she was starting to see his side of things. They met Melina two weeks before the big day, at a café by the beach. The woman cried when she saw Orestis. Orestis was more restrained, which made Eva's throat contract. Melina sat through their coffee marvelling at everything around her: the road by the Zoo, it had been fixed! And Mesa Yitonia – avenues and flyovers where before there'd been fields of snakes! The area around the Castle was as beautiful as always. But how sad some of the buildings were looking now, and what was with the Russian furriers? Eva began the afternoon feeling anxious about the meeting, protective of her fiancé, all too late, but by the end of their coffee, she'd been charmed by his mother. Melina stared with wide eyes, Orestis' eyes, at all the change that had occurred between one life and another. She looked at her son, again and again, squeezed his knee, kissed his cheek, overcome with pride at the man he'd become.

Now they watched as he danced with Kostas beneath the lit-up vine pagoda, arms around each other.

'I hope he's a better husband than his father was,' Melina said.

Eva knew he would be. She had wanted Orestis from the moment she developed an interest in boys. As their lives grew apart, no thanks to this woman, she realised how distant he really was from her. All those girls who'd had him, they wore him like a badge. Sometimes it seemed she was the only one he couldn't see. She had already decided to remain a virgin until marriage. That had nothing to do with him. But she was thankful she had waited. Now it would be even more special.

She also wasn't born yesterday. She knew that with that body, that face, he will have slept with a hundred other women, maybe even in the past month. That was fine with her, let him get it out of his system. Let him grow tired of those shallow sluts and be ready to settle down to a life with her. She had loved him even when he'd gained that weight. And now, toned and tanned and gorgeous, he was hers.

Besides, men loved a virgin. The idea that something was waiting only for them, that they were the first claimant, the sole inheritor of a land unspoiled and ready for their harvest, was an enormous ego boost. Tonight she would make him feel like a king.

In the middle of the dance, there was a change in his expression. She turned to where he was looking, at the edge of the festivities. For the briefest moment, she was convinced she'd seen Darya. Her spirit was here. It walked away from the party and vanished in the black streets.

A dream. Just a silly dream. Darya wasn't even dead.

Eva lifted her wine glass and with a 'Cheers' in English, she toasted Orestis' mother for gifting him to her.

* * *

They honeymooned in the Seychelles. Eva told everyone it was because she wanted to follow in the Archbishop's footsteps after they banished him. She enjoyed making people laugh at the same time as reminding them she was rich. And she liked touching Orestis whenever she caught another woman watching.

Once they were back in Cyprus, she began to compile photos for her exhibition. It had been easy to get one, she was friends with half the art world here. She was even planning to help her mother open a gallery. Her problem lay in deciding what pieces to show. It was well enough to invite all her moron friends to an evening launch at a former warehouse on the docks, but she couldn't attach her five-star name to two-star work. After the cruise, she'd splashed on a high-end Canon, lenses, a flash, paid for lessons in Photoshop. She had nothing left to blame but her own skills.

Photography was where she put herself. People of the past used to fear their souls being trapped in the frame but for her it was the photographer's soul that was caught. What she captured was her own interests and desires, the story she derived from a composition in a single moment, a reflection of herself. It was that woman in Tinos, looking for God. It was the boys at the harbour in Syros, hoping someone was looking. Photography was where she could be herself entirely. The ditzy playgirl was an amusement, the comedian a distraction, the prima donna an exertion of power; all a mould for self-control. The photographer was a mirror and the measure of her worth.

Things were only worth what people were willing to pay for them. Currencies went up and down, house prices rose and fluctuated. People once died fighting for cinnamon, her grandmother sprinkled it over rice pudding. Mummies were bandaged with Sappho's poetry, now Paris would struggle to sell a dozen books. Did a diamond achieve its price tag because of its beauty, its scarcity, or the dangers in its mining? It was the same with people. A maid provided a service, but how much was she valued? If she was a refugee, did that add to her worth or detract from it? People drew their worth from tragedy as much as beauty. Suffering was as much a factor in determining a human's value as brains or talent. Cyprus was precious because she was the point between Europe, Africa and Asia. She was precious because she'd been abused by all.

Darya had been an asset to Eva's father. Her beauty increased his worth. But to many, she was just a Russian, wherever she was actually from. She was a drain, she devalued their land. She was useless because she hadn't much Greek. Eva had thought so too – at first. She'd seen an empty-headed gold-digger with nothing to say. But when she asked the woman if her grandma was still alive, she caught a glimpse of the world behind those strange dark eyes. If she'd had the words to express herself, she might have risen in others' esteem. Who were you when you hadn't the words for your feelings? Eva had some experience of this herself, in London. Despite being educated at that international school, despite being fluent in English, classmates at LSE would correct her pronunciation with pitying smiles. And the words they corrected were always of Greek descent. She bit her tongue when they claimed the Southern Cypriots sabotaged the island's reunification talks. Unless they'd be happy to have half of England run by France, these guys could go fuck themselves. But her anger had made her quiet, defensive and defenceless. You couldn't control what others said about you. Maybe Darya was full of rage, or sadness; any of the emotions that take away your speech.

The last time she saw her stepmother was shortly after the will reading, which the woman hadn't even attended. Thank God for that, because she hadn't been left a cent. Eva sat in her car outside the newsagent's for half an hour, eyes stopped dead on the sun-bleached Mickey Mouse comics in the spinners, as she sipped her Chino and Whitney Houston belted in the speakers. She had never expected this of her father. She'd spent months after his marriage ranting about the Russian stealing her inheritance, but this seemed so unjust, so cruel. At first, she'd thought it was a mistake, an old will, but the solicitor had verified the date. He hadn't even left her the house.

Eva had gone to see her. She would assure the widow that the house was hers, she could live in it as long as she wanted.

Darya had answered the door. 'Thank God,' she'd said when she saw her. She'd invited Eva into the study, the smell of tobacco still in the curtains, and handed her a box. 'A present,' she'd said. 'From Aristos.'

Eva had not been able to contain her tears. It was a camera, his old Zenit. She could see there was film still in it, but she vowed never to use it. It would sit in her studio as a memento, a goal. This was the kindest thing anyone had ever done for her.

Darya had refused Eva's offer. 'This is all I want,' she'd said, and indicated an envelope with a travel agent's logo on the desk. There'd been a light in her eyes that Eva had never seen before. She would never understand this woman.

* * *

For their first anniversary, they planned a trip to London, where they would reunite with Melina and see the sights Orestis had always dreamed of. Before their flight they spent the weekend at one of the Paphos villas, to enjoy the last of the summer light. In the morning Eva woke with Orestis spooning her, hand at her breast. They ate breakfast on the veranda, then drove to the town centre. They spoke about their parents, grandparents, their family traditions. It transpired his paternal grandfather was named Ioannis.

'Do you realise,' Eva said, 'that if we'd gone full-traditional for the wedding, you would have had to change your surname?'

'Yeah. So?'

'So you'd take your grandfather's Christian name and turn it into a surname.'

'And?'

'Hello! Your grandfather was Ioannis. Your married surname would be Ioannidou.'

Orestis was stunned. He smiled, but he wasn't as tickled as she was. She wished he wasn't wearing Ray-Bans, so she could read his eyes.

Whenever they passed a pretty, barely-dressed woman, Eva wondered if her husband was watching. Would she spend the rest of her marriage searching for signs? She let him wander on, taking photos from the back as he walked beneath the gently swaying palms that dwarfed him. She snuck a picture of a plump little girl losing her ice cream. At a souvenir shop, she caught up with him and threaded her fingers through his.

'I might have been Ioannou,' he said, out of nowhere.

They drove to Petra tou Romiou to watch the sunset. Eva noticed that even when he was driving, and obeying the rules of the road, Orestis was tense. He worsened at traffic lights and junctions, or if people overtook him. She stroked his cheek, and he turned, surprised to see her there. On the beach, the waves lapping at their naked feet, he held her while the light dimmed on Aphrodite's Rock. She took photos of the

349

sunset, the sand, the shells, the water. Mediocre, all of them. It couldn't be captured. Her husband had walked further ahead as if alone on this ancient shore, which even St Paul himself had trod on. She could see Orestis, but he was too far to read. All she could gather from his posture, from the angle of his head, was that he was watching the waves, watching the whole of the sea, as if waiting for someone to rise from it.

About the Author

Polis Loizou is a playwright, filmmaker, and performance storyteller. Born and raised in Cyprus, he moved to the UK in 2001. His debut novel, 'Disbanded Kingdom', was published by Cloud Lodge Books in 2018 and went on to be longlisted for the Polari First Book Prize. His short stories and creative non-fiction have been published in Litro, the Stockholm Review, Tales From The Shadow Booth, clavmag, Untitled: Voices and Inkandescent's MAINSTREAM anthology. Having co-founded an award-winning theatre troupe (The Off-Off-Off-Broadway Company), with which he has toured the UK festival circuit, Polis has delved deeper into the world of folk storytelling to perform a couple of acclaimed solo shows. Polis currently lives in Nottingham with his husband and cats.

Printed in Great Britain
by Amazon